"WE NEED TO FACE FACTS."

Eden spoke softly. "[...] you live in Louisiana. We're both committed to careers. Even if we do love each other, what could we ever hope for except an occasional weekend together?"

"I want more than that!" Nick held her against him fiercely. "I want to marry you."

"Oh, Nick," Eden sighed. "How?"

Leaning over he nibbled at the corner of her mouth, his tongue tracing the line of her full lips with tantalizing lightness. As his kiss deepened with un-disguised desire, she moved against him, straining to press her breasts against his rock-hard chest. Finally pulling back, he softly brushed his lips against her hair. "I know we can work things out," he said.

And Eden believed him because she wanted to.

A DREAM TO SHARE

SHARE

Deborah Joyce

A SuperRomance from
HARLEQUIN
London · Toronto · New York · Sydney

First published in Great Britain in 1985 by
Harlequin, 15–16 Brook's Mews, London W1A 1DR

© Deborah Joyce 1984

ISBN 0 373 70108 X

11–1285

Printed and bound in Great Britain by
Cox & Wyman Ltd, Reading

AUTHOR'S NOTE

At one time the main thoroughfare from New Orleans to Baton Rouge was a small winding road that clung to the banks of the Mississippi River. Along its shores prosperous sugarcane growers built magnificent plantation homes.

A broad interstate highway has now shortened that route, but for those who have the inclination, it is still possible to travel down the river road and visit these restored homes. Belle's Folly is a composite of several and does not exist as such, but insofar as possible, it is described authentically.

The author would like to dedicate this book to those citizens of Louisiana whose hard work in preserving their heritage is continuing to bring pleasure to many visitors.

CHAPTER ONE

EDEN FLUNG BACK HER HEAD, inhaling deeply as she stared out across the rippling water that sparkled under the glittering rays of the Louisiana sun. Under her feet, an ancient ferry creaked protestingly as it carried her across the broad Mississippi River with the uneven rhythm of a lumbering green-shelled turtle.

Reaching into her thin leather purse, she pulled out a pair of sunglasses and thrust them on, pushing back the thick blue black strands of her shoulder-length hair. Transparent gray lenses did little to help, leaving her sapphire-blue eyes and magnolia-white skin exposed to the blinding sunlight. A trace of French ancestry was evident in the classical oval face, the delicate eyebrows and fine bones. With these features and her full curving mouth that always hovered on the edge of a smile, she created a stir that made men's heads swivel whenever she passed.

Beside her on the ferry, a man with dark reddish hair and a rumpled business suit twisted uncomfortably, his fair complexion flushed from the searing heat. Eden was aware of his intense stare and turning, she followed his gaze down to her white linen suit and turquoise cotton blouse, where the slightly open collar only hinted at the fullness of her breasts. When his scrutiny drifted down to the gently slit skirt that allowed brief glimpses of her slender well-shaped legs, she turned her head away, debating whether or not to return to her car.

"You're not one of the regulars, are you?" he asked abruptly.

Eden gripped the iron railing, keeping her eyes on the broad green levee ahead of them. "No, I haven't ridden this ferry for years."

"I knew I would have noticed you." His genuinely friendly laugh made Eden glance up and smile at him.

"Do you ride it every day?"

He nodded. "Monday through Friday. So do most of the others on here." He pointed to a sleek silver Corvette that was parked directly behind the white rental car that Eden was driving. Through the darkly tinted windshield Eden caught a glimpse of a dark head bent over a sheaf of papers propped on the steering wheel. "He's not one of the regulars, either," the man continued. "Probably an executive from one of those oil companies that have sprouted up like mushrooms around here."

"Yes, it's really something, isn't it?" agreed Eden. "I had a hard time recognizing where I was on the drive from New Orleans. I haven't been back in three years and everything's changed so much."

"Too much for me. Those newcomers don't care at all for the area. All they do is complain about the heat and the humidity." He glanced at her sharply. "How about you? Where are you from?"

Eden couldn't resist pausing, her blue eyes twinkling over his embarrassment. Relenting at length, she said, "I live in Houston now, but I'm a native of the river road. I grew up at Belle's Folly."

"I knew it! The moment I saw you I was certain I remembered you from somewhere. You're Helene Sonnier's niece."

Eden nodded just as she felt the ancient ferry settling against the dock with a jarring thud. Already car engines were roaring to life around them. "I'm in that first car," she exclaimed. "I better be prepared to move when they lift that bar."

He followed her around to the car, opening the door for her and handing her a business card from a pocket inside his suit jacket. "I'll give you a call at Belle's Folly. I hope you've come home to stay."

Aware that the engine in the powerful car behind her had sprung to life, Eden agreed absently, pocketing the card and climbing into her car. It took several moments to locate the car keys... moments in which she became quite irritated with the impatient roar of the engine behind her.

A horn sounded and she swore under her breath, jabbing the key into the unfamiliar ignition. What was wrong with that driver anyway? Didn't he know that it took several minutes after the ferry stopped completely before the operator gave the all-clear signal? That was one thing she frequently noticed about sports-car owners. They bought cars designed to go over a hundred miles an hour and herded other drivers down the highways with arrogant disregard for anyone's safety!

She turned the key and heard a grinding sound. She tried again. Nothing happened. Forcing herself to stay calm, she tapped the accelerator to the floor several times and then with slow deliberate motions turned the key once more.

A horn sounded again and with a sudden spurt of anger she leaned her head out the window and shouted. "Calm down, buster! Can't you see the bar's still down?"

The gleaming dark hair emerged from the open car window and she caught her first glimpse of the driver. His features were straight and faintly arrogant, from the tough-angled jawline to the deep cleft in the chin. Amusement emanated from the thickly lashed dark eyes and her temper boiled.

"Having trouble getting your car started?" he inquired, in tones that showed he was enjoying himself immensely.

"No, the sound of a grinding engine thrills me," she snapped, retreating inside her car and attempting to start it once more. Even in the midst of her agitation his heart-shaking attractiveness had made an impression. He probably caused havoc among women wherever he went, she decided, removing the key and jabbing it back in with a vicious thrust.

A shadow fell over her shoulder. "Would you like some help?" The sound of the deep husky voice set off an inward shiver.

Refusing to risk glancing at him, she shook her head vigorously, sending her long hair brushing against her heated cheeks. Damn! Why wouldn't this car start? It had run effortlessly on the trip down. It would be her luck to have the car pull a stunt like this when she was already nervous over the appointment to which she was hurrying.

Her car door swung open abruptly. "Move over," he commanded. "Even if you and I both agree that I won't be able to start your car, I suggest you accept my help before that impatient mob behind us gets out of hand."

She hunched over, still shaking her head stubbornly when the imperious horn sounded once more. One slim hand flew to her throat as her enormous eyes locked with his. He laughed, "That's right. I wasn't the one laying on my horn a minute ago. Now move over and let me give it a try."

He slid in and she fumbled to remove her purse in her hurry to get away from him, the heat of his body suffusing her with a radiant warmth. The slow primitive throb of her blood as she caught a whiff of an expensive masculine cologne stunned her. Maybe there was something to those claims that scents were potent forces in sexual attraction.

As he removed the key and studied it before attempting to start the ignition, she stared at him aggressively, admitting reluctantly that he was definitely the most attractive man she'd ever encountered. His superbly tailored gray silk business suit draped casually over broad-muscled shoulders and long muscular legs. The way his body filled the small front seat area made it clear that he was taller than most men.

He turned and caught her staring at him. Eden's face flushed slightly, but he appeared not to notice, frowning as he said, "I think you're right. It's not going to start."

Her eyes flared in response to the patronizing words. "So, what do you recommend I do to placate the mob? Throw myself overboard?"

He gave her a slow appraising smile, his eyes drifting down the length of her body. "While the sight of you in wet clothes does sound tempting, I wouldn't recommend such drastic action," he murmured, a glint in the dark eyes.

Anger made Eden stiffen, but she managed a cool smile. "Now that you've failed to prove the superiority of men over women in mechanical areas, why don't you trot back to your little speed wagon and leave me alone?"

His broad smile made her boil with rage, but the sound of the ferry operator's all-clear horn made her jump in alarm. Horns began to sound all over the small vessel and several shouts accompanied by rude remarks made her glance at him again. "Well? Still want me to leave you here?" A maddening grin spread across his face.

"What's the usual procedure when something like this happens?" Eden retorted icily.

"The car behind you pushes you off the ferry."

She swallowed her pride. "Since that happens to be you, I'm afraid I'll have to ask for your help."

"You have it. Put your car in neutral...." He stopped and grinned again as he saw the look of disgust on her face. "Okay, okay, no more directions. I'll push you over to the side of the road as soon as we're off the ferry."

Eden watched in the rearview mirror as he strode back to his own car. At least six-foot four of well-built, compactly fit masculinity was visible in the small square reflection. She wondered why she felt such instant unwelcome awareness of every inch of that masculine frame. Reaching up, she started to adjust the mirror so that she could watch him slide into his car, then caught herself up short. For heaven's sake, she was positively leering at the man!

To the accompaniment of a symphony of honking horns, Eden carefully maneuvered her compact white car off the ferry, almost painfully conscious of the steady pressure of the sports car against the bumper. With a sigh of relief she braked to a halt as her car rolled gently into a grassy area off to the side of the exit. The other car was still right behind her, and within moments the man who was causing her pulse rate to increase moment by moment was standing beside her open window.

"I can give you a lift to the nearest service station if you'd like." He slid one monogrammed cuff up to reveal a gleaming watch and added, "You'll have to hurry, though."

"Don't bother," Eden glared up at him. "I wouldn't want to put you out."

"It's no bother. Grab anything you need and lock up your car." As she stared at him pointedly, his eyes began to twinkle. "Sorry, I have a habit of giving directions."

"The executive type." Eden opened the car door and slid out carefully, pausing to roll up the window before picking up her thin leather purse and matching briefcase. "A man I was talking with on the ferry said you weren't a regular around here."

"The overfriendly type who followed you to your car?" It was his turn to glare.

"So you were aware of something besides those papers you were studying so carefully." Eden let a soft smile curve her mouth.

He ignored that remark, choosing to ask a question of his own instead. "And are you a regular?"

Eden opened the trunk of her car and withdrew a compact suitcase. "Does this answer your question?"

He took the suitcase out of her hand and slid it behind the seat of his own car before opening the door on the passenger side. Once inside, she carefully smoothed her skirt, her body tingling with tantalizing sensation as he slid in beside her and started the engine.

"I do appreciate the lift," Eden said, with what she hoped was the right touch of friendliness. "I'm late to an appointment as it is."

"What sort of business brings you to the river road?" He eyed the briefcase on her lap as he shifted gears, his hands with its sprinkling of fine dark hairs barely grazing her knee.

Eden eyed him suspiciously from beneath long dark eyelashes. The touch was so fleeting, it couldn't have been deliberate. His bland expression was reassuring. He appeared to be concentrating on his driving. Besides, he didn't appear to be the sort of man who would have to resort to tricks like that, she decided. "I'm meeting someone at Belle's Folly."

As she started to explain about the old house he turned to smile at her with genuine delight. "Belle's Folly. Then you must be one of the architects from that firm in New Orleans. I'm Nicholas Devereaux."

Eden smiled back at him rather blankly, so he continued, "My company is River Road Oil Services. We're the ones you've been working with to try to make something of that old crumbling mansion."

Eden experienced a tiny bolt of irritation, but she managed to retain a vestige of the smile on her lips. Let him think she was an architect for the time being. This must be the head of the company that had leased her house. Larry Holmes, the real estate agent who was handling the property for her, hadn't given her the owner's name. But he had groaned when describing what they were up against. "What sort of problems are you having?" she asked, trying to inject a note of sympathetic interest into her voice.

"Well, you must at least have seen photographs of the property." He braked to allow a car to pass and then continued. "It's a monstrosity, a total anachronism, but we're desperate. We've got to have more office space, and it's the only building large enough in the area. More than fifty rooms! It's hard to believe people actually lived in places that large."

"I've been inside many of these old houses," Eden murmured slowly. "It seems to me you could make lovely use of them for office spaces."

"Not without extensive remodeling." His voice was adamant. "I can't expect my employees to work efficiently in some moldering old mansion, and I'm willing to pay a lot to have it changed to suit them."

"So what's the problem?" Eden said lightly. "Surely the architectural plans have given you lots of ideas."

He turned a look of dazzling approval on her and Eden felt her determination waver. She studied his deeply tanned face, his dark eyes surrounded by a fine network of laugh lines, his relaxed friendly smile. "Your firm has done a great job! Unfortunately, the problem is the owner. Evidently she's the maiden niece of a woman named Helene Sonnier."

Eden had to fight from gasping her outrage at his words. Maiden niece indeed! So she wasn't married. So she was on the downhill side toward thirty. Did that mean she was to be categorized as a maiden niece? "Surely that expression is a little outdated," she managed to reply coolly.

"You're right," he admitted. "I was quoting my office manager. I don't know anything about the niece, actually, but I did meet that formidable woman, Helene Sonnier, at a charity benefit shortly before her death, and I can just imagine what we're up against if this niece is anything like her."

Eden was savoring the pleasure of telling him who she was, actually tasting the words on her lips, when they pulled to a halt in front of a small service station. Before she could open her mouth, the owner was leaning in the window. "What can I do for you folks today?" His weather-beaten face matched his friendly tones as he inspected them both carefully. "Why it's Miss Eden, isn't it?"

"Hello, Hank," she said, smiling back, recognizing the ancient little man with a surge of pleasure.

"It sure does make me happy to see you again. Yes ma'am, it does. Miss Eden Sonnier."

Eden groaned inwardly as he said her name, feeling the unmistakable tensing of the overpowering masculine frame beside her. Nick explained the situation with her car as rapidly as possible, his voice clipped. Within moments Hank was shuffling across to his small office to call the rental company.

"Sorry, but he's right," Eden couldn't resist teasing. "I'm the maiden niece." After one look at his disgruntled face she couldn't restrain her laughter. "You really put your foot in it that time. You should be more careful, you know."

"You could have said something." His face was tight, his expression unrelenting.

"You didn't give me a chance." Eden was enjoying his discomfort. It made him seem more human, somehow.

He gave in finally, with fairly good grace. "I apologize. You're far too beautiful to be called anyone's maiden niece." His eyes were bold, darker than ever, as he let his gaze drift over her flushed face and windblown hair. Reaching out one hand, he lightly traced her delicate cheekbone and then outlined her suddenly still mouth. "I can see a lot of your aunt in you. Are you as formidable as she was?'' His voice dropped to almost a whisper on the last words.

Eden was saved from replying by Hank's return. ''Got it all fixed up for you, Mr. Devereaux. They'll have their own people pick up the car. You can leave the keys with me.''

''I suppose I'm still at your mercy,'' Eden spoke reluctantly after Hank had moved away. ''Would you mind dropping me off at Belle's Folly?''

''I thought you were meeting my office manager in our present offices this afternoon.'' Nick's gaze had narrowed somewhat.

''Not until three o'clock.'' Eden glanced at her watch. ''I'm supposed to meet Larry Holmes, the real-estate agent, at the house. He's driving me over so that he can attend the meeting, as well.''

''You've got less than an hour. Why don't I take you to the office and you can call Larry from there?''

''No thanks.'' Eden tried to soften her refusal. ''Larry wanted to brief me a little on how things are going.''

''They're not going,'' Nick declared flatly. ''And you're the reason they're not going.''

''Now wait a second. . . .''

''The situation is simple.'' Nick maneuvered the car back onto the road, driving faster than he had before. ''My company has a five-year lease on the property. We want to make changes. You knew we wanted the house for office space before you leased it to us. Now you're balking.''

''I'm not being stubborn, Mr. Devereaux. I simply want to make sure that we do what's best for everyone involved.''

"My name is Nick," was his only reply.

"Okay then, Nick, what's so unreasonable about what I'm asking. I only want to preserve Belle Folly's natural beauty."

"It's expensive and it's taking up too much time."

Eden started to open her briefcase. "I've drawn up a few suggestions of my own. I believe we can remodel the house to suit your purposes without destroying any of the original architectural details."

"Save your explanations for my manager. You'll be dealing with him." Nick was staring straight ahead, his hands sure and competent on the wheel. After a quick look at his set face, Eden leaned against the back of her seat and closed her briefcase.

They subsided into uncomfortable silence, and Eden tried to concentrate on the familiar panorama of scenery outside the car windows. On either side of the road were thick woodlands, luxuriant with tropical undergrowth. Small country lanes led off the main highway and snatches of yellow and crimson wild flowers dotted the green fields. About to comment on the scenery to Nick, she suddenly caught her first glimpse of Belle's Folly.

Like a proud old woman left living long after her friends have all passed on, the mansion looked strangely out of place. Graceful, tall fluted white columns surrounded the two-story square structure on all sides, hallmarks of the Greek Revival style of architecture that characterized many of the old plantation homes in the South. Long shuttered windows lined both upper and lower galleries, and from a distance she was able to ignore the peeling white paint, crumbling brick fences and tumbledown outbuildings.

Eden sat quietly as the car turned into the wide avenue, lined on either side by massive live oaks dripping with tangled strands of silvery gray Spanish moss. Nick stopped the car in front of the double staircase that led up to the wide entrance. Without speaking, he got out, removed her suitcase and came around to the passenger door.

As Eden stepped out of the car, she found herself standing far too close for comfort to his lean masculine frame. "Thanks for the lift," she said stiffly.

His expression softened as he looked down at her, his eyes obviously appreciating the way the sun glinted off her blue black hair and fair skin. "This place suits you," he said softly, his breath fanning the feathery soft hair around her temples. "I can just see you in twenty yards of ruffles, waltzing down those steps to greet the latest man in your life."

"And do you see me carrying a briefcase?" Eden's voice was dry, the thread of humor underlying it again. "I hate to remind you, this is the twentieth century, Nick."

"And is there one?" he asked.

"One what?"

"A latest man in your life?"

Eden grinned at him and grasped her suitcase firmly. "Thanks again for the lift. I'm sure I'll be seeing you again." She hurried up the steps, pausing at the top to wave back at him, aware that he was watching her, still standing with one arm on the roof of his car.

Larry was waiting by the front door, his usually placid face looking worried and strained. "Eden! I was beginning to wonder where you were." He hurried over to meet her, staring down at Nick. "Why that's Nick Devereaux. You didn't tell me you knew him."

"I've just met him. On the ferry." Eden watched as Nick drove off, scattering gravel as his tires crunched over the overgrown drive. "That rental-car firm you recommended left something to be desired. The car refused to start again when it was time to leave the ferry."

Larry ignored her reference to the car, following her into the house anxiously. "So you've met Devereaux. Did you discuss the house with him?"

Eden didn't answer, her eyes adjusting gradually to the dim light, seeking out the familiar stairway that descended at a gracious curve into the wide hall. She flipped on a switch that controlled an enormous crystal chandelier, but it only cast a bluish gray light over the smooth mahogany chairs and tables.

Unlike the gleaming surfaces that she remembered, there was a film of dust over all the furniture, and she could detect cobwebs dangling from the ceiling corners. Larry's comments about the rundown condition of Belle's Folly in his last phone call had not been an exaggeration in the least.

"Can you imagine this as the office of a successful, high-powered oil-company exec like Nick Devereaux?" Larry pointed toward the parlor on the right side of the entrance hall.

Eden followed his gesture, tilting her head to one side, turning her full attention on the room as if she was evaluating it for some prospective client. Even in its dusty condition the room was magnificently impressive. The wooden floor was covered with a lovely Oriental rug that had been woven in a palette of muted colors. In one corner, beyond the Victorian sofa, was an ornate Oriental screen. A rare matching pair of Chinese garden stools were poised behind the striped maroon-and-gold satin sofa. On either side of the formal fireplace stood twin armchairs covered in rich brown leather.

Opulent forest-green velvet drapes trimmed with colorful fringe cascaded to the floor in luxuriant puddles, the sign of wealth in the early days of this part of the country.

Larry seemed to be reading Eden's thoughts as she mentally assessed the value of the furniture. "You could make a bundle off the junk in this room alone," he said.

Ignoring his disparaging reference to the priceless antiques, she reminded him, "Enough to pay the taxes for a good many years."

His reaction was instantaneous. "That's no solution, Eden. Maybe you need a quick tour of some of the abandoned houses around here to see what vandals have done to them."

"Something is obviously bothering you, Larry." Eden turned and eyed him consideringly. His fair good looks and thin body were scarcely changed; he still reminded her of the small boy she had grown up with here on the river road. She was beginning to have second thoughts about her decision to choose Larry's realty firm to handle the details of leasing Belle's Folly. When the housekeeper who had been living there alone decided it was time to retire, Eden had realized she couildn't afford to leave the place sitting empty any longer.

"This visit of yours," Larry spoke slowly. "I could have solved this problem with River Road Oil Services...."

Eden waited for him to go on, but after a long silence she said, "I think I'm the only one who can explain how I feel about that company's proposal to demolish the interior of my home."

Larry still looked unhappy. "You have to realize that old plantations like yours aren't exactly hot news on the marketplace these days. You're damned lucky I found someone willing to lease it for the five years at the price you're asking."

Eden had to struggle with her rising irritation. "Lease, yes! But tear down the walls and remove most of the furniture? No way! I explained to you when I gave you the listing that my eventual goal is to restore Belle's Folly and present it to the local historical society as a museum one day."

Larry laughed indulgently. "Dreams, Eden. Nothing but impractical dreams. Can you imagine what it would cost to restore Belle's Folly?"

"Better than you," she said curtly. "Have you forgotten that's my line of work? Besides designing interiors for contemporary homes, my company has been involved in the restoration of several older homes in the Houston area."

"I guess I didn't realize that," he admitted, patting her on the shoulder in an infuriating manner.

She moved away, taking quick stock of the large dusty room. "It wouldn't take as much effort as you're thinking. Particularly if I were in charge of the restoration." Had Larry always been this patronizing?

"Try not to antagonize Fred Borman." Larry's voice held the merest hint of a sigh.

"Fred Borman," Eden repeated musingly. "Is that the office manager Nick mentioned?"

"Yes, he's the office manager. But he seems to have full authority to make decisions in this matter. At least, he's the only one I've had much contact with."

Eden shrugged, keeping her back turned as she eyed the huge fireplace that dominated the center of the room. Perhaps it was more of a problem than she was admitting. Everything Larry was saying made perfect sense from a business standpoint. Belle's Folly was only one of a score of rundown plantations along this winding river. Its beauty was faded, its usefulness long since outdated. If she had an ounce of sense she'd let this oil company have it with no strings attached, be glad that at least someone was using the old structure.

Hopelessly sentimental; that must be her problem, she concluded. Her own condominium in Houston was completely modern, with rattan furniture and scads of glass. And just because she happened to be the last of the Sonniers, a powerful, aristocratic Southern family who had once ruled a small empire on the banks of the Mississippi, she need not imagine it was her duty to uphold all the old traditions. It was time she snapped out of these delusions of past grandeur and settled once and for all for the realities of the life she'd carved out for herself in Houston.

"I think Mr. Borman will find me reasonable," she told Larry. When he didn't reply immediately, she went over and sat on the uncomfortable carved sofa. "How did the oil company hear about Belle's Folly? Through an ad in the local paper?"

Larry settled cautiously on the edge of a worn upholstered chair before answering. "No. I've been dating Fred Borman's personal secretary. Her name's Karen Anderson. I'd like for you to meet her, Eden."

"Do I detect more than a casual interest?" she teased, recalling Larry's marriage to his high-school sweetheart had ended in divorce several years earlier.

He grinned over at her, his blue eyes sparkling with enthusiasm. "You might say that. The problem is, Karen's so busy with work and taking care of her six-year-old daughter that she seldom has much time for me."

"Hmm," laughed Eden. "Surely you can do something about that. Doesn't a realtor have a lot of experience overcoming objections?"

"How about you? Any special man in your life? I wouldn't want you to follow in your Aunt Helene's footsteps."

She rejected the idea immediately. "I'm not a man hater! As a matter of fact there is someone in my life. He's my assistant in the company."

"Now that's a switch. Haven't you heard the old saying about men seldom making passes at a gal who surpasses?"

Eden laughed wryly. "Not Tom Evans! He's one of the new breed of men. However, he might not agree that I'm his superior. His expertise is antiques, but a couple of years ago he decided to branch out and become involved in interior design. I grabbed him up the moment he became available."

"When can I expect a wedding invitation?"

His inquisitiveness grated until she recalled that personal questions were a way of life in the small-town atmosphere in which they had grown up. Her inquiries about Karen might have been equally offensive. "Don't hold your breath," she said lightly, trying not to analyze why the thought brought such a negative reaction.

Larry glanced at his watch. "Only a few minutes before we're due for our appointment. Has this quick look convinced you that the oil company is right in pressing for those changes?"

"Whose side are you on, anyway?"

"Yours," Larry returned promptly. "It's my job to advise my clients of what's best for them even if it's not what they want to hear. I know more about the real-estate market around here than you give me credit for."

"I'm not disagreeing with that." Eden stood up and slipped into her suit jacket. "It's hard to believe it's been almost three years since my last visit here."

They started out the door together. "That was for your aunt's funeral, I believe." Larry paused to lock the door, fiddling for several moments with the ancient lock. "When are you planning to return to Houston?"

Eden hesitated only a moment before answering. "As soon as possible," she said firmly. "I'm due to leave on a buying trip to Hong Kong, but if necessary, Tom will handle that for me.''

Larry whistled as they reached his car. "Wow! Local girl makes good and all that. Your life must be exciting now, Eden.''

She grinned back at him impudently. "I'm glad you approve.'' As soon as they were settled in the car she added, "I do enjoy my work. I've been lucky.''

Larry drove slowly down the tree-lined drive, his movements cautious and not nearly so competent as Nick's had been less than an hour before. That reminded her of her transportation problem. "I'm going to have to ask you for a ride back to Belle's Folly.''

"No problem. I hope you'll stay with mother tonight. She said to tell you there are plenty of spare bedrooms.''

Eden shook her head decisively. "I intend to stay here. If the phone's still working, I'll give your mother a call and thank her for the invitation.''

"All the utilities are on, awaiting your decision. You're welcome to use one of my company cars while you're here.''

"Thanks, that would be great.'' Eden relaxed back in her seat.

They rode in silence along the winding road, Eden mentally reviewing her arguments against making massive changes to the interior of the house. Not that she wasn't willing to agree that the place needed modernizing.

Would Nick be present at this meeting? The thought was oddly pleasing. He was different from most of the men she met, successful and confident, without seeming arrogant. He seemed to be able to laugh at himself and that was refreshing. As nice as Tom was, he had no sense of humor, so it was interesting and stimulating to meet a man who could look at life without taking it all too seriously.

She was confident that she and Nick could work something out about the house, but Larry seemed to feel that the decision rested entirely with this Fred Borman. Did Nick truly delegate decisions to his subordinates or would she ultimately find that her real opponent was the head of the company?

Looking out the window, she felt her muscles tense as she recalled those fleeting moments when he had touched her in the car. She hadn't mistaken the spark of understanding, the instant unsettling sense of familiarity that she had seen reflected in his eyes. She was willing to bet that he was looking forward to seeing her again with as much pleasure as she felt at the thought of seeing him.

CHAPTER TWO

PUFFY WHITE CLOUDS in the blue sky gradually changed to ominous shades of gray and thunder rumbled in the distance. A typical summer-afternoon shower in the bayou country began splashing huge drops of rain on the car's tinted windshield.

Larry swung off the road into a paved parking lot filled with vehicles. Amid a jumble of metal storage tanks, pipes and the ubiquitous barbed-wire fences, Eden glimpsed a one-story office complex.

"What's wrong with the building the company is in now?" she asked.

"They've outgrown it. Their operations are scattered from New Orleans to Baton Rouge, and Devereaux wants to consolidate in this area. Karen says the company is expanding almost daily and your land, with a building as large as Belle's Folly, seemed ideal."

"Profits must be sky high," she said dryly.

Larry laughed. "All to your benefit. No one else has shown the least interest in leasing Belle's Folly."

"No one?" Eden's voice was plaintive. "I was hoping maybe some rich doctor who loved antiques might want it. Or how about a writer who wants to live in a place loaded with atmosphere?''

"With outdated plumbing and no air conditioning?'' Larry reminded her as he selected a parking slot between two sleek cars. The rain was coming down harder and he stared at his watch morosely. "Can you believe I left my umbrella at the office? Maybe I better go on in. I wouldn't like to keep Fred waiting.''

"I'll come, too,'' Eden insisted, slipping out of her white linen jacket. "I'll hold this over my head and make a run for it.''

They hurried across the parking lot until they reached the glass doors. Once inside the building, Eden brushed droplets of moisture off her jacket and slung it casually over one arm, hoping her naturally wavy hair hadn't decided to turn into a mass of tangled curls.

With her experienced decorator's eye she assessed the furnishings in the impressive reception area with a note of approval. From the low leather couches to the collection of handwoven Indian rugs that were artfully displayed on the wall, she had to admit that Nick Devereaux's company reeked of style and elegance. . .a fitting reflection of the man himself. She wished it wasn't quite so modern, though. That didn't bode well for the future of Belle's Folly.

A willowy young woman with curly brown hair was seated behind a switchboard. Her eyes brightened with recognition when she spotted Larry. "I'll buzz Karen and tell her you're here. She needs someone to cheer her up. . . .''

"Sorry, Lucille, I've got an appointment for my client with Fred," explained Larry, smoothing down his blond hair. "Could you do me a favor? In case I don't see Karen, tell her I've worked it out so we can have that dinner date tonight."

Faintly embarrassed, the receptionist glanced covertly at Eden. "Yes, sir. I'll ring Mr. Borman for you." Within seconds she spoke briskly. "He'll be right with you. Please have a seat."

Eden sat down on one of the couches and smiled over at Larry, keeping her voice low. "What's the problem with Karen?"

Larry sighed. "Trouble with Fred."

Eden made a face. "What kind of trouble?" It wouldn't hurt to know a little about this man who Nick said would decide the fate of Belle's Folly.

Speaking in little more than a whisper, Larry responded. "Nothing too major. Frankly, I find Fred agreeable enough. Sometimes when he's busy he is a little brusque, but I've told Karen she's going to have to develop a thicker skin."

"Maybe Fred needs to become more sensitive," retorted Eden. The sound of footsteps made her glance up, and she saw a stout man with dark-rimmed glasses entering the room.

Larry jumped to his feet. "How are you, Fred? I brought Eden with me just as I promised. She's as eager as you to get this little difficulty straightened out."

Fred stared at Eden with hard grayish green eyes as she rose to her feet. She returned the gaze just as aggressively. "I wasn't expecting such a beautiful opponent," he said after flashing a sudden artificial smile. "Somehow, I had gathered the impression that Miss Sonnier was far older than myself." His eyes raked over her with a look of sly approval that made Eden's toes curl.

"You must have confused her with Helene Sonnier, the former owner of Belle's Folly," Larry hastened to explain. "Eden inherited the property recently, although she now lives in Houston." .

"What a pity you had to make this tiresome trip." Fred placed a hand under Eden's elbow to guide her down the hall. She flinched away from his possessive grip as he continued, "Now that I see you, I'm sure we'll have no problem reaching an agreement."

No one was at the desk outside Fred's office when they reached the end of the hall. Eden spotted a nameplate with "Karen Anderson" printed in bright red letters. Larry risked a quick glance down the hall before they followed Fred through the door.

Once seated inside the office Fred continued his admiring survey of Eden. It was all she could do to submit without some token sign of protest. "What seems to be the problem, Eden?" he asked after several tense moments.

She gave him an icy look. "I have no intention of having Belle's Folly demolished inside."

His eyes blinked rapidly behind the thick lenses. "That's a harsh assessment, my dear. We have had preliminary plans drawn up by an outstanding architectural firm. Do you realize how much it's going to cost us to turn that old place into a modern office building?''

"Mr. Borman," Eden began.

"Fred." His smile was ingratiating.

"Fred, then," Eden replied after a brief pause. "Why, exactly, is River Road Oil Services willing to spend so much to remodel a building they've only leased for five years?''

Fred spread his hands in front of him, touching fingertip to fingertip as he pursed his lips and stared off in silence. "Five years is a long time," he began finally, "and we had thought about possibly buying the old place when our lease expires. The building itself is not too attractive for our purposes, but the land would meet our needs for increased space.''

Eden shot an accusing look at Larry. Had he known about this? She'd had no idea that anyone had been discussing buying the house. It wasn't a possibility she wanted to think about. "Belle's Folly is an architectural gem as she stands," she declared. "When your lease expires, I hope to restore her to her former elegance." Eden ignored the mental warnings that told her she ought to at least consider the possibility of selling. Her sentimental feeling for the old place overrode all other considerations.

Fred didn't seem impressed. "Ah, a traditionalist, I see. What a rare trait in a beautiful young woman. I, too, hate to see the old landmarks vanishing, but I'm sure you'll agree that your ideas would take a lot of money. Something you evidently don't have or you wouldn't be forced to lease the place." He leaned back in his chair and Eden knew by the triumphant gleam in his eyes he thought he had neatly backed her into a corner.

Her nerve faltered, but the knowledge that Belle's Folly was in better condition than any of the other available plantations gave her the strength to lean forward. "Perhaps we need to tear up the lease," she suggested.

The middle-aged man shifted in his seat, as ready for battle as she was. "I don't think anything that drastic is called for. I have assured Mr. Devereaux that something can be worked out."

When? As Eden leaned back once more, her mind toyed with the pleasurable thought that Nick might have interceded on her behalf since their meeting. "Do you have that preliminary sketch to show me?" she asked.

"Certainly." Fred reached into a side filing drawer and drew out a sheet. "You'll see that we plan on removing the walls in the parlor and . . . ."

"Those walls are made of the finest Jamaican mahogany, hand carved by a master craftsman. Why would anyone want to replace them with bland painted plasterboard?" she demanded.

"To let in more light." The office manager's voice was rising.

Larry intervened adroitly, proving to Eden that his success in handling real-estate transactions was well deserved. "Fred, Eden agrees that you have to modernize the old place. Let's give her a chance to discuss her ideas."

The stout man subsided in his chair, removing his glasses and wiping them with a tissue. He was careful to avoid any eye contact with Eden. "What changes would you approve?"

"I'm an interior designer, Fred," she answered quietly. "I'd like to take this sketch and draw up a new plan that would ensure that no irreversible changes would be made to my old home."

"The employees won't stand for a gloomy atmosphere," he returned, determination darkening his eyes. "The only way Mr. Devereaux agreed to this lease was if it could be modernized."

"I realize that you were considering a long-term plan for the property," Eden's voice took on an undercurrent of adamance. "But now that you understand my position, perhaps you'll be willing to reconsider your ideas. There are many ways to bring light into a building and not all of them involve major structural changes."

"Inexpensive ways?"

"You spend a lot on public relations, I'd bet," said Eden. "May I remind you that it won't help your company's reputation when this community hears that you're planning to destroy one of their most outstanding historical landmarks?"

Larry's mouth curved into a quick grin as he glanced at Eden admiringly. He smothered it quickly. "How long will it take you to complete your plans for Fred?"

"And how much will it cost?" Fred added sarcastically.

Eden's eyes brightened with amusement. "No charge. Count it as my contribution to local history."

Writing off her business trip to the Far East, she calculated rapidly, "Two weeks should do it. Do you want me to work with your architectural firm?"

Fred sighed. "By all means, include them." He drew out a card and slid it cross the Danish birch desk toward Eden. "Here's their number in New Orleans. Please show me your plans along the way so I can see if I can live with them. If there was any other suitable building within miles. . . ." His voice trailed off grimly, leaving no doubt of what he wanted to say.

"I'm sure you'll agree, Fred, that Eden is being generous to donate her time to this project." Larry stood up as he spoke. "She's a very successful businesswoman in Houston and she has a tight schedule." He turned to Eden. "Will it be too difficult for you to arrange time off?"

"I'll manage, but I hate having to put a heavy load on my employees." She stood, shaking out the rumpled linen jacket. Tom, she knew, would redouble his efforts without a murmur. It was possible he might even appreciate this opportunity to show her he was ready for more responsibility.

Fred rose more slowly, glancing down at a desk calendar. "Please set up an appointment for our next meeting. Would tomorrow afternoon be too soon? I'm anxious to get some idea of what you have in mind."

"Tomorrow would be fine," assured Eden. "I'm equally anxious to hear what your specifications are." The three of them went out into the hall.

Fred frowned at the empty desk. "Where is that Karen? I haven't seen her in over an hour." With an irritated gesture he grabbed the appointment calendar and flipped the page over for the next day. "How about two? Is that convenient, Eden?"

"Excellent." She held out her hand. "Nice meeting you, Fred."

He grasped her fingers lightly. "Two, then."

"Where's Karen?" Larry muttered under his breath when they were out of Fred's hearing. "No wonder she's having trouble if she's doing a disappearing act."

He seemed a little too eager to place the blame on Karen. "Why don't you give her the benefit of the doubt, Larry? She probably has a perfectly logical explanation."

As they neared the lobby Eden glanced around for one last check, disappointed that she had seen no sign of Nick. As he knew she was here, this apparent lack of interest bothered her more than she wanted to admit.

"Hi—" the receptionist swiveled around in her chair to greet them once more "—I gave Karen your message, Larry."

"Where is she? Fred's fit to be tied, Lucille." Concern colored Larry's deep tones.

"That Fred!" Her response spoke volumes. "He must have forgotten that Nick's secretary is on vacation, and Karen agreed to take notes at the meeting he's having this afternoon. I'll call and remind Fred right now so he can quit his complaining."

Eden grinned over at Larry. "See, I was right!"

Larry nodded sheepishly, his eyes offering a faint apology. "I'm sorry you didn't get to meet Karen. How about having dinner with us this evening, Eden?"

She waited to answer until they reached the outside of the building. The rain had died down to a drizzle, but the air felt as moist as a damp sponge. "About the dinner invitation. I don't want to intrude on the little time you have to spend with Karen."

"No intrusion," he insisted. "Karen has been looking forward to meeting you, and she can probably fill you in on some of the requirements Fred has in mind for the renovation."

"That would be helpful," concurred Eden. "If you're certain I won't be in the way, I'll accept the invitation gladly."

Larry started to reply and then looked over her shoulder, a wary smile creasing his youthful face. "Well, hello Devereaux. Looks like you're a little wet."

Eden tensed, her mind racing unwillingly back to their encounter earlier in the day. After meeting Fred, she would have to reformulate some of her ideas about Nick Devereaux. Turning slowly, she forced herself to greet him with just the right touch of friendliness. "Why, hello again," she intoned inanely. "I thought you were in a meeting."

A curtain of rain, softer now, was still slanting from cloud-covered skies. The small overhang above the door protected Larry and Eden from the drizzle, but Nick seemed unmindful of it. She watched keen appreciation flicker across his features as he soaked in the details of her face. His gaze drank in her fair complexion, her large soft dark eyes, her small delicate features. "I was, but I wanted to see you before you left."

The yellow hard hat he wore was a matter of practicality. It covered his black hair, inadvertently protecting him from the rain. The image she had formed earlier of a sleek business executive was suddenly replaced by the reality of his well-muscled body, obviously used to hard work. His jacket was gone, his sleeves rolled up casually to reveal tanned powerful forearms darkened with silky black hair. Rain had plastered his shirt to his torso, leaving his broad chest and strong back clearly outlined.

"Was your meeting held in the rain?" Larry interrupted their silent communication with his teasing remark.

"In the warehouse." Nick shifted his attention to Larry. "We've been trying to straighten out some inventory problems. I got caught in the downpour on my way over here." An enigmatic smile softened his features. "Karen's still there if you want to see her."

"Great." Larry looked slightly embarrassed.

"Why don't you have coffee with me?" Nick then directed his smile at Eden, making the invitation seem warm and intimate. "We'll leave those two alone for a few minutes."

Eden's head felt light as air when she nodded in response. "That would be nice." Turning to Larry, she realized that he was hesitating, wondering if he ought to leave her behind. "Go ahead," she urged. "I'll meet Karen later."

"Here." Nick thrust the hard hat at Larry. "Take this." Glancing down at his watch, he added, "We'll see you in half an hour."

Eden waited until Larry had headed off across the cluttered yard before looking at Nick. She felt him move onto the single step beside her.

"Let's go have that coffee," Nick's voice came from right behind her ear. "I need it."

Lucille seemed surprised to see Eden again, but her eyes lighted with pleasure when she saw her boss. "Looks like you got wet," she teased, making it clear that Nick, at least, did not insist on formality from his employees. Eden liked that.

Instead of telling Lucille to serve the coffee, he surprised Eden by crossing over to a table around the corner and swinging open a cabinet door. "I'll use one of these guest cups for you," he said as Eden followed. "We wash them every third time they're used."

"Nick!" Lucille's voice floated over the dividing wall. "Those cups go through the dishwasher in the employee lounge every time."

"That's better than I can say at my office," laughed Eden. Her eyes rested on Nick as he poured the coffee, noting the tapering fit of his pale shirt and the slim cut of trousers that stretched taut over his muscled thighs. Just looking at him was a pleasure, she decided.

He turned and caught her staring and she grinned at him. "Cream? Sugar?" he asked in that sensual voice she had liked so much that afternoon.

"Black, please."

He crossed over and handed her a mug, his fingers brushing against hers and communicating a current of warm pleasure. "I have a theory about that."

His nearness made her forget what they had been talking about. "Theory about what?" she asked as he led the way into his office and closed the door behind them.

"About people who take their coffee black." He indicated where she was to sit and then pulled up a matching leather wing chair, ignoring the imposing executive chair behind his massive desk. "They're people who try to do too much every day."

She leaned nearer and checked the contents of his cup. "You take yours black," she pointed out.

He nodded. "I'm the best proof of my theory. Have you ever noticed how long some people can spend stirring sugar into their coffee? They manage to make it seem almost like a sacred ritual." His low rich laughter filled the room. "They're the people who never hurry themselves, never push themselves."

Eden's laughter was soft and musical. "I'm lucky if I get to finish a single cup. This morning I started three cups while I was packing and yet I don't think I got more than a sip or two."

"See?" Nick drained off his mug before setting it on the glass-topped table between them. Stretching his long legs out comfortably before him, he eased his body back into the soft leather. "So you saw Fred?"

Eden tensed at the change of subject. "Yes." She hesitated. She forced herself to look him in the eye. "We didn't have much to agree on, but I think we can work it out."

Nick chuckled. "Eden, you know I told you earlier that Fred has full authority in that area. I didn't ask you in here to discuss Belle's Folly, although I am intrigued by how the place got its name."

Could she believe him? Was he really neutral about the disagreement between his office manager and herself? Or was this just a shrewd business maneuver to soften her up before he let her know his true feelings?

Recklessly, she offered an invitation. "That's a long story. If you come over to Belle's Folly I can show you around while I tell you."

He merely smiled, not saying yes or no, but Eden felt he appreciated her offer. With his head down, his thick dark lashes hid what he was thinking as a bronzed thumb made lazy circles on the arm of the chair. After a long silence he spoke in husky tones. "You interest me, Eden Sonnier. In some ways you're like...." He paused, letting the silence drag out before he looked up and grinned. "For lack of anything better, I'll say you're like an onion."

"An onion!" Eden stared at him, shocked. Finally she began laughing and Nick joined in. When she was able to catch her breath, she said, "I'm afraid being compared to an onion is a first for me. Surely you can do better than that. How about an artichoke, or something skinny and expensive like asparagus?''

He tilted his head to one side and his smile deepened. ''Um, an artichoke. That might suit... prickly on the outside, tender and....''

''Okay,'' interrupted Eden with a protesting wave of her hand. ''I asked for that one, but don't think I'm leaving here until you explain that reference to an onion.''

''Onions have layers. When you start to peel one, you find another layer underneath and then another and another. I suspect you're like that. When I first saw you standing on the ferry with that gorgeous hair blowing in the breeze, I thought you had to be the most beautiful woman I'd ever seen. Then I wrote you off...decided you were probably empty-headed and vain.''

She gasped, but he ignored it, continuing, ''I soon learned that first impressions can be wrong. Although your first layer was physical beauty, underneath I encountered an intelligent independent woman who wanted to solve her own problems. Now, I find out you're a successful businesswoman, a talented designer. You're intriguing me more and more, Eden.''

''I don't think I've ever met anyone who could turn an insult into a compliment with more grace.'' Eden set her own mug down on the table, smoothing her skirt over her shapely legs before adding, ''Haven't you left out that onions can sting and make you cry? They don't smell too great either.''

''You're hard to compliment, woman,'' he

growled, his eyes twinkling at her. "How about having dinner with me tonight so I can discover the next layer?"

She managed to hide her disappointment. "I'm busy tonight, Nick, but thanks anyway." On an impulse she added, "Tomorrow's free."

His smile broadened and he sat up suddenly. "I'll be finished tomorrow evening about eight. Would that be too late?"

"It's perfect. Gives me more time to work."

He glanced at the elegant digital clock on his desk and said reluctantly, "Our half hour is up, Eden." With one fluid motion he rose to his feet and extended his hand.

Grasping his fingers, Eden slid to her feet and stood beside him. Gradually they inclined toward each other. Just as Eden was sure those lips were going to move to cover hers, a slight tapping at the door abruptly drew their attention.

Still Nick lingered. "Till tomorrow night, then?" His eyes trapped hers, leaving her in no doubt of his sincerity.

"Till tomorrow," she agreed, ignoring the uneasy knot that formed in the pit of her stomach as she remembered her meeting with Fred the next day.

THE IMAGE OF NICK'S BRONZED FACE kept reappearing in Eden's mind once she and Larry were in the car again. He had to speak three times before he got her attention.

"Dinner tonight still on?" He kept his eyes on the road as he asked the question.

"If you're certain I'm not intruding."

"One hundred percent certain. We'll stop by my office and I'll loan you one of the company cars so you won't feel like a prisoner at Belle's Folly tonight."

"Tomorrow I must see about getting another rental car," Eden sighed, yawning and then covering her mouth with a dainty hand.

"I've got salesmen on vacation right now." Larry paused to snap off the windshield wipers. The rain had slackened to a mere mist. "Just keep the car until I need it."

"Thanks!" She settled back against the seat. "Do you think Fred is really going to take any plans I show him seriously?"

"After the way you handled him?" Larry laughed appreciatively. "I almost stood up and cheered when you reminded him that the community might be on your side. None of the oil companies around here can afford to tarnish their images with the townspeople unnecessarily."

"I didn't mean it as a form of blackmail," said Eden. "I was only trying to point out that there are other considerations besides the optimum amount of light for the employees.

"It was effective, anyway. I'd remember that if he tries to give you too much trouble."

Eden shook her head vigorously. "No, that's not my style. I'll fight fair, Larry. I only hope he's willing to do the same."

Larry's office was located in an extra-large mobile home on the main highway. Eden followed him inside. After introductions, Iris Jordan, a woman in her early fifties, offered her a cup of coffee.

"We've met before, Eden," said Iris. "I attended several of the annual open houses your aunt held at Belle's Folly. When you first walked in here, I was startled by your resemblance to your aunt."

"That's the second time I've had that pointed out to me today," answered Eden.

"I don't remember mentioning that," said Larry, choosing a set of keys from a pegboard on the wall.

"Nick did." Eden took a sip of her coffee. "He said he hoped I wasn't as formidable as Aunt Helene." She glanced at Iris and suppressed a bubble of laughter. The older woman was carefully moving her spoon around her cup, stirring the milky coffee with genuine concentration.

Larry began telling funny anecdotes that Eden suspected were mostly exaggerations about her aunt. The old lady had been a character, but it would have been impossible for her to be as awesome as these tales made her sound.

She drained her cup and set it down. "I better be going now. What time shall I be ready, Larry?"

"Seven or so. I'll pick you up first. Karen's never ready on time."

"I'll be ready," promised Eden.

The car ran smoothly and within minutes Eden reached Belle's Folly. She climbed out, locating the key Larry had given her before starting up the stairs.

The house unnerved her. It was too silent, too

dark and she hurried around, easing up the blinds and opening shutters and windows to allow fresh air to chase away the gloom. Thank heavens she was going out to dinner with Larry and Karen.

The upstairs was almost as musty. Eden carried her suitcase into her old room and set it down in the middle of the floor. After drawing the shades to the top of the wide windows and allowing the light to stream in, she hung the few articles of clothing she had brought. She'd have to make a quick trip to Houston this weekend unless Fred changed his mind about working with her.

A refreshing breeze was stirring through the windows now, but Eden noted with a frown that it was whisking clouds of dust off the furniture. Combined with the humidity from outside, the room would soon be a miserable place to sleep. If she was quick, she had just enough time to give the room a dust and vacuum before freshening up for the evening. Besides, the exercise would dispel some of the tension that had been building since her meeting at River Road Oil Services.

The necessary tools were neatly stashed in the upstairs utility closet, and Eden dragged the bulky vacuum down the long hall. As she poured the lemon oil on the carved cherry furniture with its cabriole legs and lovely scallop-shell motifs, her mind kept returning to Nick Devereaux. Her instant reaction to him had been so intense that she felt an urgent need to find some simple logical explanation.

The whir of the ancient vacuum wasn't enough to

block out the sound of the husky voice she remembered. Impatiently she snapped off the machine and carried it back to the closet. Why not just admit that nothing in her prior experience had inoculated her against a man with Nick's potent masculinity?

By seven, Eden had bathed and changed into a pair of hip-hugging white cotton slacks with a red-and-navy striped classic shirt. She dusted off one of the wicker chairs on the front gallery and settled down, enjoying the early-evening sounds of croaking frogs and the scent of honeysuckle blossoms from the tangled vines climbing the pillars.

Soon she became restless and debated calling Tom to see how he had managed without her. No, that wouldn't do. She was going to follow Nick's example and allow her employees the freedom to make their own decisions. Not that Tom wasn't more than just an employee, she reminded herself.

They were a lot alike...she and Tom. Both came from similar backgrounds and both enjoyed the challenge of the design world. Their personal lives were similar, too...each valued independence above all, but their relationship was comfortable and relaxed. Or was that only another way of saying it was dull?

CHAPTER THREE

EDEN JUMPED UP at the sight of Larry's car and ran down the steps to meet him. "It's a lovely evening," she said as she climbed in. "I don't know what I would have done if you hadn't invited me out. I'd forgotten how quiet Belle's Folly could be."

Larry slanted her a knowing glance. "Changed your mind and want to stay with my mother tonight?"

Eden shook her head. "No, I won't have any problem sleeping. I intend to get an early start on those plans for Fred in the morning."

"Karen's house isn't much." Larry changed the subject abruptly. "I found it for her. The price was right and it had a big backyard for Becky."

"How old did you say the little girl was?"

"Six. Karen's husband deserted her when she was pregnant and she hasn't heard from him since."

"How does she do it?" said Eden. "It's all I can do to drag myself home and fix a small meal some nights."

"No plans for a family, then?"

Eden closed her eyes briefly. "I didn't say that,"

she protested. "I love children and I think a family is a definite possibility in my future."

Larry chuckled. "Just making certain that your aunt didn't influence you too much. Remember when I tried to date you once? She told my mother that you weren't interested in such frivolous activities. I think she wanted you to dedicate yourself to a career."

"Definitely. I got constant lectures on the subject." Eden yawned and stretched in the cramped seat. "I make my own choices, Larry. Aunt Helene didn't push me into anything I didn't want."

They turned off on a farm-to-market road and Larry stopped in the driveway of the first house. Karen answered the door wearing only a slip and a gauzy cotton blouse.

"New outfit?" remarked Larry as he gave her a quick hug.

"I stayed too long at the baby-sitter's," apologized the slim woman with sleek, short red hair. "You must be Eden. I think you made quite a hit with the boss today. He asked me for the phone number at Belle's Folly as he was leaving."

"Negative impact," laughed Eden. "I'm sure if Fred wants to call me it won't be because he's in a friendly mood."

Mischief danced in Karen's green eyes. "Not Fred. The big boss. Nick!"

"Oh." Eden was unable to hide her pleasure. "Did you give it to him?"

"Fred didn't have it." She pulled open a drawer in a battered hall table and fished out a piece of paper and pencil. "Write it down and I'll give it to Nick tomorrow."

"Why is it that all some guys have to do is smile at a woman and she melts into a puddle?" Larry complained. "Did you know that I once tried to date Eden and she turned me down, Karen?"

"Don't believe him," returned Eden, scribbling the familiar phone number at Belle's Folly. "We were in junior high school and it was his mother's idea." She handed the slip of paper to Karen who stuffed it into her purse.

"Give me five minutes and I'll be ready, you two," the red-haired woman said. "Larry, you know where the drinks are. Pour something for Eden."

They went into the small living room and Larry bent over to pick up several plastic toys from the oval braided rug before dropping them in a loosely woven rush basket. "The choice is rather limited. Karen doesn't care much for the stuff. How about bourbon or bourbon?"

"Neither." Eden sank down on a worn colonial maple sofa. She glanced around, approving of the ruffled muslin curtains and the baskets filled to overflowing with leafy green plants. There was a casualness about both this room and its owner that she liked. "I'm sorry I didn't get to meet Becky. What's she like?"

"A carbon copy of her mother. Skinny. Red haired. Freckle faced. A perfect angel as far as I'm concerned. Unless you're too booked by Devereaux, we'll plan an outing so you can get acquainted with her while you're here.''

"Sounds great." Eden faked a yawn and stretched her legs out in front of her before trying to speak in an offhand manner. "Tell me something about Nick, Larry. I assume he's not married.''

Karen yelled out from another room, "No, he's not married, Eden. He used to always bring the same date to the company parties. A really glamorous female from Baton Rouge, but she doesn't seem to be in the picture anymore.'' She entered the room, fully dressed except for a pair of leather sandals dangling from the perfectly manicured fingers of her left hand. "There may be someone in New Orleans. He spends all his weekends there," she added.

"Gossip, Karen. Idle gossip." Larry's voice was filled with affectionate familiarity.

"No, it's not!" Karen contradicted, sitting down to buckle the straps of her shoes. "If Eden's like me, the first thing she does when some guy shows interest is find out if he's married. Saves a lot of problems.'' She straightened up and smoothed down the skirt of her ivory cotton sundress. "Believe it or not, I'm ready. Where are we going?''

THE SUN WOKE EDEN the next morning and briefly she had trouble remembering where she was. Then deep contentment flowed through her and she lay still, watching a ray of sunshine chasing over the

down-filled satin comforter at the foot of her bed.
It felt wonderful not to be awakened by the beep-
beep of her electronic alarm clock. Not to have to
race around getting dressed, dreading the thought
of the rush-hour traffic in Houston.

Coffee. Thank heavens Larry had suggested they
stop at a country store on their way home from dinner the evening before. Eden had grabbed a few es-
sential groceries and chatted with Karen while she
picked out a surprise for Becky's breakfast.

Sliding to her feet, she stretched luxuriously. Not
bothering to change out of her lacy teddy, she hurried downstairs to the kitchen.

The familiar pots and pans were in their usual
place and the ancient stove proved as difficult as
ever to light. How had Camille, Aunt Helene's
faithful housekeeper, put up with it all those years?
Soon Eden was wandering out onto the gallery luxuriating in the cool morning breeze with a cup in
one hand and a fragrant, warm cinnamon roll in the
other.

Musingly, she recalled her evening out with Larry
and Karen. She had liked Karen immensely. Thursday evening she was going to have dinner at her
house and already she was looking forward to it.
Karen had been honest about her reason for the invitation. She wanted to discuss the problems she
was having with Fred Borman and thought an out-
sider might be able to see it from a truer perspective.

Eden took another sip thoughtfully. She wanted
something from Karen as well. She wanted to quiz

her more fully about Nick. Larry had discouraged Karen from talking about him the evening before, but Eden had heard enough to pique her curiosity.

She felt restless as she prowled around the entire length of the house. Was it because of the affection in Karen's voice every time she mentioned her young daughter?

I'll be twenty-eight on my next birthday, she reminded herself. *And too caught up in getting a business running successfully and making a name for myself to give marriage much thought.* She remembered a management course she's taken right after she finished her training. Marriage and children had been important goals on her list of dreams at that time. But somehow their importance had been casually set aside.

An ache throbbed inside her, revealing an empty place she hadn't been aware of before. She hurried back inside the house, rinsing out her coffee cup. What was wrong with her? She had it all, didn't she? Work she loved, a successful business, a man who made it plain he wanted her. This unaccustomed morning of sleeping late must have unbalanced her thinking temporarily.

By noon she had sketched out a rough plan for the renovation of Belle's Folly, but she wasn't entirely pleased with it. It might not be as easy to turn the old mansion into a modern office setting as she'd hoped. On the other hand, she was confident that with a little more time she'd manage to come up with a winning design.

After gathering up the rough sketches and placing them in her briefcase, she took a container of yogurt out of the nearly bare refrigerator. A trip for a more extensive variety of groceries was definitely on her agenda, she decided with a sigh.

Shortly before two, Eden presented herself to Lucille and received a welcoming smile. There was no sign of Nick in the outer office, and Eden was halfway through her meeting with Fred before she really got her mind on the subject.

"I passed some large rooms with a number of desks in them farther down the hall, Fred. Could you tell me who uses them and what specific requirements the workers have?"

Fred avoided answering any of her questions directly. When they parted, Eden felt no closer to an agreement than before, but at least she had gathered a little of the information she needed in making her plans. Fred placed an arm around her shoulder as he escorted her out of the building, which made Karen grin surreptitiously when they passed. Eden pulled away as soon as she could without making a scene. It looked as if Fred was going to require careful handling, but she had dealt with his type before.

On the drive home Eden tried to decide what to wear that evening. Now that Nick had transcended business with pleasure, she knew the few garments she had brought with her weren't adequate. Besides, he had already seen her in everything except the slacks, and there were still some restaurants in this area that frowned on women wearing pants.

She drove slowly through the small town nearest

Belle's Folly, checking to see if any of the stores on the square sold clothes. She was about to give up when she saw a sign advertising a boutique down a side street. Her abrupt turn without a signal brought a protest from the driver of the truck behind her, but she ignored it, braking to a stop at the first available parking space.

Inside she found a wide selection, but none suited until she spotted a sheer white India cotton voile, lavished with lace and tucks. That ought to throw the perceptive Mr. Devereaux. This dress was sophisticated, but romantic...sexy but demure. Anyway, the one pair of heels she had with her would go with it and that was the deciding factor in the end.

NICK WAS DRESSED CASUALLY when he arrived; brown slacks, open-necked shirt and a camel sports jacket. Casual, yet conservative enough to please even the strictest maitre'd. Eden opened the screen door and he stepped back, taking his time to give her a thorough survey. "Stunning! And very sexy! Every time I see you I'm bowled over."

"You aren't too bad yourself," she said, a slow warmth rising to her cheeks. "I'd invite you in for a drink, but the liquor cabinet is dry as a bone."

"If you stay long, we'll have to remedy that." He glanced around the hall with a bemused gaze. "Did people really live in this house once?"

"Not just people." Eden stepped back to afford him a wider view of the massive entry. "I lived here.

My parents died in an accident when I was five, so my great-aunt took me in.''

Nick glanced toward the parlor and then back to the formal dining room. Through the hand-carved double doors, the twenty-two-foot-long mahogany table was visible, with its matching graceful chairs. ''What did you do? Whisper and tiptoe around so you wouldn't wake up the ghosts?''

Eden's mouth curved in a rueful smile. ''I'm afraid not. My aunt was extremely strong willed and I'm equally stubborn. Between the two of us, we made a lot of noise.'' She lifted one slim hand and gestured toward the living room. ''Would you like to be taken on a tour?''

''Sounds great, but not tonight, I don't know about you, but I'm starving.'' He took her by the arm and they went outside.

''I'm past the stage of starving,'' Eden answered truthfully. ''My kitchen is bare, too.''

''Then I'm glad I didn't make reservations in Baton Rouge. Have you ever eaten at The Bayous? It's not very impressive from the outside, but the owners are from Austria and the food is unusual as well as delicious.''

''When I last lived at Belle's Folly, you were lucky to find a hamburger between here and Baton Rouge.'' Eden transferred her skinny purse to her left hand long enough to lock the front door.

''There still isn't much along here,'' Nick agreed, his mouth near her ear. His warm breath whispered against her skin, ruffling strands of the blue black hair. The first stars of early evening twinkled overhead, and for a moment they stood without speaking, a comfortable silence filled only by the buzzing and whirring of insects off in the thick trees.

"Do you like to dance?" Nick broke the silence finally.

"I love to." Eden tossed her hair back over one shoulder. "Is there a place to dance at this restaurant? That would make it a real find."

"Whenever the band shows up, which isn't too often," he admitted.

After they were both in the car, Eden turned to-ward Nick. "I seldom meet a man who admits to liking to dance. But then, you're unusual in many ways." Her compliment was sincere and she sensed that he realized she wasn't merely trying to flatter him.

He started the powerful engine. She was acutely aware of him in the small enclosed space: his clean male scent, the rise and fall of his broad chest, the pulse beating strongly in the tanned column of his neck.

Turning, his gaze swept over her, warming her as though she was standing in a summer breeze. "How am I unusual," he demanded quietly.

"A business man who doesn't talk exclusively about his work. Do you know, I really have no idea what River Road Oil Services does to earn its hefty profits. Or have you delegated so much to Fred that you're not certain yourself?" she teased.

His rich laughter danced between them. "I wish I could. Don't think delegating comes easy to me. I love my work and it's a constant fight not to interfere with every detail. I started out as a one-man operation and I still harbor a few vestiges of the superman complex. It wasn't until I came down with a severe case of pneumonia a few years ago that I found out things went along pretty well even in my absence. Since then I've slowly learned to change.''

"That's something I need to learn," she admitted wryly. "Does your company drill oil wells?"

"We bring in the wells, but then our responsibility ends. We're basically an investment firm. We sell shares in producing wells to people who need a place to park their money."

"So, you find the wells and then run like crazy?" She wanted to keep him talking so she could lean back and enjoy looking at him.

"It's not that easy." Nick settled back in his seat so that he could turn to talk to her. "We drill a lot of dry holes for every one that gushes."

The car engine was purring softly now, an occasional surge of power indicating that it was not used to sitting idly while its owner talked. "How did you get started?" Eden asked deliberately, trying to prolong this conversation.

"As a roustabout. I was sixteen and Job Devereaux...." Nick stopped abruptly and his hands tightened on the wheel. "My father," he explained hurriedly. "He gave me my first chance. He was a wildcatter, one of the best, before his death."

"That must have been hard on your mother. Isn't a wildcatter's life dangerous?"

Nick froze, the muscles in his cheek tightening and then relaxing before he replied. "My mother was dead. Anyway, she didn't know Job...he adopted me later." His voice throbbed with repressed tension.

Eden immediately regretted her probing questions. Nick's past seemed to cause him a great deal of pain. He hadn't mentioned his real father, perhaps he hadn't even known him. She could understand how he felt. Her own parents had died when she was five, and the most she could remember of them was that her mother had been tall and slim, very sweet, with dark hair and eyes very much like her own. Her father had been fun, always laughing, and it didn't take her long to realize that Aunt Helene had disapproved of her nephew. With more composure than she was feeling, she switched the conversation back to safer ground. "What made you start your own business?"

Nick eased the brake off and guided the car out onto the main road. He smiled over at her, a slow smile that made her catch her breath. "Do I get a turn to ask you all these questions next?"

"Fair enough," Eden grinned impudently at him. "First, though, I intend to satisfy my curiosity."

They chatted quietly until Nick stopped the car in a poorly lighted parking lot. "Recognize this place?"

Eden made out the faint outline of a squarish building. "I think there used to be a dance studio here."

"Could be. Karl and his wife opened their restaurant about a year ago. The food is excellent, particularly if you place yourself in their hands and pay no attention to the menu." He opened his car door.

She was outside by the time he came around and she laughed when he glared at her. "I'm not used to being treated so elegantly," she said lightly. "Besides, I'm absolutely starving."

"Have I mentioned how beautiful you are?" he murmured, slipping an arm around her waist.

"Mmm...." She nodded.

"And how delightful you smell?" He very gently brushed his lips against the curve of her neck, a touch so subtle she could hardly be sure it had been there.

She melted against him. *Steady there,* she reminded herself. *Don't start something you'll regret.* "Not like an onion?" she interjected lightly.

Nick raised his head and groaned, the sound barely audible. "Are you ever going to let me live that one down?"

"Sorry, I couldn't resist." Eden brushed back a strand of her hair and moved toward the doorway.

The restaurant was inviting and homey, with flowered cloths on the tables. Fat round candles cast a soft glow creating a feeling of intimacy. A squat blond young man hurried toward them, smoothing his hands on the apron he wore over khaki trousers. "I was mentioning you to my wife only tonight, Nick." He seemed delighted. "We haven't seen you for a while. Please...come this way."

"I've been kept busy," explained Nick. He introduced Eden as they were seated.

Karl nodded in Eden's direction, his smile friendly. "Would you like the menus tonight?"

Nick shook his head. "We're putting ourselves in yours and Anna's hands. I might warn you that we're both starving."

"Perfect. I will bring a bottle of your favorite wine and some of those stuffed mushrooms to begin."

"You must come here often," said Eden. She refused to admit, even to herself, that she wanted to know if some special woman usually accompanied him.

Could he read her mind? "Whenever I can't face eating alone another time, I drive over here. Anna and Karl treat me like one of the family. How about you? Do you live alone, Eden?"

"Yes, but I detest eating in a restaurant alone. I know it's stupid, but I always find myself people watching, being terribly nosy and staring at them."

Nick's eyes moved down to the shadowed clefts of her full breasts, caressing the soft flesh as surely as if he'd touched them. "I'm sure many people stare at you," he murmured, his eyes dark pools in the candlelight. "You're a special woman, Eden. I think I like this purely feminine layer best of all."

"Nick," she laughed softly. He was so direct that she wasn't certain what to say.

Karl returned with a bottle of wine and went through an elaborate tasting ceremony with both

Eden and Nick. "A toast," said Nick, touching her glass when they were alone. "May this be only the first of many happy times spent together."

Dinner was excellent: stuffed mushrooms, rice almond soup with a touch of saffron, slices of rare prime rib and fresh asparagus drenched in a lemony butter sauce. Nick sliced off a chunk of golden wheat bread and handed it to her. "I believe you haven't satisfied your curiosity about me, Eden. What else can I tell you?"

She smiled demurely. "Is that a polite way of telling me I ask too many questions?"

"Not at all." Nick seemed genuinely shocked. "I always appreciate a good listener. Actually, I usually find it rather difficult to talk about my own life, but you've got me telling you all my secrets."

"How about giving me a quick résumé?" Eden asked in mock seriousness. "Age? Work history? Hobbies? I have an insatiable curiosity."

"As long as you remember I get equal time." He buttered his bread. "Age: thirty-four. From New Orleans. Graduate of Tulane with a major in petroleum engineering. Worked at every type of job in the oil business until five years ago when I went out on my own. I haven't had much time for hobbies." He paused to take a deep breath and grinned. "Enough?"

"Ever been married?"

His eyes became serious. "No. How about you?"

"The same."

"Involved with anyone?"

The tension between them was acute, and Eden

felt tiny beads of perspiration form on the warm valley of flesh between her breasts. "I've been spending a lot of time with my assistant," she said slowly. "I'm not certain how I feel about him, except that we have a lot of common interests. How about you?"

He shrugged. "There's no one in particular." He poured some wine. "I'm certain of one thing: You're a very special person and I'm really enjoying being here with you tonight." His eyes met and trapped hers, sending a jolt throughout her confused senses.

She looked away first, picking up her fork and taking another bite of the succulent beef. "Tell me about your work, Eden," he said. "Do you enjoy it?"

"I love it! After graduating from high school I had a real fight with my aunt to let me go to a design institute rather than the college she'd chosen for me. I'm glad I won because it's the perfect job for me."

A smile touched his lips. "What do you do? I'm afraid I don't know much about interior designers."

"We're very useful creatures," she began. "Actually we save people money by helping put together all their ideas into one coherent plan. Most people don't realize what a wide range of knowledge we have to have...construction, plumbing, electrical wiring. And of course, colors, fabrics, furniture. There's always something new to learn."

He raised one eyebrow. "How do you decide what will please a client?"

"I get to know them, their likes, their dislikes. How they spend their time. I like to see how they've decorated in the past. A room doesn't work unless the person feels comfortable in it." Her eyes sparkled with enthusiasm as she warmed up to her subject.

"How about offices? Have you ever designed for one before?"

"Oh, yes." Eden nibbled at her food before continuing. "We handle as many office projects as we do residences. I have one employee who specializes in that, if that bothers you."

He reached out and took one of her hands in his own large grasp. "Nothing's bothering me, Eden. As far as I'm concerned, you and I are not involved in any business transaction." Bending over, he brushed his lips against her palm lightly, setting off a chain of delicious inner tremors.

"Nick, I can't forget that you're the owner of the company that's leased Belle's Folly," she said quietly. "I can't believe it doesn't make any difference to you what happens between Fred and myself."

He took a deep breath and sat back. "Okay, Eden. If you insist, we'll talk about it." His fingers restlessly moved an unused fork in tiny patterns on the tablecloth. "Yes, I am concerned about the outcome of your negotiations over the lease, but if I spent my time handling that I couldn't concentrate on my expertise, which is bringing in oil wells. I believe in hiring the best people and then giving them full responsibility for doing their job. I'm sure you're aware that legally we have the right to make the changes we want since you did sign that damned lease.''

"I had no idea the extent of your plans," she sighed. "When Fred said you were thinking of making an offer for the property at the end of the lease, I didn't know what to say. I thought Larry understood that I don't intend to sell if I can possibly help it.''

Nick's face was unreadable. "So Fred tells me.'' He sat silently for a moment and then said, "I suppose it's none of my business what you plan to do with the house someday?''

Eden had to smile. "An impossible dream, I suppose, but I don't want to see the dream die, not after all the years of hard work and suffering it represents for my family.''

"A very romantic view—'' Nick looked at her thoughtfully "—but perhaps in another five years you'll feel differently.''

"I doubt it," Eden said flatly, wishing they'd never started this conversation.

"I do understand now why you're so bent on preventing us from making extensive changes. I've tried not to get too involved, but from what I can see, the installation of air conditioning is going to require at least some structural changes. Surely you agree that we can't expect our employees to work in this kind of heat.''

"Of course," Eden murmured. "Is that why

Fred gave me some time to come up with alternate plans? Is he hoping I'll design something less expensive?''

''Not exactly. I asked Fred the same question yesterday.'' Nick's voice was frank and Eden couldn't doubt his honesty on this point. ''It was his opinion that you could make things sticky for us in the community. Since we're planning on making our permanent headquarters here, that wasn't too desirable.''

''So this was a little ploy to make everyone think you had made an effort, while all the while you're still planning to tear up my house any way you see fit?'' Sickening disappointment colored Eden's tones as she pushed back her plate and reached for her bag from the seat beside her.

''No!'' Nick's voice sounded equally unhappy. ''If you can come up with a design that works, then we'll use it.''

''That's a big *if*. Who's to decide if it's workable?'' Eden was still poised to move.

Nick reached across and grasped the bag, removing it from her hands and placing it on the seat beside him. Then he took both of her hands in his. ''Eden, why can't we pretend we've just met and this has nothing to do with business? I promise I'll be staying out of any negotiations you enter into with Fred. If you can convince him, you'll win. Otherwise, he'll have to do what he considers best for my company.''

''And if it's not best for my house, I suppose we'll end up on opposite sides in court?'' Eden's face was stony.

"It's not going to come to that." Nick sounded sure of himself. "Would it help if I put the final decision to a panel composed of all the administrative personnel? I'll even throw in one vote from the architectural firm, if you'd like an outside opinion."

The anger drained from her. "Will you vote?"

"I only vote if there's a tie in matters such as these. How about it?" He brought her hands to his mouth and tenderly kissed each one in turn. "Are we still friends?"

She gently disengaged one hand and traced his firm jawline with the tip of one finger. "I'd like very much to have you for my friend," she whispered.

The ride back to Belle's Folly was accomplished in companionable silence. The heavy meal, combined with the warm night air, caught up with Eden and she dozed off.

Belle's Folly was dark, lit only by the soft yellow porch light. The air was still and heavy, the pungent scent of Spanish moss mingling with the dying blossoms of wild flowers. Nick brought the car to a halt beside the staircase, coming around to wait as Eden slid out in a half-dazed state.

When she turned to say good-night, she found that Nick was right beside her and a jolt of excitement rushed through her veins. "Thanks for dinner," she whispered, her eyes widening as they adjusted to the soft darkness.

"It was all my pleasure," Nick replied, his husky murmur making Eden's breathing alter slightly. The darkness enfolded them as he reached for her, his warm mouth unerringly finding her half-parted lips. Her first instinct was to resist, but lulled by the sweet warmth of Nick's body and the promise in the evening air, she didn't even try to push him away.

Her hands crept around to his back, her fingers kneading the taut muscles, as her thighs were pressed firmly against his. Lost in the chemistry of their melding mouths, she was only vaguely aware of the moment his hands slid down to curve around her bottom and pull her into the thrusting urgency of his hips.

His unhurried kiss was teasing at first, emphasizing the depth of his attraction for her. As the lingering kiss deepened, it hinted at a passion Eden could only imagine. A shiver of mingled pleasure and anticipation trembled through her. With no thought for the consequences, Eden stepped closer into the intimacy of his male body.

As if in a dream she heard his husky whisper in her ear. "Umm, your hair smells delicious." Nuzzling his chin into the soft waves, he moved his lips through the silky strands. "It's like a black cloud, Eden." Lifting his chin, he grinned down at her, framing her face with his hands. "Does it signify a storm ahead?"

In answer, Eden lifted her face for his kiss again, and this time it was she who injected a certain reckless urgency into the melding of their mouths. The last vestige of propriety disappeared in a glowing sensual mist as Nick tasted the moist inner recesses, his tongue sipping, exploring, entering into a seductive give and take that reminded Eden of other, more intimate sharing.

Somehow, without even being aware of it, she found that she was leaning against the staircase railing, held there by the pressure of Nick's body and one long muscular thigh thrust between hers. The gauzy cotton of her dress had been pulled down, freeing her breasts to the arousing play of his large warm hands. His fingers circled the dusky peaks and the deep rose tips swelled to meet the exquisite torture of his touch.

Her own fingers worked impatiently at the buttons of his shirt to tangle finally in the matted dark vee of hair, evoking a sigh of pleasure from Eden and an answering groan from Nick.

Her back arched, lifting her breasts to the seductive exploration of Nick's fingers, and Eden felt the dampness of his firm chest. Both of them were breathing hard and as their mouths reluctantly broke apart, Eden observed the look of surprised pleasure in Nick's eyes as he gazed into the blissful depths of her own.

"Eden...darling," Nick whispered as his hands moved over her arms and along the sides of her creamy breasts with restless fascination. "You're beautiful...your breasts.... Oh, God, I never knew anything could be so soft...but then I've known you were special...since the first second I saw you.... Please love...let me love you."

Temptation beckoned before Eden forced herself to slow things down. With reluctant pressure, she slid her hands to Nick's hips, exerting steady force until he eased away from her. "No, Nick... not now...please, I'm sorry...but we have to stop."

With a muffled groan he rested his chin lightly on the top of her head. His breathing gradually slowed as he gained control. Slowly, so slowly that at first Eden wasn't sure what was happening, she felt laughter overtake him, until he shook against her. "Oh, Eden," he choked huskily. "What have you done to me? I feel about sixteen years old right now." As his laughter ended, he lifted his head and smiled down at her, his grin slightly crooked. "Forgive me?"

With one hand Eden pulled her dress up to cover her breasts, a glimmer of humor beginning to curve her own mouth. "Actually, now that I've been classed as a maiden niece," she admitted, "it's nice to know I can have this effect on a man."

Nick reached out one hand to smooth the fabric of her dress over one shoulder, helping her get her clothes back in place. Her gesture strangely intimate, Eden buttoned his shirt, her fingers lingering reluctantly on the smooth cotton after she was through.

Leaning forward to rest her forehead against his chest, she whispered, "I'm sorry I didn't know you when you were sixteen."

Nick chuckled. "Just stay around and I'll probably act that way all the time." Gathering up a handful of her gleaming hair, Nick rubbed two fingers across the strands. "I better get out of here before I start dreaming about seeing this spread out on a pillow beside me,'' he murmured frankly.

Eden fought unsuccessfully against the series of erotic vignettes his words invoked. ''Good night,'' she said hesitantly.

Nick followed her up the steps, waiting until she entered the hallway and switched on a flood of bright lights. Reaching into his pocket, he pulled out a plain business card and scribbled a number on the back. ''If you need me for anything—'' he glanced around the room with a disturbed expression ''—or if you get scared in this damned gloomy place, call me.''

''I wouldn't dream of disturbing you,'' she assured him.

Nick slanted a smile at her and as the screen door closed behind him, with a soft murmur, his words floated back to her. ''Dreams of you will be disturbing me all night.''

CHAPTER FOUR

EARLY THURSDAY MORNING, Eden opened the door to a long-legged, copper-haired man in his early twenties dressed in khaki work clothes. "Miss Sonnier?" he asked politely.

"Yes?" She peered behind him to see if the van she spotted in the driveway gave any clues to his identity.

"Roy Jones of Jones Air Conditioning," he drawled.

Eden shook her head with a grin. "Sorry, but there's nothing here that needs repairing. All the old window units seem to be working."

"I know. Mr. Borman sent me to draw up specs and give his firm a bid on air conditioning Belle's Folly."

Eden bit back her angry words. Damn Fred. This was sufficient proof that he had no intention of listening to her. "Did Fred tell you there are two plans under consideration?" she asked, pushing open the screen door and motioning Roy Jones inside.

He frowned. "No, he gave me this blueprint...." He held out the roll he had tucked under his arm.

"There's been a change," she returned firmly. "I've got a pot of coffee brewing. Why don't I explain over a cup?"

They carried the ironstone mugs into the breakfast room, settling down at a round oak table that was bathed in bars of streaming sunshine. Eden spread out some of the rough sketches she had been laboring over since sunrise. "These aren't complete, but I believe they'll show you what I have in mind." With as few words as possible she explained her plans to restore the old mansion.

He leaned over and studied her sketches thoughtfully and then raised his eyes to meet hers. "I won't have any trouble following these. It would be nice to see Belle's Folly become a first-class tourist attraction. Do the town good not to depend so much on work at the oil companies."

"Are you from the river-road area?"

"Oh, yeah. I remember you. My dad worked at the Sonnier Sugarcane Mill until it closed. When I was a kid I always loved to come to the open houses your aunt held here."

Memories softened Eden's sapphire-blue eyes. "Jones? You have a sister named Ann?"

"Right. I think she was a couple of years ahead of you in school."

"I haven't thought about those parties in years," Eden said. "Aunt Helene used to plan for them all year. She always chose the Sunday closest to the day the original house was finished by Lucien Sonnier. Do you remember those huge buffet tables out under the oak trees?"

He chuckled. "Do I ever remember them! Once I ate so many buttermilk biscuits filled with slices of ham that I was sick all night. My mom said I disgraced her."

"Do you think it's just a dream to want to leave the house to the community?" Eden asked softly.

"No way! I've got a son now and I'd like for him to see what life was like long ago. I hope you can pull it off."

His enthusiasm encouraged Eden. "I'll work on it," she promised. After showing Roy where the stairs leading to the attic were located, she returned to her sketches.

She had reached the stage where she was visualizing the individual offices for River Road Oil Services. The entrance hall was wide enough to accommodate the receptionist desk. An elegant conference room could be made out of the long dining room, and what other company would be able to boast a twenty-two-foot-long mahogany table that was a priceless antique?

The executive offices would grace the opposite side of the hall, and the present kitchen needed only to be modernized to make a superb employee lounge. Upstairs, the bedrooms could accommodate the bulk of the office staff: the landsmen, accountants, administrative assistants and their secretaries. Everything was falling into place on the sheets of paper under her deft fingers.

Nick would approve of it. She was certain of that. Although she was caught up in excitement over the project at hand, her mind had kept returning to thoughts of him all morning. There was something different about his caresses, his kisses, something infinitely more exciting than other men she knew. Even now she could taste his lips on hers. Each word he had spoken echoed in her mind, the husky nuances saying volumes more than any surface meaning.

If he had continued his seductive caresses, would she have gone to bed with him? The resounding yes that came to mind startled her. She had never been casual about lovemaking, never believed it possible that she could feel this strongly after knowing a man only a few days.

The ring of the phone interrupted her thoughts and she hurried to answer it. It was Tom, sounding slightly breathless and making Eden feel guilty over the heavy work load she had dumped on her assistant.

"I got your message," he said. "I would have returned the call sooner, but I've been at the Hewes place, fighting over the paint colors. When can I expect you back?"

"It may be longer than I thought." She added a brief explanation of how she had won the first round in her battle to save Belle's Folly. "I'll fly back to Houston tomorrow and see if I need to call any clients. If necessary, we'll ask for a delay in the completion dates."

"I'm coping," said Tom, his voice slightly aggrieved. She could picture him running his fingers through his sun-streaked blond hair that was showing faint traces of gray at the temples. At forty-one,

Tom's passion in life was antique furniture and he was recognized as one of Houston's leading authorities in the field.

Eden had first met him several years earlier, but they had only begun dating in the last six months. They made a good team and recently Tom had been dropping hints about the possibility of marriage. Was that what she wanted?

"If you don't mind," Tom was continuing, "I'll give your phone number to Alan Gregg. He and his wife want to talk to you about decorating their chalet in Colorado. He wouldn't believe me when I told him it was doubtful you'd have time."

"I don't," she said firmly. "Have him call and I'll tell him myself. If they don't want to wait, we'll recommend another firm. Any more problems?"

"The furniture you ordered for the Cullens arrived from North Carolina yesterday. I'm going out to oversee its arrangement this afternoon."

"You'll find the layout sheet in my top right-hand desk drawer. "What's this about the Hewes? What color paint are they wanting now?"

Tom laughed over the exasperation in her voice. "Two hours ago she was certain she wanted a deeper shade of mauve."

Eden sighed. "That's the third change in a month. Did you explain there would be an additional fee for it?"

"Yes, darling. She's willing to pay." His voice lowered. "I've been missing you, Eden."

Guilt returned. She hadn't been missing him at

all, she realized. The silence lengthened and Tom broke it off first, his tone dry. "Absence doesn't always make the heart grow fonder, I see," he murmured.

"Tom...."

"Forget it, darling. You have enough on your mind without me complicating things. Give me a ring when your plane is due and I'll meet you. If you make it before ten, we'll have time to run by the Terrells' housewarming."

"Damn, I'd forgotten that," moaned Eden. "I'll call you and make plane reservations."

After ending her conversation with Tom and calling the airline, Eden bit her lower lip thoughtfully. This weekend she had to explain to Tom that she wasn't ready to make any decisions about a future with him.

Late that afternoon she went through the sparse clothes in her room, desperate to locate something to wear to Karen's house. Outside, the humid bayou air was hot and heavy. The sun hadn't been warm enough to burn off the residue from the rain two days before.

She held up and rejected several garments, and then settled on the only pair of slacks she had brought. They were black cotton, wide at the top, with baggy pockets, tapering down to end with a tight fit just below her knees. Turning up her nose at the matching shirt, she hunted around in her drawers and emerged triumphant with a skinny camisole T-shirt left over from her high-school days. Its bright turquoise color would add just the right touch without looking as though she were trying to intimidate the other woman.

After a quick bath she tugged the slacks over her rounded hips and shrugged into the T-shirt, not concerned about the lack of a bra. This was an evening strictly for females. It was going to be fun to meet Becky and get better acquainted with Karen. An opportunity to learn more about Nick would be welcome as well.

When she pulled into the oyster shell driveway in front of Karen's simple frame house, she caught sight of a small girl with flaming red hair darting in and out of a lawn sprinkler. By the time Eden had climbed out of her car, the child was running toward her. "Are you Eden? My name's Becky," she shouted.

Eden knelt down to eye level with her, ignoring the droplets of water being sprayed over her slacks and shirt. "Yes, I'm Eden. That looks like lots of fun."

"It is! Guess what we're having for supper." The green eyes bubbled excitedly.

"I can't guess. Will you tell me?"

"Meatballs and spaghetti! Uncle Nick's coming by afterwards for some blackberry cobbler."

Nick? Eden's pulse skipped a beat. Was it possible Karen knew someone else by that name? She followed Becky to the front door and went inside.

"Don't dare come in here. You know you have to use the back door when you're wet." Karen's voice floated in from the back of the house.

"It's me," replied Eden, leaning over to pick up

the same toys she had seen Larry retrieving earlier. Once again she felt a tug as she surveyed the homey, comfortable atmosphere.

Karen entered, laughing. "Sorry, I didn't hear your car. I don't usually yell at my guests like that." She pointed to a chair. "Have a seat while I get us a glass of wine. I need something to help me unwind before we eat." Her fuchsia terry jump suit complemented the sleek red hair and pale complexion.

When she returned with two glasses and a bottle of chilled white wine, she sank down on the sofa and kicked off her sandals. "Whew! I hope your day has gone better than mine."

Eden accepted a glass and took a sip. "It wasn't bad. Fred played one nasty surprise on me, sending an air-conditioning firm to make a bid on his plans for Belle's Folly."

Karen nodded. "I wondered why he didn't cancel that. How's your plan coming?"

"Great! Now all I have to do is make Fred agree."

Karen's eyes slanted mischievously. "Guess who invited himself over for dessert when he heard me telling Lucille you were my guest tonight."

Eden breathed a sigh of pleasure. "Becky told me Uncle Nick was coming. Tell me she meant the one I know."

"Himself. Of course, he might just be fond of my cooking," she teased. "Honestly, Eden, you should feel flattered. He can't even hide how interested he is in you."

Eden smiled and took a sip of her wine. "Tell me a little about him."

"I don't know much, really," admitted Karen thoughtfully. "He's a great boss. Kind, considerate, a good sense of humor. But he doesn't let anyone get too close to him. When I first went to work for the company, I had the most terrific crush on him; especially when I saw how fond he is of children. Did you know he stops by here just to play with Becky occasionally?"

A stab of pain, peculiarly similar to jealousy, struck Eden. "Maybe he's interested in Becky's mother," she said in what she hoped was a casual tone.

Karen disparaged that. "Not one little ounce. He's pleased that I'm dating Larry. All the employee's children interest him, but I happen to live along the way he takes to go home."

Eden slipped off her shoes and tucked her feet under her. "If he's so fond of children, why do you think he's never married, Karen?"

The other woman shrugged. "Maybe he's been too absorbed with building up a business from scratch. I don't think he had anyone backing him, either. At least, that's what Fred said."

"Fred." Eden made a face. "Any trouble out of him lately?"

"I thought you'd never ask." Karen leaned forward and set her wineglass down on the coffee table with a thud. "Would you mind giving me a little advice on how to handle him? It may be silly, but I can't stand the way he paws me."

"Sexual harassment?" Eden took another sip from her glass. The term had become a catchword for a lot of women, yet owning her own business made her virtually immune to the problem. But as a student, she remembered a professor who had infuriated her with his behavior.

"I don't know when flirting turns into harassment," admitted Karen slowly.

"Anytime it's offensive, in my book. What does he do?"

Karen's face flushed slightly. "I told you it would sound silly," she mumbled, shifting uncomfortably. "It may just be me. I had a bad experience with Becky's father, so I may be reacting more than the situation is worth. More wine?" she asked.

Eden shook her head and Karen continued. "Probably what's bothering me most is that Fred only started this recently. At first he began just brushing against me when I was at the file cabinet. You know the type of thing. Leaning over me when I was at the typewriter until I almost had my face in the ribbon. Cornering me whenever I tried to pass him. Nothing blatant."

"Then he progressed to running his hands over my arms and making remarks about my anatomy." She stuck out her chest. "Since I'm so flat, you'll probably think I'm making this all up."

"Not at all," Eden denied, remembering Fred's leering glances. "Have you mentioned this to Nick?"

"I haven't even mentioned it to Larry." Karen looked miserable. "He knows I'm unhappy with

Fred but doesn't know the real reason." She leaned forward anxiously. "Eden, my job is everything! Becky's father doesn't pay a cent of child support, so I don't dare do anything to jeopardize my income. Do you know of any ways to discourage Fred without making him so angry he'll find a way to fire me?"

"How have you been handling him?"

"At first I tried ignoring his remarks, thinking he'd get tired of it if I didn't respond. Then last week I snapped at him to get away from me and he's doubled my work load since."

"That's terrible," Eden flared. "Why don't we discuss it with Nick when he comes tonight? He's responsible for what happens in his company."

Karen's eyes widened in alarm. "Please, don't say a word. Nick shouldn't have to interfere. It's his policy to...."

"I know," interrupted Eden wearily. "He delegates. Isn't that a convenient way of passing the buck?"

"It's not his purpose," defended Karen. "He believes in giving everyone an opportunity to take responsibility. In my case it's worked. I started out as a file clerk and now I've risen to executive secretary under his policy." She jumped up suddenly. "Do I smell something burning?"

Eden followed her into the kitchen and under Karen's instructions mixed the dressing for the lettuce, orange and almond salad. Karen continued talking as she ladled scoops of tender spaghetti onto the plates. "Really, I think I may be exaggerating the whole thing, Eden. Why don't you forget I ever mentioned it?''

"If you promise to tell me if things get worse. Nick may have to step in whether he likes it or not,'' Eden replied firmly.

Karen sent Eden in search of Becky and she located the bright-eyed little girl in her bedroom. After assisting her in washing her hands, they joined Karen at the table. "Where do you stay when mommy's at work?'' Eden asked.

"At the ABC school. We have slides and swings and a sandbox.''

Karen passed a bowl of freshly grated Parmesan cheese. "As you can see from all the bumps and scratches on Becky, she prefers the outdoors.''

"When mommy marries Larry he's going to get me a horse,'' she announced.

"That rat! He's always promising her things to sway me into marriage.'' Karen grinned over at Eden. "Between Becky and Larry manipulating me, I feel I'm losing control over my own life. How have you managed to stay single, by the way?''

"No one irresistible has ever proposed,'' said Eden, twirling her spaghetti around on her fork.

"Yet!'' finished Karen, her eyes glinting with mischief.

She was removing the plates from the table when a knock sounded from the porch. "Come in,'' she yelled.

"You're a trusting one.'' Nick's low voice made the breath catch in Eden's throat. As he came into the kitchen she studied the tall athletic-looking body clad in impeccable dark trousers and a midnight-blue shirt open at the neck. He pulled out a chair and before sitting down, planted a kiss on the tip of Becky's small upturned nose. Eden felt as if he'd touched her, too.

His eyes raked lazily and approvingly over Eden, taking in the proud tilt of her breasts. She felt her nipples strain treacherously against the snug fabric. "Good evening, Eden," he murmured huskily. "You're looking gorgeous."

"Am I gorgeous?" Becky drawled out the long word.

Nick laughed, chucking a finger under her chin. "You're always gorgeous, sweetie. Have you counted those freckles yet?"

Becky giggled. "I told you I can't count them. They slide all over my face when I try."

Karen and Eden joined in Nick's laughter. He reached in his pocket and drew out a small sack. "Look what I found with your name on it."

Becky grabbed for the sack, dumping out a cellophane package containing an assortment of miniature plastic dolls. "You're spoiling that child, Nick," complained Karen, the smile on her face negating the reprimand.

"Look, Eden." Becky held up the dolls for inspection.

"They're lovely," said Eden. "What will you name them?"

"Don't start that," ordered Karen. "She'll spend all evening on it and she's got to eat her dessert first." She scooped up the toys and placed them on a shelf. "We're taking our dessert in the living room, but you can have yours here."

Eden helped Karen ladle the warm berry cobbler into the bowls, handing them to Nick who spooned out mounds of vanilla ice cream. She could feel his breath stirring the hairs on the back of her neck as he leaned around her to place the scoops in each bowl.

She avoided looking at him until they reached the living room. He sank down beside her on the sofa, pressing thigh to thigh. "I like your outfit," he murmured.

"The T-shirt was the latest style when I bought it ten years ago," she said with a laugh, acutely aware of her lack of a bra as his intent gaze outlined the thrust of her breasts once more.

Karen joined them after settling Becky down to the task of finishing off her meal. "It feels almost civilized to be eating with adults," she sighed. "I'm tired."

"Is that a hint you're overworked?" suggested Nick.

"I refuse to answer on the grounds it might incriminate me," returned Karen. "How about you? Was your day busy?"

"Extremely. Remind me I've got to be home for a phone call at nine." He turned his head and smiled at Eden.

Karen let out a yell. "Ooh, I forgot to give you that message. How did you hear about it?"

Nick grinned. "Fred told me. He seemed a little unhappy."

"Fred's been unhappy a long time, Nick," she pointed out.

He nodded, his eyes masking any emotion. "I know. He's had a rough time." Dipping his spoon into his bowl, he scooped up a mouthful. "Delicious, Karen. Where did you find wild blackberries?"

"Larry's parents' home. They make a hobby out of growing berries. The bushes are loaded with them this year."

"I haven't had cobbler this good since I left Louisiana," chimed in Eden.

"Time you came back and settled down," murmured Nick.

Karen agreed. "Why don't you move back to Belle's Folly and play lady of the manor?"

"More like Scarlett O'Hara." Nick's eyes rested on her face.

"I'd be as poor as she was if I gave up my business," said Eden, returning his smile.

"How did your aunt live there? Off inherited wealth?" asked Karen.

"Partly. Also, she managed the Sonnier Mills until sugarcane lost its profitability. I'm afraid the inheritance ended with her, or I wouldn't be forced to lease the old place now." A tiny muscle in Nick's jaw tightened and she glanced down at her dish.

"You are going to make Fred save that lovely old mansion, aren't you?" demanded Karen.

Nick laughed softly. "Have you and Eden been discussing that?"

"No," Eden denied hotly. "We hadn't mentioned it once. I'm a little sick of the whole thing right now. All day I've been drawing plans and thinking of nothing else."

Nick leaned back against the sofa. "I know what you mean. Tonight is too nice to be discussing business. How would you three ladies like to take a ride in my car with the sunroof open?"

"Becky and I have to...."

"You don't have to do anything," Eden interrupted, setting her dish down. "Let's go for a ride and we'll do those dishes when we get in."

"No, I'm serious. I've ordered some cosmetics and the saleslady is supposed to deliver them this evening. Why don't you two run along?"

Nick shook his head. "It's terrible enough to invite myself to your dinner party, Karen. I'm not about to run off with your guest."

Eden felt a pang of regret as he rose to leave. It vanished from her mind as she heard a loud crash followed by a wail from the kitchen. Nick ran down the hall, followed by Eden and Karen.

He was already bending over Becky when they reached her, one glance at the chair lying on its side beneath the shelf telling the whole story. "Where does it hurt, sweetheart?" Nick's tender tones were soothing the child.

The sobbing slowed down. "All over, I think," said Becky.

Long strong fingers traced lightly over the child's arms and legs. "No bones appear to be broken, but she's got a cut by the side of her eye."

Karen closed her eyes and Eden reached for her. "No, go and get Nick a wet cloth. I'm always like this over injuries."

"It's not serious," said Nick after he cleaned off the cut with the cloth Eden handed him. "It might require a stitch or two. Why don't I take Becky to the emergency room at the hospital?"

"You have that phone call," reminded Karen, her color regained now that the cut was out of sight under the cloth. "I have a friend down the road who's a nurse. Her house is much closer than any hospital. I'll run Becky over there and see if she thinks it needs stitches."

"I'll stay here to get your cosmetics delivery," said Eden. She went into the living room and located Karen's shoes and purse while Nick lifted Becky in his arms, eliciting a giggle from her as he pretended to count the elusive freckles.

They went out to the car, and Nick gently placed the child into the seat beside her mother. "Hold this on your face," he instructed.

When Karen pulled out of the drive, Eden turned to Nick. "I really admire Karen. It must be a tremendous responsibility to raise a child all by yourself."

Nick nodded in agreement. "My mother tried raising me alone, but she finally had to give up." They walked toward the house, Eden stretching her legs to keep up with his long stride.

Before reaching the door, Nick stopped. He encircled her waist with his hands and turned her to face him, his mouth brushing against her cheek.

"All day long I've been wanting to smell that honeysuckle scent of your hair, Eden." He pulled her toward him until her head rested against his chest. "I've wanted to hold you like this all day."

Eden wrapped her arms around his waist, breathing deeply of his clean masculine scent, reveling in the warmth of his body, her pulse throbbing slow and sweet. No words were necessary, she thought. She felt she had known him forever. Was it really only a few days ago that she hadn't even known he existed?

Her hands moved up around his shoulders and caressed the dark strands of hair on his neck. Leaning back, she offered him her lips and he reached for them eagerly.

The gentleness of his kiss surprised her, and she felt herself flowering under his ministrations as he kissed her again and again, moving from her lips to her cheek, eyelid, ear and down to the soft column of her neck.

"You're so lovely," he murmured. "When we're apart I wonder if I've only imagined you."

His mouth closed over hers, his tongue moving instinctively over her lips and then invading her mouth with a gentle assault.

With tender hands he stroked along her sides, seeking and finding the curve of her breasts. She moved under his tempting intimate caresses as his palms covered the aching swells, his thumbs slowly circling the tips through the thin fabric. His mouth left her lips and moved to her throat, murmuring, "Eden, what are you doing to me?"

"Nick." His name rode on the crest of her emotions. "We've only known each other a few days...."

"I've known you forever. We only *met* a few days ago," he returned in a low voice. His hands stilled and she wanted to press them against her breasts again.

The strong fingers trailed down to her waist, and he moved away from her, smiling down with a quizzical gaze. "If I had more time tonight, I'd try to convince you that we've known each other forever."

"What time is it?" she whispered, her eyes shifting away from the intensity of his, willing him not to guess how much she longed to move back into his embrace.

He glanced at his watch. "We have time to go inside and talk a few minutes."

"I'd like that." She started in and he followed, close behind her, flicking off the lamp and leaving the room suffused with a soft glow from the hall light. He pulled her gently down onto his lap as he settled himself in an overstuffed armchair.

"I never got my turn to ask you questions last night," he reminded.

"My life is an open book," she retorted. "It's not too exciting, I'm afraid."

"How does a Louisiana girl like you feel about living in Houston?"

Eden leaned back and settled her head against his shoulder. "Houston has been good to me. I've grown to love it." The regular rhythm of his heart distracted her for a moment before she remembered, "I'm going to Houston tomorrow for the weekend."

Nick's disappointment was obvious. "I was hoping to persuade you to have dinner with me again."

"Sorry, my plane leaves early tomorrow evening. I have to be back for a housewarming. One of my clients wants to show off the results of our work."

Nick slipped one thumb under the strap of her T-shirt and idly slid it down over her shoulder, revealing the smooth swell of one creamy breast. "Can I offer you a lift to the airport?"

Eden smothered a sharp gasp as his fingers followed the curve of her flesh. "Thanks. I'd like that." She caught a glimpse of his watch and reminded him, "Your phone call!" Sliding off his lap in a fluid movement, she replaced her strap and stood smiling at him uncertainly.

He stood, resting his hands gently on her shoulders. "Would it be okay if I came by around two tomorrow?"

"Two?"

"I was hoping you could give me that tour of Belle's Folly you've been promising." Nick's composure seemed more shaken than hers and Eden liked the feeling that gave her. It made what she felt more real. It was happening to both of them and he felt it as much as she did.

With a euphoric sense of happiness she responded, "Two would be fine. I'll have my things packed so we'll have plenty of time to look around."

Nick reached out and slid his hand beneath her chin, his eyes communicating his reluctance to leave. "Until tomorrow, then?"

Eden's smile held a world of promise and pleasure. "Until tomorrow."

CHAPTER FIVE

A LIGHT RAIN FELL throughout the morning the next day, wrapping the old plantation in a soft misty cocoon that matched Eden's contented frame of mind as she finished drawing her plans. Glenna, the woman who handled the office projects could check them and if they were satisfactory, one of the assistants would render them into neat blueprints bearing the stamp of the Sonnier decorating firm.

Snatches of the lyrics of love melodies filled her head, and she found herself moving around the room in rhythm with the slow dreamy music. Love. The word kept insinuating itself into her mind, but she veered away from it. In her vocabulary love had never played an important part. She and Aunt Helene had never put a label on their feelings for one another, and Eden couldn't remember that they had ever expressed any affection. The older woman hadn't been one to hug or kiss anyone, and she had raised Eden to be like her, cool, undemonstrative, protective.

Strange that Nick, who seemed to have had none of the advantages of real home life, should be so relaxed about expressing himself to her. He was elusive, though. There was no doubting that. Despite the fact that he had been open about his growing feelings for her, she sensed that the real Nick Devereaux was rarely seen. Perhaps it was only with her that he was able to reveal glimpses of his true nature. The idea gave her such delight and satisfaction that Eden stopped what she was doing abruptly.

Strolling over to one of the wide floor-to-ceiling windows, she stared out at the misty grounds. The rain had soaked through the tangled overgrown shrubbery making the various greens, from olive to emerald to lime, seem more intense than usual. As she watched, two squirrels darted onto the porch, cavorting and leaping, their obvious abandon causing her to laugh.

Nick. Always there on her mind, his image so strong that she had only to close her eyes to see him. Deep inside she feared that her attraction to him was not in her best interests. Her business in Houston was at that delicate stage where it demanded as much attention as a newborn baby. Decorating firms were a dime a dozen there and she had worked unceasingly to get ahead of the pack. Her dream was that one day Sonnier's would be the most prestigious decorating firm in the southern part of the United States, a name synonymous with quality and excellence.

Then what do you want from Nick?, she asked herself angrily. *A casual fling?* The idea was oddly depressing, and uneasy at the trend of her thoughts, she forced herself back to work.

Karen called at noon. "I don't think I thanked

you for straightening up the house last night. I couldn't believe you'd washed all those dishes?''

"How's Becky today?''

"Recovered and lively as ever. I checked with her school a few minutes ago, and the teacher said she's got all the other children jealous of her bandage.''

Karen paused to answer a call on another line and then returned to talking to Eden. "Nick's been going around with a satisfied smile on his face all day. How long did he stay?''

Smiling in remembered pleasure, Eden said, "He had to leave in time to catch that call. Did I tell you he's driving me to New Orleans this afternoon?''

Karen groaned. "Nick's already mentioned it twice. Sounds like things are going great between you two.''

Eden decided that events were moving a little fast. After all, she didn't want people assuming things before she even knew what was happening herself. "He's not making a special trip,'' she said casually. "Didn't you mention that he spends most of his weekends in New Orleans?''

Karen lowered her voice. "According to Kay, his secretary, he's there every weekend. I asked her what the attraction is, but she doesn't know. All she has is an emergency answering-service number where he can be reached if anything comes up here at the company.''

Keeping her tones light, Eden refused to give in to the temptation to ask more questions. "Hmm... Nicholas Devereaux, mystery man. Sounds like an exciting TV series. Wonder what his secret could be?''

Laughter filtered over the phone. "I'll keep delving into the matter for you. If a secretary can't find out, no one can."

Eden decided it was time to change the subject. "How's your boss?" she asked firmly. "Any problems today?"

"More of the same." Karen sighed expressively. "He asked me out to lunch today, and when I refused he spent the rest of the morning nitpicking every job I did."

"What about Larry? Can't you say you're having lunch with him? Surely Fred knows you're seeing him."

"Yes," Karen replied slowly. "But Larry and I aren't engaged or anything and Fred knows it." She paused and Eden could hear the steady plop-plop of raindrops outside.

"It seems like a copout to drag Larry in for protection," Karen finally continued. "I'm determined to solve my own problems. I don't want to become dependent on Larry."

"Mmm...I can understand that," Eden agreed thoughtfully. "Why don't you march into Fred's office this afternoon? Force him to have a little talk. Sometimes bringing things out in the open works best."

"Not with Fred," Karen said vehemently. "He wears his sensitive male ego on his sleeve." Her voice lowered suddenly. "Now I've done it. He just came around the corner and it'll be murder if he heard me. Have a good trip and we'll plan on lunch together when you return." She quickly hung up.

Eden spent the rest of the afternoon before Nick was due making a thorough inventory of the furnishings in Belle's Folly. Before anything was stored she wanted Tom to come and appraise the valuable items. If all went well, she'd have the excess things hermetically sealed and stored until the lease ended.

Lunch was a quick sandwich, followed by a steaming cup of coffee, which she drank while sorting through a box of old photographs. Her efforts were rewarded when she discovered a yellowed envelope labeled "Household Inventory." The photos were old, outdated, but they might give Tom an idea of what was here.

She became so engrossed in her work she had to rush her bath and was in the process of putting the finishing touches on her makeup when she heard the sound of the powerful engine in Nick's car.

Dressed in the white linen skirt and turquoise blouse she had been wearing when they first met, she hurried down the stairs and reached the porch by the time he braked to a halt.

The rain had stopped, a watery sun coming out to begin the process of drying out. Leaning over the railing surrounding the gallery, she caught a glimpse of Nick's black hair through the open sunroof of his car.

"Hi," she greeted as he emerged into the sunlight. "Weren't you afraid of getting wet?"

"If it's not Scarlett herself," he returned, even white teeth flashing in his bronzed face.

"I suppose you think you're Rhett Butler," she flung back.

"I didn't want to have to point out the similarity, but I'm glad you noticed. All that's missing is the rakish mustache."

He bounded up the steps two at a time. "Shall I grow one and make the fantasy complete?"

A surge of surprised pleasure washed over her. There was no way she could refrain from showing her delight in his presence! *Careful,* she warned herself. She wasn't used to things moving this fast with any man. Maybe this old plantation spun a web of magic around those who met on its shadowy grounds.

She tilted her head to one side and surveyed him provocatively. His long legs were encased in a pair of casual gray cotton slacks, a striped white-collared polo shirt emphasizing his strongly muscled chest. The evidence of his years of hard work was revealed by his lean body, his tanned skin. "There's only one Clark Gable," she concluded.

His hands swept out and encircled her waist, pulling her against him with sweeping grace, his dark eyes filled with laughter. "I can see you're not easily impressed, Miss Sonnier."

His velvety voice set her heart racing as their gazes caught and held. Spontaneously Eden wrapped her arms around him, stroking the wide shoulders. "I couldn't wait to see you today, Eden," he said tenderly, brushing the soft cloud of hair back from her forehead and kissing her gently.

His mouth was warm, intimate, as he placed gentle caresses on her eyelids, her cheeks, the tip of her nose. Raising her head, she signaled her pleasure with an encouraging smile and quivered at the sensuous darkening of the black eyes gazing down at her.

Leaning over, he nibbled at the corner of her mouth, his tongue tracing the line of her full lips with a tantalizing lightness.

"You taste as good as you look." His warm breath was arousing, sending a stab of desire coursing through her. Her lips opened in welcome. Their mouths melded with breathtaking speed, their tongues entangling tenderly. When the pressure of his mouth deepened and he covered her lips with suffocating hunger, she moved against him, straining to press her breasts against his rock-hard chest.

Too soon it was over and she let her eyes roam his face. "If you want that guided tour, I think you'll have to stop this," she managed to say.

"You'll have to stop looking so desirable, then." He seemed equally affected as he stepped back, releasing her before he leaned against the railing.

"This old porch could tell a lot of stories if it could talk," she said lightly.

"Were all your lovers as captivated by its spell as I am?"

"Lovers?" she smiled into his eyes. "Haven't you forgotten I'm the maiden niece?"

A wide grin creased his face as he reached out, taking her hand in his before whispering huskily, "You've certainly got me under your spell."

Eden laughed and returned the pressure his palm was exerting, sighing inwardly. She really wished she weren't so attracted to him. The sweet responsiveness of her own body when he was near was new to her, unfamiliar territory to be explored at her own risk.

Underneath the cautious warnings of her mind, her heart insisted nothing was going to stop her until she sorted out his attraction for her. A vague suspicion entered her thoughts; was she seeing him as an opportunity to break free, to grab a taste of the life she'd been too busy to experience?

Evading his gaze, she began to speak in a stilted tour guide's voice, "There are several tours available at this plantation. Which one would you prefer?"

"The grand tour, of course." He straightened up to stand beside her, the look in his eyes making her knees buckle, despite her resolution to slow things down.

"We'll pretend you're a visitor to Belle's Folly in the year 1847."

"Who are you?" His eyes, their admiring expression frankly revealed, never left her mouth.

"I'm Belle, naturally."

"What's your folly?"

Eden regarded him thoughtfully, her lips curved in a delightful smile. "Belle was the French bride of Lucien Sonnier. She was reputed to be so beautiful that he could deny her nothing. When she insisted on having thirteen architects draw up plans for her home before she was satisfied, everyone in the community dubbed the place Belle's Folly.''

"Poor Lucien," Nick murmured, pulling her against him as they started down the stairs. "If she was anything like you, he didn't stand a chance."

They walked down the brick path until they reached the ornate white wrought-iron entrance gate. Turning, they both took in the sight of the old mansion, splendid and impressive in the soft glow of the afternoon sun. A small sigh escaped Eden as her eyes moved over the avenue of bearded oaks casting dark pools of shade on the deep green of the grass.

Her skin prickled knowing Nick's gaze was resting on her, examining her slender curves, her shining hair, the cool oval of her delicately featured face. "You really love this place?" he whispered, gripping her hand more tightly.

His words reminded her of the struggle she was involved in to save her home, and she removed her hand, pointing toward the magnificent structure. "Who wouldn't? The original building is that part in the center. The two symmetrical wings on either side were later additions, added as the family grew. Lucien and Belle had twelve children."

His hand went around her waist and pressed her back against him. "I can understand that, too."

It was more difficult to ignore her racing pulse this time. Looking up at Nick, she found that he seemed faintly puzzled. "If they had twelve children, how did it happen you're the only Sonnier left?"

Eden grinned. "To poor Lucien's dismay, almost all of the children were girls. He was definitely outnumbered, especially since it's rumored they were all as beautiful and headstrong as Belle. The elder three sons died during or shortly after the Civil War, leaving no one to carry on the family name except my great-great-grandfather, the last child. He was a surprise; they hadn't planned on his arrival."

Nick brushed his fingers along the curve of her neck, setting off a chain reaction of explosive responses deep in her body. "Perhaps that explains why you're so enchanting, so full of surprises yourself."

She found herself staring at his hands. They were strong hands, large, but their touch was incredibly gentle. She wasn't used to being with anyone who touched so much, so naturally. What would it be like to feel free enough to reach over and touch him, run her fingers along the firm line of his jaw, tease the thick hairs that grew down along the back of his neck?

Realizing that he was staring at her, half-amused, half-perplexed, she hurriedly resumed. "See that tower at the back," she said, pointing. "It's known as the *garçonnière*, or boy's house. When the male members of the family became young men, they moved in there. That way their comings and goings were unobserved."

"Very convenient," Nick murmured. "What did the lads do their mother wouldn't approve of?"

Eden pushed back the fringe of hair that threatened to cover her eyes. "You could probably fill

that in better than I.'' Indicating the tall levee fronting the house, she continued, ''The river boats
traveled up and down the Mississippi, bringing
gamblers, ladies of the night, what have you. I'm
sure they found plenty to get them in trouble.
Legend has it that the mothers in the community
warned their daughters not to go near the dangerous Sonniers.''

Nick laughed aloud, pulling Eden tightly against
him and leaning over to kiss her mouth briefly.
''Are you dangerous?''

''What do you think?'' she countered, returning
his kiss with light pressure of her own.

''Very, very dangerous.'' He kissed her several
more times before reluctantly breaking away.
''Shouldn't we be going inside for the rest of the
tour?''

Nick was openly admiring as they strolled hand in
hand through the house. Eden kept up a running
commentary on the ornate wood-paneled walls and
ceilings in the dining room and parlor. It took will-
power not to point out what lovely offices these
rooms would make, just as they were.

''This is my favorite spot,'' she told him when
they reached the morning room with its light
lavender walls. She pointed to the frieze along the
ceiling. ''Those birds and flowers are the origi-
nals.''

''It's incredible,'' said Nick. ''I can't imagine
what it would have been like to live surrounded by
all this beauty.''

''I took it for granted,'' Eden admitted. ''I'm

sure it influenced me. Interior design is as natural to me as breathing is to most people.''

''The size of this place amazes me.'' Nick's gaze swept around the spacious room, the high ceiling. ''It seems such a waste for two people. Not like the place where I grew up. There we had more people than space. I never even dreamed anyone could live like this until I was a teenager. The first time I slept in a room alone, I was thirteen.'' He grinned at the memory. ''I couldn't sleep at all. The silence was terrifying.''

There it was again. A glimpse of that elusive background, a tantalizing peek at what had made Nick the person he was today. She remained silent, still, hoping he would say more, but the moment was over.

''Upstairs?'' His voice was brisker.

They climbed the stairs together, the chemistry between them increasing with each step. Eden continued to point out the architectural features and tell amusing anecdotes about the Sonniers. When they reached the large central hall, she pulled open the door to her room, barely allowing Nick a glance inside. ''Mine,'' she stated shortly, closing it quickly and moving down the hall to the next door.

''This is the nursery. Many of the toys were brought over from France for the children of Lucien and Belle.''

''My God, you must have grown up thinking you were a princess.'' Nick's smile softened the words, but still Eden stiffened, wondering if he was being critical.

"Actually, I was quite lonely here." She instantly regretted her admission. She'd never admitted that to anyone. Aunt Helene had constantly reminded her she was fortunate to be a Sonnier, more fortunate than the poor children whose parents died and left them homeless in some institution. No one had ever known how much Eden missed her parents, missed the warmth and sharing of a real family.

"I'm sorry if my remark hurt." Nick's voice was neutral, but his expression was compassionate.

She led the way across the hall, flinging open the double doors. "This is the master suite."

Nick followed her, lounging in the doorway with unconscious grace, his eyes widened in shock. "Don't tell me anyone actually slept here?" The sweep of his hands lumped the rosewood English-style four-poster bed, the lavish folds of brocade and the matching drapes all together in his disapproval.

"It would make me claustrophobic," she agreed. "Next door is my favorite bedroom. It belonged to Belle and was known as her boudoir." They entered a smaller room furnished with a New Orleans style daybed, chaise lounge and rocking chair, all upholstered in a pale blue taffeta that matched the color on the walls.

"You like this room because it's the perfect setting for you." His husky voice built a bridge, crossing the space between them, shutting out the world. Eden was inexplicably shy. Hadn't she known this moment was coming? It had been there from the beginning; this attraction, this sense of déjà vu, as if they were lovers in the past, meeting again, reopening old passions.

The silence between them was patently sensual yet comfortable and undemanding at the same time, as if they had forever to get to know each other. But she knew that sooner or later, one of them was going to make the first move. Somehow, she realized it had to be her who took that step. She needed to find this missing part of herself, the feminine, sensually sensitive woman she became with this man.

She wasn't certain at what point they began moving closer, her head lifting, his descending, until the feather-light touch of his lips brushed delicately against her forehead. Everything was so warm, so right, so good.

She opened her eyes to look into his, searching for the clues that would tell her this was something important, not just a passing fancy brought on by convenience, circumstances, close proximity.

The answer she wanted was clearly evident in the tenderness radiating from his eyes.

"Eden, you were sent to enchant me," he whispered, his voice thick with undisguised passion. "Did you know you've been driving me wild, knocking me off balance since the moment we met?" His voice dropped to a sensual murmur as his hands roamed restlessly over her back, his fingertips tracing her straight spine, sliding down to cup her smoothly swelling hips.

Eden relaxed in his arms. Her fingers flattened against his chest, moving slowly upward, pausing to savor each dip and hollow until her hands met and clasped behind his neck.

Nick trembled beneath her hands, letting his mouth close hungrily over hers, arousing her deeply.

Eden's every sense was heightened, the tension almost painful. The room was quiet apart from the gentle whirr of a lone air-conditioning unit down the hall. Sunlight filtered in slender bars across the polished floor, throwing their faces into shadow. Each nerve ending in her skin was alert to his lightest touch. His mouth tasted of promise, of passion, of caring.

Her lips found his throat, moving with whispery softness up to his chin, across his cheek until their breath mingled in intimate communion. With absolute certainty she knew she both needed and wanted him. Longed for him. Her head fell back in deliberate invitation, her smooth creamy throat bared in tempting abandon.

With the force of a barely restrained dam, Nick allowed his hands to slide to her breasts, cupping them through the frail fabric of her blouse.

His thumbs flicked the swollen tips, the delicate fabric slipping and sliding with the rhythm of his caresses. Pushing back her hair, his mouth and tongue traced tantalizing circles on the small indentation above her collarbone. Her pulse raced maddeningly, beating frantically in response to his sensitive touch.

In one swift movement his hands found the shadowy hollow between her breasts, sliding straight down, loosening the buttons, revealing her satiny flesh to his rapt gaze. Gently he pushed the garment from her, ignoring it as it drifted soundlessly to the floor.

Eden felt free before him, as if the baring of her body was revealing a whole new side of herself, a surprise not only to him but to her as well. Leaning forward, she rested her breasts against the rough cotton of his shirt, looking up to find he was watching her with fascinated intensity.

"Nick," she breathed. "What is this effect you have on me?" Her hands found the hem of his shirt, searching underneath until they felt the warm, velvety texture of his back.

"Let yourself go," he murmured against her lips. "Let me feel your fire." His face darkened with passion and suddenly he could restrain himself no longer. Not letting her move so much as a centimeter away he backed up to the daybed.

When they were both lying on the narrow structure, he freed his hands of all restraint, letting them roam over her, following their path with his lips until her breasts rose to meet his every caress, swollen and tingling, rosy with warmth.

Eden could make no protest when he discovered the catch on her skirt and released it, pushing it off her body along with the brief lacy panties that barely spanned the curving splendor of her hips.

Murmuring soft indistinguishable endearments, he kissed the tips of her breasts and her belly. He lavished her thighs with caresses, letting his fingers drift up the long smooth length of her legs, parting her thighs until he could move in gradually diminishing circles around the downy triangle that covered the core of her femininity.

His touch was good, it was exciting, much as she had imagined it would be just this morning. Eden longed to share the feelings he was evoking in her, ached to let him know the explosive reaction he was unleasing. The touch of his hands communicated to her very soul, making a celebration of body and breath.

Gently stilling his hands, she shifted his shirt until he could slide it off. His chest was fantastic, beautiful; his shoulders and arms revealing firm muscles indicating a life that hadn't been easy. Thickly matted hair veed down across his flat stomach, and Eden snaked her fingers into it until she found the buried nipples, delighting as she felt him stir against her.

Their mouths met now with fiery passion, his hands coming up to stroke her throat, his callused thumbs outlining her trembling jaw.

"I want you too much, Eden," he groaned, moving his body to cover hers, trapping her legs beneath the steel length of his own. Slowly he parted her legs with his, settling his body over hers, murmuring encouragement as she shifted restlessly beneath him.

Starting with her breasts, he began covering her body with kisses again, leaving no secret place undiscovered. His mouth felt like liquid fire as it moved over her belly, his tongue teasing the small indentation of her navel. With only the slightest movement then, his lips were caressing the creamy flesh of her inner thighs, building up an explosive hunger in her loins as his touch circled that central core, which was aching for assuagement.

"Nick...." Her body tensed as he sought and found her with sure certainty. Arching her neck, she pushed at his shoulders futilely, suddenly unsure yet reveling in his every movement.

"Let me, Eden...relax...don't think...just let yourself feel for once...let me make you feel."

Eden fought a brief mental struggle, her innate reserve warring silently with the overwhelming pleasure he was giving her. It went against her protective nature to become vulnerable in any man's arms. Passion beat strongly, in time with the throbbing within her, winning against all restraint. She arched her hips, a primitive sensuality guiding her movements. Her fingers dug into his shoulders as he moved with her, taking her away from the present, lifting her higher and higher until she caught a brilliant glimpse of never-before-guessed-at enchantment.

"Nick," was all she could whisper when it was over. "Nick," as unfamiliar moisture prickled behind her closed eyelids. Nothing quite like this had ever happened to her, leaving her spent, shaken, fully aware of herself as a woman.

He moved to lay alongside her, the brush of his trousers against her bare skin bringing a sudden flush to her cheeks as she was forced to acknowledge what had happened. She, the cool, reserved, always-in-control Eden Sonnier, had totally lost all control in the arms of a man she knew scarcely anything about.

She had a swift intense need to look at him, to see whether she could read his feelings from the play of expressions across the strongly molded face.

"Eden?" His voice matched the faintly vulnerable curve of his mouth.

"Nick!" The warm pronouncement of his name made no attempt to hide the depths to which she had been moved by his tenderness.

As the movement of the sun behind a cloud plunged the room into dusky afternoon somnolence, their gazes caught and held. It was a moment rich in communication, their eyes asking and answering a myriad of nonverbal questions. Eden reveled in the richness of the moment, not yet ready to examine what had happened, not yet ready to move to the next stage of their relationship, whatever that might be.

Nick's arms wrapped around her, holding her close against him as she lay in his arms. "I didn't mean for this to happen," Eden murmured drowsily, not even sure that she had said the words aloud until she felt the deep rumble of Nick's laughter against her body.

"And I suppose you think I planned it," he returned lightly, smoothing a stray strand of silky hair away from her temple.

"You know that's not what I meant," she protested, half-indignantly.

"I haven't yet got to the stage where I can think clearly around you, Eden," Nick admitted huskily. "Let's not try to figure out where things are going yet."

Eden didn't answer. She couldn't. She knew what he meant. This overwhelming attraction between them seemed to have a life of its own. This was a side of love that she had never seen. She'd always approached her relationships calmly, rationally, but this time she was leading with her heart.

The increasing shadows in the room made Eden sharply aware of the passage of time. They had been lying entwined for who knows how long and for a moment she thought Nick might have fallen asleep. As she stirred against him, he glanced at his watch with obvious reluctance. "Good lord, what time does your plane leave?"

"Seven." She sat up, grateful for the shadows. She'd never realized how vulnerable nakedness could be. "I can't miss my plane!"

"We have time," he confirmed. He reached for his shirt, then leaned over to quickly brush her lips with his own. "Eden," he murmured. "I wish I could persuade you to forget Houston and stay right here this weekend. I haven't even begun to learn all the things I want to know about you."

When Eden didn't answer, he added, "I'm sure glad we decided to lease this place. Otherwise we wouldn't have met." Outlining the curve of her shoulder, sliding his fingers along her silky arm, his eyes communicated a message Eden couldn't help but understand.

Levering himself to a sitting position, he tactfully got to his feet and crossed to a door in the corner. "Is this by any chance a bathroom, or do you even have modern plumbing here?"

Before she could answer, he opened the door, glanced inside and shut it behind him. She looked around the room and located her clothes, reaching for them and then vigorously shaking the wrinkles out of the linen skirt. Her mind was refusing to think about what had happened. The explosive intensity of her responses had shocked her, leaving her feeling unsure, a little wanton, yet embarrassingly eager to explore this new relationship. This kind of lovemaking, with its free and easy expression, without any seeming expectations or demands, was new territory to her. With as much dignity as she could muster without a stitch of clothing, she crossed the hall to her own bedroom, retrieving her abandoned blouse and undergarments as she went.

Nick was waiting when she came downstairs. "Everything closed up here?" he asked, taking her small suitcase.

She nodded, not meeting his gaze. "Larry's promised to check on the house while I'm gone. I'm leaving the keys to his company car here on the table in case he needs it this weekend."

He strode over beside her and grasped her chin firmly in his hand, tilting it gently until her eyes met his. "What's wrong, Eden?" Understanding glimmered in his eyes as he pulled her into his arms for a quick hug. "Maybe things are moving a little fast between us, Eden," he said huskily, his voice drawing her like a magnet. "This is new to me. I have to keep reminding myself that we've only just met, that it takes longer than this to find you care for someone. If you think I'm pushing you, tell me to slow down. Promise?'' His expression was uncertain, yet Eden couldn't help appreciating the honesty of his words.

She swallowed, her mouth dry. It would be so easy to fall in love with this man. He was so sensitive, so caring, so generous. Was it wise to trust her feelings? Nick was an overwhelmingly attractive person and yet what did she really know about him?

Thankfully, he didn't press her for an answer. ''When are you returning?'' he asked when they were on the highway leading to New Orleans.''

''Sunday afternoon.''

He glanced toward her, smiling. ''May I meet your plane? We could have dinner in New Orleans before we came back.''

She deliberately held herself aloof, disturbed by how quickly her life was leaving her own control. ''That would be nice. My plane's due to arrive at four Sunday.''

His eyes narrowed. Her withdrawal hadn't escaped him. She was beginning to realize that very little evaded his notice, despite his seemingly casual and carefree attitude.

Looking directly at him, she spoke, her voice low but firm. ''Don't rush me, Nick. I'm a very independent woman.''

His hands tightened on the steering wheel, but his voice didn't rise an inch. ''Did I say anything about demanding dependency?''

She shook her head, brushing her hair back, aware of his swift intake of breath as her arm brushed his shoulder. "I have an idea you wouldn't tolerate a dependent woman," Eden murmured.

"I'd probably tolerate almost anything out of you, Eden." He refused to let her escape. "I told you I've been made a captive."

She glanced at him sideways. "I've never had a captive before. What shall I demand of you?"

"How about a thousand and one nights of love?"

She laughed softly, an incandescent bubble of humor making her feel strangely light-headed. "I don't think that could be worked into my schedule right now," she responded. "Maybe I can fit you in after I finish my next twelve projects."

Silence fell between them, a comfortable silence that worked its magic on Eden. She slowly relaxed, allowing herself to review what had happened between them.

"Hungry?" Nick's voice broke the silence as he glanced at the dashboard, noting the time. "If we make the next ferry, we might have time to get something at the airport."

"Thanks, anyway, but I get a meal on the plane." Eden smiled, the curve of her mouth widening as she saw the admiration in his eyes.

Their perfectly timed arrival at the ferry prevented him from answering as he guided the car onto the waiting ramp. When they were safely on board, they got out of the car and walked over to the railing.

Nick slipped an arm around her waist and she leaned against him, letting the soft breeze ruffle strands of silky hair across his face. "I predict this is going to be a long weekend," he inserted quietly.

"Do you have a home in New Orleans?"

She felt his arm tighten. "In a way. I stay with friends." Though the barrier was down, he would only let her see so far and then she was shut out. Perhaps in time.

"That's nice," she murmured, settling against him more securely.

"Eden, you drive me crazy," he whispered suddenly. "Why don't you tell those Texans you're coming home where you belong?"

She glanced up, candor in the blue eyes. "I'm not certain where I belong, Nick. You'll have to give me time to find out for myself."

CHAPTER SIX

"READY FOR COFFEE?"

Eden looked up to see Tom in the doorway of her office, his meticulously fit body clad in a pair of impeccable cotton slacks and a casual striped pullover that probably cost a mint.

Her hand stilled on the heavy book of wallpaper samples she was fingering. From her perch on a tall stool in the corner she smiled. "Not quite yet, Tom. Give me a few more minutes."

"Sure," he agreed in a smoothly cultivated voice. For once Eden found herself being critical of the man who had been her best friend and co-worker for some time.

It wasn't fair to compare Nick and Tom. The two men were totally dissimilar. Nick had lived a life of few advantages, spending most of his time until the past few years outdoors. Everything about him was alive, vital, as if he had some mysterious communion with the forces of nature. He obviously played as hard as he worked, and from what she had observed he kept the two fairly separate.

Tom was an artist, but as talented as his work was, there was something restrained about it. As if he had never really broken free of the rigid rules and mores that inhibit the creative process. Tom needed the security that Sonnier's provided, the prestigious location and clientele that fueled the firm.

As he vanished down the hallway she berated herself. Since arriving in Houston the night before she'd been a million miles away. Or, she admitted honestly, she'd been back in New Orleans. A sleepless, night filled with images of the past week, hadn't helped. Everything about her ordered, refined little world here in Houston screamed in protest at the way she had been behaving.

Entering the converted house that now served as her showroom had brought her sharply back to reality. Yet a subtle change seemed to have come over her office. The bright bouquet of Texas bluebonnets on her receptionist's desk had been a jarring note. Normally, Eden made sure that anything displayed in the main rooms was personally approved by herself. The smooth silvery gray wallpaper and cool stark marble floors conveyed just the touch of subtle sophistication she hoped impressed her customers. Her usual feeling of wellbeing was missing, however, and when Linda, the receptionist, spotted her in the doorway, her eager young face blanched as she hurriedly grabbed for the offending bluebonnets.

"Miss Sonnier," she breathed. "No one told me you'd be in this morning."

Eden smiled benevolently at the younger woman, aware that her own stomach was tied in knots. "Never mind, Linda. They add just the right touch of springtime." Watching relief spread across Linda's face, she recoiled. Good Lord, had she become such a tyrant? That much anxiety over a bunch of wild flowers? She had to admit her employees did have reason to fear her. She demanded excellence. Her determination to make Sonnier's succeed sent her on an endless quest for perfection.

The effects of that quest had been reinforced less than fifteen minutes later when her junior design assistant had arrived. "You beat me here," Jenifer Tate had gasped in dismay.

"I couldn't sleep." Eden found herself apologizing, desperate to relieve the tension in the other woman's face. When she still didn't smile, Eden asked gently, "Anything wrong?"

"Nothing." Jenifer nervously smoothed the skirt of her navy two-piece suit that Eden suddenly realized was totally out of character. These were creative people she'd hired! What was happening to them? Had her insistence on overseeing every detail stifled their own personalities? Jenifer had come to her from a leading New York design school. In two years she'd gone from sporting unique, ethnic clothing and waist-length hair to this conservative navy suit and a neatly coiled chignon. Worst of all, Eden hadn't even noticed it happening, had probably even made approving comments.

"Sit down, Jenifer," she said as gently as possible. When the other woman was seated in the maroon-and-silver striped wing chair, one of a pair that graced Eden's spacious private office, she continued, "Any problems while I've been gone?"

"Everything's fine," Jenifer assured her but her

hands twisting in her lap belied her calm. Suddenly she burst out, "I know you aren't going to approve, but a new account came in this week and I've already prepared a design portfolio."

Eden started to protest, then bit her tongue. As part of office protocol, it was understood that Eden did the initial consultation whenever a new account was opened. Despite the work load this arrangement imposed, she felt it vital that her own touch be included in every Sonnier design. "That's a bit unusual," she stated slowly. "Any special reason?"

Jenifer stared down at the floor before replying, her voice slightly belligerent. "I'm an interior designer, Miss Sonnier. I'm tired of spending all my time implementing your ideas. If you're not willing to let me advance, then I'm going to have to seek a new position." The last words came out in a rush.

Eden leaned back in surprise. This was a shock. Full-scale mutiny from quiet agreeable Jenifer. "I'm sorry if you feel you've not been allowed to advance," she said evenly. "Surely your pay increases have expressed our continued satisfaction with your work. I thought you found this job challenging."

"It's not the money," Jenifer declared miserably. Taking a deep breath, she plunged on, "It's you, Miss Sonnier. You're always looking over my shoulder, directing every little thing I do. I'm a good designer and I want a chance to develop my own skills."

Eden felt sick. Was Jenifer right? Was she so anxious for Sonnier's to be the best, that she had turned into a tyrant? With as much grace as she could muster, she apologized quietly. "Perhaps you're right, Jenifer. I hired you because I was very impressed with your qualifications. It's not fair of me to refuse to allow you to express your talent. Why don't we go over the financial details of your new account and then, as long as our client remains satisfied, I'll assign you to do this job yourself."

Jenifer's eager smile was salt in the wound. Eden barely listened to the enthusiastic barrage of details that followed. In fact, she'd had to excuse herself, telling Jenifer they'd continue their discussion later. Though Jenifer left with a new sense of hope, Eden was mentally kicking herself for not having seen what was happening. Nick's voice suddenly came back to her. He'd told her that freedom was the environment that worked best for his employees. It seemed perhaps he was right.

Sliding down off the stool, Eden strolled across to the closet in the far corner and swept open the door to reveal a full-length mirror. Normally she only used this to check her appearance before meeting with a client. Today she wanted to assess herself. Perhaps seeing her reflection would help put things into perspective. Had she been too wrapped up in herself to notice what was happening to the people who worked for her? It was all well and good to tell herself that what she did for Sonnier's ultimately benefited every one of them. But if they were unhappy, what was the point?

Personal relationships were difficult for Eden. The distance between herself and Aunt Helene, the isolation of her childhood, had been a disadvantage. No one looking at her would ever know. They saw only her background, the huge mansion, the privileged environment that had shielded her against so many of life's realities.

Now she was forced to confront herself. Why did she want Sonnier's to be number one? Sure she liked money. Who didn't? But it was more than that. She needed the thrill of achievement, she needed to feel she'd done something that brought approval from others. In concentrating on that goal, she'd alienated herself.

On the surface Nick was her complete opposite. He was sure of himself in a nonoffensive manner, and he seemed to truly like almost all the people he came into contact with. Away from Houston, removed from time by Belle's Folly's timeless ambience, events had moved quickly between Nick and herself. Perhaps those moments spent with him had opened her eyes, widened her perspective, revealed the lack of meaningful relationships in her life.

Suddenly impatient, Eden slammed the door and went in search of her purse. Time for lunch and time to get her mind back on work. The unaccustomed time away from her usual environment had interrupted the rhythm and routine of her life, giving her too much time for introspection.

Passing Jenifer's desk, she noticed that the woman's hair was trailing in wisps from the tightly coiled chignon as she pored enthusiastically over the stack of plans on her desk. Eden smiled ruefully and called a hasty goodbye.

Tom's office was at the other end of the long hall, occupying what had once been a very masculine, and very cozy library. The original paneling was still intact, but there the adherence to tradition ended. Tom's desk was a slab of Italian marble, carefully chosen to emphasize the Tabriz rug on the polished floor.

He was talking on the phone and she paused in the doorway, not willing to interrupt. "I'll be over around five," she heard him say with resignation. "Can it wait until then, Neva?"

Eden moved into the room, flashing him a sympathetic smile as she sank down into a leather chair in a startling shade of cinnabar. Tom's bluish green eyes looked tired; the deepened grooves on his face told her he hadn't slept any better than she the evening before.

"Trouble again?" Her concern indicated her understanding of the problem. Tom had been divorced from Neva for several years, but his ex-wife still depended on him, calling for his help constantly, using their two teenaged daughters as the catalyst.

"This time it's the garbage-disposal unit." Tom ran a hand through his thick hair, his manicured fingers managing to leave his hair looking neat as always. "I tried telling her all she has to do is push the reset button under the sink. The woman's helpless, absolutely helpless."

"Why don't you just tell her no," Eden asked reasonably. "She can call a repairman just like anyone else."

"I know, I know," Tom replied. "It's just that somehow I can't rid myself of the feeling that I'm responsible."

"Umm...poor Tom," Eden sympathized. Actually she could never really relate to Tom's problems with Neva. The woman seemed attractive enough. She had just never learned to be independent. Tom handled it well, though, and Eden rather admired his responsible attitude.

"Ready for lunch?" she asked with a half smile.

"Where?" Tom perched on the edge of his desk and looked approvingly at her tailored skirt and blouse. Tom was a perfectionist as well. That attention to detail was what had built his reputation in the design world. Since coming to work for her firm, they had gotten along admirably, finding they had much in common. Was it true that opposites were more suited, Eden found herself wondering, or were she and Tom compatible in all the ways that counted?

"How about that new Italian place," Tom suggested, bringing her attention back to lunch.

Seated at a red-linen-covered table a few minutes later, where they had a view of an attractive courtyard, Eden relaxed and looked over the menu.

"Our special today is Linguine *Bucaniera*," a low-voiced waiter hovered over her to speak in her ear. "It's a fantastic combination of fresh linguine tossed with Gulf shrimp and our own *marinata* sauce."

"Sounds delicious." Eden smiled over at Tom. After placing his own order, he leaned back, waiting until the waiter was out of earshot before he spoke.

"Don't you think it's time you leveled with me about what's bothering you?"

Eden's hand stilled on her goblet of water. When she didn't answer, he added, "You've been in another world since I picked you up at the airport last night."

Eden bit her lip and glanced away, unwilling to answer his question. How could she answer when she wasn't sure what the matter was herself?

"Eden," he quietly insisted, "why don't you give up your crusade to save Belle's Folly if it's bothering you this much?"

"There's much more to it than that," she said, swiveling to face him once more. With a throaty laugh she added, "I'm probably just a little tired this weekend, Tom."

"I've seen you tired lots of times. But never curled up like a snail in its shell. Last night at the Terrells' housewarming you looked as if you were a million miles away."

She smiled weakly and took a sip of water. "I've never liked the social side of this business."

"But darling, you're an expert at it! That's where we get ninety percent of our clients. With your looks...."

"Looks? I much prefer to think that Sonnier's is developing a reputation for flair and quality."

Tom chuckled, his fingers reaching for one of the freshly baked rye-and-sesame breadsticks that the waiter had placed on their table. "That sounds more like the old Eden. I was afraid she had disappeared somewhere deep in the heart of the bayou country.''

He buttered a breadstick and handed it to Eden, his fingers brushing against hers. When she tensed at his touch, his eyebrows rose. ''Have I suddenly become repulsive?''

She shook her head wishing he weren't so attentive to the slightest detail. ''Tom, I've been thinking about us.''

''Something tells me I'm not going to like what you've been thinking.''

She eyed him levelly. ''I'm sorry, Tom, but I have to be honest. I've realized I'm not in love with you.''

Tom waited as crisp green salads were placed before them. Finally he answered in a cool voice, ''Love? Eden, I'm perfectly aware that you're not the type to ever fall in love.''

Eden stared back at him, taken aback at the lack of feeling in his tones. ''What kind of a remark is that?''

He carefully picked up his fork and tasted the salad before responding. ''Good dressing,'' he murmured. Catching a glimpse of her mutinous face, he said, ''Face it, darling. You're a cool customer. You were brought up without affection and it's made you tough and self-sufficient. I had to learn the same lesson by going through a disastrous marriage.''

Eden lifted her own fork and then put it down abruptly. ''Was your marriage to Neva so disastrous?'' Gathering up her nerve, she said, "Or did Neva just want more of you than you were willing to give?"

The silence between them was uncomfortable. The conversation had taken a personal turn that shook them both. *But that's ridiculous,* Eden chided herself. *I've thought of marrying this man and yet we've never gone beyond the surface.*

There was no mistaking the pain on Tom's face, even though he made an effort to hide it. When he spoke, he attempted to be casual. "Neva and I were happy at one time. It was just one of those things. She never really grew up."

Eden hated to keep probing, but something told her Tom needed to talk to someone. All this time they'd been working together, she'd never realized that his offhand manner could be a cover-up for feelings of hurt and bewilderment. "Perhaps you never encouraged her to grow up?" Eden said gently. When he didn't answer she added, "Maybe we're both alike, Tom. Maybe we're a little selfish."

"Selfish!" Tom's reply was indignant, but a sheepish smile creased his face.

Eden quickly launched into a description of her conversation with Jenifer earlier that morning.

"Yes, I see what you mean," Tom said finally. "But I'm not sure what went wrong, with Neva I mean. I'll agree that you and I tend to be single-minded. That's why I felt we'd make such a good team. It's what makes us successful, you know. Neva never appreciated that side of my character. Perhaps that's the price of success."

Eden took a few bites of the linguine that had arrived during their conversation. "This is a great restaurant," she remarked before taking up the conversation again. "Maybe that's also why we can't seem to sustain love relationships. You're divorced. I've never married. Maybe we deserve each other."

"Eden," Tom protested. "What happened in Louisiana that's made you start thinking so much about love?"

Eden felt a warm flush rising to her cheeks and saw his eyes narrow as he noted her unusual confusion. "Maybe being away from all the work here gave me time to look around and see how other people live. Do you realize I have no really close friends?" She took a sip of wine and went on, "Except you, of course. But would we be friends if we didn't work together? And what do we actually know about each other. We avoid personal subjects as if they were the plague!"

Tom shifted uncomfortably and then glanced over at her, his face thoughtful. "Since Neva and I split, I've learned it's better to keep your feelings to yourself. You don't get hurt that way."

"Maybe not," Eden agreed, "but isn't it a miserable way to live?" They were both silent before Eden began speaking again. "I made a new friend in Louisiana. Her name is Karen and she has the most delightful little girl."

Tom glared at her and shook his finger warningly. "Don't let sentiment cloud your vision, my dear. You're not the motherly type."

"Damn it, Tom," Eden protested vigorously before she realized he was grinning. "See what I mean? You and I are always making generalizations like that about each other."

He shrugged. "I guess I don't know you as well as I thought."

Eden started to expand on that theme and then stopped. There was no use getting mad at Tom. He was the best friend she had. But that only pointed out how shallow her life had gotten. Her relationship with Tom was superficial. There was nothing much between them except business. Yet somehow she had thought that would be sufficient. While their plates were removed, Eden ordered coffee.

"How much chance do you think you have with this crusade over your house?" Tom asked.

"It's scarcely a crusade, Tom," she replied, gazing longingly at the cart of tempting desserts being wheeled past to the next table. "Frankly, I'm not sure whether I'm wasting my time or not. I'd like to think that there's some hope for the house in the future. I've a vague idea of turning it over to the community as a sort of historical donation. However, this oil company does have the lease for the next five years, and if they destroy the authenticity of the house, there won't be much left to do except see if I can sell the land."

"Why care? Is it some kind of ego trip? I bet the community couldn't care less about the old plantation."

"You're wrong there." Eden recounted the story

of Roy Jones and his interest in having a museum to show to his young son.

"Then that's your answer!" Tom leaned forward. "Why not have the local press do a story? That ought to put pressure on your oil company. They won't dare touch the place."

"I couldn't do that to Nick," countered Eden. Just speaking his name brought her pleasure. Since leaving him at the airport in New Orleans, she had been able to concentrate on little else, remembering his kisses, his caresses, his sensational assault on her senses. God, what was she doing? She'd never let any man occupy her thoughts to this extent. No wonder Tom was surprised by the change in her.

"Nick?"

The atmosphere was thick with tension. "Nicholas Devereaux, the owner of River Road Oil Services."

Tom looked out across the crowded restaurant and then turned back to her abruptly. "That's who it is."

"What do you mean?"

"I should have known there was a man involved somewhere. I've never seen you in this mood before, Eden."

"That's just what I've been trying to tell you." Eden spread her hands out and shrugged her shoulders. "We're good business associates, Tom. But there's more to life than business."

"Nothing else so satisfying." His face took on a closed expression and Eden suddenly felt there was no use pushing the conversation. This luncheon had been eye opening, though.

Tom signaled for more coffee and turned back to her. "Perhaps it will do you good to have a romantic fling. You're younger than I am and maybe you need to get it out of your system."

His attitude was so patronizing that Eden simply murmured, "I'm glad that you're so understanding." He seemed to miss the slight edge of sarcasm in her voice.

With sudden determination she added, "Tom, we really don't know each other at all, do we?"

"I felt we did, Eden." His hand paused in the act of reaching for his cup.

"Let's give each other some time, shall we? I know we've talked about marriage, but I think it was just convenient for both of us. Let's not date for a while, you know, just be friends. I think we'll find we're better friends than lovers."

"Don't bet on it." Tom's reply was flat. "Sizzling affairs seldom last and I'll be here waiting come September when the cold winter looms."

Eden refrained from replying, choosing instead to change the subject. "Have I told you how well I think you've been handling the business during my absence?" she commented.

"Why, thank you, Eden." He waited while she paid the check with the company credit card and then added, "Frankly, I'm like Jenifer. It's been nice having you gone. You do have a tendency to check up on everyone, including me. Sometimes I think you don't have much confidence in me."

"I need to learn to delegate more," she admitted. "After all, you are my second-in-command. When I return we might see about that branch office. You'd make a great manager."

A broad smile creased his face at her unaccustomed compliment. "I'd appreciate that, Eden."

Her vote of confidence soothed the hard feelings between them and they left the restaurant as friends.

IN BED LATER THAT NIGHT, Eden found that she was looking forward to seeing Nick again. Anticipating it with more pleasure than she could quite admit. Coming back to Houston had opened her eyes to the narrow life she'd been leading. Being with Karen and Larry, as well as the developing relationship with Nick, seemed more and more attractive. There was more to life than work and if she could only relax, perhaps she'd find her own life immensely enriched.

CHAPTER SEVEN

EDEN STEPPED ONTO THE DEBARKATION RAMP at New Orleans International Airport on Sunday afternoon with her pulse racing at the thought of seeing Nick again. She gripped the handrail and started down, moving gracefully in the feminine ankle-strap heels that complemented her softly flowing coral dress. The afternoon sun was blinding, but the breezes lifting her dark wavy hair made the temperature seem almost pleasant.

She saw Nick the moment she entered the terminal gate. He was wearing a light cream tropical-weight suit that emphasized his lean muscular frame. There was enough time to study him as he stepped aside to let several small boys push ahead in their rush to greet an arriving couple. He glanced down at the children, his features softening, the firm mouth breaking into a tender smile that radiated to his dark eyes. As he turned his head she saw a scrape accompanied by a dark bruise on one tanned cheek.

Catching sight of her, he started forward, his smile deepening. Halting a few feet away, he subjected her to a brazen inspection that took in her windblown hair, the silky drape of her dress against her rounded breasts and long shapely legs. "I've missed you," he said quietly, huskily, holding out his hand.

She grasped it and he pulled her forward, wrapping his arms around her, seeming oblivious to the presence of others around them. Unused to displays of public affection, it took Eden a moment to relax, but her overwhelming pleasure at being with him again soon overcame her self-consciousness. "I've missed you, too," she murmured, a warm weakness spreading through her.

He lowered his head, his mouth hungrily closing over hers. She found herself returning the kiss with equal fervor. As she drew back, he said shakily, "Let's get out of here so I can kiss you the way I'm longing to."

She stepped back, her eyes shining with agreement. "What happened to your cheek?"

"Oh, that? It's nothing. Do you have any luggage?"

She nodded, fishing in her purse for the ticket. "How much can that car of yours hold?"

"I'm willing to rent a truck to haul everything you own," he answered.

"Why do you say that?" Her brow wrinkled as she tried to sort out his meaning.

"Because it would mean you listened to me and you're moving back home," he explained.

"Home, Nick?" Eden laughed. "You've leased my family home and I have a perfectly lovely condo in Houston."

He shot her a glance out of the corner of his eye

as they walked toward the baggage section. "I can think of more satisfactory arrangements."

"Including a way for me to commute daily to Houston for my work?" She forced a light quality into her voice to cover the sudden tightness in her throat. This was treading too close for comfort. Their life-styles were still miles apart, no matter how close they were becoming. "How were your friends this weekend?" she said, changing the subject.

He touched his cheek. "Rough."

"Did a jealous husband do that to you?" she teased.

He threw back his head and laughed. "Nothing that exciting. I got this when I tried to teach some little boys how to play soccer. I haven't figured out yet why I'm the one who landed on the bottom of the pile."

She pointed out her blue suitcase and bulging canvas bag, and Nick extracted them from the slowly revolving ramp. As they walked toward the parking lot, he said, "How was your weekend? Very dull and boring, I hope?"

"Beast! As a matter of fact, you're right. Friday evening I went to that housewarming and was bored out of my mind. Absolutely no one listens to anyone else at those functions, but everyone talks at the top of their voices."

He grinned, swinging open her car door and then going around to the rear to put her luggage inside. Eden slid into the seat, smiling ruefully as she realized how accustomed she was becoming to having these little gestures performed for her. *Don't let yourself be spoiled,* she warned herself.

Once inside, Nick turned to her. "Mind if I run one errand before we start our tour of the Quarter?" His eyes traced fiery paths over her face and down her throat as his fingers stroked through her hair.

His gaze made her suddenly breathless and she nodded mutely. Lips twitching, he said, "You mind?"

"No. . . ." She gave into impulse and traced the line of his jaw with a fingertip.

He turned away and started the engine. "If we're going to make it to the Quarter, you better go easy on me. You know how powerfully you affect me." With that he urged the powerful engine into reverse.

After exiting from the parking lot, he pulled into the traffic on the interstate. "You're not going to believe this, but there are many parts of New Orleans I've never visited," she said.

"It will be my pleasure to be your guide. When's the last time you were in the French Quarter?"

"Years ago. My senior year in high school, to be exact. And I was heavily chaperoned then."

He chuckled. "You won't need a chaperon tonight. I'm here to protect you."

"Who's going to protect me from you?" she murmured rather shyly.

He removed one hand from the steering wheel long enough to grasp hers before exiting off the freeway. They drove through brick-paved narrow streets lined with handsome masonry and homes enveloped in forests of wrought iron. Everywhere there were masses of tropical greenery and brightly colored flowers peeping out of courtyards guarded by ornate gates.

"What a lovely neighborhood," she said.

"One of the oldest. I grew up near here."

She glanced around with more interest. "Where?"

"Several blocks away," he replied noncommittally. "Don't you think New Orleans has the most interesting street names: Royal, Broussard, Lafitte, Chartres, Magazine?"

His swift change of subject puzzled Eden. Was he telling her subtly to stay out of his private life? Nick braked to a curb beside a curlicued iron fence that bordered a tiny neighborhood cemetery. It held rows of raised stone tombs, one of the burial grounds unique to this flood-prone state. She glanced over at Nick inquiringly.

His face was shuttered, yet Eden couldn't miss the vulnerable way he held his body, as if he was waiting for her reaction. "Nick?" she whispered.

"This is where Job's grave is, Job Devereaux, the man who adopted me," he said tersely. "If you'll give me a minute, I'll check to see if fresh flowers have been delivered. I never know if the florist is doing his job."

"Mind if I come?" Eden kept her voice light, her smile friendly and warm. "Most of this weekend I've been leaning over a drawing board. A little exercise would be welcome."

"Please," he said, and Eden wondered if she imagined that he looked relieved.

He grasped her hand tightly in his as they started down a narrow grassy path until they reached a section far from the street. "Here," he said abruptly.

An enormous spray of flowers covered one of the plots. "From you?" she asked.

"A standing order every week." His voice was clipped and Eden tried to hide her surprise. "Job meant a lot to me. He was one of the best of the wildcatters, and he passed along everything he knew about the oil business to me."

Eden studied him in silence. Why did she feel that somehow Nick had brought her here for a purpose. It was almost as if he wanted to tell her about his life but couldn't. She would have to tread very carefully. Funny, she knew how it felt to be unable to express one's deepest feelings, but she had thought Nick was relaxed and open. Perhaps everyone had something in their past that caused them pain. Eden glanced again at Nick, enjoying the sight of his wind-whipped hair lying thickly over his high brow. "How old were you when he adopted you?"

"Sixteen. Actually, he hired me to work as a roustabout one summer. When it was time to return to the home, he suggested I stay with him. Since I was a minor, the sisters had to refuse. Never one to let obstacles stand in his way, Job proceeded to adopt me." Nick's mouth curved in a nostalgic smile as he ended his explanation.

The home? Eden was dying to ask questions but she sensed that he would withdraw if she pressed too hard. "It sounds like it was a good decision. Did he live long enough to see you become such a success in the oil business?"

Nick shook his head. "No, and he might not consider me a success. Job never made a lot of money but he had a good time. He used to warn me not to be a drifter like him, though. He was convinced no one would ever visit his grave when he died."

"And here we are," Eden murmured, touched by this insight into Nick's past. The tenderness with which he regarded Job reflected how much the man had meant to him.

Nick put his arms around her, drawing her close. "I'm certain of one thing. Job would approve of my bringing a wonderful lady like you here. Do you know how lucky I feel when you smile at me?"

"Nick," she whispered, moving even closer as he tightened his arms around her. At this moment, she surrendered to the feelings that had haunted her all weekend.

He bent to kiss her and she eagerly responded as his mouth, warm and hard, closed over hers, his tongue tangling intimately with her own. She slipped her arms under his suit jacket and encircled his warm back, pressing her legs against his hard thighs.

They drew back at length, slowly returning to a sense of their surroundings. "Have you ever been kissed in a cemetery before?" he asked.

"Perhaps it's not in very good taste," she admitted reluctantly.

"Nonsense," Nick retorted, throwing back his head and laughing. "I know Job would approve and I bet some of these other good Southern ladies and gentlemen could have taught us a lot about loving."

Pointing toward a wrought-iron bench that graced the base of a low-hanging tree, he asked, "Shall we sit down for a few minutes?"

Eden led the way, turning to face him once they were seated. "Tell me about Job," she requested softly, hopeful that he wouldn't feel she was prying.

Nick laced his fingers together and clasped them around one knee. "Job was a caring person. Even though he had no family of his own, by choice, he gave me my first real taste of homelife."

"Then you never knew your parents?" Eden held her breath after asking the question, but the look on Nick's face relieved her worries. He looked pleased that she had asked, as if he had been hoping to talk about this but hadn't quite known how to start.

"I never saw my father," he said slowly, as if testing her reaction. "In fact, I'm not even sure who he was." He waited, not saying anything else.

Sensing that her reaction would determine whatever else he told her, Eden trod carefully. "And your mother?"

The shuttered look came over Nick's face again, lines of pain creasing his forehead. "My memories of my mother are sketchy. She was in and out of my life until I was eight, then she died." He stared off across the cemetery and Eden sat quietly, not saying anything.

Finally he turned to face her, leaning forward, his face intense. "Maybe this is stupid, Eden," he said, looking her fully in the eyes. "For some reason I want to tell you about her. I've never discussed her with anyone."

"I know what it's like to lose your parents," Eden replied, touching his hand lightly.

"And there the similarity between us ends," Nick said dryly. "My parents were nothing like yours," he enunciated harshly. "My mother never married my father. She was young and never thought much, just seemed to do everything based on feelings."

"Aren't you being rather hard on her?" Eden's voice was firmer than she felt. "We all make mistakes. Perhaps she loved unwisely, is that any reason not to appreciate her for her good qualities."

Nick looked chagrined. "You're right, you know." Taking one of her hands, he played with it idly as he continued. "I don't feel angry toward her. It's just that she would never let go. After I was born she refused to let me be put up for adoption. Instead, she would go and work for a while and then come take me with her. Everything would be fine for a few months and then something would happen. She'd get sick or lose her job." Here he paused to consider Eden. "She was a bar hostess, worked in some of the big hotels and restaurants downtown. I guess that's where she met my father. But she never told me anything about him."

Eden heard more than his words were saying. He didn't need to fill in the details for her. She could sense the pain he had experienced, the feeling of never having really belonged anywhere, the longing for a real home and family. "What happened to her?"

Nick sighed and released her hand. "She died when I was eight. She was so run-down that when she got sick she couldn't recover. After she died I couldn't talk to anyone for days. I guess I had mixed feelings toward her. I hated the way she moved me back and forth. Yet she was my mother and I loved her."

"She must have loved you very much." Eden grasped his hand again and stroked it comfortingly.

Nick's brief reluctant smile erased some of the tension from his face. "You're right. I suppose I should remember that about her. She did the best she could."

Eden tilted her head to one side and regarded him. "Somehow, I think you loved her very much," she said softly. "But you feel guilty because without you, her life wouldn't have been so hard. You resent how hard she worked to keep you because it makes you feel responsible." Even she was surprised by her speech when she finished. Would Nick be offended?

He stared at her, speechless for a moment. "What makes you think that..." he began and then stopped sheepishly. Smiling at her, he whispered, "You surprise me, Miss Sonnier. Such wisdom from someone who looks so cool. Maybe you're in the wrong job."

Eden felt embarrassed. "That was inexcusable, I

suppose. Sorry if I stuck my nose into your business."

"Aw, but what a pretty nose." Nick put his arm around her and pulled her up against him. "Thanks for listening. I really needed to talk about my mother. I wanted you to know about my background, in case it bothered you."

"Bothered me?" Eden glared at him.

"I can't trace my lineage like the noble Sonniers." Nick pretended to be amused, but Eden sensed his diffidence.

"Are you a snob?" she demanded indignantly.

Now it was his turn to feel embarrassed. His eyelids partly closed to shield his reaction. "Sorry," was all he said, yet Eden knew he considered the differences between them greater than she did. She only saw the mature Nick, the successful businessman with the power to make his own choices and a life-style that fit in well with any group. Maybe he felt handicapped by his background. Only time would allow them to feel at ease in each other's company.

"Thanks for telling me about yourself, Nick." Her softly spoken words sealed the bond between them, and soon they were laughing again as they moved back to the car. "Where to now?" she asked once inside the car, pulling down the sun visor and checking in the small mirror to see how wind tossed her hair was.

"The Vieux Carre, New Orleans's chief tourist attraction. We have a couple of hours before our dinner reservations, so we'll stroll the streets and have a drink at one of the jazz bars. Sound good?"

"Mmm...wonderful. Are we going to have one of those evenings that the tourist brochures say are unforgettable?"

His smile was very white against his bronzed face. "Unforgettable!" he agreed.

They parked the car in a garage inside one of the high-rise hotels on the fringe of the Quarter and strolled down a narrow street, stopping to study and comment on the artfully displayed quality merchandise of the antique shops, art galleries, small intimate salons and jewelers.

"You're the expert on these," Nick said in front of an antique furniture store. "Are they authentic?"

"You can trust a reputable place like this, but a novice needs to beware of fakes in some stores."

"If I decide to buy any antiques, I'll take you along," he said, hugging her against him. She responded by pressing her mouth softly against his neck. He moved her even closer to him, kissing the top of her head lightly.

From down the street came the sound of music. A crowd was gathering and they joined in, pushing their way through the jostling throng. They reached a circle gathered around an elderly man playing a mouth organ as he executed a rhythmical tap dance in the middle of the street. The noisy crowd joined in, clapping in time to his steps as some sang or hummed the tune. When the man finished, there was a round of applause, and Nick and Eden joined the others who were placing money in the entertainer's bucket.

"Have you ever been to Preservation Hall?" he asked as they started down the street again.

"Yes, I love it. If I remember right, that's the home of jazz."

He nodded. "When you watch the enjoyment of the players and their total spontaneity, you can believe it."

Twilight had come and all around them neon lights were starting to flash, doors opening on bistros as they continued down the street. Through open doorways Eden could see performers on raised stages inside the darkened interiors gyrating to the sound of the sweet trumpet music flowing enticingly into the street. Spices and chicory blended with the tangy odors of the bayou night.

"Don't you feel at home here?" Nick whispered in her ear. "As they say, once a Cajun, always a Cajun."

"It's strange, but until this visit I thought I had turned my back on Louisiana forever. I've made a good life for myself in Houston."

"What made you go to Houston in the first place?"

"It's a long story." Eden answered.

"Then let's go in here and have a drink while you tell me." He pointed to one of the jazz spots and they slipped in, sliding along the wall to reach one of the wooden tables without disturbing the performing piano player. When the music ended, a waitress came to their table. "Like a hurricane? You get the glass to take home as a souvenir."

Nick grinned. "What's a memorable night in New Orleans without its most famous drink? Are you game?"

Eden nodded. When the waitress left, Nick turned to her. "Now, tell me what made you leave home."

"School. I chose a design institute in Houston. My last year there I started work as an apprentice at one of the design studios. One thing led to another and when the right opportunity came along, I started my own business."

Nick reached over and took her hand, as if he hated to spend a moment not being close to her. "Ever given any thought to starting a business in New Orleans?"

She shook her head. "Too competitive. The decorating studios here are a close-knit group who've fought hard for their status. Houston has new money, new opportunity. If one's willing to work hard, the sky is the limit."

Nick considered her thoughtfully. "I'm surprised you're so convinced New Orleans is a closed market. You strike me as being a very strong person, so I wouldn't think a little competition would stop you."

Eden refused to be baited. "Perhaps I will consider it, someday." She tossed her hair back and smiled. "This weekend I did talk about opening another branch office with my chief assistant."

"Tom?" Nick's eyebrows drew together in a frown.

"Yes," Eden confirmed. "He feels we need to

expand, but I'm not sure. I want Sonnier's to be top line, and if we spread ourselves too thinly, we might end up opting for quantity instead of quality."

Their drinks arrived and they leaned back in their wooden chairs, sipping the sticky sweet rum concoctions, listening to the haunting sweet sounds of a trumpet mingling with the piano.

She glanced at him obliquely, keenly aware of his clean male scent, of the rise and fall of his broad chest, of the strong tanned column of his neck and the pulse beating rapidly in his throat. She drank in his profile: strong chiseled features; dark straight hair; long thick lashes. Handsome, dynamic, exciting and yet so much more. Nick had his layers, too, and the more she knew of him, the more he intrigued her. They had open lines of communication between them, seemingly free to agree or disagree on any subject, no need to put on an act to please each other.

"We'll have to leave now if we're going to keep that reservation." Nick turned to find her watching him. He signaled the waitress and paid, starting to refuse her offer of a bag to carry their glasses home.

"Please bring the bag," interrupted Eden.

Nick looked at her quizzically. "I can't believe an interior designer would approve such tacky souvenirs in her home."

"I hate sterile environments, homes that look as if they've just been readied for a magazine photographer's arrival. I think everything in the decor should have personal significance for the owner," she said, slipping her glass into the padded bag the waitress offered.

"You're full of surprises," murmured Nick as they rose.

They made their way through the crowded sidewalks, sticking close to avoid being separated by tour groups. The restaurant Nick had chosen had an elegant masonry facade, but once inside the foyer Eden could see it was a conversion of one of the creole-style homes so prevalent in the area. The hostess greeted Nick by name, calling for one of the waiters to lead them to a reserved table.

The cloth was snowy white, the menus large and leather-bound and entirely in French, the second language of many Louisiana natives. Nick refused drinks from the bar, and the wine steward arrived within minutes to engage him in a lengthy discussion.

Eden listened in fascination. Where had he learned all of this if he had been a roustabout at sixteen, rescued from some kind of home by a man who sounded like little more than a drifter? Had there been some woman later on who had exerted enough influence over Nick's life to smooth down the rough edges and complete his education? The idea left a bitter taste in her mouth, and she berated herself for being jealous. No one was lower in her estimation than someone who used a relationship to deny another person the right to his or her own experiences and thoughts in life.

The meal was superb. The intimate setting. The flickering candlelight. Soft music mingling with delicious food as course followed course: succulent raw oysters on the half shell, a clear lobster bisque laced with a trace of sherry, delicate veal sautéed with fresh mushrooms in a tangy lemon-butter sauce.

"Dessert?" Nick's eyes darkened in the dim light.

"Sorry, but I couldn't possibly. It was all so wonderful." She looked at him through lowered lashes and enjoyed his instant response.

"Then coffee," he insisted. The waiter stepped forward as if on cue and Nick ordered *cafe brulôt*. "We're probably going to have to take the long way home tonight. It's too late to make that last ferry."

She glanced down at the thin gold watch on her arm. "Time has gone by so quickly. I had no idea it was this late."

He reached out and picked up her hand, pressing it against his cheek before kissing the soft palm with a seductive caress that melted her heart. "That's very flattering, Eden."

Her smile emphasized her sensual response to him. "Careful," he cautioned huskily. "When you look like that, I forget all about where I am."

Her blue eyes sparkled. "Do you realize we haven't known each other one whole week yet?" She left the intimate events of Friday afternoon at Belle's Folly unsaid, but the memory permeated the air.

"We were fated to meet," he said quietly. "Everything we've done in the past has only been a prelude, a preparation for this time in our life." His tones underscored the current of excitement, pulsating and electrifying, that zigzagged between them.

Nick was right, Eden realized. The amount of time you knew someone wasn't all that important. No one could deny there had been an instant rapport that grew steadily with each encounter, culminating in the rising tide of their feelings this evening.

Nick sat quietly, studying her face. The silence lengthened and Eden's heart raced painfully in her chest. He brought her hand to his mouth and kissed each finger slowly, tantalizingly, tenderly. "Eden," he whispered, "would you think I was crazy if I told you I think I'm falling in love with you?"

She was staggered. Love had such awesome implications for her. As if it were something separate with strings...no, ropes...attached, binding two people together and cutting off all other options. Was she incapable of falling in love as Tom had accused? She swallowed convulsively.

"Don't..." he said, covering her mouth with one finger. "I promised to give you time and I mean to keep my promise."

"Thank you, Nick," she whispered, telling him with the expression in her eyes how much his words had meant to her.

At that moment the waiter wheeled in a polished mahogany serving cart. In the center sat a silver bowl atop a tray surrounded by brandy-soaked sugar cubes. Eden watched in fascination as the waiter combined the steaming hot coffee from a pot with the cognac, cinnamon, cloves and citrus peels already in the bowl.

The waiter blew out the candles on their table, plunging them into instant darkness and with a flourish struck a match, igniting the cubes. They flared into running slivers of flames that engulfed the streams of *cafe brulôt* he was deftly ladling up and down. Eden's breath caught in her throat as she watched the dramatic scene, her eyes locking with Nick's in an intimate embrace that captured the pure magic of this moment.

"You've come home, darling," he whispered. "Home to Louisiana and home to me."

CHAPTER EIGHT

RELAXING IN THE CAR, sunroof open to the gentle night breezes, Eden leaned her head on Nick's shoulder, enjoying his nearness. Her mind was blank, free at last from the tensions of the past few days. She allowed herself to luxuriate only in the moment.

"Go to sleep, darling," Nick murmured in her ear, reaching in front of her to flick on the car stereo. Her eyelids drifted downward as she surrendered completely to the mounting crescendo of the music surging through the encapsulated intimate space. The waves of sound increased with a growing urgency and then subsided so poignantly that she was almost moved to tears.

The next thing she knew someone was shaking her gently yet persistently. Eden blinked several times, pushing away and sitting up.

"Wake up. We're here," Nick murmured.

"We can't be here already. We just left," she mumbled.

His hands came out to gently knead the tired muscles of her shoulders. "You slept the whole way. Are you awake now or would you like me to carry you inside?"

"I'm awake." Smiling ruefully at him, she added, "I deserted you. I bet you've been bored driving back with me snoring beside you."

"You don't snore. You look gorgeous when you sleep." Nick leaned across her to flip open her door, his arm grazing her breasts and driving the last vestiges of sleep from her mind.

Nick came around to her door and held her elbow lightly as she got out. He accompanied her up the steps and waited while she located her key and opened the front door. Fully awake now, she turned to him, smiling expectantly. "I'll make us a pot of coffee."

Nick started to accept and then stopped. "Eden, if I come in, I can't promise I'm not going to want more than coffee. Since I have promised to give you more time, I'm not sure that's fair."

Eden's emotions took a nose dive. She didn't want him to leave, yet how could she repeat her offer without sounding as if she wanted him to come in and make love to her. *Well, isn't that exactly what you want, my girl,* she asked herself. While she debated, Nick took a step backward.

"Would you like me to go in and check under all your beds to make sure there's nothing to go bump in the night before I leave?"

Eden managed an indignant, "No thanks! I thought I'd convinced you I wasn't the maiden niece."

Nick's laugh deepened as he reached past her and swung the door open. With sudden decisiveness, Eden stepped into the darkened hall. "On second thought, Nick," she said quietly, "perhaps you'd better check the house. After all, it is quite late." For a moment, as he remained stationary, his face impassive, she felt her nerve falter. Perhaps he didn't want her but no, that wasn't true. He'd told her tonight that he might be falling in love with her, and even though she had not yet admitted it to herself, she was beginning to believe that this was the man she loved.

"Nick..." she whispered more firmly, extending her hand toward him. "Come, put your arms around me. Please," she added.

As he stepped through the door, his tall frame blocked the light from the porch and Eden could not see the expression on his face. "Are you sure?" was all he asked. Eden's answer was in her touch.

With no hesitation he drew her to him, swinging the door shut behind him before wrapping his arms around her. Eden's purse slipped to the floor unheeded as his hands caressed her buttocks and moved her close to him.

Eden trembled as he kissed her eyelids. Her lashes fluttered beneath his lips. She flattened her hands against his chest, feeling his muscles tense beneath her fingertips. With a will of its own, her body seemed to mold against his. Was it only Friday that he had held her like this, bringing her such joy with his touch?

His mouth came down over hers in a swift and passionate movement, his tongue penetrating the sweet recesses and taking secure possession. "Eden, Eden," he murmured, moving his mouth only long enough to rain kisses along her smooth jaw. In growing desire his lips sought her ear, nipping seductively at the lobe. His breath fanned against her cloud of hair as he spoke. "Do you want me to make love to you, Eden?" he asked between arousing kisses. "Because that's what I want and if you want me to stop, you'd better make me leave now."

Eden pushed herself away from him and moved to the foot of the stairs, her hair wildly cascading around her pale face. Slowly, she extended one hand and said, "I want you, Nick. I have from the moment I saw you."

Nick and Eden were silent as they went upstairs, even when they reached her room and she swept open the door. No light was burning, but the wide-open window let in the glow of misty moonlight.

Words weren't necessary as their bodies communicated the sweet language of passion. Inside the room, Nick lounged against the door, watching her as she kicked off her shoes and turned to face him.

"Undress for me, Eden," he requested softly, adding "please," to let her know how important this was to him. Her reserved nature fought against her desire. Slowly she slid off the silky coral dress, letting it fall with a soft whoosh around her feet. Stepping out of the dress, she stood before him in a brief slip, her legs smooth and white in the moonlight. With sure movements she peeled off the slip, adding it to the pile on the floor.

Her breasts were proud and firm, rounded and creamy white, untouched by the sun. Her slender hips balanced the generous swell of her breasts.

Naked now except for pale lacy panties, she swept her hair back, letting it tumble onto her shoulders. She stood before him unashamed.

Nick's eyes were riveted on her. Moving toward her, he stopped briefly, to devour her with his gaze. His pleasure in her body was evident in his expression.

Unable to withstand his scrutiny any longer, Eden placed her hands on his hips, pulling him to her, sliding the jacket off his shoulders in a smooth motion that freed his arms to wrap around her.

His strong brown hands sought her breasts, covering the rosy tips and cupping the smooth swelling flesh. Eden's breath whispered against his neck in a sigh of pleasure. Their bodies gently revolved as they moved, their mouths clinging in fiery passion until they lay coiled on the bed, their bodies sensuously entwined.

They kissed, teasingly at first and then more insistently. Eden's hands moved freely over his back, loosening his shirt from the band of his trousers so that she could feel the smooth warm skin of his back under her fingers. Nick broke away from her reluctantly, rising to take off his shirt and trousers until he stood naked at the side of the bed.

Eden drank in the sight of his beautiful body sculpted by a life of physical labor. Not an ounce of spare flesh marred the taut muscular skin of his abdomen, his hips narrow and lean, his shoulders wide and hard. Eden's eyes skimmed the vee of dark hair that tapered to reveal his masculine arousal, and as if she had touched him there, he groaned and moved to lay beside her again.

Drawing her beneath him, Nick guided his knee between her thighs, his eyes never leaving hers as he stroked her warm flesh. Eagerly she pulled him to her as his hands touched her rose-tipped breasts, his lips following in swift pursuit. Gently his fingers slid down her hips to find her warm and ready for him, and when Eden responded with sensuous movements and restless hands, he increased her pleasure almost beyond endurance.

Eager to express her answering passion, Eden grasped his hips and pulled him against her, letting her fingers sink into the smooth skin of his buttocks.

When Eden thought she could wait no longer, Nick was there, parting her thighs, sliding between them, entering her with a powerful thrust that joined them for all time. With his hands beneath her, he held her hips tightly as they moved instinctively. They rode upon a wave of ecstasy so great that they cried out together before they slowly drifted back down from the heights.

"Eden, I love you," she thought she heard him whisper, the words barely penetrating her afterglow of passion. Her reserve would not let her answer. Not yet. But to herself she repeated the words over and over until they could be tasted on her lips when he kissed her.

Outside, a rising wind rustled through the trees, drowning out the buzzing insects from the bayou swamps. At some point Nick fell asleep, cradling her in his arms, his head pillowed on her breasts. Eden didn't move. She lay still beneath him, listening to his even breathing.

When she awoke, the dawn sun was streaking through the open drapes, undulating in wavy patterns across the floor, highlighting her discarded clothes. Eden snuggled down into the sheets with a contented sigh, her mind sleepy, her body comfortable and satisfied in a way she'd never known.

In her dreams she was wrapped in Nick's arms, reliving the moments they had shared. Reaching out her hands, she felt for him and then sat straight up. The bed was empty.

Not only was the bed empty, the room was empty and it felt as if the whole house were empty. Eden groped for the small traveling alarm clock she had set beside her bed. Quarter to six. My God, at what unearthly hour had he left her?

Feeling a surge of disappointment, she started to lie back down, and then her eyes fell on a sheet of her own notepaper, propped against the lamp on the table across from her. Sliding out of bed, she crossed the room, sunlight dancing off her naked body and sifting through the tangled strands of her black hair.

"Eden," the note read. "Have I told you lately you're gorgeous when you sleep? I rose early and didn't have the heart to wake you. No wonder you're so thin. There's nothing in your refrigerator! I'll stop back by around seven with breakfast." His name was sprawled across the bottom of the page.

Eden's spirits soared and she hummed quietly as she headed back to the bed. Wrapping the sheet sensuously around her body, she lay on her back, staring at the ceiling and thinking about Nick. How like him to remember the little things, to bring her breakfast even at the start of his own busy day. She'd never met anyone so successful who could be as relaxed and carefree as Nick was. Having learned early to create his own happiness had made him particularly sensitive to the happiness of others.

The shrill ring of the telephone caught her attention and Eden slid out of bed, throwing on a frilly cotton robe and padding down the hall in her bare feet. Was it Nick?

"Belle's Folly," she said swiftly into the receiver.

"Well, Ms Sonnier, I hope I haven't interrupted your sleep or anything else important," Tom said dryly.

"Tom! Has something happened?" she asked immediately.

"Sorry to call so early, but I tried and tried to call last night and never got an answer." His petulant voice was demanding an explanation, but Eden had no intention of giving one to him.

When she didn't reply his voice changed, taking on a boyish excitement. "Do you remember the furnishings and accessories in the Jed Morgan home in River Oaks?"

"Yes." Eden fumbled with the phone cord, wishing there were some place to sit in the hall.

"They're ours for one-fourth of their value if we can act tonight. Jed called me several hours ago and he offers them to the firm if we can promise the money by nine o'clock tomorrow morning. It seems he's having trouble with his brother, you know, the one who's his business partner. He wants to liquidate his assets before they're frozen. What do you think?''

The news left her breathless. Jed Morgan and his wife were friends of Tom's, and she had gone with him to their palatial mansion several times for parties. She closed her eyes, evoking images of the nineteenth-century Japanese furniture, the French and American Art Deco accessories and the scenic paintings on the shoji panels. It was a decorator's dream and there would be no difficulty reselling the items to eager clients. She wouldn't mind owning them herself for that matter.

The figure he named, while considerably below the value of the items, was still staggering enough to make her pause. ''How about it?'' Tom asked impatiently.

''Are we doing anything illegal? Could the stuff be taken from us by the brother?''

''Not if we act quickly. If your conscience is bothering you, Jed assures me that his brother is doing the same thing with his own assets.''

''It's not that. As iong as it's legal, it's not our problem why the goods are being sold.''

She paused a second longer, nervously drumming her fingers on the table beside her, considering the financial risks and then said firmly, ''Let's do it, Tom. I'll call my banker later this morning and make certain that my line of credit will cover that amount. I'll call you back after lunch.

''Damn, I admire your decisiveness.'' Tom's voice quavered with excitement. ''Sorry if I woke you up.''

"You didn't," she assured him. "I'll get back to you the moment I know anything."

As she hung up and went to turn on the shower, her mind was seething. The possibility of obtaining a treasure trove like this was a real plum for a decorating firm. Nervously, she wondered if she ought to return to Houston. What if Tom messed things up, didn't handle the situation right? She'd hate to lose the furniture now that she had her heart set on it.

Stop it, she warned herself. *You promised Tom you were going to let him take care of things while you were gone. Relax and trust him. It's arrogant to think no one can do anything right except yourself.*

An hour later she paused to survey herself critically in her dresser mirror. Her blouse was a soft cotton printed voile, sheer and unbuttoned to reveal the shadowy cleft between her breasts. Her skirt was a simple wraparound, a crisp green that brought out the highlights in her coal-black hair.

Coming down the steps, she glanced into the living room and met the censure of Belle's eyes shining from the portrait hanging over the marble mantel. The painting was one of the major art treasures in the house, and legend had it that no matter where you wandered in the room, the eyes of the beautiful woman followed you.

Eden put her hands on her hips and faced the portrait squarely, "What's wrong, Belle? Don't you approve of me? Is it Nick you don't like or is it my life in Houston?"

The solemn stare of the sapphire-blue eyes so like

her own unnerved her and Eden suddenly began smiling. This was ridiculous. Over the course of a week and a half, she'd been reduced to talking to portraits. Was Nick such a powerful influence on her life? Nick. She savored the name in her mind as she sank down into a soft chair.

She glanced up and her eyes widened. Blinking rapidly, she decided she was only imagining the expression in the beautiful Belle's eyes had changed. With a grin she stood up and headed for the kitchen. Enough of that. She had work to do today and Nick was on his way over.

Hearing a car crunching over the unpaved drive, she hurried to put coffee on. "Eden?" a masculine voice called.

"Nick!" She hurried to the door and flung it open, wrapping her arms around his waist as he stepped inside. "Good morning. Isn't it a breathtaking day!" she enthused. Her voice was muffled as she burrowed her face against his crisp dress shirt. His skin, tangy and freshly shaven, was warm beneath her cheek.

"Breathtaking," he agreed, crushing her willowy softness against the hard length of his body.

She lifted her head, leaning back to gaze hungrily at him, waiting as he lowered his head slowly, his lips brushing across hers with a feathery kiss. Their mouths met, their tongues entwining with such intensity that Eden felt dizzied by her response.

She moaned, yielding to the insidious warmth that stole through her. As he reluctantly released her mouth, she whispered, "I'm wrinkling your shirt, Nick."

"And I'm crushing our doughnuts," he murmured, holding up a bedraggled sack. "I'm here to collect on that coffee I smell."

"It's almost ready," she said, struggling to regain her composure as she reached for the doughnuts. She peered inside at the square, lightly browned fried morsels, sprinkled with grains of glistening cane sugar. "*Warm beignets!* Where on earth did you get them?"

"A woman down the road from my house sells them, fresh from her kitchen. You're supposed to place your order the day before, but I talked her out of a dozen."

"You can be very persuasive, Mr. Devereaux," Eden agreed, twisting her fingers in the cloth of his shirt with one hand.

"If you keep looking at me like that, neither one of us will get to work today," he warned, and Eden dropped her hand, laughing affectionately.

"Let's eat in the breakfast room," she suggested, leading the way toward the kitchen area.

He poured the coffee into the two mugs she took from the cabinet, and they carried them to the round oak table. Sitting in the bright sunshine, Eden told him about her call from Tom, her eyes sparkling with enthusiasm as she described the Morgan furniture.

"If you need to make that phone call to your banker, don't let me stop you," Nick offered. "I can't stay long. I've got a conference at eight."

"I'll take care of it later this morning," Eden answered, smiling at him over the rim of her mug.

Nick took a sip of the coffee. "Only a native can make chicory coffee like this," he murmured appreciatively. "How do you manage in Texas?"

"It's not available in most restaurants," she conceded. "At the studio, I keep a pot on all the time."

He offered her one of the doughnuts and she bit into it. "It's sinful for something to taste this good. Sinful and fattening."

His eyes raked down over her curves with warm approval. "You're far from having to worry about that. Just well-rounded in all the right places."

She reached for another doughnut. "Don't blame me if I get a little too well-rounded, then," she laughed.

His eyes darkened with growing feeling. "Can you come to dinner at my house tonight?"

"I'd love to." The sight of her notebook on the table made her hesitate suddenly. "Now it's me who can't stay long. I've got to get my plan finished for Fred before the week's over. He suggested Friday for our meeting."

Nick's expression hardened. "I thought you two had agreed on two weeks. That won't be up until next Tuesday."

Eden nodded. "That's right, but Fred wanted Friday. Do you think I can change the meeting?"

He eyed her. "Don't ask me. You're a businesswoman. You know how to demand that someone keep to their original agreement."

"Don't get angry," she murmured, frowning. "I'll call him today and change it."

He sighed. "Why is it I get the feeling you still don't believe I have no part in making the decision regarding Belle's Folly?" He stretched out his long legs and leaned back.

"I can't understand how you can stay so aloof about something that concerns you. I'm having a hard enough time not flying to Houston right now to direct this Morgan deal."

"Then I'd hate to be one of your employees. Don't you delegate at all?"

Eden frowned, remembering the events of the weekend. "Yes, but I still keep on top of everything that's happening."

He chuckled. "Then you're not really delegating at all. Your employees know that in the long run they can always depend on you to rescue them from any mistakes they make. How do you expect them to grow, to feel responsible for the outcome of their decisions?"

Eden glanced down. "I guess I haven't given anything but the success of the company much thought." Her eyes met his aggressively. "If it fails, I'll be the one held accountable."

"I know," he answered softly, his brown eyes filled with affection and caring. "There aren't any easy formulas to follow when you run your own business."

The warmth of his words dispelled the tension that had been building between them since the mention of Fred. Eden held out a fresh doughnut. He grinned, leaning over to take a bite of it, his large muscular hand covering hers firmly. "Hmm, this tastes good," he said, nibbling on one of her fingers.

"Help," she yelled.

He pulled back and reached out for the notebook, flipping it open. "How are your plans going, Eden?"

Eden glanced at him surreptitiously. Nick was certainly different. Most men would only have talked about the night before, but here was Nick, calmly eating doughnuts, talking about any and every subject. This was a kind of compatibility she had never known with any other man. Although the intensity of their lovemaking had been wonderful, Eden was beginning to realize it was only a part of the growing feelings between them.

"The blueprints are being worked up this week by one of my assistants. They'll be express mailed as soon as they're finished. Right now I'm getting ready to call the subcontractors to get competitive bids for the work. I do have one problem, though."

"What?"

"The architectural firm. Fred gave me their number and told me to work with them, but they won't return my calls. I get as far as the receptionist and I'm put off every time."

His eyes darkened dangerously. "I'll call them as soon as they open today, and I guarantee you'll get a return call immediately. Any other problems?"

She shrugged, suddenly uncomfortable. "I'm handling everything."

She watched as he lowered his eyes, his voice husky. "What's going to happen if the vote goes against you, Eden? What will it do to our relationship?"

She shook her head, wishing the subject hadn't come up. She didn't want anything to spoil the memory of last night. "I'm not sure. I'll be angry at first, I think. If you tell me that your company can't afford it or you can't work with my plans, I'll probably learn to handle that. I'll be happy to compromise as long as the negotiations are professional and not personal. Now that I've had a chance to look over Fred's plans I realize they aren't that different from my own. The air-conditioning installation is our biggest bone of contention."

He reached for her hand and began brushing his thumb across her palm, radiating warmth throughout her. "Eden, even if I hadn't put Fred in charge, I still wouldn't be capable of making this decision based on sound business principles. Naturally, I'd like to give you the world. I've fallen in love with you. But I don't think you want to win on that basis. You entered a fair fight and I hope you win. Then we'll both feel good."

She nodded, her throat choked. "If I lose, I'll try to remember what you just told me, Nick. You're being more than fair. It's Fred I don't trust."

His voice was normal as he dropped her hand. "Nonsense. Fred is as objective a businessman as you'll find. Anyway, this committee is set up so his vote won't be the deciding factor." He glanced at his watch, making a face. "I have to run now and we've spent the whole time talking business when what I really wanted to tell you—'' his voice lowered and he pulied her to her feet, drawing her into his arms ''—what I really wanted to tell you is that I love you.'' Dropping a swift kiss on her parted lips, he stepped back. He knew he wouldn't leave if he held her closely much longer. ''How about tonight?''

''Sounds great.'' Eden looked at him warmly. ''Can I bring anything?''

''Yourself,'' he murmured, brushing her cheek with a kiss full of promise before he left.

CHAPTER NINE

By NINE Eden had called her banker. He was the first loan officer she had approached when thinking of opening her own firm, and his enthusiastic endorsement had forged a friendship between the two. It was no surprise to her when he gave his immediate approval to extend her line of credit to cover the purchase of the Morgan furniture.

Immediately afterward she called Tom and they discussed arrangements for moving the furniture to their showroom. Only those items too large to fit into the storage room would need to be stored commercially. "Let's get all of the items photographed and we'll make up a brochure for our clients to browse through," she finished.

After hanging up, she felt on top of the world. It seemed almost everything was going her way today, and she found herself humming an old tune as she worked. Part of the reputation of any decorating firm depended on being able to find the exact item a client wanted. If someone had his heart set on a particular chest or chair, you could be sure he would praise you to the skies if you found it for him. The Morgan collection would give her a head start, for it included a variety of items highly in demand.

Her conversation with Nick had brightened the day, as well. After the satisfying events of the evening before, she'd been unsure how things would be in the light of day. Though he had appeared nonchalant, Eden knew he had expressed his true feelings for her during their night of tender lovemaking. As for her feelings about him, well, they were definitely getting warmer every day. She had never been one to fall in and out of love. Anyone else would have declared herself in love already, but it was a gradual process for Eden and she wanted to relish every moment of the experience, not rush anything.

A brief phone conversation with Karen at ten confirmed a meeting for lunch and at twelve Eden was waiting at the quaint little tearoom that operated in tandem with the boutique shop she had located in the village.

"Tell me about your weekend," Karen asked over the menu.

"Dull. Hard work. I was exhausted by the time I returned to New Orleans, and my employees didn't appreciate being kept all day Saturday, either. They usually work a half day."

"Not that part of the weekend. I'm talking about the time you spent with Nick. Do you know how he got that scratch on his face?"

In spite of herself Eden blushed. "Don't look at me. All I know is what he told me; he got it playing soccer. As for the rest of your question, I had a marvelous tour of the Quarter with Nick last night, thank you. How was your weekend?"

"Super. Larry took Becky to the circus in Baton Rouge, and I had a whole Saturday afternoon to do absolutely nothing except rest."

"How romantic," teased Eden.

Karen grinned. "Believe me, it was—after Becky went to sleep that night."

They were interrupted by a waitress hovering over their table. After they both ordered the luncheon special, Eden asked, "How about you and Becky coming to dinner at my house tomorrow night?"

"Larry usually comes over on Tuesday nights, but I could change that."

"Better yet, have him come with you. He's been so busy I've barely seen the two of you together since I got here."

"I'll take you up on that," agreed Karen. "I'm dying to get a better look at Belle's Folly. Larry showed the place to Fred and me before the company leased it, but I was so busy writing down notes for Fred I barely got a chance to see it. It's so fabulous I can hardly believe it's real."

"Then come as soon as you get off work and pick up Becky. That way you'll have lots of time to go through it. Larry can join us later—" She broke off at the sight of the spinach and bibb lettuce salad piled high with artichoke hearts and boiled eggs. It was accompanied by an array of petite tea sandwiches and a melange of fresh fruits. "I am going to gain so much weight!" she protested.

"Don't worry about it," Karen soothed.

"No, really. In Houston I never have time to eat

much. I'm always too busy to do anything more than grab whatever is available. Everything is so laid-back here. It's a wonder I wasn't fat as a child."

"I know what you mean," Karen commiserated. "Fortunately, I'm just a skinny redhead," she joked. "I never seem to gain weight no matter how much I eat."

They ate silently for a few minutes before Karen spoke again. "Fred cornered Nick as soon as he came in this morning and asked for a conference on Belle's Folly. They stayed behind the closed office door for at least an hour."

Eden lay down her fork with a frustrated bang. "Why that...."

"Yes?" giggled Karen. "If you can't think of the right name for Fred, I've got several select ones."

Eden grinned. "I can come up with enough on my own. That Fred. Trying to influence Nick. Any idea what they were talking about?"

"Nope. Fred took the blueprints in with him and he didn't look too pleased when he came back out. Maybe Nick told him you were going to get your way whatever Fred thought."

Eden shook her head firmly. "Nick will never do that. He promised me he'd get a consensus of opinion from everyone concerned. He won't take sides and I believe him."

"Don't forget that Fred may not be playing fair," warned Karen.

"Is he giving you any more problems?"

"Not this morning. I'm bending over backwards

to do my work efficiently and without any errors. That way, if he wants to accuse me of anything, he won't have any proof.''

Eden nodded approvingly. ''In the long run, that's the way to win.'' She glanced at the clock on the wall. ''And just to be sure, I'd say we better leave so you can get back on time.'' She grabbed for the check before Karen could reach it. ''My treat today.'' On the way out to their cars she explained about her fabulous opportunity to acquire the Morgan furnishings. ''This was my celebration luncheon.''

EDEN TOOK A LONG LEISURELY BATH that evening, leaning back and relaxing in the warm water as she let her thoughts drift to Nick. Either he had assumed she knew where he lived or else had forgotten to give her his address. Karen had drawn her a map, explaining that he was leasing the home of a family who were living overseas, friends of his, she believed.

Eden got out of the tub and toweled herself dry before rubbing a perfumed cream over her body in long smooth strokes. She dabbed a matching fragrance on her wrists and throat and then slipped into her most alluring lace briefs and bra.

A glance in the mirror at her flushed cheeks made her take a long deep breath in a deliberate attempt to slow down her racing pulse, but it was useless. She couldn't deny it any longer. She loved him. She wasn't ashamed of wanting him, needing him, longing for his touch. What it might mean for the future was unimportant tonight. All that mattered was knowing that he was there, as eager to see her as she was him.

She had a difficult time choosing from the garments she had brought with her from Houston. What did he have in mind when he mentioned dinner? A formal meal prepared and served by a maid or some fast food he'd picked up on the way home? She discarded that idea...hamburgers and French fries didn't seem his style when entertaining a lady. Maybe that went with whoever he played soccer with.

No, he was definitely more the romantic type, candlelight and wine and all the trimmings. She chose a soft red wrap skirt with a matching blouse that clung in all the right places. She applied her makeup with a deft touch, stroking smoky gray eye shadow above her eyes and black mascara on the long lashes. Her sapphire-blue eyes shone like multifaceted jewels when she finished. The phone rang while she was combing her hair.

"I forgot to tell you where I live." Nick's voice was a welcome sound.

"Karen drew me a map," Eden explained.

"Then I'll see you soon," Nick said before he hung up.

The map Karen had drawn appeared easy enough to follow, so Eden finished dressing leisurely before leaving. When she reached the turnoff where Karen lived, she honked her horn and waved at Becky who was once again playing in the lawn sprinkler.

After continuing down the farm-to-market road

for several miles she began looking for the white fence Karen had described. She had almost despaired of finding it when it loomed ahead of her, and she veered into the gravel driveway with an abrupt swerve.

The nondescript entrance had not prepared her for the impressive sight of the magnificent white-stucco-and-glass house towering from the midst of rolling green lawns and lush trees. Suddenly her stomach clenched and an unusual sense of intimidation swept over her as she stared at the opulence of her surroundings. How had Nick had the nerve to ask her what it was like to live in a setting as splendid as Belle's Folly?

Although not yet completely dark outside, it still seemed strange that there were no lights twinkling from the windows of the palatial home. A discreet white sign caught her eye and she read the For Sale notice with misgiving. Perhaps she was at the wrong home, she decided, glancing back down at her map as she slowed the car almost to a halt.

"Over here."

The sound of Nick's voice startled her and she leaned out the car window, searching for the direction it had come from.

"Park over here," he shouted when she finally located him. He was dressed in white cotton trousers and a red-and-white striped polo shirt, his dark hair gleaming even more vividly than usual.

She drove in the direction he had indicated and parked the car. "Are we eating outside?" she asked as she stepped out.

His eyebrows rose. "I hadn't planned it but we can, if you like."

She grinned, pointing toward the house. "There aren't any lights on in that presidential palace over there."

"That's because it's vacant," he said, running his gaze appreciatively over her full breasts and slender legs before pulling her to him for a kiss. "You're looking beautiful, as usual."

Pleased by his compliment, she returned his kiss with a lingering one of her own. As they walked down the path, he explained, "The friends of mine who own this estate are spending several years traveling around the world on their yacht. I live in their guest cottage." He guided her away from the main house, following a curving path until they reached a small white wooden cottage fronting on a private lake.

"Ooh, how lovely," exclaimed Eden. "Is that sailboat yours?"

He nodded. "It's a small one. If you'd like we'll try it out some day when the wind is right."

When, Nick? Have you forgotten I'll soon be gone? The unwelcome words popped into her mind, but she said nothing. "I'd like that," she said quietly. And perhaps she would be back here again soon. After all, she hadn't given their future much thought. She'd been too busy enjoying the present.

He held open the screen door and she stepped inside, glancing curiously around Nick's home. As if he could read her mind, he said, "Don't try analyzing me from what you see in this house. One of the reasons I agreed to live here was that I wouldn't have to bother buying furniture.''

"Bother?''

He nodded. "Until recently I've been too busy to even think about it.'' Pointing to the sofa, he said, "Have a seat and I'll get you something to drink. What would you like?''

"Scotch and soda,'' she said, sinking into the pale blue cushions. She surveyed the room, looking for personal items: photographs, memorabilia, books. She located nothing and felt disappointed in spite of herself. Unconsciously, she had been counting on learning even more about Nick during this visit to his home.

She, who had always been too busy to even notice other people, was suddenly determined to become an expert on Nick Devereaux.

After handing her a drink, Nick sat down beside her, his shoulder touching hers, creating an intimacy that made it natural to move closer to him.

"Tell me what type of decor you would choose for me if you were decorating my home,'' he said, his voice close to her ear.

She lifted her eyes to take a long intent look at him, thinking once more what a devastatingly attractive man he was. He returned her smile, brushing his lips lightly across her cheek. "Well?'' he prompted.

"I'd need to know more about you, much more, before I could even begin to plan a home for you.''

"I'm all yours,'' he murmured, his free arm going around her shoulders and drawing her against his chest. "Ask me anything you'd like to know."

"Okay." She took a deep breath and looked at him directly. "Why aren't you married? Why no children for a man who's obviously so fond of them?" She brushed her fingertips across the scratch on his cheek and added, "After all, you give up your weekends to do something that involves them."

Nick's eyes turned serious and he looked down at his hands. "I haven't married because I haven't met anyone I'd like to be with when they grow old. You're the first person I'd like to share arthritis rubs and orthopedic stockings with," he teased.

"You're impossible." Eden moved more closely against him and pretended to glare.

"As for the children," he began, smiling down at her. "As far as I know, equality of the sexes hasn't extended to the point of men bearing children. And as I have no wife...."

"You could adopt," Eden suggested. "Like Job did."

Nick fingered his glass. "Job was an exception. Not many men could have acted as both father and mother to a son."

"Do you want children?" Eden felt she had to ask the question. Nick's offhand manner wasn't quite up to the truth she'd grown to expect from him.

He started to make a glib remark and then stopped. "All right, Eden, if you want the truth. I'm not sure about children. After all, I don't know that much about my own parents. I don't even know my father's name. Is it fair to have children when they might inherit some genetic problem I don't know about."

"Have you tried to find out?" Eden took a long swallow of her drink, wondering if she had been right to lead the conversation down this path.

"No," he admitted after a long pause. "I'm not sure I want to know."

What could she say to that? Anything she said would sound like a platitude. Finally she spoke. "One of these days the time will be right and you'll have to know."

"You're right," he agreed, his eyes becoming warm and sensual as he regarded her. "The subject has been on my mind a lot lately."

Now it was Eden's turn to put a halt to the conversation. She wasn't quite ready to start talking commitment even if Nick was. Glancing down at his fingers that were idly tracing a pattern on the bare skin of her arm, she commented, "If you keep that up, I'm going to be incapable of thought."

"Then let's not think for a while," he said huskily, setting his glass on the table beside him and removing hers from her fingers. He turned toward her, threading his hands through the silken curtain of soft glowing hair, pulling her face against his. The pressure of his mouth was urgent as their lips met.

She reached for him blindly, her arms encircling his neck, flames sparking through her like a raging forest fire.

"Beautiful, beautiful lady," he whispered, moving his lips across her face and slowly down the slender column of her throat. "All day I've been longing to kiss you here." His lips brushed against the shadowed hollow between her breasts. "And here." He pushed aside the fabric with his lips and continued his seductive trail across the creamy flesh, planting a kiss each time he murmured, "And here," until she was trembling with ecstasy.

He pulled back with a groan. "If we're going to have that dinner while it's hot, I think I better see about getting it on the table."

"May I help?"

"Bring along your drink and we can talk while I finish," he suggested.

The kitchen was small but well equipped with a built-in microwave along with the usual array of time-saving appliances. Nick pointed to a stool. "Sit there, sweetheart."

Eden sniffed appreciatively. "Shrimp gumbo! I love it. May I sample a bite?"

He measured out a spoonful and brought it to her lips. "Perfect," she raved. "Do you share your recipes?"

He grinned. "Gladly, but I ordered our meal this morning from the same woman who made the doughnuts. She runs a small catering service out of her home."

"And here I thought you were the perfect man!"

"What is that supposed to mean?" he growled playfully, slipping his arms around her, holding her firmly beneath her breasts.

She leaned back and pulled his face down to hers, kissing him on the mouth. "You are the perfect man, Nick. Even if you don't know how to cook."

"I do. A little anyway," he said, returning her kiss.

They sat together at a small round table in front of a glass wall facing the lake, tasting the thick spicy gumbo filled with pieces of shrimp, okra and rice, thickened with just the right amount of filé powder. When they finished, Nick insisted she stay seated while he brought out slices of ham loaf with honey mustard sauce and petite biscuits dripping with melted butter and strawberry jam. They drank a bottle of wine between them and then had coffee laced with a chocolate liqueur that left them feeling totally relaxed and satisfied.

"What did you do at work today?" Eden asked, leaning back in the chair she had turned to face the lake.

"I found out some bad news," Nick said truthfully. "I have to leave tomorrow."

"Leave?" She turned her stricken blue eyes toward him, suddenly feeling as if all the joy had gone out of the evening. "Where are you going?"

He sighed. "Don't make me feel worse, Eden. There's no way I'd leave if it weren't an absolute necessity. An opportunity has come up to obtain some oil leases on federal land in Alaska and it's too good to pass up. I'll be back as soon as possible."

Her mouth was dry. These next few days that had

promised to be glorious suddenly stretched before her like a barren desert landscape. "Tell me what you'll be doing," she said slowly, her voice calm.

He answered in deep rich tones, "The Bureau of Land Management has opened up these leases on federal lands to speed the development of domestic reserves. The law limits any firm or individual to 300 thousand acres, so it's a mad scramble for each of us to stake our claim to the best lands."

"What's the procedure?"

He glanced at her briefly and seemed convinced she was sincerely interested. "We have to have the land surveyed to define the legal boundaries so no claim jumpers can come in."

"You make it sound like another gold rush," laughed Eden, fascinated by the enthusiasm in his voice.

"It is! Liquid gold! Oil and gas reserves may offer us our last real chance for energy independence. The potential in Alaska is enormous, Eden. We're talking about wells that pump six thousand barrels a day!"

"Are you making the trip alone?"

"No, a couple of geologists will be with me. We're leaving tomorrow afternoon and I'm going to do my best to be back by Sunday at the latest." He glanced over at her cup, which was almost empty. "More coffee?"

"No thanks, I couldn't hold another drop. Everything was wonderful, Nick."

"Then how about a walk around the estate? It's a fantastic place."

Eden touched her lips with her napkin. "I'd love that."

He rose and drew her up to stand beside him. "Are you staying with me tonight, Eden?"

She hesitated, overwhelmed by her desire to be with him, yet equally aware that this night could be little more than the end of a brief affair with a man she might never see again. "I want to."

His voice was low. "Then what's the problem?"

She met his intent gaze fully. "I'm staying, Nick, but I'm not sure I should."

He pulled her into his arms, kissing her slowly over and over again. "I'll make you sure," he said when he drew back. Without elaborating, he said simply, "I know we can work things out." And she believed him because she wanted to.

They went out into the moonlit evening and walked down a path that was lighted by discreet muted spotlights, hidden among green leafy plants lining the edges. The night air was perfumed with flowering jasmine and honeysuckle blossoms and filled with the sounds of nature.

They walked down to the edge of the lake and Nick pointed out the boat house and a gazebo that was used for outdoor parties. "Maybe next week we can go sailing and grill steaks there."

"Next week I'll be returning to Houston," she replied, her voice slightly strangled.

"I've been giving that some thought. There are ways to work that problem out, you know."

"Ways? I can't really think of any. I live there. You live here. It's as simple as that," she snapped.

His eyes darkening, he gazed down at her. "We'll work it out, Eden. I know we will. I'm not rushing you, but I know we have something special between us and no amount of distance can put a stop to that." Smiling tenderly, he reached over to caress her cheek.

She returned his smile. "I hope you're right, Nick." Glancing around, she said, "How about showing me the swimming pool. From the brief glance I got it looked fantastic."

"It's shaped to follow a natural ravine with a waterfall at one end," he explained. "A national magazine featured it about a year ago. Perhaps you might have seen it."

"Sounds fabulous," laughed Eden, suddenly determined to enjoy this glorious night with Nick.

They strolled through the trees, emerging into a small clearing and stopping at the pool's edge. Eden gasped with pleasure. "It looks exactly like a lagoon in some South Sea Islands movie. No one would ever guess it was artificially tiled."

"Want to swim?"

She shook her head. "I ate so much I'm sure I'd sink to the bottom. Do you swim a lot?"

"Nearly every day. We'll swim later when you feel like it." He leaned over, forging a path of kisses over her cheeks and eyelids. "I can't believe you're really here with me tonight, Eden."

"Believe," she whispered, closing her eyes to more completely enjoy his caresses.

Her hair fell down her back in a silken drape, smelling sweet and fragrant. His lips clung to her with a vibrant gentleness that sensitized every nerve ending in her yielding body. "Nick," she moaned.

"Eden, my love." He molded her lips beneath his firm sensual mouth, nuzzling and tasting, nibbling and savoring, sipping the honeyed sweetness as his tongue entered the welcoming recess with demanding thrusts.

She stood on tiptoe, her fingers welded to his strong back muscles, the heat of his body infusing her with desire. His sure and sensuous hands stroked her back, slipping down to the curve of her bottom where he pressed her against his throbbing need.

Her only reality was that of excitement and anticipation consuming her like raging flames. She felt an urgent need to rip away the confining clothing that separated them, to touch skin to skin as they became one. She grasped his back as his hands found the ties on her wrap skirt, and the seductive silk fabric slid over her hips to fall in a puddle on the grass beneath her feet.

He moved her back from him, gazing with undisguised passion at her slender legs as his fingers stroked the creamy flesh into pillars of fire. Her blouse followed her skirt and then the bra, before his eyes feasted on the rosy peaks of her breasts. "Darling," he breathed. "Let me look at you. I can never get enough of the sight of you."

His voice trailed off as his hands cupped her straining breasts in large warm palms as he continued his sensuous survey. Wave after wave of pleasure swelled through her as his relentless hands tenderly caressed her breasts, his fingers gently urging the tips into taut throbbing crests of desire.

He leaned down, to cover each pink-tinged perfection with moist kisses. His arms went around her and he sank to the ground taking her with him.

"Here?" His eyes searched hers hungrily and she nodded, wanting nothing more than to have Nick making love to her there, under the stars, in their own secluded haven.

CHAPTER TEN

AN UNEXPECTED TEAR slid down her cheek as she watched him stand and remove his clothes. The tear should not have surprised her, for she knew this moment held a significance far beyond anything she had ever felt before. She knew now, without one lingering doubt, that she loved Nick. And she accepted that he loved her, too. They belonged together. Their mutual understanding and trust was almost mind shattering.

She felt completely free to let go, to revel in the glories of their passion without fear. Tonight she was set free, free from her restraints, free from her fear of showing her real feelings, free to love and be loved in return.

Her eyes followed the path of his hands as they pulled his shirt over his head and then removed his trousers and briefs. She marveled over the width of his sinewy shoulders, the firmness of his chest, the taut stomach and slim hips, his magnificent manliness, alive with passion.

She held out her arms and slowly, very slowly, he stretched out beside her on the soft cushiony bed of grass and half covered her body in sensual possession. His lips touched her forehead, sliding down to her closed eyelids before planting tantalizing kisses on her ears, her cheeks, the tip of her nose. "I love you, Eden."

"I love you, Nick." Her voice rose barely above a whisper. His hands stilled and she opened her eyes to see his face poised over hers, his own eyes filled with wonder.

"Did I hear you right?" he asked.

She wrapped her arms around his neck, pulling his lips to hers, repeating, "I love you, Nick. I love you." Words never said unreservedly to any man before. Words that were frightening and powerful. Words that contained the power to change one's life. She knew she would have to confront all this later, but it seemed totally inconsequential to the glory and magnificence of this moment.

Their mouths melded together, their tongues tangling hungrily. His hands slipped under her to press her hips against the driving proof of his desire. Her breasts rubbed sensuously against the hair on his chest and he moaned deeply. She wanted to give him as much pleasure as he was giving her.

His mouth left hers to trail across her throat and descend to her breasts, cupping one in a large hand as he took the taut nipple into his mouth and pleasured the aching fullness with gentle care. Her sounds of satisfaction lingered on the night breezes as his mouth continued downward.

With agonizing slowness his tongue played across her flat stomach as he reached between her slender legs, probing, exploring, teasing, tantalizing, delving into her hot moist responsiveness until she began to move with him, digging her fingers into his hard sinewy muscles, hearing words of love flowing from her throat.

Nick's breath fanned across her breasts once more, taking a nipple in his mouth, rolling his tongue over it until her desire rose to uncontrollable heights. Pushing against his shoulders, she surprised him by taking the lead, gently pressing until he lay back and let her make her own slow heated exploration of his body. He trembled as she tasted the length of him with tender kisses, enjoying the freedom to discover all his pleasure points, watching the myriad of emotions cross his face as she found those that brought him the most pleasure.

"Enough," he groaned, swiftly moving over her, thrusting urgently into her creamily lavished warmth, then slowing to a plunging glide that she rose to meet with a desire as great as his own.

Moving together, building slowly, their rhythm grew in intensity and exquisite harmony as they rode out the fire together. Overtaken by a flowering explosion, she cried out her happiness, which echoed in the shudders of his body. Beneath her fingertips she felt the perspiration that formed on his spine as he cradled her in his arms, his whispered words of love filling her with deep and lasting joy.

For an inestimable length of time they lay locked in the intimacy of their embrace, at one with the stillness of the night. The soft lapping beat of the waterfall, the sighing of the leafy trees in the evening breezes. The scent of flowering jasmines that clung to a trellis beside them. Nick and Eden. Two united into one. Now and forever.

She knew she would never be the same. Even in her rapture, she had her share of doubts and worries, banished only by an effort of will. Moving beneath him, she felt Nick brush back her hair and tasted his kiss on her lips.

"Ready for that swim?"

Her eyes widened. "You're joking, I hope."

He shook his head. "I'm deadly serious, my love. Nothing like a little swim before going to bed."

"I'll watch." She sat up, gathering her skirt and blouse, laughing gently at him.

Nick stood, his bronzed body gleaming in the moonlight. "Let me get you a towel from the bathhouse." Within a short time he was back with several large towels that he dropped at her feet. He quickly crossed to the pool.

Poising on the edge of the diving board, his lithe body tense and alert, he arched into a perfectly executed dive and entered the blue lagoon with only a slight rippling of the clear water. His dark head emerged within seconds, shaking off the moisture, his white teeth gleaming as he smiled over at her. "Join me, darling. The water's a perfect temperature. Not too hot and not too cold."

His enthusiasm was infectious and she slipped the towel from her shoulders and started forward, aware of the appreciative gleam in his eyes as he surveyed each curve of her body. She fought off a bout of shyness and moved to the edge of the pool, where she sat down to test the water with one foot.

"No diving?"

She shook her head and he chuckled. "Why have you gone suddenly shy on me?"

She threw back her head and tilted her chin. "Are you sure no one can see us? Something tells me there are eyes peering out of those bushes."

"Racoons, maybe. No one is within miles except me. And I'll admit to watching you. You have a body I can't help but admire."

She slid into the water and swam toward him, long gliding strokes that brought her to his side quickly.

He reached for her, pulling her against him and tangling his legs around hers, his mouth nibbling at her neck until they began sinking. "Help," she gasped, breaking free and swimming away.

Laughing, he gave chase, reaching her just as she arrived beneath the waterfall. Pulling herself onto a large flat rock, she inhaled deeply, pushing him away with her feet as he tried to join her. "Were you trying to drown me?" she managed.

"No, I was trying to kiss you, woman," he protested, moving past her and hauling himself on to the rock. He wrapped his arms around her and she turned to him, the sensation of skin against skin unbearably sweet. "God, how am I going to leave you?" he murmured against her mouth.

She nestled close into his arms, guiding his large hands to the fullness of her breasts. "Don't leave."

He sucked in his breath. "You're very persuasive."

She moved away. "Perhaps I'm not being fair," her blue eyes twinkled as she spoke. Glancing down at the water and splashing her feet in random circles, she added, "I know you have to go to Alaska. Anyway, I have work to do myself. Race you to the other end." She slid into the water without warning and started off, swimming with her longest strokes.

She felt him behind her and then overtaking her and he was waiting at the other end when she arrived. "I won. Are you my prize?" he teased.

She smiled provocatively. "At your service, sir." Her eyes rested on Nick as he lounged against the rock, the water breaking against the taut muscles of his chest.

"Be careful," he warned, his husky voice betraying his response to her nearness. "I'm at your mercy, Scarlett."

She moved forward, a coil of anticipation tightening her abdominal muscles. Brushing her hands through the hair on his chest, she slowly trailed them down his flat stomach, letting her cheek come to rest on his shoulder.

Looking up, she studied his profile, the thick dark brows, strong nose, the sensual span of his lips. Her hands moved lazily across his shoulder, sliding down leisurely to tangle in the furry mat on his chest. His hard-muscled torso contracted beneath her touch and she edged closer. *What a fantastic man,* she thought. The beauty of the night, the isolation of their setting had all combined to focus her attention on this man who had become so important.

Nick spoke and she could feel the rumble of his voice beneath her fingertips. "Don't stop...keep touching me...I love you, Eden."

Eden drifted dreamily in the water, stroking, caressing, occasionally lifting her lips to exchange a lingering kiss. Suddenly Nick was alive under her touch, gathering her close in his arms, lifting her from the pool to lie on the mossy bed of grass.

This time it was Eden who led them on their journey to fulfillment. Moving above him, she paused to savor the everchanging expressions on his face before allowing him to guide her in joining them in joyous union. Caught up in the intensity of their rhythm, she let him know her delight without hesitation. With the soft music of the waterfall behind them, they crested with the gentle waves of the lagoon, rising into a realm of transcendent ecstasy and slowly drifting down.

"Come to Alaska with me?" Nick asked, his mouth nuzzling her ear as they lay entwined.

"I can't, Nick. My work...." She stopped. "This trip isn't exactly going to be a vacation for you, is it?"

"Good lord, no," he verified. "I don't know what I was thinking of. You do have that effect on me, Eden. But you're right. It's not the place for you. You'd be miserable, just waiting around in a hotel for me with your own business left behind." He paused and seemed to hesitate. "I know I haven't told you this, but I do realize that your work is part of you. It's one of those layers that makes up the whole person. Surely we can keep our relationship separate from our businesses, not let anything come between us."

Eden lifted her head, starting to reply when she caught a glimpse of movement in the bushes to the left of his head. Seconds later she was staring directly into a pair of bright eyes ringed by black circles. As she watched, a soft furry animal, not much bigger than a small terrier, sidled out of the bush and stared at her.

Cautiously, Eden whispered, "I hate to tell you this, Nick, but more than our work is about to come between us."

"What?" he asked, stopping from sitting up by the gentle restraint of her hands.

"There," she pointed at the small creature who was standing motionless.

Nick rolled over until he could follow the direction of her gaze. "That's Dixie," he explained, laughing and holding out his hand to the curious raccoon. "Come here, Dixie, I want you to meet Eden."

"What is he, your pet?" Eden groped for one of the towels they'd left lying on the grass, wrapping it around her toga fashion and tucking it in above her breasts.

"He happens to be a she," Nick corrected her. "She lives here by the pool. I've gotten into the habit of feeding her whenever I come over here to swim."

"Now that you mention it, she does seem to be hungry." Eden considered the raccoon's expression thoughtfully, taking a step backward as Nick cajoled Dixie into moving closer. "Will she bite?"

"Dixie?" Nick and Dixie both gave her a reproving look.

"Sorry." Eden leaned forward and slowly stroked the fuzzy fur. Dixie gave her a reproachful look and Eden added, "I have a feeling I'm going to be blamed if we don't find something for Dixie to eat."

Nick grabbed his own towel and wrapped it around him, gathering up their clothes with swift movements. "We'll go back to the house now. Dixie will follow along behind us. I just remembered. We haven't eaten our own dessert yet. Hungry?"

"Ravenous," she said, standing still while he gently toweled her hair dry under Dixie's watchful gaze.

They walked hand in hand back to Nick's house, its light a welcoming beacon guiding them to its warm haven. Dixie trotted along swiftly behind them, not about to miss out on whatever dessert was going to be.

When they reached the house, Nick pointed to his bedroom. "Look for a shirt to slip into. You'll find plenty in my closet," he directed.

She went inside, her curiosity active again as she looked around the room whose every wall was lined with furniture. A large low platform bed dominated the room, covered with a blue-and-brown plaid bed sack that she recognized as a designer brand. A large roll-top desk was open, displaying cubby holes filled with papers.

Above the desk was a bulletin board jam packed with scribbled notes, business cards and a few photographs. Eden went closer and examined them. One large black-and-white photo was of an older man who Eden surmised was Job.

The other photos included one of a much-younger-looking Nick posed with a group of children around his age. They seemed to be wearing matching T-shirts, but she couldn't make out the insignia. All in all, the pictures revealed nothing more about Nick than she had already known. Despite his obvious success, Nick seemed to have very few ties in life and his personal possessions certainly did not reflect his wealth. For both of them this relationship was a first, an awakening of unfulfilled needs, an acknowledgment that at some point everyone had to make choices if they wanted love to last.

Walking back to the closet, she started to look through the neat racks of clothes. Nick entered the room behind her, a pair of worn jeans barely skimming his hips, his chest and feet bare. "Finding everything you need?"

"I hate to muss up one of these clean shirts."

He smiled and reached over her shoulder for a blue checked cotton sports shirt. "This ought to do. It's soft enough for your silky skin."

"Where's Dixie?"

"She's waiting on the porch. Very impatiently I might add." Indicating a door on the opposite side of the room, he said, "The shower is through there. Come out to the kitchen when you're through."

The bathroom was large and bright, well stocked with towels, bath salts, and had plenty of counter space. Nick's shaving gear was spread over one side of the counter, but apart from that everything else was neatly stored on shelves.

Eden quickly showered, luxuriating in the warm spray of water, washing her hair with the shampoo she found in the shower caddy.

Quickly toweling herself dry, she slipped on the shirt. It fell in generous folds just below her hips, leaving her legs silky and bare. She found a comb in her purse and struggled with her tangled hair, finally giving up and leaving it to dry in stubborn waves around her face. Nick would certainly be seeing her in her natural state tonight. Without a blow dryer and curling iron, her hair fell in waves and curls, standing out around her head and giving her a slightly exotic look.

Before returning to the kitchen she studied the titles of the books on his bookcase. They were mostly technical manuals, about geology, petroleum engineering, energy-related subjects. But there was a more-revealing shelf filled with spy thrillers, mysteries and a few westerns, as well as a very old and well-worn Bible.

Nick was working in the kitchen when she came out, carrying on a one-sided conversation about food with Dixie, who was curled on a mat just inside the door. Looking up, he cast an approving glance at the shirt and said, "That never looked better.'' Eden perched on a high stool near the stove, her bare legs swinging free.

''How come Dixie is so tame?'' she inquired, eyeing the racoon.

''She's been here for quite a while. I inherited her with the house and now that the owners are gone, she depends on me to supplement her diet.'' With an apologetic glance, he added, ''She's already devoured a can of sardines while you were in the shower, but now she insists she's staying for dessert.''

''That's fine with me,'' Eden agreed, stroking the animal's fuzzy back with her bare toes. Dixie looked up adoringly and Eden was completely won over. ''What are we having?''

''Lemon crepes,'' he promised. ''That is, if you don't tempt me into forgetting all about them.'' He eyed her long bare legs and came over to stand in front of her, sifting his fingers through her damp curling hair. ''It's been at least a half hour since I kissed you. Come here.''

Eden planted a quick kiss on his nose and then pushed him away. ''Stay away,'' she warned. ''Dixie and I are waiting for dessert.''

He chuckled. ''Don't worry. I have every intention of impressing you with my culinary skills. Why don't you have a glass of champagne while I show you my wizardry.''

He removed a bottle of champagne from the refrigerator and deftly unleashed the cork so it bounced neatly against the tile backboard of the sink. She held out one of the empty glasses sitting

on the counter and he poured the bubbly liquid into
it.

Feeling a furry nudge against her foot, she looked
down to see Dixie looking up at her expectantly.
"Don't tell me you've trained this animal to like
champagne. That's horrible. I ought to report you
to the humane society."

Nick looked over and shot a reproving glance at
Dixie. "She wants any food that's offered, whatever it might be." Sliding his foot over to nudge the
racoon back onto her mat, he added, "Sorry, this
time you're out of luck."

"Where did you learn to cook?" Eden asked,
after tasting the champagne and licking the effer-
vescent bubbles from her lip.

"At the home. The sisters there invented
women's liberation. Boys had to learn to cook,
scrub, sew. You name it, whatever jobs were going
were distributed evenly among the sexes." His grin
was disarming as he beat milk into a bowl of flour
with a French whip. "How about you? Did the
maiden niece learn all the womanly arts?"

"Hardly. Aunt Helene had grandiose ideas for
me. I was to run the Sonnier mills and have a
retinue of servants to care for me." Memories
clouded her eyes and she said, "The housekeeper
who moved out of the house and left it empty for
you to lease was our only servant besides the outside
help on the land. But Aunt Helene kept right on
with her dreams."

"How do you manage now?"

"I learned to clean and cook a basic menu while I

was in design school. But sewing?'' She shook her head. ''Are you available to make couture garments?''

''Nothing that frivolous, but I can darn a sock and do a mean seam on an apron.'' He broke several eggs into a bowl, beat them and dumped the contents into the batter, adding melted butter at the last.

She leaned over and watched closely as he melted more butter into a long-handled crepe pan, swishing it around until it was completely covered. He carefully measured out the batter, explaining, ''One-and-one-half tablespoons, no more, no less.''

As it spread over the pan he tilted it until it bubbled, flipping it with a spatula and letting it brown on the other side. Removing each crepe from the pan, he repeated the process until all the batter was gone. Fascinated, she asked, ''Who really taught you to do this? Not the sisters, I bet.''

A slow flush crept up his neck and she laughed. ''Ah, Nick. Tell me about her.''

When he finished cooking the last crepe, he turned to her. ''A woman I dated for several years used to fix these.''

''What happened to her?'' Eden found that it didn't hurt to ask the question. She realized that the woman no longer meant anything important to Nick.

''You wouldn't have liked me, then.'' He gave her a rueful grin. ''I was busy finding myself and nothing much meant anything except the company. When I finally grew up, she and I realized we had outgrown each other.''

Eden looked down at her glass and took another sip. "In some ways I wish we'd met earlier," she said thoughtfully, "but then I think that's what we like about each other. The sum total of what we are today."

Nick's gaze caught and held her own, communicating his understanding in wordless silence. Striding over to the freezer compartment above his refrigerator, he took out a carton of butter-pecan ice cream. She watched as he selected several crepes and placed a large scoop in the center of each, folding them over and placing them in a glass dish. Over the top, he ladled a lemony yellow sauce and slid the dish deftly into the microwave, allowing it to heat for only seconds before handing it to her.

"All this? For me?" She sliced off a morsel and tasted it, sighing. "This is out of this world, Nick. I am impressed."

Deftly preparing a dish for himself, he set it in the microwave and reached for a paper plate. Eden watched. "Don't tell me that's for Dixie. Are you sure she should have something this rich?"

"Sure," Nick said, warming it in the microwave and then placing it on the floor in front of the racoon. It was gone in seconds and before Nick could start on his own dessert, Dixie marched to the door and waited to be let out. "Good night, Dixie," he said with a low chuckle as she disappeared into the darkness.

"Does she do that often?" Eden waited until Nick had seated himself on the stool beside her before asking the question.

"A couple of times a week. During the winter months we keep animal feed out in several spots around the grounds. There's a lot of small animals around here and the owners enjoy keeping them fed."

Eden finished her dessert and slid off the stool, going over to the sink.

"Wait," Nick protested. "I leave the mess to my cleaning lady. Tomorrow's her day to come."

"You mean we get to forget these dirty dishes?"

"Right, my love. We're going to spend every minute we have left doing more pleasant things."

Eden's only reply was a slow smile, but that seemed to satisfy Nick.

CHAPTER ELEVEN

"MORNING, LOVE," Nick said, smiling as he emerged from the bath with a terry wrap around his waist. Eden caught her breath at the sight of the crinkly dark hair on his bronzed muscular chest. Shiny beads of moisture glinted amidst the tangled mat, magnified by a bright shaft of sunlight streaming through the window.

"You didn't!" Eden pushed herself up against the headboard, pulling the sheet up under her chin.

Nick stopped, frowning, and she laughed, stretching her arms over her head with a sigh of satisfaction. "I wanted another swim this morning and you've already taken your shower."

He sat down on the bed, gathering the lush thick dark waves of her hair with one hand and piling it on top of her head. "Where do you get your energy, darling? I barely crawled out of bed this morning." His lips nuzzled her cheek.

"The thought of all the calories I've consumed since I came to Louisiana has suddenly loomed in front of me," Eden moaned. "Besides," her voice dropped to a low whisper. "You've given me new energy." She pulled his head closer and brushed her mouth against his slowly, tantalizingly, seductively.

Never had she felt more gloriously alive. Nick's love was energizing her with an exciting glow that radiated life and vitality, filling the sparkling blue eyes with rainbows.

He broke loose, stripping back the sheet and patting her bare bottom playfully. "Come on, water nymph. If we go now we ought to have time for a leisurely. . . ."

"Swim?" she finished, blushing as her eyes met his.

"What else?" He picked her up and kissed her thoroughly before striding down the hall and pushing open the screened front door.

"Wait," Eden protested. "Are you sure we can't be seen by anyone passing by?"

"Absolutely certain. The pool is completely hidden. But if you'll wait I'll get some towels to wrap in while we walk over." Within minutes he returned and draped a towel around Eden before moving her against him, their mouths melding together in a sweet, savoring, lingering kiss.

Padding over the carpet of dewy grass beside Nick, Eden found herself thinking what a delightful spot this was. "I noticed the house is for sale, Nick," she commented, gesturing toward the large main house that could barely be seen through the trees.

"Yes. Jay, my friend who owns the place, has decided to make sailing around the world a permanent thing."

"What will happen to your cottage when the house sells?"

Nick slowed down and gazed back at it thoughtfully. "I'll probably have to leave it. The cottage was originally designed as a sort of guesthouse for Jay's extended family. Guests could maintain their independence there by doing some of their own cooking. While someone else might not want it, I doubt they would sell it because there's no access except past the main house."

"Where will you move?" Eden brushed away a persistent insect and then grabbed to keep her towel from slipping.

"I don't know." Nick stared up at the main house. "Jay offered to let me have first chance at the property."

"Are you interested?"

"It's a big step for me," Nick grinned at her. "I'm not sure I know how to put down roots. Perhaps that's my background coming out or just some facet of my personality."

Eden didn't reply, but as they walked on she began to understand Nick better. The things he had told her about his early childhood would have made anyone feel unstable, unsure of how to go about putting down roots. Nick had withdrawn into himself, afraid to depend on any one place or any one person for permanence, despite his liking for people. She had fought to break free of the deep-rooted past of her own family by going to Houston, starting a new life, a new business.

Together perhaps they could establish something meaningful. Nick needed to learn to put down roots, not to fear that they would decay and disappoint him. She needed to appreciate the necessity of roots, to trust that they wouldn't strangle and choke her. But slowly, slowly. It would take a while.

Their early-morning swim was a blissful blend of perfectly heated water, cooling flower-scented breezes, bare skin brushing against bare skin and renewed desire that quickened into the ancient, sensuously moving rhythms of a medley of love and passion.

Back at the cottage, Eden asked, "When do you need to be at work?"

"Soon. I'll have to catch a bite to eat there."

She shook her head, giving him a playful shove as they stood in the living room. "I'm in no hurry. You go on and get dressed and I'll fix us something to eat."

He grinned, revealing his gratitude. "Make yourself at home in the kitchen. I think you'll find everything you need."

Eden worked quickly in the kitchen, cracking egg shells on the side of a yellow bowl and beating them with a wire whisk, adding small chunks of ham she located in the refrigerator to the sizzling butter in the skillet.

When he came into the kitchen, dressed in a superbly tailored summer-weight blue wool suit, she glanced down at the towel still draped around her breasts and made a face. "Is the maid allowed to eat at the table?"

He gently disengaged the towel, whipping it off and letting it drift to the floor while he cupped her breasts. "Am I allowed to pick the menu?" he murmured.

She pushed him back. "Nick! Enough! Our omelet is getting cold." Pulling the towel from his hand, she fastened it under her arms securely while he left the room, chuckling loudly.

Back in a moment, he handed her a soft terry robe and waited while she wrapped it securely, letting the towel drop from beneath the hem.

His eyes darkened with some unnamed emotion while he watched. "Omelets are something I can have anytime but you—" he paused, sighing "—you're the most wonderful thing that's ever happened to me...I don't want to leave you...." His voice trailed off.

"Only until Sunday," she reminded, turning back to the stove before he could see the pain in her eyes.

They carried their plates, piled high with the fluffy omelet, buttered toast and thin slices of melon, onto the porch, perching on the wooden railing as they ate facing the lake.

After Nick finished and was drinking his coffee, he said, "Promise you won't leave Belle's Folly until I return?"

She nodded, smiling. "I took your advice and called Fred yesterday afternoon. He agreed to change our momentous meeting until Monday morning at ten. That means you'll be back." A glint of mischief shaded her blue eyes.

He exhaled his breath sharply. "Eden, you know I'm not attending that meeting. No matter what happens, we have something between us that is entirely special and separate."

She lowered her eyes. "I know, Nick. It's not easy for me to divide up my life into airtight compartments the way you do. Everything's one indivisible whole to me...myself, my love for you, my business in Houston, Belle's Folly. They all connect whether I like it or not."

His low tones were serious. "I've probably had more practice than you shutting off things I don't want to think about. After a while, it gets easy."

"I envy you. But I'm not sure it's right, even for you. Eventually everything floods back in and you might not be prepared to handle it."

"I always have," he replied, but Eden noticed that his eyes were uncertain. Setting down his cup, he leaned toward her. "I have to go now. Don't forget to leave everything for Mrs. Hankins to clean. And don't bother with locking the door when you leave. She knows I'll be out of town, so she'll lock things up when she's finished."

His arms went around her in a comforting embrace. The potent smell of his expensive cologne, the warmth of his body pressing against her breasts and thighs, the pressure of his mouth on hers a reminder of his earlier words of love. "You and I need to talk when I get back, Eden."

She released him reluctantly. "I know."

"Once things are settled here, you'll be going back to Houston. We'll need to decide how we're going to see each other." He grinned at her, his good humor back. "What do they call it these days? A commuting relationship?"

"Right." She shielded her eyes against the deepening rays of the sun.

"I'll call you tonight if I get a chance. Otherwise, once in Alaska I'll be out in the field, away from any phones." He started down the lane and then turned. "If any of those Texas types call you while I'm away, tell them it's too late. You're all mine now."

"Same for those Eskimo maidens," she called, watching as he got into his car and roared away.

TWO PICKUP TRUCKS were waiting in front of Belle's Folly by the time Eden returned home. Trying to ignore her bare legs and wrinkled dress, she rushed to open the door for the carpenter and electrician who were there to estimate costs for the work that needed to be done.

The rest of the day was equally busy, giving her no chance to be alone with her thoughts of Nick. Around noon she made a quick trip to the nearest country store to buy fresh vegetables and chicken, as well as fruit. Conscious of the rich food she had been eating, she stuck to simple foods, adding a loaf of rich homemade bread in case Larry or Karen were extra hungry.

Stopping by a beverage store, she selected a bottle of Scotch, as well as sherry and several varieties of wine to stock her empty bar.

Under the tangled plants in the kitchen garden at the rear of the house, she located a few fresh herbs.

Throughout the afternoon the smell of a savory casserole bubbling in the oven filled the air with a pleasant aroma.

Tom called twice and she found herself moving quickly back into her other life, the world that didn't include Nick. Tom seemed reluctant to go on their annual Hong Kong buying trip without her, and finally Eden suggested he offer the trip to Glenna, reminding him of her new policy of allowing her employees greater opportunity.

Karen arrived before six with an excited bouncing Becky. Eden leaned down and picked up the lively redheaded child, giving her a hug and a kiss. "I tried calling you several times last night," Karen said, tossing her purse down on the marble-topped table in the entrance hall. "Hope your phone's not out of order."

Eden glanced over Becky's shoulder at her, flushing in spite of herself, and Karen began laughing. "Of course. That's where you were. Why didn't I think of that. Things must really be great in that department."

Eden nodded, not willing to commit her happiness to words. "Did you need me for anything important?"

"As a matter of fact, I did." Glancing down meaningfully at Becky, she added, "I'll explain later. Meanwhile, I'm dying to see the house."

Becky clung to Eden's hand, the small warm body pressing eagerly forward and interrupting with constant chatter as they wandered from room to room. Karen tried to curb her daughter's conversation so she could talk. "I've been wondering why you don't open up this house one last time for the community in case the vote goes against you. There are a lot of people like me who didn't live here when your aunt was alive who would love to see inside this place. The old-timers need another go at it for nostalgia's sake."

"You mean have an open house like my aunt did?" The thought was exhilarating but also overwhelming. "I don't think I could get everything ready. Those things used to be pretty elaborate."

"I don't mean anything fancy," Karen protested quickly. "The house is fine exactly as it is. I'm sure we could find enough people in the area willing to bring refreshments. Those could be set out on tables on the lawn."

"Well...." Eden still wasn't sure about the idea.

"Why not? We could get Larry's secretary to handle it. She's always telling us about the parties your aunt used to give. All we'd need is to let the word get out that volunteers are needed and you know how this community would react. They're the greatest!" As Becky voiced her added enthusiasm, Karen continued, "Let everyone see the old place again. It's a marvelous opportunity for the children and even for some of the natives who haven't actually been inside one of these old mansions."

Eden didn't want to commit herself, but nevertheless she nodded. "Let's think about it. If Larry agrees, we'll call his secretary and see what she says. Even if only a few people come, it would be fun.

And if the vote goes against me, at least I'll feel my time spent on Belle's Folly wasn't wasted.''

"Wasted?" laughed Karen, arching an eyebrow. "I don't think Nick would like to hear you say that.''

"You know what I mean," returned Eden, wondering what Nick would think of the idea. She'd tell him about it if he called tonight. The important thing she'd have to do is warn everyone involved not to mention her problems over the house with River Road Oil Services. She didn't want the community involved in that.

"Why don't I call Larry now," Karen suggested and while she made the call, Eden took Becky upstairs and showed her the nursery. "Here are the toys that I played with when I was a little girl," she explained. "Some of them are well over a hundred years old.''

"May I play with the dollhouse?"

"Yes, darling." Eden took an elaborate Victorian house from a shelf and set it carefully on the floor. Getting down beside her, she handed out each exquisite piece of miniature furniture, telling Becky how some of the antique articles were used.

Within minutes Karen returned with news that Larry's secretary, Iris, was thrilled with the idea. "She'll call you later this evening to discuss it. I'm sure there's still time to get an announcement in Friday's paper. What time on Sunday will it be?''

"It was always held from four until eight." Eden jumped up. "If you'd like, Becky, if you're real careful, you can stay here and play with the doll-house while your mother and I talk.''

After making a list of what they would need to do in order to open the house to the public, Eden and Karen settled down in the living room with glasses of sherry. ''Why did you call last night?'' Eden asked. ''Is something wrong?''

''Fred.'' Karen rolled her eyes expressively. ''I took your advice and tried to talk to him in his office the other day. It was impossible. If someone pretends they don't understand what you're talking about, you can't get far with them. I finally gave up, but he's back at it again.''

''There's got to be some way to stop him.'' Eden sipped her sherry and stared at Karen. ''I still think you ought to tell Nick.''

''I'll probably have to. I just hate to start something like that.'' Karen sighed expressively. ''You know, running in with my little tales. To a man these things sound petty anyway. No one but another woman understands how frustrating it can be to have a man constantly making innuendos and touching you. Even when I tell you, I feel embarrassed because listed out, the incidents seem trivial. They add up to a very uncomfortable situation, though.''

''Oh, I do understand,'' Eden sympathized. ''But I know that eventually you're going to have to do something about it. And the longer you wait, the harder it's going to get.''

Larry's arrival put an end to their discussion. He seemed enthusiastic over their plans for Sunday and after dinner, they spent the rest of the evening planning. Iris called them to say that the women's club had taken over all arrangements for bringing light refreshments.

"I hope we haven't overextended ourselves," Eden said worriedly near the end of the evening.

"I don't think so." Karen looked down at their lists. "Iris's club is bringing refreshments. Larry is borrowing some chairs and tables from the church to set out on the lawn. Iris and I will come over Thursday and Friday evening to help you get the house ready, and there will be an announcement in Friday's paper."

When Eden still looked unsure, Karen persisted, "We're keeping things very simple, Eden. Mostly everyone wants to see the old house. Don't worry if there's a little dust or if things aren't perfect."

"Everyone's willingness to help has really surprised me," answered Eden, wearily rubbing her eyes. "To think, I almost believed my assistant when he told me no one would even be interested in Belle's Folly."

"Horse feathers," said Karen. "I'm a long way from being a native of this area, but even I feel a sense of pride in the old place. I guess everyone wants roots in the past, so it will remind us of how others managed in life."

Larry leaned over and kissed Karen. "We'll depart on those sage words, hon, and let Eden get some rest. She looks wiped out."

Eden stood up as they did. "Thanks a lot, Larry."

Karen giggled. "Tsk. Tsk. Tough night last night, Eden?"

"Out with you!" retorted Eden laughingly.

While Larry went upstairs to retrieve the sleeping Becky, Karen continued to tease. "Are wedding bells going to be ringing soon?"

Eden shrugged. "I live in Houston. Nick lives here. How can that be worked out?"

"Simple. Give up your business and move here. Nick's got so much money you'll never have to work again." Karen's voice was choked with laughter.

"Sure, Karen." Eden glared at her. "Just like you. Why are you so worried about Fred firing you when Larry's begging you to marry him?"

Karen flipped back her hair, the close-cropped mop of red flying out at an angle. "Because I've had a rotten experience and I have a child to think about. You're free, Eden, and so is Nick. Surely you won't let an interior-design business make you lose someone as marvelous as that."

Eden felt her stomach knotting. "What would I do with my time? Attend teas? Twiddle my thumbs waiting for Nick to come home and entertain me? Since I was no older than Becky, I've always known what I wanted to do. Running a business is in my blood."

Karen gave an understanding nod but added, "Remember, you're not going to meet someone as right for you as Nick twice in a lifetime. Try to make it work and at least give him equal billing with business."

Larry descended the stairs with Becky limply over his shoulder like a sack of potatoes. Eden reached up to give her chubby cheek a quick kiss and the little girl lifted her head, eyes half-closed, mumbling, "Thanks for letting me play with your an-tees, Eden."

"Antiques," Karen corrected automatically above Larry and Eden's laughter.

Eden remained on the front porch, waving until their car disappeared from sight. Too sleepy to clean up, she dragged her weary body upstairs and was asleep almost as soon as she managed to change into a gown and crawl between the cool sheets.

CHAPTER TWELVE

EDEN AWOKE ABRUPTLY to the sound of a ringing phone. Opening her eyes, she realized that light had barely begun to filter into the room. Who could be calling at this hour?

Throwing back the covers, she went quickly out into the hall and answered the phone, more to stop the annoying sound than because she really wanted to talk. These early-morning calls were becoming routine.

"Belle's Folly," she managed on a sigh.

"Darling, I'm being cruel, but it's the only chance I'm going to have to talk to you."

She sank down on the Oriental hall runner and leaned against the wall, thrilled to hear Nick's deep husky voice. "Nick, are you in Alaska?"

"No. Seattle. We barely made our plane in New Orleans, so I didn't get a chance to call you from the airport there." In the background she heard the sound of chattering voices amid an announcement about the departing planes.

"How long before you leave?"

"We should have been gone hours ago, but they had trouble with the plane. We're at the gate and it will be any minute. I waited till now to call because

I didn't want to interrupt your sleep." His voice lowered. "I'm missing you like hell, Eden."

"It seems like too long since you were here," Eden agreed, wishing that he weren't so far away.

"I can't talk long because others are waiting for the phone, but I wanted to ask you something." Nick's voice hesitated. "Please listen and promise that you'll at least think about it while I'm gone," he said in a rush.

"What, Nick?" Her sleepiness evaporated and she was instantly alert, sensing whatever he had to say was important.

"If your plan for Belle's Folly is approved, would you consider taking on the job of overseeing the remodeling yourself?" As Eden started to speak, he said, "No, wait. Let me finish. I wanted to ask you now, before the vote is taken on Monday. This has nothing to do with my wanting you near me, although I want that very much, as you know. I think you'd be the best person for the job. They're your plans and if they're chosen, you should be the one to oversee them."

"Nick," she protested. "What about my business in Houston? I'm already behind. I can't take on your project and forget everything else."

"I know that," he assured her quickly. "I've thought it all out. My company plane could carry you back and forth so that you could take care of business in Houston as well. I know it would be difficult, but decorating firms frequently take on jobs outside their immediate area."

"That's right." Eden was still overwhelmed.

"But those jobs are usually not as extensive as Belle's Folly. It's going to take a lot of work whatever plan is chosen. I'm not sure I have the time for it."

The background noise worsened and Nick sighed. "Promise me you'll think about it. We'll see how the vote goes on Monday and discuss details if your plan is approved."

"I'll think about it, Nick," she relented. "It would mean I'd get to see you more often."

"I tried not to let myself think about that when I asked you," he agreed quietly. "I love you, Eden. I can already see that being away from you is going to be tough."

His voice was muffled and then he came back distinctly. "I've got a man who's threatening to commit murder or suicide if I don't let him have this phone. See you Sunday or before, darling. Love you."

"I love you, Nick." The phone went dead and Eden slowly replaced it in the cradle. The thought of staying on at Belle's Folly was tempting, but she had a business to run. Could she manage both?

"Damn," she said aloud to the empty hallway. She hadn't mentioned the open house on Sunday. Nick would have to learn about it when he got back. Hopefully, it wouldn't be too much of a surprise.

Later in the morning she called Tom, eager to find out how things were going in Houston. "When will you be back?" he demanded as soon as she got him on the phone.

"I'm not sure yet," she replied. "We're having our final meeting on Monday morning." Before she could tell him about Nick's offer, she was interrupted.

"Jed Morgan is insisting that he get his check for the furniture by next Wednesday at the latest. I called the bank and you've got to pick it up and sign the papers yourself."

"I'll check with the bank," Eden told him and she hung up.

After an unsatisfying conversation with her banker, she called Tom back. "You're right, Tom," she said. "It looks as if I'll have to try to get back by Tuesday morning so I can take care of things. I'll let you know what flight I'm returning on."

"Think again," he warned. "Our papers say that there's an airport strike brewing in New Orleans."

"Surely they'll settle it," Eden groaned. It had been days since she'd read a newspaper. Somehow being at Belle's Folly removed one from the realities of the world. Quite a difference from Houston where everything moved at a fast clip and one had to be constantly on top of things to survive.

"I wouldn't count on it. Go ahead and make a reservation, but you'd better make alternative plans."

"I suppose I could rent a car and drive," Eden sighed, wishing she'd driven over the past weekend.

"Why not take the train?" Tom suggested.

"The train?" Eden's mind refused to comprehend the idea. "What a horrible thought."

"The train from New Orleans takes overnight to

get to Houston.'' Tom's voice warmed with enthusiasm. ''About four years ago Neva and I took
the girls over and came back by train. It's nicer than
you think. It beats driving all night.''

Eden still wasn't convinced. ''I'll check on it,
Tom. Whatever I decide, I will be back, don't
worry.''

After hanging up, Eden called Amtrak and found
out about the train. She could get a reservation for
Monday, so she went ahead and made one before
calling the airport. The airline representative confirmed what Tom had told her, giving her little hope
that planes would be flying on Monday.

The rest of the week passed too quickly. Wednesday. Thursday. Never enough hours in each day to
do all that needed to be done, but Eden loved it this
way. There was less time to miss Nick, less time to
worry about the meeting on Monday, less time to
figure out ways to have it all in life.

All, naturally, meant being with Nick in Louisiana while working her usual twelve- and fourteen-
hour days in Houston. Whoever said dreams should
be based in reality?

Plans for the open house went smoothly and with
each day that passed Eden grew less concerned
about it. She worked with Karen and Iris on Thursday night, and among them they managed to make
the old house look fresh and clean enough to show
to the public. Aunt Helene would never have approved of their arrangements. Her parties had always been formal and elaborate, but new times had
come to Belle's Folly, in more ways than one.

Fred was the first to spread gloom across Eden's halcyon skies. He arrived Friday afternoon, mounting the stairs with a belligerent sound that made Eden open the door to investigate. "Hi, Fred. What do you think of the old lady today?" she asked, waving her hand to include the whole estate. The spring weather had cooperated fully, bringing myriads of fresh flowers to the wild gardens and bright green leaves to the shrubs and trees.

"What's going on?" he demanded, puffing slightly from exertion.

"Haven't you heard about the open house on Sunday? Karen told me she posted an announcement on the employee bulletin board in the lounge."

"I seldom spend any time in the employee lounge," he said, his jaw tight.

"Come in and have some coffee," Eden offered, noting the dark circles under his eyes. For the first time she felt stirrings of sympathy for him. Nick's unvarying trust in him must have softened her initial negative reaction. "I had no idea you might object. My understanding is that River Road Oil Services doesn't begin paying on the lease until the end of the month," she reminded.

They sat in the parlor that smelled faintly of lemon oil from the vigorous cleaning it had undergone the night before. Fred seemed mollified somewhat by Eden's hospitality, listening as she told him about how the event had been one of the highlights of her life while growing up.

"Perhaps I misjudged your motives," he admitted when she finished. "When I heard about it, I assumed this was some kind of publicity stunt to gain support for your side."

Eden sat the fragile china coffee cup down hard, her mouth set in a straight line. "Absolutely not, Fred. The people in this community have no idea that I want to restore Belle's Folly as a museum someday. If I thought community opinion could have raised enough money to buy it, I would never have offered it for lease in the first place. The common opinion around here is that the old plantation is going the way of so many others and this is their last chance to pay tribute to it."

"Then I apologize," he said grudgingly. A little warmth crept into the gray eyes. "I should have trusted Nick's high assessment of you."

Eden flushed with pleasure. "I hope you're planning on attending the open house."

"I'll see." He stood, thanking her for the coffee, then adding, "My vote on Monday will not be affected by it."

"I didn't expect it would. What will you base your vote on?"

"The bottom line will be cost."

"I can appreciate that." And she did. That was Fred's job and she could see now why Nick relied on him so. But it didn't make her feel any better as she watched him driving off. The blueprints had arrived from Houston and most of the cost estimates were in. The figures showed it would take more work and money to preserve than to destroy the inside of the old home. She hoped some of the people who would be voting agreed that such destruction would be too unthinkable to allow.

THE WEATHER WAS OBLIGING on Sunday, producing one of those balmy days that inspire poets. Brightly blooming flowers cast pools of myriad colors against the jewellike green of the lawn. Although the grass had begun to grow again after the winter frosts, it was not yet too high. The shade of the large oak trees invited leisurely strolls over the massive grounds.

Iris's battalion of ladies from the women's club arrived early to set up their folding tables and prepare urns of coffee and iced tea as well as setting out trays of cookies and cakes. Their hard work was evident in the abundant supplies and Eden couldn't express her appreciation enough. It made her feel good to see that so many people remembered the Sonniers. Aunt Helene would have been pleased.

By early afternoon, more ladies had arrived to take up stations inside the house for the tours. Karen and Iris had suggested that people be allowed to wander through on their own, with ladies posted to make sure that nothing was broken or disturbed.

Eden had chosen to wear a street-length silk dress with a billowing skirt, her only concession to the past being the loan of a dress to Becky that she had once worn herself. She knelt before the little girl, carefully tying one of the ribbon bows that dotted the tiers on the long skirt. "You look beautiful, darling. Go see yourself in the mirror."

Becky preened in front of the glass, turning slowly and then showing a gappy smile to Eden. "I look gorgeous," she declared. "I promise to take very good care of this dress."

"I'm sure you will. Now run along and help your mother at the front door."

When she scampered off, Eden went out onto the upstairs gallery and surveyed the parking area before beginning her official duties as hostess for the event. Still no sign of Nick's sports car. All morning she had been hoping he would call. Better yet, that he would come by and they could have some time to spend together before the open-house festivities began.

He had taken commercial flights on this trip and if he didn't make it back tonight, he might be stranded by the strike planned for the next morning. It was certain to be a surprise to him to find her unavailable when he had made it plain he expected them to be together when he returned from Alaska.

With a small sigh, Eden turned away from the colorful panorama below her and resolutely concentrated on all that needed to be done. A small but steady stream of people had begun to arrive and soon the tours of the house would be starting.

By six o'clock the grounds were filled and cars were having to park out on the levee across the road. Eden was amazed at the number of people who had turned out to have a look at the old place. Many of the guests were longtime neighbors, but there were also many new faces, some of whom she suspected were tourists who had seen the sign out front and decided to stop in.

Karen stopped her on one trip back to the kitchen for fresh iced tea. "Have you ever seen anything like it?" she enthused. "I've met more people tonight than I have during the three years I've lived here."

Eden nodded. "I'm amazed at all the interest the people have in the old place. The younger ones as well as the old-timers hate to see it dying."

"Well," Karen said, looking up at the old house, "whether you or Fred wins tomorrow, at least someone will be using the building. It won't be like one of those skeleton houses you see up and down the river."

"You're right." Eden shuddered at the thought of Belle's Folly succumbing to such a fate. Even seeing the place turn into an office building was better than that. "Any idea when Nick should get back tonight?"

Karen glanced down at her watch. "The plane was due in about five, last I heard, but nobody knows for sure if Nick was on it. His schedule was running tight in Alaska."

After she hurried back with the tea, Eden began circulating again. For the next hour Eden was caught up in a constant whirlwind of activity. How had her aunt managed those elaborate affairs of the past? Even this small-scale open house required enormous effort.

The stream of guests showed no sign of winding down, and Eden began to wonder if it would all be over at eight after all.

She was getting anxious to see Nick. There had been no time to really consider his offer of staying to oversee the plans for Belle's Folly. And at this point, neither of them knew what the outcome would be tomorrow. She assumed that if Fred's plan was chosen, the architectural firm he had engaged would be directing the renovations.

At seven she went to the kitchen to make fresh coffee, grateful for the generous supply of ground coffee that the women's club had provided. She was measuring some into a large urn when she heard firm footsteps approaching.

Eden caught her breath and turned expectantly. Somehow, she sensed that it had to be Nick. He reached out for her, the skin stretched tightly across his face as he pulled her into his arms and held her close. She clung to him, her arms around his neck, wordless, needing only to feel his warmth, to bury her face in his neck, to feel his cheek against her hair. God, it felt good to have him with her once more.

His head turned, his lips seeking hers with searching intensity. She was the first to break away, suddenly conscious that someone could walk in at any moment. "Nick, it's wonderful to see you," she managed breathlessly.

"What's going on here?" He made no effort to stop her when she stepped back from him. "I could see the lights for miles. At first, I thought it might be a fire." There was a depth of emotion in his voice that told her how deeply the possibility had affected him.

"It's an open house," she explained lamely.

He smiled. "Yes, I was told that at the gate. When did you decide to hold this?"

"It just snowballed. First Karen mentioned it and I realized it was the same time of year that Aunt Helene always held hers. Then Iris, Larry's secretary, joined in and got the women's club excited about it and well, here we are...." Her voice trailed off. "Nick, how did your trip go?"

The dark eyes were warm and compelling. "Great as far as business was concerned, but I missed you like hell."

"I missed you, too. This is a lot to walk back into." She gestured toward the crowd outside. "You look awfully tired," she said softly, noticing the deep lines of fatigue in his face, the dark shadows under his eyes.

He gave her a slow smile and then said, "Why don't I deliver this coffee for you and then we'll see about spending some time together."

"It'll be hours before I'm free here, Nick." Eden felt torn. As much as she wanted him to stay, she realized that he needed rest. It wasn't fair to ask him to wait until the crowd had left and the volunteers finished helping clean up.

"I understand," he commented quietly. "Why don't we plan on seeing each other tomorrow?"

"Tomorrow!" There was anguish in her voice. "Couldn't you stay here, have something to eat? I can cordon off one of the bedrooms and you can rest while I'm finishing up."

He shook his head, smiling at her in a way that

made her pulse do double time. "I'm so exhausted that if I ever drop off to sleep, it will take an earthquake to move me. I'll go on home and get rested. We'll talk first thing in the morning." He pulled her against him, his hands caressing her back through the thin fabric.

"More bad news, Nick," she mumbled against his shirt, hating to tell him. He held her away from him just far enough to look down into her face. "I have to leave tomorrow evening."

"Tomorrow?" he repeated blankly.

"Problems in Houston. Nothing serious," she added as he looked concerned. "My presence is required, though."

"Damn," he groaned, letting his hands fall away from her and stepping back.

"Sorry." She stiffened, feeling that he had no right to be upset.

"I'm sorry, Eden," he apologized, but a tight withdrawn expression that she hated had settled upon his face. "First I've been gone all week on business and now you have to leave. Those are the breaks, I guess."

There was no time to discuss her future involvement with Belle's Folly. Eden couldn't help but realize that no matter what happened, it wasn't going to be easy to keep up a long-distance relationship.

"Will I see you tomorrow morning?" she asked.

"After the meeting," Nick whispered as he closed his eyes and rested his cheek against the top of her head.

Feeling that the list of touchy topics was lengthening by the moment, Eden forced a soft smile. "Go on home, Nick. Get some rest."

She sensed his gratitude as he pulled away and placed a hand under her chin, bending down to drop a light kiss on her parted lips. "Timing is everything," he said gently. "Things will work out, Eden, if we have the patience to see them through."

"I know," she agreed, meeting his gaze with a candid understanding in her own. "Tomorrow, then?"

"Tomorrow." He turned and left the room quickly, his fatigue evident in the droop of his shoulders, the heaviness in his firm strides.

Eden followed more slowly, in some ways disappointed that he hadn't stayed but also relieved that the meeting to decide Belle's Folly's fate would be over before they talked again.

Out on the lawn, a man came out of the dusk, accompanied by a woman and a small boy. "Let me carry that for you, Miss Sonnier," he offered, taking the heavy urn from her hands.

After they had put it on one of the tables, he turned to her and she recognized Roy Jones, the man who ran the air-conditioning firm. "This is my wife, Fay," he told her, and Eden acknowledged the introduction with a smile. He pointed toward the little boy scampering off across the lawn. "My son. I'm so glad he's getting to see inside the house tonight." Roy's face seemed to contain a restrained excitement that Eden couldn't quite understand.

"It's nice to have everyone here," Eden commented kindly.

"Don't you worry, Miss Sonnier." Fay patted Eden on the shoulder. "Nobody in this community will stand by and let your house be lost. It's a wonderful part of our heritage."

Eden managed some reply while giving the couple a sharp look. What were they talking about? With a flutter of rising tension Eden recalled her conversation with Roy the day he had come to make his bid. Surely he hadn't repeated the conversation to anyone else besides his wife.

Oh well, she reassured herself as she went on to greet more guests. At least the vote was early tomorrow morning. What harm could it do if Roy did tell people of her desire to make a museum of the place someday? It couldn't influence the meeting at this late date.

It was long after ten before the last person left Belle's Folly, the remaining guests lingering to chat on the wide galleries and beneath the sweeping oaks in the cool evening air. Eden felt as if she was sleepwalking as she said goodbye to the stragglers and made sure that the doors were all locked, the lights out.

Briefly, she considered calling Nick to say goodnight, to ask him about his trip. Glancing at her watch, she noted the time and decided it would be cruel. More than likely he had been asleep for hours. He had looked more than exhausted. Tomorrow would be soon enough.

Whatever happened tomorrow, she was determined not to let it interfere with their growing love for one another. If her plan was approved, the idea of taking on the job herself was looking more and more attractive.

CHAPTER THIRTEEN

DESPITE HER FEARS that anticipation of the meeting would keep her awake, Eden fell instantly into a deep and dreamless sleep. The alarm sounded at six and she forced herself downstairs in search of a cup of coffee.

After sipping the steamy liquid and feeling more alert, she went to the phone and called the airport. "Yes," the disembodied voice intoned in her ear. "The strike seems to be on. No planes will be leaving New Orleans today unless they reach an agreement, which seems unlikely at this point."

Eden quickly dialed the Amtrak number and confirmed her train reservation before giving Tom a quick call to let him know that she would be arriving in Houston the next morning.

Gathering up her notebook and pen, she slipped into a robe and went out onto the upper gallery to look over her notes one last time. The dew hadn't yet been burned off by the sun and it glinted on the low-hanging Spanish moss like misty cobwebs. The sight of a lone squirrel reminded her of Dixie and she wondered if Nick was swimming this morning. He would be going into the office early today after being gone for several days.

If her plan didn't win, when would she be seeing him again? He had promised that no matter what happened, their relationship would continue. But no matter how much they wanted to, could they work things out? More and more people were maintaining long-distance relationships these days, and New Orleans was not that far from Houston. Still, pitfalls loomed.

Even if she stayed to direct the remodeling, that would only be a stopgap measure. No matter how much they cared for each other, they were both firmly committed to their own careers, firmly established in differing locales. It would take more than romantic love to keep things going over the long haul. Both would have to exercise great understanding, loyalty, integrity. Were they up to it?

Going back into the house, she tidied the kitchen quickly, emptying the refrigerator and making sure everything was turned off. Checking that things were closed up downstairs, she went upstairs to dress and pack. There would be very little time this afternoon if she was to catch her train.

Dressed in a new black linen suit that she hoped lent her an air of self-confidence and authority, Eden arrived early at the offices of River Road Oil Services. Lucille gave her a "thumbs up" sign that brought a smile to her lips as she entered the building. "Fred's in a dither," the receptionist whispered. "As usual he's taking it out on Karen and she's in the lounge crying in her morning coffee."

Uncomfortable being the recipient of all this gossip, Eden only nodded and went down the hall to the lounge. If things with Fred had gotten to this point, Nick would ferret it out in short order.

Thankfully, Lucille had exaggerated the situation and as Karen poured a cup of coffee for Eden, she explained, "Fred is convinced I didn't get the numbers right when he dictated a letter the other day."

"Shorthand?"

"Yes, he doesn't like machines."

Eden took a sip of the coffee. "Didn't he read the letter over before he signed it?"

"No, it was one of those cases where he was going to be gone and he directed me to sign it for him. Now it's his word against mine, but I know I'm right. I wouldn't have written it down wrong."

"Is it very serious?"

Karen shrugged. "He'll get over it."

"No, I mean was the mistake very serious?"

"I really don't know. I offered to call the man and take the blame if it would make Fred feel better, but he refused and demanded a conference with Nick. I guess all hell's been breaking loose in the main office. Typical after the big boss has been out of town."

Eden's eyes softened as she remembered. "Poor Nick. He looked so exhausted last night."

Karen looked surprised. "Did he come by?"

"Yes, but when he saw what was going on he left."

"Did you tell him you have to go back tonight?" Karen glanced down at her watch and frowned.

"Yes." Eden didn't want to think about that right now. "You'd better get back to your desk. I'll talk to you before I leave."

"How about lunch?" Karen emptied her coffee cup and prepared to go back to work.

"Nick...." Eden hesitated.

"Of course," Karen's smile was wide and genuine. "You'll want to be with him. We'll talk later. How about giving me your number in Houston in case I don't see you before you go."

After Eden gave her a business card, Karen left the room. Eden made a quick trip down the hall to Nick's alcove, but one glance at the number of people in the reception area convinced her she didn't stand a chance of seeing him before the meeting. When she returned to the hall where Fred's office was located, Karen directed her to the main conference room. Several people were already seated around the long table when she entered the room.

Introducing herself to the men and women present, she took her seat, sizing up the committee with an experienced eye. Two members of the architectural firm were there, a man and a woman. After Nick had intervened, she had talked to both of them several times on the phone and although both were cooperative, neither one had dropped a hint as to how they felt on the issue.

The others present were accountants, employee representatives and a banker from New Orleans. Fred was the last to arrive and his face was flushed as if he had been running. "Sorry to be late," he said. "I hope everyone has read over both pro-

posals and studied the blueprints and artist's rendi-
tions of the changes.''

His abrupt manner annoyed Eden and for the
first time that day she felt her fighting spirit emerging. If he thought she was going to be denied the
right to explain her plan to this board, he better
guess again!

"Any questions?" he asked.

Eden forced herself to remain quiet with the
others while he continued, "Then let's take a look
at these cost sheets that I've prepared and we'll
compare...."

"If you don't mind," interrupted Eden. "I'd like
to go over my sheet and explain each item on it."
She flipped open her briefcase and pulled out a
sheaf of papers.

"Some of these people have tight schedules. We
wouldn't want to keep them tied up too long."

A tall woman who had identified herself as an
accountant spoke up. "Everyone was told to arrange time for this conference, Fred. I'm sure we
are all most eager to hear Ms. Sonnier's explanation."

Fred cleared his throat noisily. "Please begin but
keep it brief."

As Eden held up the artist's rendition of each
proposed change, the group leaned forward and
began asking questions. They seemed to be a
talented lot of people and their inquiries reflected
intelligence and open-mindedness. Even Fred
showed more interest than she expected and once,
when she asked if she were taking too much time, he

insisted she continue. When she finished, she saw a gleam of approval on several faces.

"Well done, Eden," Fred surprised her by saying. "Now, we'll have to turn our attention to the difference in costs so we'll have a balanced presentation." Eden forced her spirits to remain high, even though the figures were less auspicious than she had hoped.

The vote was taken by secret ballot and Fred called for Karen to come in and collect them to be counted. While they waited for the results, drinking freshly brewed cups of coffee, Eden felt at peace. No matter what happened, she knew she'd tried. That was all anyone could ask of themselves.

Karen came in grinning. "Sorry, folks, but it's an even tie."

Fred sputtered, "But that's impossible." He glanced around the group and began counting.

Karen stopped him. "Did you forget that John is in the hospital? There are twelve of you."

"Oh, no," groaned Fred. "Nick warned me not to let this happen and I completely forgot about appointing anyone to take John's place." Shaking his head helplessly and showing an uncustomary loss of poise, he added, "This week has been something else. Will you go and tell Nick what's happened?"

"Great! What's the old story about killing the messenger who brings bad news?" She left, laughing softly, not really looking worried.

She came back within minutes, looking much more sober. "Nick insists on seeing you, Fred.

More coffee anyone?'' she asked with false brightness.

Eden felt tense, wondering what was going on in Nick's office. With difficulty, she forced herself to respond to the conversation around her. Everyone made a determined effort to stay away from the subject of their vote and the minutes dragged by interminably.

Eden had to admit the plans were very similar. It was really a matter of choosing one of two fairly equal ideas. What Fred's plan lacked in artistic care and concession to historical merit, it more than made up for in price.

When Fred returned, he closed the door behind him and strode over to the table. ''The big boss is in an uproar,'' he announced with raised eyebrows. ''I quote: 'Tell them to get off their duffs and vote again. I'll be damned if I'm going to step in.' ''

Laughter was general, but Eden's was forced. Was she the only one who realized what a spot Nick was in if he had to vote? He hated to mix anything personal with business. Fred opened the floor for questions and a general discussion broke out, lasting for a half hour, before everyone agreed they were ready to vote once more.

Karen stayed in the room this time, nervously fingering the ballots as she counted. ''Sorry, folks, it's another tie,'' she announced.

''That's impossible,'' said the woman from the architectural firm. ''I changed my vote.''

''So did I,'' groaned one of the accountants.

Fred threw up his hands and grabbed up a phone, punching a button hastily and speaking firmly into the receiver. "Kay, tell Nick he'll have to cast a vote. We've tied and it's still no go."

This time there was no attempt at conversation as they waited. Everyone glanced toward the door when it swung open and Eden stared in surprise as Nick strode in. His intense glance fastened on her for only a moment, but it was enough to put a chill right through her. What was wrong?

'Okay," he spoke harshly, his face tense and tired. "I don't know what's been going on in here, but I've got too many more important problems to waste much time on this."

Eden felt a rush of emotions as she listened. He looked so tired, and from what she had seen and heard so far this morning he had plenty of problems to deal with. But was her presence here, the debate over her property, so trivial to him? That hurt. And moreover, why was he so angry? Where was their closeness, their understanding. She attempted to catch his eye, but he avoided looking at her.

"Ms Sonnier's plan will be accepted, Fred." A sigh of relief rustled through the room, barely audible and hurriedly silenced when Nick continued abruptly, "I'll leave you to get the keys from her so the remodeling can begin without any more delay."

He left as abruptly as he had entered. There was a stunned silence for several minutes and then Karen said, "Congratulations, Eden. I think you won."

A general babble of congratulations filled the air and even those who admitted voting against her appeared to be pleased with the decision. "Good public relations," admitted Fred, as he offered his hand. "Someday we'll probably take credit for having the owner's cooperation in changing the old mansion."

Eden's voice was husky. "Thanks, Fred." Her mind was on Nick. Something had happened to bother him and it wasn't only the problems that had arisen while he was gone. It was something to do with her. When could they talk?

"If you'll give me those keys. . . ." He hesitated as she looked at him blankly. Of course, that was what was really bothering her! Nick hadn't mentioned his offer of having her do the work herself. Fred seemed to know nothing about it and from Nick's manner only moments before, she wasn't sure the offer was still on.

"This afternoon." She put Fred off with a vague smile. "I have more packing to do and I'll need to have you a set made as these are the only keys I have."

"Sure," he said. "Let me know how soon you can have your furniture moved and stored. We'll want to get to work quickly."

"Has Nick told you what decorating firm he'll be using?" Eden decided to tentatively sound him out.

"No. I imagine he'll leave that up to me."

"Oh, I see." But she didn't see. She didn't see at all. Suddenly she had to talk to Nick. Now. This minute.

She strode past a surprised Lucille in the lobby and had to stop to catch her breath as she reached

Kay's desk. Ignoring the other people already waiting, she said, "I need to see Nick immediately."

"I'm sorry." Kay's eyes were round with surprise as she looked up at Eden. "He has several appointments."

Eden steadied her voice. "Is anyone with him now?"

"No...." Kay glanced down at the calendar on her desk. "But I don't think...."

"I'll only keep him a minute." Eden brushed past Kay and swung open the heavy office door, closing it firmly behind her. Nick was seated in his high-backed executive chair, staring out the window facing away from her. She leaned against the door, her heart pounding from her excited dash down the hall. Studying his profile, she realized that he seemed more than tired, discouraged almost.

He suddenly became aware of her presence and swung around, his eyes first widening and then closing halfway, shielding his expression from her view. "Didn't Kay tell you I'm busy?"

"Busy?" Eden stepped forward and settled down in the chair across from him, smoothing her skirt as she kept her voice reasonable and calm. "It looked like you were staring out the window when I came in."

When he didn't say anything she continued, "Look, I know you're upset because you had to vote. You hated to get involved that closely with the decision. But it's over and it was close. The plans were almost equal. I'm sure no one could accuse you of letting your personal feelings guide you."

"I know that," he snapped impatiently, picking up a pen from his desk and fidgeting with it in a manner that made her want to pluck it from his fingers. He began tapping it against the desk, the sound ominous, signaling not only impatience but also an alert, as if he was warning her to stay away.

"What's wrong, Nick?" Eden asked the question with a return of her cool, direct manner.

"It's you." His voice rumbled with frustration and the pen tapping stopped abruptly as he rose from his chair, coming around the desk with brisk strides to tower over her. "Your underhanded methods of business."

"What!" Eden jumped up to face him. "What on earth are you talking about? This is me, Eden, remember?"

"How could I forget?" he said, but the words lacked all warmth, sending a chill that gripped her with icy coldness.

"You'd better explain yourself." Eden's voice was operating on remote control, as if someone else were pulling the strings while she tried to cope with his change of attitude.

He spun around and snatched up a stack of papers, sticking them in front of her nose. "These, Eden. These petitions asking...no, demanding...that I don't do anything to demolish Belle's Folly. All postmarked Friday, Saturday. What have you been telling these people while I've been gone? All I wanted to do is rent an office building and arrange it so my employees could work at desks with a modicum of relief from the heat. You—" here his voice stopped and took on a deadly quiet she'd never heard before "—you've turned it into a damned self-righteous crusade. Why didn't you at least prepare me so I could have known what I was facing?"

Numbly she reached out and took the papers, flipping through them carelessly, her eyes barely focusing on the list of scrawled signatures filling all the lines. Who could have started this? And so quickly! So few people knew of the fight. No one had mentioned anything about this at the party last night. Slowly she forced herself to try to make out names. The members of the women's club, their husbands, neighbors. "I'm sorry, Nick..." she began.

He turned and moved back toward his chair. "Save the apologies. Maybe you learned those business tactics in the big city, but here in this part of the country we still believe you never gain anything by hitting below the belt."

"I didn't know about it." She spoke each word clearly and slowly.

"I trusted you, Eden. I thought we understood each other. You didn't need to do this!"

"I didn't, Nick," she repeated slowly. "I knew nothing about any of it."

"I find that very hard to believe." His voice was still deadly quiet.

Eden sifted through the papers again, reading them carefully. Midway through the stack she came to a letter on stationery from Jones Air Conditioning. A warning bell sounded in her head and she read the letter with a sinking heart, remembering how excited Roy had been at the open house the night before.

"May I use your phone?" she asked Nick.

Without waiting for his affirmation, she quickly dialed the number on the letterhead, asking for Roy when a secretary answered the phone. Their brief conversation confirmed her suspicions and when she hung up, it was to find Nick sitting quietly behind the desk, waiting.

"You heard?"

"Enough," he replied tersely.

"I mentioned my ideas days ago to Roy, casually, not knowing he'd try to take matters into his own hands. When he heard about the open house, he wanted to help, so he called the women's club and they offered to circulate petitions."

Coming around to stand beside him, she touched his shoulder with her hand. "I'm sorry, Nick."

His hand came up to cover hers and he turned, pulling her into his lap, sighing against her ear. "I suppose the company will recover. We're being touted as the black villains right now, but maybe when everyone sees the old place still standing they'll forgive us."

"Oh, Nick, I wouldn't have had this happen for the world. I made a point of making Larry and Karen promise not to discuss this with anyone."

"I was so angry when I came in this morning," he admitted honestly. "And hurt." She could tell the admission was difficult for him. "I didn't realize how much of myself I'd turned over to you until

I saw how easily my feelings could be shattered.'' Burying his face in her hair, his words were muffled, ''I love you too much, Eden. I've an idea it isn't good for me.''

''I'd never hurt you, Nick,'' Eden said softly, leaning back against him. ''You mean too much to me.''

''I don't like it when my personal life gets wrapped up in my business life.'' He stroked her arm gently, his hands tightening around her.

''I warned you that you couldn't keep your life marked off in separate compartments,'' Eden said in a low voice. ''No matter how much you want to avoid admitting it, we're involved on a personal level as well as business. There's no way to keep them totally isolated.''

''You can't run a business that way, Eden,'' he protested even as he pulled her more closely into his lap.

Eden stiffened. ''Are you saying that your offer is withdrawn, that you no longer want me to oversee the direction of my plan?'' She saw no point in beating around the bush. She wanted the truth laid out before them.

''Eden, I love you,'' he said tautly.

''That's not what I'm asking,'' she probed relentlessly.

''You're the one who just reminded me that they're not two separate subjects.'' He tried to turn her to face him, but she resisted just enough that his hands dropped away from her.

''There's something else wrong, isn't there?'' Her voice was cool and composed.

"I want you more than anything, Eden," he whispered hoarsely. "But somehow I feel over-whelmed." Gesturing toward his cluttered desk, he said, "You're leaving today and yet I've got to stay here and face all this. There doesn't seem to be enough time for us and I'm not sure how to make that time."

"You know I have a business to run," Eden spoke reasonably, calmly. "What did you expect me to do, drop everything and stay here to be with you? I've already been gone too long."

"I know that," Nick protested.

"Perhaps we haven't been realistic about what we could mean to each other," Eden went on softly. "The truth is that I live in Houston, you live here. We both have careers which require constant atten-tion and effort. Even if we do love each other, what could we ever have except an affair, an occasional weekend together?"

"I want more than that!" Nick held her against him and Eden could feel his body trembling.

"What did you expect?" Eden repeated. "Did you think I would drop everything, leave Houston, leave my business and move back here to be with you?"

Nick took a long time to reply. "I suppose if I thought about it at all, I pictured you moving back here, starting some sort of interior-design business here."

"Contrary to popular opinion, Nick—" Eden tried to keep her voice even "—interior design is not a hobby which women take up to keep themselves busy before marrying. For me, it's a full-time competitive business. I've worked years to achieve what I have in Houston.''

''I realize that. But can't you see that it's impossible for me to leave this area as well? I have a large company here and a lot of people depend on me.''

''Maybe we're expecting too much too soon,'' she said quietly and slid to her feet, eluding his embrace. ''Let's give ourselves some time to think it over,'' she suggested in a calm tone of voice that cost her a tremendous effort. ''I'll call you later in the week and we can discuss things then.'' She left the room before he could speak again.

She was proud of the way she smiled at Kay and the receptionist before leaving the building, revealing nothing. The drive back to Belle's Folly passed quickly and she hurried into the house, going into the living room and sinking down into one of the overstuffed chairs.

The room was dark, warm without the chilled air usually provided by the lone window air-conditioning unit in the corner. Her mind wrestled with the events of the morning. Why had her neighbors gotten up that petition? She hadn't needed it. She was sure that Nick would have chosen her plan even without their pressure. But she didn't like the feeling it gave her.

Now the question would taunt her. A niggling doubt to crop up and make her wonder if she had won fair and square. Not until this moment had she realized how important it was to her to know that it was her skill as a decorator, not her relationship with Nick, that tipped the scales in her favor.

Nick was confused as well and that didn't surprise her. For both of them, their love had burst out of nowhere with a life of its own. It hadn't been based on reality and a relationship based on dreams and hopes wouldn't stand the test of real life, real problems.

She cared deeply for Nick, yes, she loved him. But how he ranked on her list of priorities was still unclear. Perhaps it was good this separation had come along to slow them down. Would they feel differently once they were both back to their usual routine, in their own environments?

If she pressed Nick, she knew that he would give her the contract to do the remodeling. Once he made the offer, he would stick by his word. But is that what she wanted? She was an interior designer. Her work was usually related to creating gracious homes for a select clientele. Belle's Folly needed structural work and that wasn't her forte. Besides, she wasn't a local designer. She didn't know the suppliers, had no contact with the New Orleans design world.

Suddenly it didn't seem like such a good idea to leave her own life behind, to rush headlong into a situation here that would cut her off from the ties she had spent the last ten years building in Houston.

She would go back to Houston this evening, maybe even let Tom oversee the removal and storage of the furniture Nick's company wouldn't be using from Belle's Folly. If, after a span of time, Nick and she managed time together again, they would work things out. This time it would be right, it would be a true compromise between their two life-styles. If she came here, it would all be on his turf, his terms, and she wasn't willing to give up her independence to that degree.

How was it the old saying went? You can't reach a compromise unless you both know where you're starting from. Before she and Nick could have a future together, they would have to find a mutual starting point.

With a sigh, she kicked off her shoes and went over to the sideboard that held the liquor. Locating an almost-empty bottle of sherry, she poured the remainder into a glass and sipped it slowly. Only a few more hours before she had to get on her train. She had been going to ask Nick to drive her, but she was reluctant to call him. He was too busy. It wouldn't be right to add more pressure to his already overtense day. And she wasn't sure they should see each other again right away.

The phone rang and she tensed, feeling both relieved and disappointed when she heard Karen's voice on the other end. "I wanted to say goodbye, Eden."

"Sorry I didn't get a chance to talk more. You all seem pretty busy there today."

"That's for sure," Karen groaned. "Nick is still tied up in his office. You didn't have lunch with him."

The comment was a statement, but Eden could sense the question behind it. "He was busy."

"Oh," was all Karen said, leaving the conversation open-ended.

"Have you heard about the petition?" Eden asked reluctantly.

"What petition?"

Eden explained briefly and from the silence on the other end of the phone she could tell Karen was as horrified as she had been. "Do you want me to talk to Nick?" she offered breathlessly.

"We've already talked it over. He understands that it was an accident." Eden leaned her forehead against the wall and sighed. "Things are fairly complicated right now, Karen."

"You'll figure out what to do." She sounded much more confident than Eden felt. "You and Nick are right for each other. Any fool can see that. Just give each other time. Be patient."

"Patience isn't my strong suit," Eden said dryly.

"Give it a try," Karen advised briskly. "When are you leaving?"

Eden explained her problem of transportation. "I need to return Larry's car."

"Why don't you drive it on to New Orleans," Karen offered. "Larry and I will have dinner in town tonight and pick it up on our way home."

"That's too much trouble for you," Eden objected.

"Nonsense," Karen laughed. "It'll get me out of having to fix dinner for him. My excuse to have a night on the town."

"Thanks," Eden said, feeling truly grateful. After listening intently as Karen told her where to leave the car and instructed her to drop off the keys at the information desk inside the train station, they hung up.

As she was getting ready to leave that afternoon, Eden realized that neither of them had mentioned plans to see each other again. Was Karen so confident that Eden would be back to see Nick? These last two weeks had been the most eventful of her life. She'd made more new friends than she had in years and she had seen another side of life that offered temptations as well as drawbacks. Now it was time to set her priorities in order.

CHAPTER FOURTEEN

IN SPITE OF HERSELF she felt a surge of anticipation as she parked the car in front of the train station that evening. How long had it been since she had ridden on a train?

After checking her luggage with the baggage master, Eden was one of the first passengers to go on board. The Orient Express, it isn't, she decided as she inspected the padded blue seats and chose one by a window. Through the blurred pane she watched as crew members checked out the wheels below.

More passengers straggled on and Eden found herself wondering why it wasn't packed since no planes were operating. When the conductor passed she asked him and he explained that the news was reporting that planes would be flying at midnight.

Great, she thought. Well, at least she would be able to get some rest. She leaned back, closing her eyes, and felt the train lurching into motion before she drifted off to sleep.

Later, she wasn't sure how much later, she woke up abruptly. She had slumped down into the seat and her eyes opened to see long legs, encased in sharply creased trousers, stretched out beside her own. Glancing up, she gasped when she recognized her seatmate.

"Nick!"

He was smiling, fatigue lines still creasing his face. "Any chance you might like company?" The hesitancy in his voice revealed more than the words.

"Oh, Nick," she whispered, her eyes roaming restlessly over his wide shoulders, his neatly compact hips and long legs. He looked so good and suddenly nothing else mattered except that he was here.

She stretched out her hands and he caught them in his bronzed grip, drawing her to him and wrapping his arms around her so that she was pressed as closely to him as the space allowed. "Eden, I couldn't let you walk out," was all he said as he searched for her lips with his own, his body trembling.

Slowly, gently, he slid his hand around her neck and covered her mouth with his own, his breath warm and intimate as it mingled expectantly with hers. Eden felt that nothing could be more wonderful than to be held by him like this and she caught his lower lip gently between her teeth with growing passion.

They were lost to everything around them, oblivious to anyone passing in the aisle until the conductor paused, clearing his throat before moving on and bringing them to awareness of the other passengers.

"How did you get here?" Eden was still surprised by his presence.

"Karen told me you were taking this train." Nick

let his hands slide possessively down her arms, looking at her as if he could barely restrain from pulling
her to him again. "She offered to get me a reservation. I had to drive like a madman to get here."

"She's a true friend," murmured Eden, a stab of
gratitude piercing her at the thought. It was nice to
have friends. "But all that work...." She protested
as she realized that Nick had left his office."

"It can wait," Nick responded seriously. "You
can't."

Eden didn't quite know what to say to that. Her
own eyes wide and muted to a steel blue, she said,
"But why?"

"Eden, we need to talk. We need time together."
He grasped one of her hands and squeezed it tightly. "I want to spend as much time as I can with you.
It's that simple. I need to learn more about you,
about your life away from me."

Looking away from his intense gaze, Eden became aware that an elderly woman across the aisle
was blatantly involved in their conversation.
"Nick!" Her eyebrows lifted as she waited for his
gaze to follow hers.

"Listen, Eden," he leaned over and dropped his
voice to a whisper. "I've got a stateroom."

"On this train?" Eden looked at him in surprised
pleasure. "How did you manage that?"

"Karen and I spent half the afternoon on the
phone," he explained. "Want to share it with me?"
The question was dropped in a casual, offhand
manner, but Eden wasn't fooled.

"Of course," she assured him. "Try and stop

me." Looking down at the worn seat they were sitting on, she said, "Is there any chance I'd say no? The thought of this for a whole night isn't too thrilling."

Nick retrieved her overnight bag from the overhead compartment and they wended their way through the narrow aisles. The woman who had been eavesdropping stared at them disapprovingly, but Eden smiled sweetly at her as they left.

They had to cross several cars before reaching a narrow hall, where Nick stopped in front of the door near the end. Eden followed him inside and stopped to stare around. "This sure does beat the coach car!" she exclaimed.

It was a deluxe stateroom, paneled in a rich dark wood that glowed with polish. A double bed, couch and club chair were all covered in a pale shade of blue while matching shades concealed the bank of windows on the outside wall.

Nick watched her, a small smile on his lips as she turned to him once more. He bent his head, his eyes darkened by a soft inner light as he kissed her thoroughly. "Maybe if we're lucky the train will break down," he whispered, his lips full and warm against hers.

"Don't wish such on the other passengers," she reprimanded gently. With deliberate slowness, she loosened his tie, sliding it off and tossing it onto the couch. "If you think I can feel relaxed with you dressed like you're planning on attending a board meeting...."

"Go ahead," he challenged huskily. "Take off anything that bothers you, sweetheart."

His jacket slid off his shoulders with a swift movement of her hands and she tossed it onto the bed. She unbuttoned the top three buttons of his shirt, pressing her lips against the exposed skin, feeling the pulse in his neck quicken. Lifting her head, she rested her cheek against his and felt the hint of roughness along his jawline from the day's growth of beard. Her lips lingered on his throat, savoring the taste of his heated flesh.

With rough impatience his hands tangled in the strands of her hair as he brought her face up for his kiss. "Eden," he breathed. "You're driving me crazy."

"Can't take it?" She taunted softly and watched as his eyes took on a fiery glow.

Their kiss started slowly but soon increased with a tempo all its own, assuaging the hunger that had grown during their enforced separation. Drawing on their knowledge of one another, each sought to bring the most pleasure to the other.

Nick shifted down to the couch and brought her with him, cradling her on his lap as he stretched out his long legs. "Eden, I need to talk to you and if we keep this up I won't be capable of thinking, much less talking."

"Okay," she agreed reluctantly, still letting her fingers roam in tender exploration over the curve of his ribs beneath the cotton shirt, his flat abdomen, his muscular arms.

Nick groaned and caught her hands in his, ceasing her restless movements and drawing her more fully against him until she was lying back in his arms. Looking down at her, he swept her hair back from her face and said, "Eden, you know I love you. But I want more than an affair with you. Meeting on trains, having you come over to dinner and stay the night. That's not enough for me."

Eden froze, sensing that he had something he needed very much to say but wondering if she was ready to hear it. "Eden," he let his lips brush over her forehead. "Eden, I don't feel like I have a right to ask you to marry me. But that's what I want. I want to marry you and live with you for the rest of my life."

"Nick," she whispered, thrilled by his words, yet not knowing what to say. Finally she said the only word that kept running through her mind. "How?"

"I know," he groaned. "Marriage usually means two people living under one roof, but we're both committed heavily to separate cities. That's why I had to come with you today. I need to see how you live in Houston. I need to know about your life there."

"Nick, I do love you." She traced along his jaw with trembling fingers.

"Look, if we give it time, if we try to get to know as much as we can about each other, we'll find a way to keep what we've got and have each other as well."

"Oh, Nick." She buried her face in his shoulder. "Being married to you would be wonderful. But not yet. I'm not ready. Don't push me."

"Promise you'll let me stay around and I'll go as slow as you want." He held her snugly, tightly.

"I won't send you away," she agreed, wondering even as their lips met again if she was making a mistake.

TIME PASSED TOO QUICKLY and it was near nine when Eden reluctantly loosened herself from Nick's arms in the darkened room. They were still lying on the couch. Nick had fallen asleep, his breathing even and quiet and she had watched him for a few minutes. In sleep his face was relaxed, vulnerable, and she felt a surge of tenderness shake her body. Not for anything would she willingly place in jeopardy the love Nick was so warmly and openly offering her.

Going into the adjoining bathroom, she splashed cool water on her face and wrists, drying slowly on the fluffy white towel laid out on the counter. Reaching into her purse, she pulled out a comb and managed to restore order to her hair before touching up her makeup and smoothing out the wrinkles in her suit.

Going back into the stateroom, she tiptoed past Nick's sleeping form and opened the closet where he had set her overnight bag. A dark suit bag hung inside with Nick's initials in silver letters. She reached into her own bag and pulled out a fresh blouse, a pale print in a virtually wrinkle-free fabric she loved.

She was standing in her slip, preparing to get into the blouse when she became aware that Nick was watching her. "Feel better?" she asked, pausing in her movements.

"How long have I been asleep?" He squinted at his watch.

"Not long." She shrugged into her blouse and began fastening the tiny buttons. "Hungry?"

"Very!" He sat up and grinned at her. "In fact, I haven't eaten at all today."

"The dining car is open a while longer according to that timetable." She gestured at the card on the closet door.

"Shall we go eat?"

Within minutes they were in the hallway, pausing when they reached the vestibule between the cars and looking out at the passing landscape. The shrill roaring of the wheels as they flew over the tracks made conversation impossible. The floor rumbled and rocked beneath their feet and Eden was thrown sharply against Nick as they rounded a curve. "I've got you," he whispered against her ear as she was caught and held in his strong arm.

"Yes, I think you have," she replied, just loud enough for him to hear, giving him a slow smile that made her meaning unmistakable. His grasp tightened.

The dining car was almost empty and the waiter hurried them to a table, his red jacket a spot of color against the sea of white tablecloths and gleaming white china. Once they were seated, though, the service was slow and restful. They ate slowly, watching the night rushing past outside the wide windows, occasionally catching a glimpse of a town out on the horizon.

"What about Belle's Folly?" Nick asked when

the waiter removed their plates and brought coffee.

"Your offer, you mean?" Eden took a sip and winced at the scalding temperature of the liquid.

"Do you think you could manage it?" Nick seemed hesitant to press her. "I don't want you to feel you have to take the job."

"Give me a day or two in Houston to see how things are going there. I'm not sure I'm the best person for the job," Eden explained. "You'd probably get it done faster with a local firm."

"It wouldn't have your touch." Nick was stubborn.

"What do you mean, my touch?" Eden protested. "You haven't seen my work."

Nick reached into his inside suit pocket and pulled out two papers, folded together. Their slick surface revealed immediately their source. "This was in a magazine I found at the airport in Seattle." Nick unfolded the papers.

"The Harrison's house," Eden said slowly. "But that just came out this month. They shot the photos for that feature last fall. It was one of my favorite decorating jobs."

Nick glanced down at the lush colors, the luxurious rooms. "It shows," he said simply.

"What were you doing reading a decorating magazine?" Eden couldn't get over her surprise.

"I stopped to buy a paper and there was the magazine with Showcase of Houston Decorators across the front. I was sure you'd be in it and you were." He looked inordinately pleased with himself.

"I can't imagine you being interested in a decorating magazine." Eden looked him over with amusement.

"I'm interested in anything that concerns you."

Eden glanced down at her coffee cup as he refolded the paper and put it back in his pocket. "What do you say, Eden? Will you think about taking on the work?"

"I'll try." Eden promised.

When they returned to their stateroom, the attendant was just leaving. "I've turned back your bed and given you fresh towels," he explained. "Would you like to be called shortly before we arrive in Houston?"

"Yes, about a half hour before," said Nick, handing him a tip as Eden turned off the light and went over to the window. "This has been a very surprising day, Mr. Devereaux," she said softly as Nick joined her.

"Tired?" he asked, rubbing her back lightly so that she turned and leaned against him, lulled by the rocking motion of the train.

"Mmm. . ." she said, pressing her cheek against his shoulder and lifting her face to his. Their mouths met and lingered as they savored the taste and feel and texture of each other. Eden clung to him. Her desire swelled and she gave herself over to the love rising on a tide swiftly and surely within her.

There was no time for a reluctance that neither of them wanted. Passion rose between them with its own sharp, sweet insistence and they surrendered utterly, completely.

Nick's hunger was palpable, his need to touch her, to hold her, arousing. His hands caressed her as he removed each layer of her clothing until she stood naked before him.

Eden helped him remove his own clothes, exploring his taut flesh with eager fingers, anxious to feel the reality of him beneath her hands. His earlier words of love repeated themselves in her mind, and Eden felt reassured as she sought to give him pleasure as great as he was giving her.

Their passion flowed molten and hot, joining them into one being and sending them off on a journey that left them more joined, more united, than either thought possible. In the darkened room with the world whizzing by, they lay wrapped in each other, tasting the sweet honey of shared love.

Nick's whispers of love were exciting and Eden moved him closer to answer, letting him know that he was loved and needed, precious to her. They spiraled downward together into deep and dreamless sleep, wrapped in each other's arms, secure with their feelings for now and forever.

POISED AS EVER, Tom betrayed not the slightest surprise when he spotted them in the terminal and hurried toward them the next morning. "Welcome to Houston, Nick," he said when Eden introduced the two men.

As they moved toward the baggage section, Tom questioned Nick about oil investments and Eden was grateful for the opportunity to get her bearings. Time spent with Nick always left her removed from

the world, and now she had to face the demands of
her life there. First, the business. Was it doing as
well under Tom's control as it had when she was in
full charge? Were new clients being brought in
while the needs of the old ones were being met? The
challenges of her business always gave her a shot of
adrenaline and she tapped her foot impatiently,
waiting for the baggage handlers to bring her cases
to the ramp.

Eden settled into the middle seat of Tom's gray
Mercedes, smiling at Nick as he slid in beside her.
She moved closer so that their thighs touched,
pressing together in a not-too-obvious way.

"Where to?" Tom asked.

"My townhouse. I need to get my car. Then, you
tell me what's on the agenda," Eden replied.

"We've planned a little celebration at the office." He glanced over at Nick and smiled broadly.
"We had no idea we'd be welcoming both the victor
and the vanquished."

Nick's eyes narrowed slightly as he smiled at
Eden. "Vanquished is right. Eden is one smart businesswoman."

"Luck, my dear Mr. Devereaux," she said.
"Tom, the deck was stacked in my favor."

"As usual," said Tom. "I am glad you rescued
the old lady from the wrecker's ball. How about the
furniture?"

"You're not getting your greedy hands on it,"
teased Eden. "A few of the larger pieces are going
to be incorporated into the executive offices. The
rest will be stored for now. I'll need you to ap-

praise it and photograph it before anything's moved.''

"Fantastic," Tom's eyes gleamed at the thought of seeing a new group of antiques. He concentrated on maneuvering through the usual Houston freeways, looking now like crowded parking lots as everyone fought to get to work on time.

When they reached the driveway leading into the elegant townhouse community where Eden lived, Tom pulled to a halt. "I don't want to rush you, but some of the staff have appointments by nine."

"No rush. We'll be there in plenty of time," Eden assured him, following Nick out of the car and waving goodbye.

When they entered the ground floor of her home, Nick stopped and looked around. "This is a treat." He smiled at her tenderly. "A chance to see how a decorator decorates her own home. Something like sneaking in a dentist's bathroom to find out what kind of toothpaste he really uses."

Eden grinned and set her bag down on the floor while Nick deposited his collection in a heap near the door. Hurrying around the room, Eden swept open the long flowing drapes that shielded the solid wall of glass on the back from the Houston sun. Light filled the room and Nick wandered around, expressing his approval of the cathedral-ceilinged living area with its solid rattan love seats, low glass-topped tables and colorful Oriental rugs.

The room was warm and despite its size, it had a comfortable, friendly atmosphere. There were very few accessories in the room, Eden preferring to keep her walls fairly bare and her tables free from clutter.

"How about some coffee?" she asked, leading the way into the compact kitchen with its steel-blue walls and pure white cabinets. Here was Eden's only concession to collecting, for the open shelves were filled with all manner and size of blue-and-white china.

Nick sat down at her small round breakfast table. "The next time you're at my place, I want to show you around the main house. Now that I see your home, I know you'd love it."

"What's it like?"

"Huge soaring windows. Rooms that sort of flow into one another." He shrugged. "I really don't know how to describe it."

"For an oil-field roustabout, you're not doing so badly," she teased. "When do you expect your friends back?"

"They've already removed their furniture. The house is empty now and until it sells, they won't be back."

"What a life!" Eden turned away from the coffeepot and smiled at him.

Nick caught her gaze with a warm glance. "I'm glad I'm getting this chance to see you here in your home. And to visit your company. Now, when I'm away from you I can visualize what you're doing, what you're seeing...."

"Was it worth leaving all that work behind?" She poured a mug of coffee and set it in front of him, laughing in protest as he caught her and pulled her onto his lap.

"I only wish I could stay longer." Nick held her gently, his embrace warm and loving.

"When will you have to leave?" She hated to ask yet she had to know.

"Tonight." Nick's voice was muffled against her hair. "I'll be waiting to hear whether you're going to take that job."

"I'll do the best I can." Eden twisted to look him in the eye. "You can count on that."

"From now on I'll always look at trains a little differently," he whispered before claiming her mouth in a brief kiss.

Warmth rose in her cheeks as she smiled, "Me, too." Reluctantly she left him to make a quick change of clothing before the day's work began.

CHAPTER FIFTEEN

SEVERAL PEOPLE WERE ALREADY WAITING in the lobby when Eden and Nick walked into the offices of Sonnier Decors a short time later. The decorating firm was located in a converted home in the Montrose area of Houston. The former garage of the home had been glassed in and the wall between it and the old living room removed to form a stunning showcase for one-of-a-kind decorating accessories.

This morning, Linda had set out a beautiful bouquet of spring flowers and Eden nodded at them approvingly as she paused beside her desk. "This would look fabulous with that suit," Linda enthused as she leaned over to pin a spray of delicate white flowers on the lapel of Eden's rose linen jacket. Handing her a stack of phone messages, she added, "Tom's waiting for you in your office."

Eden led Nick down the hallway, pausing as he stopped to peer into one of the workrooms, where the staff was already at work among the littered desks. Even with her standards, there was no way to avoid the natural clutter of a design studio. Fabric samples were draped over chairs, wallpaper books were stacked in all four corners and Eden nodded an acknowledgment as Glenna, her Rapidograph moving swiftly across her drawing board, looked up and smiled.

"That's Glenna," Eden explained as they moved on. "She handles most of our office projects."

Nick smiled at the older woman and then eyed Eden inquiringly as an apparition in battered army-surplus fatigues swept past them. "Good morning, Barry," she said patiently and grinned affectionately as the other man went on down the hall. "Barry," she said. "He may look disreputable, but he has a fantastic knack for finding just the piece I need to satisfy a picky client. His only problem is that he frequently gets mistaken for a repairman, but he steadfastly refuses to change his mode of dress."

With a surge of pleasure Eden realized that it was good to be back in her office. Despite the happiness of the past two weeks, she had still missed her office desperately. Here was her natural environment. Here she felt oriented, comfortable, challenged, accomplished.

"Very nice." Nick's eyebrows rose as he entered her spacious office, his gaze traveling rapidly over the soft silvers and grays, the splashes of maroon and steel blue.

"Champagne?" Tom pointed to the bottle he had open and ready, bending to fill one of the waiting glasses.

"Is this the way you work?" Nick accepted a glass with a smile. "Wonder if my employees would get more done if I tried this?"

"A tempting thought," Tom agreed. "But this is

an exception. We're glad to have Eden back. We've missed her." Jenifer, coming in to get a glass of the bubbly liquid, added her endorsement to the statement and Eden felt a glow of warmth at their friendly welcome. After her last visit she hadn't been sure if they weren't getting along better without her.

Jenifer was wearing a full, red circular cotton skirt in three tiers, lavishly embroidered with multicolored geometric patterns. Her frilly white eyelet blouse swept wide across her shoulders, highlighting the shimmering waves of hair that she had left free to fall down her back. The change in her appearance was no less startling than her enthusiastic smile and attitude as she greeted Eden.

"How's your new client?" Eden asked and with that they were off into a discussion of furniture, suppliers and colors that left Tom to entertain Nick.

"Time for your appointment at the bank," Tom reminded her a while later.

"Oh, no," Eden protested, glancing down at her watch with a frown. "I was hoping to show Nick around the office before we went."

Tom suggested, "Why don't you leave him here to have a look around on his own. You're sure to be finished by lunch."

"Go ahead," Nick agreed with a smile., "I need to call and see about a plane reservation for this evening. Hope the planes are flying again or I'll have to see if the company plane is free."

"They settled the strike," Tom assured him dryly. "It'll cost the taxpayers in your area a mint, though. Hope your profits are hefty."

Eden felt a twinge of guilt as she and Tom left moments later. She'd been hoping to have some time with Nick today, but judging by the phone messages she'd stuffed in her purse and the papers she'd seen on her desk, she had her work cut out for her. Anything Nick wanted to learn about her, he would have to scope out on his own.

Everything went smoothly at the bank and after she and Tom had driven the check to Morgan's office they returned to pick up Nick for lunch. He was waiting in the lobby, perched uncomfortably on the edge of a fragile chair, looking decidedly out of place.

"Sorry we took so long," Eden apologized breathlessly. "Did you have a look around?"

"Don't worry. I've found the wait very educational." His deep voice held a note of that reserve Eden was growing to dread. She had tried to tell him how things were here in Houston, but until he could see for himself, he hadn't understood.

Over lunch Nick repeated his offer about Belle's Folly, Tom asked several pointed, specific questions about terms and money that Eden and Nick hadn't discussed. Turning to Eden, he said, "The offer sounds fair enough. I'm sure we could handle it. It would be good for Sonnier's to branch out a bit. We need contacts in other cities."

"We're so busy," Eden commented.

"Once you get the major contractors lined up and the work is under way, it will be a matter of overseeing things from afar.'' Tom was relentless and Eden eyed him speculatively. He seemed to have struck up an instant rapport with Nick and she felt that he was, ever so gently, nudging her toward him.

"I'm still not sure Nick wouldn't be better off with someone local, someone who could be right there to spot trouble,'' she persisted stubbornly.

"I'm willing to risk that,'' Nick inserted smoothly. "It seems easier for us to work with you, since you developed the plans, than to find somebody new at this late date.''

Feeling that she really had no choice, Eden finally consented. "I'll give it a try.'' Looking at the two men mutinously, she added, "But I refuse to budge from my office for at least two weeks. I need to get caught up on things here.''

"That's fair enough.'' Tom looked at Nick, waiting for his agreement.

Nick replied more slowly, his eyelids coming down over his eyes so that Eden couldn't see their expression. "If you insist, I suppose it can wait until then.''

The afternoon went as quickly as the morning had, Eden caught up in numerous tasks and fielding a seemingly endless procession of phone calls. Nick sat patiently in her office, leaving to have coffee with Barry and then returning about five. "May I take a taxi and not bother you anymore?'' he asked.

Eden pushed back from her desk and stood. "Of course not, Nick. I want to drive you to the airport. Really I do.''

"But can you afford the time?"

"I'll make it up by working late," she assured him, reaching for her purse. On the way out she stopped by Tom's office to let him know she would be returning. The other employees were preparing to leave except for Jenifer, who was still hard at work at her own desk.

Nick was quiet on their way to Hobby Airport on Houston's southeast side. Eden's attention was taken by the thick traffic, something she had not missed at all during her stay in Louisiana. Maneuvering her compact car through the crowded freeways, she spoke little until they reached the airport.

Finding a metered parking spot, she pulled in quickly and shut off the engine, turning to Nick as she removed her key. "I'm glad you came with me, Nick. I'll miss you."

His voice was quiet, uncommunicative. "I'll miss you more than I can say."

Eden thrilled at his words. Yet there was something disturbing, something hanging in the air, which held her back.

"Would you like to go ahead and check in? Then I'm sure we could find a coffee shop and get something to eat." Her suggestion seemed to go unnoticed.

"You don't need to come in," Nick finally answered in a clipped voice.

"Nick," she said patiently. "I'm sorry I've been so busy today. I really am."

Nick turned toward her in the small space, his knee brushing against hers. "I'm not angry, Eden," he said gently, his eyes softening as he looked at her. "I feel awkward. I'm not good at saying good-bye." His hands reached out toward her and then dropped.

"I don't want to say goodbye, either," she said in a low tone. "But I'll be over in two weeks. Or maybe you could come here this weekend?"

"Not this weekend." Nick shook his head. Sighing heavily, he spoke again. "I've just realized, on the drive over here, that we're going to have to get used to saying goodbye. That's not a pleasant thought. I have so much I still want to say to you and do you realize, I haven't even kissed you all day?"

"We can remedy that." Eden's eyes sparkled and she leaned toward him until her lips brushed his cheek. Nick reached for her, fastening his hands on her slender waist and drawing her to him as their lips met, warm and hungry for the taste of each other.

"Ouch!" Eden's moan divided them. "The gear shift," she explained, pointing down at the offending object. "It's poking me. These damn small cars may be good for conservation, but they sure are hell on romance."

Nick reached over and caught her hand in his, letting his other hand trace along her jaw. "Two weeks, Eden?" he asked. "Promise?"

"Two weeks," she agreed.

"Let's cut this short," he said huskily. "I don't want to say goodbye. It'll be easier if I go in alone." Lifting her hand to his lips, he kissed it before adding, "Besides, you need to get back to your office. I don't want you working too late tonight."

"I wish I could convince you not to go," Eden admitted in a ragged whisper.

"And I wish I could stay." With a sudden decisive movement, he opened the door and got out of the car, reaching into the tiny back seat for his bag before slamming the door shut and coming around to her side. Leaning in the window, he dropped a swift kiss on her parted lips and said, "I'll call later in the week," before striding across and entering the airport.

Watching his retreating back, Eden slowly started her car. Like it or not, when she was away from Nick, she was beginning to feel as if part of her was missing.

THE REST OF THE WEEK went by quickly. After several long days at her office, Eden began to feel on top of things again. It was amazing how much could happen during a short absence. Jenifer was handling her project in a way that made Eden feel very proud of her, and the rest of the business was progressing even better than she had hoped. This was going to be a good year for Sonnier's, and the contract for Belle's Folly had financial rewards to offer as well.

Over lunch on Friday Tom revealed why he had been so eager for her to take on the job. They were sitting in the booth of a nearby coffee shop when he dropped his bombshell.

"I do like your Nick even though I haven't fully recovered from losing you," Tom began.

"You look content enough to me." Eden eyed him approvingly. "Sure you haven't already replaced me?"

"As a matter of fact...." Tom looked embarrassed and Eden's eyebrows rose. "I've been seeing Neva again."

"Neva!" Eden couldn't hide her surprise.

"After our conversation, I suggested to Neva that she go back to college." Tom took a bite of his salad and continued, "She got so excited about it that it reminded me of how she'd been when we first married. Maybe you were right after all." He showed no more inclination to discuss the subject and Eden took the hint.

"About Belle's Folly. Do you think you can continue to handle my being gone periodically?"

"I can handle it," assured Tom. "There is one thing, though."

"Yes?" Eden speared a recalcitrant piece of spinach and lifted the fork to her mouth.

Tom took a deep breath and plunged on, "I'd like to buy in as your full partner."

Eden's fork fell back to her plate with a clatter. "Partner?" She eyed Tom with a look of shock.

Tom seemed more sure of himself now that he'd broached the subject. "Partner, Eden."

Slowly she took a sip of her water and considered what she would say next. "If you'd like a larger base salary or a higher percentage of the work you handle...."

"I want to be a partner," he said stubbornly.

"Tom, you can't imagine how much I've appreciated your work. I depend on you."

"And paid me well for it," he said dryly. "It's not the same thing at all, Eden. You're the boss, I'm your employee. That's not good enough for me anymore. I'm not getting any younger and I want to secure something for myself. I think we could both benefit from a partnership."

"What are your terms?" Eden asked warily.

They spent the rest of lunch discussing Tom's proposition. Eden still wasn't convinced, but she promised to think it over. Tom looked inordinately pleased with himself and magnanimously grabbed the check at the end of the meal.

AT HOME THAT EVENING, Eden relaxed in a warm tub, her hair pinned up in a knot on top of her head. The scented water soothed her tired muscles and she leaned back, closing her eyes.

She should have seen it coming. Tom was an expert in his field, not one to remain second fiddle to anyone for long. But partners? For so long, Sonnier's had been her sole domain. Could she bear to share that with anyone? Tom's offer had been generous and it would bring new capital to the firm, making it possible for them to expand and hire new employees. That would mean Sonnier's would change, grow larger, more impersonal. Would that help her achieve her goals?

Stepping out of the tub, she wrapped herself in a luxurious teal blue bath sheet and padded into her bedroom, leaving the lights out as she crawled between the sheets without bothering to put on a nightgown.

Her life had seemed emptier since she left Louisiana. Before meeting Nick, she hadn't been aware of this void, hadn't known that anything was missing. Now she had seen a glimpse of what it meant to have a relationship like that with a man. It was wonderful. Two minds, two souls, two hearts, two bodies, all complementing each other, with the promise of immense fulfillment.

Always before, she had thought of marriage in terms of some vague future with a man like Tom, a businesslike relationship that would provide the framework for home, family. But now that Nick had come along, she had begun putting faces to that family and it was all frighteningly real, demanding that she make choices. Now Tom was asking that she make choices as well. With a frustrated sigh, she turned over on her stomach and forced herself to go to sleep. Perhaps tomorrow would provide answers to her questions.

SHE HAD PLANNED to go into the office on Saturday morning, but when she woke sunlight was streaming into her bedroom and a glance at the clock informed her it was nearly ten. Her body felt rested, though, and her mind was refreshed. After a leisurely cup of coffee, she dressed in a pair of tan linen slacks and a sleeveless jade-green cotton shirt, pulling her hair into a neat chignon at the nape of her neck.

Settling down at her breakfast table, she began

going over the figures Tom had provided for the proposed partnership. By lunchtime she was beginning to consider approving the plan. It was sound and showed great thought and care. This was no whim on Tom's part. He was serious about wanting to join Sonnier's future and his ideas provided Eden with a whole new viewpoint. She still wasn't sure about his expansion ideas. The thought of branch offices in other cities might prevent her from maintaining Sonnier's quality.

The phone rang at noon and she jumped, hoping it was Nick. He had promised to call and until this morning she had been too busy to realize that he hadn't done so. It was Karen.

"How's Houston?" she asked, but her voice didn't match the bright cheerfulness of her words.

"Still as lively and busy as ever." Eden settled back in her chair and waited to find out what was bothering the other woman.

It didn't take long for Karen to enlighten her. "It's Fred again," Karen explained. "Or I should say it's me."

Eden waited for her to go on and when she didn't, she asked, "What's happened?"

"I made a big mistake," Karen said, her voice breaking slightly, and she stopped a minute before continuing. "On one of the payroll vouchers. I mixed up the figures and we overpaid a whole section of workers. By the time Fred discovered the error it was too late to stop the checks, so we had to ask each employee for the money back. It was very embarrassing for Fred and now he's furious at me."

"Karen!" Eden's stomach knotted when she heard the story. With Fred so upset at her anyway, she couldn't afford to keep making serious mistakes.

"I know," Karen went on anxiously. "It's just that he's making me so nervous. I've never had trouble like this on a job before. His suggestions are getting more blatant now. In fact, I got the impression that if I'd spend a few evenings with him, he'd gloss over my mistakes so that no one would ever know."

"That's obscene!" Now Eden was really mad. "You've got to put a stop to this. Right away."

"How?" Karen sounded absolutely helpless.

Eden debated silently for a few moments, trying to come up with a possible solution. Nick had to know about this. But now that Karen had made another bad mistake, it wouldn't do for her to take her story to Nick. He would find it hard to believe her with Fred's evidence to counteract her statements. Then an idea clicked in Eden's mind. An idea she'd read in a recent magazine.

"Buy yourself a small tape recorder," she told Karen. "You know, one of the ones that use microcassettes. Get yourself a couple of full skirts with big pockets and put the recorder in a pocket next time you go to work. Every time you're alone with Fred, turn on the recorder. It may take lots of blank tape, but you're bound to catch him red-handed one of these times."

Karen giggled. "You'd better make that 'red-mouthed.'"

"This is no time to joke," Eden retorted. "You'd better take this seriously or you might find yourself out of a job."

"Thanks, Eden," Karen agreed solemnly. "I don't know what I'd do without you."

Eden bit her lip but couldn't help asking, "How's Nick?"

"I haven't seen him much," Karen said slowly. "He's been so busy all week that no one has seen much of him. He's in New Orleans again this weekend."

Eden felt her first twinge of concern. What on earth could he be doing in New Orleans on his weekends? And why hadn't he called her? Not wanting to involve Karen, she refrained from asking any more questions and they soon hung up.

ON MONDAY she told Tom she was considering his offer of a partnership. "First I want to talk it over with my banker and lawyer," she explained when his face took on a glow of enthusiasm. "If they say no go, then it's out."

"They won't," he said complacently. And he was right. Both men endorsed the idea wholeheartedly and her banker even went so far as to say it would make her company's future.

She left the lawyer to draw up the final agreements and told Tom she would accept his offer on Wednesday morning. "Thanks, Eden," he said warmly, and for the first time Eden found herself thinking that perhaps it was a good thing after all.

That afternoon she held a conference with each

of her employees, listening to any problems they might have and explaining the terms of her new agreement with Tom. Jenifer expressed her pleasure over the forthcoming partnership and said, "You're changing. And I think it's going to make things a lot better around here."

Her assessment was true in more ways than one, Eden thought wryly as she went home that night. She was changing. For the first time in ten years she was finding it hard to put her career first. Even in the midst of her business conferences this week she had wrestled endlessly with thoughts of Nick.

Marriage. That was the big question. There was no doubt that she loved Nick. But marriage to him was another thing. It took a lot more than sensational lovemaking to make a good marriage nowadays. Could she and Nick afford to gamble on their love for one another being enough to sustain a marriage?

She knew Nick would ultimately want children. She had always wanted children as well, but she'd always thought of it as some far-distant future thing. Now she had to face facts. Before long she would be thirty. The biological time clock was beginning to count down for her, and before long she would have to decide about children or it might be too late.

Nick called late that night. "I love you, Eden," were his first words and Eden melted, longing to be with him to hear those words spoken.

"I've missed you, Nick." She lay on her back in the middle of her empty bed, wishing he weren't so far away. The room was dark, she had gone to bed early, and she had been almost asleep when he called.

"Sorry to call so late," he apologized, "but I've been working like crazy to get caught up on everything before you come back here."

"I'll be there Friday night," she said, making up her mind suddenly. After all, she was caught up here and there was no reason she needed to work this weekend. Why not go Friday instead of Sunday?

"Are you flying over or shall I send my plane?"

"Neither," she laughed. "I'm driving. It will only take about six hours and it will give me a nice break."

"I'll be by on Friday night," he offered, "but I can't stay. I have to go to New Orleans again."

"Oh." That was all she said, but it communicated a world of frustration to Nick.

"I want you to come to New Orleans on Saturday," he continued. "I want you to see something."

"What?" she asked, but he wouldn't tell her and when she hung up she felt unsettled, feeling suddenly that she knew very little about Nicholas Devereaux.

ON FRIDAY MORNING she packed a small suitcase and closed up her town house. Later she sat in Tom's office, going over her checklist for Belle's Folly. "I should be back by next weekend," she explained. "The initial start-up will take me about a week and then we'll see how often I'm going to have to travel back and forth."

"Where are you going to be living?"

Sinking back in her chair, she sighed. "I'm not certain, Tom."

"With Nick?" he probed gently.

"It's never come up, but I'm sure I'm welcome."

"But you're not sure you want to?"

"I'm doing well," she protested. "I'm letting you be my partner. Don't rush me into things, Tom."

He laughed. "So I am. Love is much more serious than a partnership. It hurts too much to find out you've made a mistake. You're probably wise to maintain your independence with Nick until you know one another better."

"And until I'm not handling an account for him."

"Can you live with your friend, Karen?"

"I wouldn't want to crowd her. She and Becky have precious little room as it is."

Suddenly she snapped her fingers and sat up. "Of course. I'll stay in the *garçonnière*, the tower house. It's small and needs to be cleaned up, but it has an air conditioner and it's furnished. Aunt Helene used it as a guesthouse occasionally."

"Sounds ideal," Tom agreed.

"It is. I'll be right there by the main house, but I won't be in the way of the workmen once they start their work. Now," she said, glad to have settled on that, "when will you be coming to help me photograph and inventory?"

Tom consulted his calendar and suggested, "How about Wednesday?"

"Great." Jumping up, she went around to the side of the desk and kissed him on the cheek. "Keep me informed on your progress with Neva," she demanded, grinning when he flushed.

Around one o'clock, Eden finished her last-minute work and left her office. It was a strange sensation to be leaving the company knowing that this time she had an almost partner. Strange, but nice to know that someone else was here who felt as much in charge of things as she did.

With the windows of the car down and her hair blowing in the warm early-afternoon breezes, she drove across the nearly empty freeways, beating the heavy Friday rush-hour traffic.

As she drove through the flat, Texas Gulf Coast terrain, passing alongside the grotesque oil refineries sprawling beside the cities of Orange and Port Arthur, Eden sang along with the radio. She was going to see Nick and suddenly the whole world looked rosy.

The route grew increasingly green as she entered Louisiana and stopped for a hamburger and coffee in Lake Charles. After that her impatience to get settled in at Belle's Folly grew. When at last she turned off the freeway onto the winding river road, her pulse quickened. The grassy levees built to keep the Mississippi River from flooding each spring were a brilliant shade of green and the swaying green stalks of sugarcane brought back memories of trips to the fields with some of her aunt's foremen.

They had always cut off big stalks for her and peeled them back, giving them to her to suck out all the sweet juice as a special treat for their boss's niece.

As she pulled through the entrance gate to the plantation, Larry's car passed by on the road behind her. He reversed and followed her through the gates. "Welcome home," he said as Eden got out of her car. "Karen told me you weren't coming until Sunday!"

Eden stretched her tense muscles and enjoyed the feel of the breeze lifting her hair off her sweat-dampened neck. "I finished up my work early and decided to spend the weekend here. How's Karen?"

"I'm not sure." Larry looked worried. "She's asked me not to call her at work for the last few days, so I don't know for sure what's going on." He frowned as he helped Eden remove her suitcase. "Something is going on and Karen won't let out a peep."

"Think it's something bad?" Eden took out her house keys and started up the steps.

"No, not exactly," he replied. "Any idea what's bothering her?"

Eden gulped but shook her head. It was not her business to tell Larry anything Karen didn't want him to know. "I'll call her when she gets home."

Larry stayed long enough to drink a cup of coffee but left soon thereafter. "I have an appointment to show a house at eight."

After reopening the windows and shutters

throughout the house, Eden hurried out to the *garçonnière*. As a child it had always been her best treat to go with the housekeeper to clean the small rooms. She checked the stairs as she went up them, but everything seemed to be fine. She could clean the small place out and once the workmen began arriving, it would provide her with a place to stay on her trips back and forth. She wasn't ready to commit herself to staying at Nick's house all the time.

The main house was still moderately clean from the open house. When Tom arrived on Wednesday she would have a moving firm hired to transfer and store the pieces Nick's company wouldn't be using. As she went into the living room, she saw a small sports car pulling in at the gate in the twilight.

She was waiting in front when Nick pulled up. Leaning in the window, she laughed with pleasure. "Hi, mister. Looking for anyone?"

His eyes darkened. "I've found her." He reached out, drawing her face closer until their lips met in a lingering exchange. His mouth was warm and loving as it moved over hers, the scent of his skin musky and intoxicating. Eden felt a surge of desire welling up from deep within her as she curved her fingers around the back of his neck. As his mouth parted hers, his thumbs sensuously stroked the small hollow at the base of her throat.

"It's good to have you back," he whispered as he reluctantly drew away.

"Are you coming inside?" Eden leaned both elbows on the edge of the car and looked him over lovingly, noting that he still appeared tired and that dark circles still underlined his eyes.

"I'm late as it is." Nick consulted his watch and pointed out the time.

"Tell me—" Eden leaned into the window further "—why all this rushing to New Orleans on the weekends?"

"It's something I'd rather show you than tell you." Nick reached into his pocket and pulled out a small index card. "If you want to find out, come to this address around eleven tomorrow morning."

"Mmm. . . ." Eden glanced down at the card that showed an address she didn't recognize. "This sounds awfully cloak and daggerish. Don't tell me you're a spy."

"Nothing so exciting, I'm afraid." Nick's hand reached out to capture one of hers. His eyes, dark and unreadable in the gathering darkness, locked with hers.

"If you'd like, we could have dinner in town tomorrow evening and spend the night there."

Eden felt her pulses begin to race maddeningly. "Sounds delightful." She tried to keep her voice even.

"Damn it, Eden." Nick's own voice was suddenly gruff. "I hate having to plan every moment alone with you. It makes me sound like all I want is sex and you know that's not true. I love you, damn it."

"Heavens," Eden protested faintly, "you don't have to sound so fierce about it."

Nick gazed straight ahead for a moment and then gave her a sheepish smile. "Tomorrow?"

"I'll be there bright and early," she promised.

His car disappeared down the lane and she stood staring after it, wishing it were tomorrow already.

CHAPTER SIXTEEN

KAREN AND BECKY ARRIVED shortly after she got up the next morning. "Anyone home?" Karen shouted from the front porch.

"Coming," yelled Eden. She hurried down the stairs, buttoning her blouse. She had dressed quickly in a pair of olive-green cotton twill pants and a tailored khaki blouse that emphasized the translucent quality of her skin. Her hair was full and slightly curled from the early-morning humidity.

Swooping Becky into her arms, she gave her a quick hug and a kiss. "I brought you a surprise from Houston. Run upstairs and look for a sack on the round table in the nursery."

Karen followed Eden into the kitchen, watching as she put water to boil for some instant coffee. "Guess what," said Karen, her impish smile reminiscent of Becky's. This morning her red hair was a spot of color against the pale beige short jumpsuit and matching sandals she wore.

"Tell me what's got you up and around so early on a Saturday morning?" Eden flung the question at her as she peered into the refrigerator, frowning as she realized she had forgotten to pick up any cream or rolls at the grocer's.

Reaching into her purse, Karen brought out a minirecorder and set it on the table. Flicking a lever, she glanced expectantly at Eden. Fred's voice filled the room, a suggestive undertone evident as he made several remarks filled with sexual innuendos.

When the voice stopped, Eden grinned. "You did it!"

"Yesterday," Karen said, nodding, and flipped off the recorder, replacing it in her purse before Becky could come into the room. They could hear the little girl clattering down the steps.

"What do I do with it now?" Karen asked as she reached for a cup of the steaming coffee. "Play it back for him and tell him I'll play it for Nick if he doesn't stop?"

"Exactly," Eden nodded. "But first, make a copy of the tape. Just in case."

Karen sipped her coffee and groaned. "It all seems so underhanded. I hate doing things like this."

"Sometimes that's the only way to handle someone like Fred." Eden smiled sympathetically. "Wonder why he acts like that?"

"I know," Karen grimaced. "I've tried to figure it out myself. He's not that attractive, I guess, but still, you'd think he wouldn't have to resort to behavior like this to get attention. His wife is dead, you know."

"What happened to her?"

"I'm not sure. He never talks about her. She died before I came to work for the company." Karen paused as Becky entered the room. "Why don't you go out on the porch and play?" she requested. "Mommy will be out in a minute."

As Becky took her toy and left the room, Eden poured herself another cup of coffee. "Has he always bothered you with his remarks?"

"No," Karen sighed. "This started about six months ago. Something just seemed to snap and he's been getting worse ever since."

"Maybe all he needs is to be brought up short and made to see how ugly he's been acting," Eden said briskly. "But meanwhile, try to avoid making any more costly mistakes."

"I will," Karen replied fervently.

AFTER THEY LEFT, the house seemed quiet. Eden finished applying her makeup and then sat out on the porch to work for a while before driving to New Orleans. It was difficult to concentrate. She couldn't help wondering what Nick wanted her to see. Was he going to introduce her to his soccer team or was there something else he wanted to show her? She had packed a silk dress and another slacks outfit along with her cosmetics so that she could take him up on his offer of a night in New Orleans.

Finally it was time to leave. When she reached the outskirts of New Orleans, she stopped at a service station to refill the gas tank and ask directions to the address Nick had given her. "Best thing to do is to buy a map of New Orleans," drawled the attendant. He pointed toward the rack.

Eden chose one and spread it out on the hood of

the car, searching through the list of streets until she located the right one and then following the number and letter given until her finger reached it. It was a section close to town, not too far from one of the major freeways, so it wouldn't be too difficult to find.

By the time she reached the street, she had begun to feel nervous. The homes in the area were large and stately, although some were slightly run down. A row of huge trees lined each side of the street, their leafy branches almost touching as they cast deep shade over the route. When she neared the street number, she slowed down to a crawl until she found the block number where Nick was supposed to be.

Glancing over, she realized she was at the end of the block, with only a huge brick fence surrounding what looked like several acres. She stopped the car and got out, walking toward the gate until she was close enough to read the words on a metal plate inlaid in the brick.

All Saints Orphanage. Founded: 1837. She glanced back down at the paper and then up again. The home. Nick had referred to it several times, the home where he had grown up.

She tried the gate and it was locked. What now? Without thinking she rattled on it several more times and an elderly man passing by stopped and leaned on his cane. "You'll have to ring the bell," he said politely, pointing to the opposite post.

Feeling foolish, Eden thanked him. "Is there anyone here this time of day?"

His eyes brightened. "Oh yes, children tend to stay put in an orphanage. The gates are locked to keep the youngest ones from wandering away, you know. After you ring, you best be prepared for a little wait. It takes the sisters a while to walk out from the main office."

"Thank you." Eden gave the old man a friendly smile before walking over and firmly ringing the bell.

The man seemed reluctant to leave. "Beautiful day, isn't it?"

"Lovely. Do you live near here?"

"Yes, down the street." He pointed at a large cottage-style home that appeared to have been made into a boarding house. "Are you here to visit one of the children?"

"No." Eden shielded her eyes against the sun and tried to peer past the gate. "I'm looking for someone." She turned back to the man. "I had no idea I was coming to an orphanage."

"Really? It's been here a long time, but like everything else, it's changing now. The children don't even wear uniforms or take walks every day in those straight lines like they used to."

They both turned their heads as they heard the firm click of heels on the brick walkway. A tall thin woman, her iron-gray hair partially concealed by a gray-and-white headdress, came toward them. Although elderly, she moved with a youthful grace that revealed her years of hard work and discipline. Her matching gray dress was street length, the starched fabric rustling quietly as she moved.

"Mr. Beauregard, how are you?" she said in a crisp clear voice.

"Fine, thank you, sister. You have a visitor." He nodded toward Eden and the woman swung her dark piercing gaze in her direction.

Swept by the same feelings she had experienced as a small child when one of her teachers caught her in some misdeed, Eden stuttered slightly. "I'm here to see Mr. Nicholas Devereaux. Is he here?"

A smile removed any traces of sternness from the elderly woman's face. "Ah, you want to see Nick." Quickly, she unlocked the gate. "Do come in, dear. Would you like to wait for him in the office or shall I take you out to the playground?"

"The playground." Eden felt as if she'd stepped into a time machine and was being rapidly transported backward into a past age.

The sister continued, "I'm Sister Theresa. If you haven't eaten yet, perhaps you'd like to join us. Nick will be bringing the children in for the second seating."

As they moved down the walkway, Eden introduced herself. "I'm Eden Sonnier," she spoke quietly.

"A friend of Nick's," returned the sister. "He's mentioned you to me several times. I knew you were coming today." The curve of the path they took led to a grassy playing field. Sounds of childish shouts and laughter filled the air. "Before you leave, stop in and have tea with me, Eden. I'd like to get to know you."

"Of course, sister," Eden replied.

A plump girl of about eight, blond pigtails flying in the wind, ran toward them. "Who do you want, sister?" she called.

"Uncle Nick, dear."

"Can't find him. He's playing hide-and-seek. With the boys," she added. "Girls aren't allowed."

"How utterly chauvinistic of him," teased Sister Theresa, smiling as Eden burst out laughing. "We'll sit here on this bench while you go and locate him, Jenny. Tell him he has a visitor."

When they were seated, the sister smiled over at her. "Nick tells me you are an interior designer."

Nick must have been doing a lot of talking, Eden decided as she said, "Yes. In Houston. I've taken on a special project for Nick here."

The sister shocked her by leaning over and patting her hand in a motherly gesture. "He really cares for you, my dear. Take good care of our Nick. He's very special to us."

Eden smiled vaguely, trying to assimilate all this new knowledge of Nick. The pieces in the puzzle were falling into place now. His weekends in New Orleans, the soccer team and the scrape on his cheek. But why had he not told her about all this before?

A shadow fell across her shoulder and she turned as Nick came striding toward them, a wide smile on his face. He was wearing faded jeans and a torn T-shirt, his worn tennis shoes crossing the ground between them in firm strides. Two small boys followed closely behind him, imitating his stride.

"Eden! You came," he called over to her, pleasure evident in his broad grin and dark gleaming eyes.

Sister Theresa stood up. "Come, boys," she said, scooping up the youngest child in her arms and nodding firmly at the other. "Let's leave Uncle Nick with his visitor."

Aware of the rise and fall of Nick's chest muscles under the knit shirt and the long expanse of muscular legs revealed by his close-fitting jeans, Eden smiled up at him in welcome.

"Nick, I hope you'll invite Eden to lunch with us today. Please bring her inside soon," added the sister over her shoulder as she moved off.

Nick settled down on the bench beside Eden, his knee brushing her thigh as he adjusted his body to the narrow seat. With one arm settled firmly along the back of the bench, he caressed her shoulder as he smiled down at her. "What do you think of it?" His gesture took in the smooth lawns, the shady trees, the old buildings and the children playing in the distance.

"Is this where you grew up, Nick?" Eden reached over and put her hand on his leg, tracing an idle pattern with her fingers along the firm muscles.

"Until Job adopted me," Nick explained. "I was born in the hospital down the street and came here when I was only a few days old. Except for the times my mother took me—" here his gaze darkened and he stumbled a little over the words "—I spent almost my entire childhood on these sheltered grounds."

"And Sister Theresa?"

"She's been here forever, I guess." Nick's face softened and Eden felt his love for the elderly woman. "I couldn't imagine this place without Sister Theresa."

"She's surprising," Eden said, grinning at him. "Warned me to take good care of you."

Nick looked embarrassed. "Damn," he muttered, running a hand carelessly through his hair.

Eden grinned even more broadly. "Does Sister Theresa allow that?"

"She's been known to slip a couple of times herself, but don't tell her I told you so." Nick winked at her wickedly.

"I'll bet." Eden pretended to be shocked.

"I am glad you came today," Nick repeated as he shifted closer on the bench. "I've been wanting to tell you about what I do with my weekends, but I was afraid you'd think it was childish of me."

"Of course not!" Eden let the love welling up inside her shine in her eyes.

"Eden," he groaned and enfolded her in his arms, giving her a melting glance from beneath hooded lids. As his lips moved to cover hers, she caught his special scent and breathed deeply of it, reveling in the nearness of his body. She returned his kiss with equal fervor, tracing the outline of his lips with her tongue and arching toward him so that her breasts brushed against his chest.

As his hands slowly slid up to rest just beneath her aching breasts, she drew back and murmured,

"Watch it or you'll be a bad influence on the kiddies, Devereaux."

He chuckled and reluctantly let his hands drop. "Come on and let's have some lunch, sweetheart."

When they entered a large ivy-covered brick building, Eden turned to Nick. "Are you allowed to eat dressed like that?"

"Sure. The old days are gone forever around here."

"And about time, too," said Sister Theresa as she came toward them. "Why don't you two sit here at my table? That will save squabbling among the children over who gets to sit on either side."

The food was different from what Eden expected, too. Exactly what children liked: thick grilled beef patties, homemade hamburger buns, crusty country-fried potatoes and one of the best chocolate cakes she had ever tasted. During the meal, Nick kept up a running conversation with the other sisters and a young couple who were apparently also weekend volunteers. He included Eden as if it were the most natural thing in the world to have her here beside him.

Eden couldn't help laughing at herself. If someone had told her a month ago that she would be delighting in sitting in the cafeteria of an old orphanage with a roomful of noisy, exuberant, sweaty children, she would have suggested they seek help of some sort. Was it possible to change so rapidly, or had this side of herself always been there, waiting for someone like Nick to come along and free it?

When the meal was finished and the sisters rose, the blond girl who had found Nick earlier ran up to them. "Will you play with us?" she asked Eden. "Let's have the girls find Uncle Nick's boys and then they can find us."

Nick glanced inquiringly at Eden, but she sensed that he hoped she wouldn't reject the little girl. "If you don't mind, the kids would love it," he said, his dark eyes compelling, communicating more effectively than words his desire that she accept his world and life here.

"Why not?" Eden agreed laughingly, and the little girl rushed off with a big grin.

The youngest children were herded off for naps, but the older ones clustered around Nick and Eden when they went outside. Several of the oldest walked off in disgust when they heard that hide-and-seek was the game of the hour, but there were enough left to make it exciting.

"Girls get to hide first," said Nick.

Eden shook her head. "We'll take our chances. Got a coin?"

"Not on me."

"Neither do I. We'll race you." Choosing one of the tallest girls, she pointed to a tree. "Pick out a boy and the two can run to that tree. That'll decide who gets to hide first."

"Always independent, aren't you?" Nick shook his head and looked at her sideways as he moved to direct the race.

Within minutes the game was in progress and Eden allowed herself to be led into nooks and crannies all over the grounds, only to be located within a short time by giggling boys. Nearly an hour later, trying to locate a more secure hiding place, she was running around a hedge when Nick came up beside her. "What are you doing here?" she demanded. "You're supposed to be covering your eyes while we hide!"

"I'm helping you," he said, sweeping his hand down her back and then grabbing her hand. She pulled away from him, but he persisted, leading her into the shadows of a recessed doorway.

"Nick!" she protested weakly as his mouth came down to cover hers, his arms wrapping around her and settling her securely against his hips.

"I've been waiting to do this all day," he murmured. "Don't try to get away."

Their mouths met with such heated urgency that they were finally forced to separate, laughing in breathless delight at the fire rising between them. Nick's fingers played restlessly with the buttons on her shirt, sliding between them to tantalizingly caress the smooth skin between her breasts. "Eden, it's been too long, much too long," he whispered huskily as he moved to reclaim her mouth.

She put one finger against his lips and stopped him with a seductive smile. "You need to learn patience, Mr. Devereaux."

"That's not in my vocabulary where you're concerned." He brushed her finger aside and rained light kisses down the side of her face, his calloused fingertips stroking the small hollow at the base of her throat where her pulse beat erratically.

"The game," she reminded him when she could speak.

"I'm more interested in what's happening between us," he murmured hotly.

"Enough," she said firmly and pushed him away, stilling his roughened breathing with light fingertips against his chest.

The sound of running feet and childish laughter put a stop to their intimacy and soon they were caught up in the game again. Eden was exhausted by the time one of the sisters came out to collect the children for their story hour.

Nick went with the older boys to pick up the playground equipment, and Eden made her way to the main office where she asked for Sister Theresa. "She's in her office," said one of the younger women, pointing down a hall. "She's expecting you."

Sister Theresa's office was bright and bare, and although the furniture was old, everything was polished and shining, making it seem new and fresh. After asking one of the older girls who helped out in the office to bring tea, Sister Theresa came over and sat down, gesturing for Eden to do the same.

"I wanted a chance to get to meet you, and know you better," the older woman said with a smile. "Nick means a lot to us and anyone special to him is special to us."

"He's a wonderful person," Eden said softly.

"That he is, my dear."

"How long has he been working with the children?'' Eden asked the question more to keep the conversation going than anything else.

Their tea arrived and Eden helped pour it before Sister Theresa replied. ''Nick always kept in close touch with us, even after Job Devereaux adopted him. I suppose we were the only stability in his life.''

''He seems to really love the children.''

''They're very important to him,'' the sister agreed. ''And they need him.'' She took a swallow of the hot tea and winced before continuing. ''His own mother was one of our girls, you know.''

Eden looked at her in surprise. ''I didn't know that.''

''Yes,'' Sister Theresa sighed. ''She was a young thing when I first came here to the orphanage, a very independent, stubborn girl. Nick was born when she was only eighteen and she never really managed to get her life together after that. There was very little we could do to help her, though.''

''And his father?'' Eden hated to ask the question but she couldn't resist.

The sister fixed her with a penetrating look that seemed to strip away all pretences. ''Why are you asking? Would that make a difference in your feelings for Nick?''

''Of course not!'' Eden was taken aback.

''I wasn't sure,'' the sister said calmly. ''Some people set great store by their background. And the truth is that we know nothing about Nick's father. Evelyn, his mother, would never tell and we don't force anyone to reveal anything about themselves that they don't want to. That's not our way."

"I'm sorry, sister. I wasn't trying to pry," Eden said. "I was hoping that it would tell me something more about Nick."

"I understand." Sister Theresa spoke soothingly and her smile reestablished the friendly atmosphere in the room.

Eden decided it was time to switch the subject, much as she would have liked to learn more about Nick. Anything Nick wanted her to know, he would tell her himself. "Tell me more about the children," she asked.

Sister Theresa nodded approvingly at her. "They're only temporary residents these days. None of them stay more than a few months at a time."

"What happens to them?"

"These children all have one or both of their parents still living. For one reason or another, sometimes financial problems, sometimes marital difficulties or illnesses, they stay here with us. Any available infants are adopted as soon as they're born, and even our few older orphans seem to be adopted more quickly these days."

"It must be hard on the ones who have to go back and forth," Eden spoke softly, remembering Nick's face as he had told her about his mother.

"More than hard." Sister Theresa was decisive. "It's very disruptive. That's why we try to make life here stable, serene. At least for the time the children are with us, they'll know what it's like to have a secure environment.''

The sound of Nick's laughter floated down the hallway and Eden smiled at the sister. "What are you two in here talking about?" Nick swept the door open and grinned at them.

"You, of course," Eden said lightly, setting down her teacup.

"I'm sure you can find something more interesting than that to discuss."

"If you've promised this young lady a night on the town, you'd better get cleaned up." Sister Theresa eyed his clothes reprovingly.

"I hate to take Nick away if he usually spends the evening here," Eden began quickly.

"Go on, both of you." The sister smiled and waved them out the door. Standing, she moved around and grasped Eden's hand. "I hope you'll come back to see us. You're welcome with or without Nick, anytime."

"Thank you." Eden's voice was filled with genuine appreciation of the offer. "Goodbye."

NICK'S CAR WAS PARKED in a lot behind the main dining room. "Why don't you follow me to the hotel?" he suggested.

"Are you the type who runs yellow lights and leaves a trail of dust for anyone trying to keep up?" Eden hesitated.

"Here." He reached into the front seat and pulled out a map. "I'll show you where it is and then if you get lost, you can't blame me."

"That's big of you." She pretended to be cross.

The hotel he named was not one she was familiar with, and Eden carefully copied down the address, promising to meet him in a few minutes. He walked her back to her own car, taking out a key and unlocking the gate before kissing her lingeringly. "I'll see you soon," he whispered and she nodded.

The hotel Nick had chosen was actually an old cottage home in the heart of the French Quarter that had been converted into a guesthouse in recent years. Eden drew her car to a halt behind Nick's sports car and breathed a sigh of delight.

Set on raised blocks, the cottage was a low-slung, two-story building with wide dormer windows shuttered in blue and an inviting double French front door in the same rich color. Gay blotches of red, purple and other rich hues were provided by wildly growing bougainvillea which twisted around the iron grillwork fence surrounding the guesthouse and its gardens. Stepping out of the car, Eden reached for her overnight bag and turned to find that Nick was standing behind her.

"This is delightful," she enthused with a spark of real pleasure lighting her eyes.

"I was hoping you'd like it." Nick seemed pleased by her response. "Let's go inside."

Nick demonstrated his thoughtfulness again when he went to the desk to register. They were given separate rooms on the same floor. The desk clerk seemed totally uninterested in them and for that Eden was grateful.

The front desk was of hand-carved wood that had been painted to look like marble. *Faux marbling* was what they called it here in Louisiana.

The custom had started when plantation owners discovered that the heat and the humidity rotted the boards in houses, causing heavy real marble flooring and mantels to fall through their supports. Artisans who specialized in the special effect had flourished along the river, and Belle's Folly boasted one such fireplace mantel, in the room Eden had planned to make Nick's office.

To the left of the main entryway Eden could see a large living area that seemed to have been made into a lounge for the use of the guests. To the right was a small dining room. As Nick followed her gaze, he commented, "They only serve breakfast and lunch. We'll be going out for dinner."

Eden was grateful for the silk dress she had packed as she followed him up the stairs. Her room was at the end of the wide hallway on the second floor, Nick's was directly opposite. Handing her the key to her room, Nick stepped away from her door.

"Are you coming in?" she asked, feeling somewhat awkward when he didn't say anything.

"Eden, I don't want you to feel that you're being pressured into anything," he replied in little above a whisper.

"I don't," Eden responded succinctly, and smiled slowly, warmly. "I love you, Nick," she said simply.

His answering look was seductive, promising much to come. "I'll give you thirty minutes to rest while I clean up. Then why don't we have a drink in the garden downstairs."

"Fine," she said and went into her room.

It was dim, restful and cool, secluded from the busy crowded streets below. That was one of the delightful things about New Orleans. Even in the midst of the French Quarter, each house and hotel seemed to maintain its own cloistered environment with cool gardens, shuttered windows and sweeping old trees.

Eden wandered around the room, noting the wide four-poster bed with its hand-worked crochet spread, the marble-topped mahogany dresser in one corner, the two overstuffed chairs in front of a brass-fronted fireplace. The whole room was a delightful blend of past and present, with pastel floral wallpaper and a matching muted carpet.

Quickly unpacking her bag, she hung her dress in the adjoining bathroom to steam out the wrinkles while she bathed. The dress was a slim kimono-style silk in vibrant deep purple with a contrasting black obi belt. She had brought along strappy black heels and fine black stockings that emphasized her slender legs. The deep slit in one side of the skirt only showed when she walked.

Pinning her hair up in wispy tendrils on top of her head, she stripped off the now-limp cotton slacks and shirt and her brief bra and panties. After running a tub of steamy scented water and cleansing her face at the large sink with its hand-fashioned faucets, she soaked for fifteen minutes.

Her brief glimpse of Nick's orphanage had told

her much about his life as a child. No wonder he found it difficult to talk about. The orphanage was another world, an oasis far away from his present life-style. She felt pleased and touched that he had shared it with her.

But it presented more problems. It was clearly obvious that they counted on Nick's presence on weekends. If she and Nick continued their relationship, would she be taking him away from people who meant much to him? But what other time did they have?

Not wanting to let something unpleasant intrude on her present happiness, she slipped out of the tub and wrapped herself in the thick white towel left hanging beside the tub. Padding into the bedroom, she dried off leisurely and then wrapped the towel around herself once more.

She was reaching to release the pins from her hair when she heard Nick's door open and his footsteps in the hall. His knock came a moment later. Turning to face the door, she called softly, "Come in."

Nick came in and shut the door behind him, stopping when he saw her standing across from him, wrapped only in the towel. For long moments, he drank in the sight of her appreciatively, his gaze returning again and again to her bare white shoulders, her long legs revealed by the towel that ended just below her hips. "I've never seen your hair up like that before," he said at last, his voice low and husky.

Eden reached for the hairpins again, but his voice stopped her as he crossed quickly to stand in front of her. "No, let me do it," he said roughly, his hands trembling slightly as he carefully loosened her hair and let it fall down around her shoulders.

Placing his hands on her bare skin, he buried his face in the thick strands of her hair. "Your hair is like silk, Eden," he uttered the words into the muffling curtain of hair. "I lie awake at night dreaming of the way it looked on the pillow when you were beside me in bed. In the morning light it's the color of new oil, the rich, thick ebony of crude as it spouts up from the earth like liquid gold."

"You're always making the funniest comparisons." Eden lifted her eyes to look at him, hooking her fingers through the loops on his trousers underneath the light jacket he wore. "First I was an onion and now I'm like crude oil. I don't know whether to be flattered or insulted."

"I'm just a rough wildcatter, honey," Nick apologized hoarsely. "But I do know one thing. There's nothing rough about you. You're like refined gold, delicate porcelain, the highest quality. Sometimes I don't know how you can stand to have me around."

"Don't say things like that," Eden protested fiercely, moving closer to him and pressing herself shamelessly against the length of his body.

"I love you so much," he murmured. "Sometimes I'm not sure I should let you get so close."

The admission had cost him dearly. Eden could sense that. Very carefully she chose her next words. "You mean everything to me, too, Nick."

"Eden," he said searchingly before claiming her

lips in a soul-shattering kiss that tasted, nibbled, explored, coaxed and promised, all at once. Eden leaned back slightly to facilitate the movements of his fingers as he fumbled with the edges of the towel, unfastening it and pushing it away from her body.

Her breasts, aching with longing for his touch, pressed against the rough cotton of his shirt, and Eden pushed the jacket off his shoulders, reaching for his tie and loosening it while he planted kisses along her smooth bare shoulder.

As her fingers sought and found the buttons that would release his chest from the confines of the shirt, his lips moved urgently over hers, drawing a sweet response from deep within her that left her hopelessly under his spell.

With a muffled groan, Nick could hold back no longer and he moved his arms so that she could help him shrug off his shirt and stood patiently while she unfastened his belt and pushed the trousers from his hips. At last they stood unclothed in the dim room and the desire that had been tightly leashed for the past few hours began to unfurl.

Holding her tightly against him, he drew her down beside him on the bed, stretching out his length until they were pressed together, cheek to cheek, shoulder to shoulder, hip to hip, their feet entwined.

They kissed passionately, too eager to stop for tender exploration, fierce with a need that would not be denied. Nick's fingers sought and found the gentle swell of her breasts, cupping them and circling the nipples until they stood out firm and hard against his palm.

Eden found his male nipples with her fingertips and leaned down to torment him with flicking movements of her tongue, enjoying the rough texture of his matted hair against her cheeks.

Laughing softly with the delight of holding each other again, they moved on the bed in relentless pursuit of what would give each other the most pleasure.

Muscles rippled in Nick's bronzed arms as he levered himself slightly away from her and took his time surveying her cloud of hair spread on the white cover of the bed, her smooth firm breasts, rosy with the effects of his sensitive touch.

His chest was massive above her, the dappled sunlight through the shuttered windows spotlighting the rough planes and angles of his body. Through the thin fabric of his dark briefs, the proof of his desire was evident and with a soft moan Eden pushed the fabric from his hips, grasping the firm flesh of his buttocks as he moved to gather her close again.

Somehow they moved beneath the cool sheet, Nick throwing the heavy spread back to fall against the burnished mahogany bedposts. His hand found her breasts, stroking the soft satiny skin and lifting it lightly, brushing the nipple with his lips. The rose-hued tips stood out firm and flushed with a fiery desire, aching for the feel of his mouth against the taut buds.

As she writhed beneath his touch, murmuring his

name on choked outbursts of breath, his other hand played across her abdomen, dipping in at the curve of her waist, sliding down over the swell of her restless hips.

His hand slid between her thighs to cup the moist warmness waiting for him there. A groan escaped from his throat as she opened to him more fully and let him find her ready for his touch, prepared by the exquisite power of his caresses.

"Oh, Nick," she whispered, hesitating only a moment before touching him with coaxing, stroking movements of her hands that elicited a shuddering response in his body as it lay stretched over hers.

His muttered words of love and encouragement were breathed into the tangled web of her hair, and Eden reveled in the trembling response of his body to her arousing, feather-light touch.

"God, Eden, I can't wait any longer." Nick groaned the words in a hoarse whisper as he parted her legs fully and settled between them firmly, penetrating her receptive warmth with a swift movement that brought a sigh of satisfaction to their mingled lips.

"I'm only half alive until I'm with you like this," Nick whispered into her ear with a seductive warmth that added to the flush on her heated cheeks.

"Love me, Nick," she urged against his seeking mouth and then, as their lips played out a symphony of their own, they began to move to the ageless rhythm of the tide of desire rising between them.

With each thrust of his hips, Eden rose to meet him until they were rocking together, pressing closer and closer, seeking higher ground until they left the earth completely and moved into a realm of pleasure so deep and so profound that their urgent cries became a medley as they were forever joined in a newly forged and seemingly unbreakable unity.

CHAPTER SEVENTEEN

THE CLINK OF SILVER on china was muffled in the opulent, heavily draped, dimly lit restaurant where they sat later that evening. Nick's broad shoulders were emphasized in a dark suit that complimented the flat black sheen of his hair. A recalcitrant lock of that hair fell across his forehead and as Nick reached to brush it back, Eden recalled to mind the past two hours. A satisfied smile curved her mouth and Nick eyed her curiously. Soon his expression changed to one of knowing pleasure as he noted the blush mounting beneath her high cheekbones.

"Penny for your thoughts," he offered in a wickedly seductive whisper as the waiter moved forward to bring them a bottle of chilled white wine.

"Oh, I think they're worth much more than that," Eden replied enigmatically, looking up to smile as the waiter hovered over their table.

Her ankles crossed and uncrossed beneath the table before she tentatively stretched out one nylon-clad foot and brushed it against Nick's trouser leg. He shot her a chagrined look as he struggled to carry on a conversation with the waiter about dinner. Eden ignored him, taking advantage of the long starched linen tablecloth to move her foot daringly up the side of his leg, sliding beneath the fabric of his trousers and inching her way along his firm muscles.

"Dessert?" He looked up at the waiter vaguely, seemingly having trouble concentrating on the conversation at hand.

Eden smiled innocently at him, all the while continuing her seductive assault beneath the table.

"We'll order dessert later." Nick gave in finally, unable to maintain his composure under her gentle ministrations. He heaved a sigh of relief as the waiter moved away.

Eden leaned back in her chair slightly, replete with a delicious dinner that had begun with delicately cooked shrimp in a pleasingly hot red sauce and continued with a delectable filet of trout sautéed with tender young zucchini and tomatoes. They were now awaiting the arrival of their salads and after that, Eden doubted her ability to make room for dessert.

"You better stop that," Nick warned as she let her foot play with his trouser leg.

"Why?" she asked, the picture of innocence.

"You know why," he whispered. Reluctantly she let her foot slide away, the memory of their warm and wildly passionate lovemaking darkening her eyes to a deep sapphire.

After lying in his arms quietly for a while, Eden had reached up to place a line of kisses along his bronzed shoulders.

"Ready for dinner?" Nick had asked softly, and Eden had looked into his eyes, dark and so near her own that she blinked several times.

"I was almost ready to go out when I was suddenly led astray," she explained, and he kissed her thoroughly and approvingly. "Too bad we can't go to dinner like this." He surveyed her slender length with a regretful sigh. "But even the French Quarter isn't ready to allow people to go that far yet."

Eden had sat up slowly, untangling herself from his arms and attempting to restore some sort of order to her disarranged hair under his watchful gaze. Reclining back on the white fabric of the sheets, he drank in the sight of her, noting the lift of her breasts as she moved her arms up to her hair, dropping to linger on the firm flesh of her stomach, the dark triangle of her femininity.

"I'll be happy to volunteer to wash your back," he offered, pretending to be serious even as his eyes twinkled.

"Umm. . . ." Eden tilted her head to one side as if considering. "Maybe. . . ."

"Come here." He drew her to him and wrapped himself around her, claiming her mouth again with loving attention before leading her into the tiled bathroom.

Remembering the feel of his hands on her breasts as he soaped them gently, the suds sliding down to reveal the proudly pointed tips, she glanced at his arms, covered now by the crisp white shirt, the dark jacket. In the tub, the bubbles had collected on the sprinkling of dark hairs that graced his forearm, and Eden had tangled her fingers in his matted chest hair, offering to wash his back in the same seductive tone in which he had made his previous offer.

He had taken her up on it and, one thing leading to another, it had been some time before they were ready to go out to dinner....

"Eden?" Nick's voice recalled her to the present and she smiled across at him, a sudden rush of love threatening to overwhelm her. She needed this man, needed him more than she had ever needed anything in her life. It was hard for her to admit to needing anyone or anything, but she freely admitted it to herself now.

"I do love you so." She leaned across the table to whisper the words and saw the answering flush in Nick's tanned cheeks. He grasped her hand and held it tightly.

"We've never had that dance," he said suddenly and as Eden gazed at him blankly, he explained, "I offered you a dance our first evening out together, but we didn't ever have it. How about it?"

"Sounds wonderful," she agreed and indeed it did.

Nick took a sip of his wine and then looked across at her. "What did you think of Sister Theresa?"

Eden smiled softly, remembering the kindly older woman. "She's delightful!"

"The home means a lot to me." Nick played idly with one of her hands resting on the tablecloth as he spoke. "Even though the children come and go, it makes me feel good to know that I can help out in a small way."

"Why do you keep it such a secret?" Eden asked. "No one at your office seems to have any idea what you do with your weekends."

Nick looked slightly embarrassed. "If they knew, they might make a big fuss about it, or they might think I was doing it for the wrong reason. I'm not trying to impress anyone with how generous I am. I get as much out of those weekends as I give. There's nothing altruistic about it."

"You do help a lot," Eden said gently. "Even from the short time I was there I could see how much they all rely on you."

"I'm not the only person who helps." Nick downplayed his involvement. "Several of the other former residents come regularly to help with sports or music or to help tutor the children who've had to miss school for one reason or another."

"The home is more or less your family, isn't it, Nick?" Eden asked the question and then wondered instantly if he would be hurt by it.

For a long time he didn't answer, but finally he said, "I guess you're right. I never really thought about it that way."

With the arrival of their salads, they were forced to return their attention to the meal, but within a short time they were outside the restaurant. "Where to?" Eden asked, sliding her arm through the curve of Nick's elbow and resting her fingertips lightly on his jacket sleeve.

"Why don't we walk along until we hear a band we like," Nick suggested. "Most of these places have a dance floor of sorts."

The night air was warm and heavy with the scent of a veritable army of flowers, and they walked slowly along, savoring the sights and smells and sounds of Bourbon Street on a Saturday night. Other couples jostled past them and several open doorways beckoned with dim lights and throbbing music. Finally Nick indicated a small bar where a collection of musicians seemed to be reveling in playing romantic, ageless love songs. "Here?"

He led Eden inside and waited as she laid her purse on the small table indicated by the waitress. Without letting her sit down, he led her on to the small dance floor where only one other couple was moving to the slow sweet music.

The melodies were seductive, invoking a stirring of nostalgic memories mingled with the promise of future good memories. Eden melted into Nick's arms, gratified to find that he moved effortlessly with the music, his innate rhythm allowing her to follow his steps without even thinking.

She wrapped her arms around his shoulders, her hips brushing his as she stepped closer into his embrace. His large hands slid sensuously down her spine, his fingertips urging her to meld with him. His breath whispered against her ear and she turned her face into his neck, pressing a light kiss against the tanned column beneath her mouth.

The spell of the dim lights and haunting music was insidious and as they moved together Eden dissolved against him, her pulse quickening as he slid his fingers up her back and brushed the curve of her breasts at her sides. His thighs insinuated themselves against hers, rubbing through the silky fabric of her dress, causing it to cling to his sharply creased trousers.

Eden felt that tonight was theirs, indeed that the whole world was theirs. She whispered into his ear, a hundred avowals of her love that soon had Nick raining kisses over her hair and eyelids, seeking her mouth in the dim light.

"We better start moving or else people will be watching us instead of listening to the music," Eden warned suddenly, noticing that the attention of several people at nearby tables seemed to be focusing exclusively on them.

"Who cares?" Nick muttered as he sought her lips again.

"Nick!" she protested faintly as he let her draw back from him a little ways, reluctance in every touch of his hands.

They danced for a long, long time, stopping only now and then to return to the table. Nick's need to have her near him seemed insatiable and Eden relished this romantic streak in him. Where some men stumbled around on the dance floor as a chore or duty, Nick held her closely and firmly, enjoying every moment.

Finally, they were forced to leave. The musicians began folding up their instruments and music and the last straggling couples left the bar. "Somewhere else?" Nick suggested, but Eden could sense that he wanted to be alone with her.

"The hotel?" she asked and he nodded. "Shall we walk?"

"Yes, let's," she agreed. It didn't take long to stroll back to the guesthouse, whose shuttered windows and scented gardens seemed closed for the night.

This time they came together swiftly, their passion rising sure and strong and inevitably to a conclusion both ecstatic and poignant.

EDEN WOKE LATER in the night and turned to find the bed empty beside her. For a moment she was disoriented but slowly regained her senses. Moonlight was slanting into the room, bouncing off the shiny mahogany bedposts, falling in dappled shadows onto the muted wallpaper. The shutters on the long low window across the room had been thrown open, and through the slightly open window she could hear the humming of night insects in the humid air.

Nick was sitting in front of the window, his lean frame stretched out in a chair he had pulled over from the fireplace. Eden slid out of bed and reached for her robe, wrapping it loosely around her body and moving quietly over the carpet to stand beside him. "Nick?"

"Did I wake you?" He stood up hurriedly and put a hand on her shoulder.

"No," Eden said, noticing the tension in his set jaw, the shadows in his eyes. "Is something wrong?"

Nick went over and got the other chair, motioning for her to sit in the spot he had vacated. "No," he assured her, but Eden wasn't convinced. "You look bothered by something," she persisted.

Nick looked at her for a long moment, his palms rubbing together in an unconscious gesture. "Eden, you are going to marry me, aren't you?" his low voice spoke suddenly into the uncomfortable silence.

Eden sat back in her chair, crossing her ankles and fan-folding the hem of her robe nervously. "I love you, Nick," she said finally. "I just don't know about marriage. We're so different, you and I."

"Does that bother you?" Nick pursued the subject relentlessly.

"It bothers me that our lives are so different. How can we make that work? We haven't even talked about the future. Not really. What do you want out of marriage?"

"I want the usual things," he said quietly. "A wife who shares my love, a home, companionship, good times together, maybe children later on."

"And you think I can provide those things?" Eden gave him a direct look. "Are you sure I'm the type of person you need?"

"Eden," he spoke urgently, hurriedly. "We don't always pick the sort of person we fall in love with. Sure when I thought of marriage I always thought in terms of something stable, a permanent homelife, children. But it's you I love. I know we can find a way to make things work."

Eden looked over his shoulder, staring out at the moonlit gardens below, her mind in turmoil. She had been wrestling with these same thoughts for days. It wasn't her nature to enter so fully into physical intimacy, to give her love totally and completely, without thinking in terms of commitment. No matter how independent she had become, no matter what she had made of her life to this point, she still ultimately wanted marriage. It was just that Nick wasn't at all the sort of person she had thought of marrying. He didn't fit her life-style.

As she hesitated, Nick persisted. "This is beginning to seem too much like an affair to me. Maybe you'll think I'm old-fashioned. I don't know." He paused and laughed shortly at himself. "I am old-fashioned, Eden. Oh, I'm not saying that there haven't been other women, you know that. But since the moment we met, I've known we were different. The kind of love I have for you demands the fulfillment of marriage."

"When would we ever see each other?" Eden sighed and looked away. "You have your weekends at the orphanage. I'll be in Houston a lot during the week. You travel frequently." She lifted her head and spoke firmly. "Even if we married it would be impossible."

Nick rose and drew her toward him, settling back down in his chair with her on his lap. Eden stiffened for a moment and then relaxed against him. "Come on, Eden." He caressed her face with his callused fingertips, looking at her tenderly. "Don't fight so hard. Sure it's a challenge, but let's try, anyway."

For long moments the silence in the room was palpable. Even as Eden gazed into his eyes, she realized the hopelessness of fighting her love for him. She had been less than honest with herself. It wasn't in her nature to pretend that love and caring of this sort could exist happily apart from a committed relationship. She wanted marriage with Nick, wanted it desperately, and it was fear of failure that was holding her back. A fear that she would disappoint him, hurt him, wind up destroying what was so precious between them.

"Okay, Mr. Devereaux," she capitulated suddenly. "We'll get married. But first you have to give me more time. I refuse to be rushed. I want things to be right."

His kiss was tender and gentle, all that she could hope for, and she wrapped her arms tightly around him as he lifted her and returned to the bed.

THEY HAD BREAKFAST in the garden the next morning, a quiet and peaceful Sunday morning characterized by gentle breezes and warm spring air. Over a bowl of fresh succulent melon, Eden and Nick made plans for the week.

"I'm going to meet with Fred tomorrow," Eden said, breaking a buttery croissant in half and handing one portion to him.

"Friendly, I hope." Nick's glance was teasing as he watched her expressive face.

"An armed truce," Eden said, grimacing. "Fred and I will never be close."

"Fred isn't so bad." Nick speared a piece of melon and ate it rapidly before continuing. "He's had a tough time. That's made him seem abrasive to people who don't know him well."

"Oh?" Eden was curious to find out more about the man who was giving Karen so much trouble. "Karen said his wife died several years ago."

"She was ill for a long time." Nick's voice was sympathetic and Eden could sense his genuine concern for Fred. "He loved Nancy very much. She was a lovely person, but after a party one night, she was injured in a car accident. Fred was driving that night and I think he still blames himself."

Pausing to take another croissant, he looked across at her. "Nancy had to be completely cared for the rest of her life. Fred refused to let her spend those last two years in a nursing home. He spent every spare moment of his time devoting himself to her care. It left him with no life at all."

Eden took a sip of freshly squeezed orange juice and thought about what Nick had told her. Did Karen know any of this? Perhaps they had all been a bit hard on Fred. No one would be happy under those circumstances, but still, that didn't explain his off-color suggestions to Karen.

If only she felt free to mention it to Nick. She was sure Karen was wrong about how he would receive the information. Nick would never tolerate any employee being harassed, and even though Fred was a good friend of his, she knew he would be fair. But Karen had made her promise not to mention it to anyone, especially Nick, and she wasn't about to betray a confidence, no matter how close she felt to Nick.

It made her feel awkward, knowing something was going on in Nick's company that he wasn't aware of himself. It violated the feeling of trust and honesty between them. With firm resolve, she decided to have a talk with Karen. The situation couldn't be allowed to continue.

They spent the morning exploring the French Quarter by daylight. It had an entirely different character in the morning sun, an old-world flavor highlighted by narrow town houses with trailing balconies, the ever-present New Orleans gardens, quiet parks and a mixture of languages and cultures.

By afternoon, gray clouds were beginning to gather on the horizon and Eden eyed them doubtfully. "Looks like we're going to have a rainy drive back. Perhaps I ought to get started." In a bad thunderstorm, the narrow river road could be difficult to negotiate.

"Are you coming to my house?" Nick asked as they returned to the guesthouse to get their bags.

Upstairs in the hallway, Eden paused with her hand on the door. Nick had wasted his money getting two rooms, she thought ruefully. Still, it had discouraged any comments from the desk clerk or staff.

"Well?" She realized Nick was regarding her quizzically.

"Nick, I'm not going to stay at your house," she began firmly.

"Don't like the company?" He was laughing on the surface, but she sensed his defenses building up.

"I'm an independent lady," she said, placing her hand softly on his arm. "I'm here to work, Nick. Like you're always saying, business and pleasure don't mix. I'll get more done if I'm alone.''

"I can understand that," he said after a brief pause. Drawing her to him after a quick glance down the hall, he kissed her lightly. "I can understand it, but I don't like it."

"Thanks for a wonderful weekend." She placed her head on his shoulder and leaned against him, savoring his warmth. "I wish it didn't have to end."

"It wouldn't if you'd marry me," he said brusquely, his fingers pressing into her arm.

"Nick, you promised!" She extricated herself from his embrace and looked at him reprovingly.

"I promised to give you more time," he replied shortly. "I didn't promise not to keep reminding you that I want us to be together."

Eden shied away from entering into another discussion about marriage. She wasn't yet sure enough of herself to know how she really stood on the issue. "I won't forget," she whispered. "I love you, too, you know."

His mouth descended to move urgently against hers and Eden responded by meeting his probing tongue with a now-familiar surge of desire.

"Tomorrow night?" he whispered huskily against her lips. "Have dinner with me again at my house?" As she hesitated he urged, "Dixie and I are missing you."

"For Dixie, anything," Eden laughed and pulled away.

"So it's not really me." Nick pretended to be insulted, his dark eyes twinkling with amusement. "It's really my racoon you love!"

"See you tomorrow, Nick," she said firmly, and blowing him a swift kiss with one slender hand, she turned away from him.

CHAPTER EIGHTEEN

THE RAIN THAT HAD THREATENED on Sunday afternoon didn't arrive until Monday morning. After a thorough drenching, the rain stopped, but the clouds continued to hover ominously.

Eden set about her work diligently, spreading out her plans on the dining-room table and spending the first two hours of the morning on the phone contacting the various people who had made bids to do work on the property.

She had stopped the night before and picked up a few groceries before spending the rest of the evening setting up the *garçonnière* for her stay. She wanted to be out of the main house well before work started.

Tom called midmorning to confirm his arrival early Wednesday morning. "I'm only going to stay the day, Eden," he said firmly. "It shouldn't take longer than that to photograph and inventory the major pieces."

"I'm having everything removed from the house during the working stage," she told Tom. "That will make it easier for the contractors and insure that nothing is damaged."

At ten Karen called to let her know Fred was on

his way. "I can't talk now," she said in a low voice, "but this has been some day so far."

Eden remembered her earlier determination to talk with Karen and said, "How about lunch tomorrow?"

"Sure," Karen replied. "Meet you at the same place at twelve?"

"Fine," Eden agreed, and hung up, going upstairs to check her appearance before Fred arrived. She was wearing one of the practical pairs of slacks she had packed to wear during the week. None of her usual suits would be sensible for work here at Belle's Folly. People along the river road weren't used to being greeted at the door by someone who looked like they'd stepped from the pages of Vogue. The contractors would feel more at ease seeing her in slacks and a casual shirt.

Fred was trudging up the steps when she returned to the main hall. As she opened the screen door, she saw past his surface belligerence and noted the lines of fatigue and depression etched into his forehead. Her good-morning was unusually soft as she stood aside to let him enter.

"Coffee?" she asked as she led him into the dining room and waved him toward one of the curved mahogany chairs.

"Please," he said brusquely, heaving a gruff sigh as he lifted his briefcase onto the surface of the long table.

Once they were both seated, sipping out of steaming mugs, Eden pulled out the charts she had been working on. "We'll need to get the subcontracted work under way as soon as possible,'' Eden said. ''But first I need to get a firm deadline set for when you want to be in here.''

''September,'' Fred said arbitrarily.

''Isn't that rather ambitious?'' Eden frowned, considering the schedule in front of her.

''If you can't do it, perhaps we should get someone else.'' Fred seemed primed for an argument and Eden smothered her impatience with difficulty.

''Fred,'' she turned to him and spoke earnestly, ''we're going to have to work closely on this project. We might as well clear the air before we get started. If you don't want me doing this job, please tell me why not.''

Fred appeared startled by her directness and for a moment it seemed he wouldn't answer. Finally he said stiffly, ''I didn't mind your plan being chosen. But when Nick told me you were going to be handling the job yourself, I couldn't believe it.'' He shook his head as if still puzzled.

''I am the owner of the property,'' Eden began carefully.

''You know the only reason Nick chose you.'' Fred looked over at her and spoke the words with a machine-gun rapidity that cut through the air between them.

''I assume he chose Sonnier's because he felt we would do the best job for him,'' Eden returned coldly.

''Oh, come off it, young lady.'' It seemed that once Fred got started he couldn't stop. ''He has a thing for you. That's the only reason you're here this morning. It's downright stupid to use a Houston firm when we've got people right in New Orleans who could finish the project sooner and better.''

Eden felt a freezing anger to her core. What Fred was saying sounded hateful and petty and it hurt. She wanted to think Nick respected her firm, respected her professional ability. She'd never curried favor to get a job in her life, and it chilled her to be accused of that sort of behavior.

''I suggest you talk this over with Nick,'' she said abruptly. ''Meanwhile, until I'm removed from this project officially, we'll continue our work.''

Ignoring the way that Fred bristled beside her, she pulled the schedule back in front of her and tapped her pencil agitatedly against the table. ''We'll work toward a September deadline. Now, let me show you exactly how I plan to move this project along.''

Their ensuing discussion lasted for almost an hour. By the time Fred left the atmosphere had thawed somewhat, but Fred didn't make her job any easier. He did promise to go to New Orleans that afternoon to offer contracts to the various companies who had bid on the work at Belle's Folly. If things went as planned, work on the air conditioning and plumbing might begin by the end of the week. With Fred here to check on progress, she could return to Houston with a clear conscience, free to sandwich in the decorating details between her other obligations.

Fred had brought her an inventory of the furniture that the company would bring from its own offices. Together with the pieces she had offered from the contents of Belle's Folly, they had almost everything they needed. That left her free to concentrate on her main concern: tying the old in with the new, making Belle's Folly into a functional office space without taking away the essence of its timeless beauty.

At five she stopped work and showered, changing into a cool strapless sundress and matching sandals in a pale shade of silvery blue that highlighted her blue eyes and contrasting black hair. Closing up the main house, she left a light burning in the *garçonnière* and got into her car for the drive to Nick's house.

Karen's house was dark and quiet as she passed, so Eden didn't get a chance to see either her or Becky. After her talk with Fred today, she was afraid she might end up being the one asking for advice on how to handle him rather than giving it.

The ominous storm clouds that had plagued the area all day were gathering in force by the time she pulled into Nick's driveway. He hadn't arrived, so she parked and strolled over to the main house. Peering into the windows to get a glimpse of the darkened rooms, she grew curious to see the inside.

Within minutes she heard the sound of tires crunching over the shell driveway and ran to meet Nick. He braked to a halt when he saw her, unfolding his frame from the small car to fold her in his arms and bury his face in her fragrant hair. "Mmm, you're a welcome sight," he murmured.

Her heart took a wild roller-coaster ride as he tilted back her head and bent slightly, his lips moving compellingly against hers. She stroked the smooth skin of his neck, clinging to him as a rush of feeling swept through her. She belonged here, in Nick's arms, safe, secure, cherished.

His arms encircled her, molding her against him and she could feel the firm male thighs, his body distinctly disturbing as she pressed tightly against him and elicited a groan from deep in his throat.

"Miss me today?" he whispered against her ear.

Unwilling to admit just how much she had missed him in the short time since their weekend, she simply nodded, her hair brushing his shoulder in a soft gleaming fall of velvety black. "I've been trying to get a peek in the main house but didn't have much luck."

He reached in his pocket and got out his keys, flipping through them until he found the one he was looking for. "I've got a key to the front door. Want to take a look now?"

"I'd love to." They held hands as they walked down the tree-shaded path in the deepening dusk. "How old is this house?"

"About five years." Nick flashed her a smile that made her heart stop momentarily before racing at double its normal rate. "Jay had it built when he retired, but they've barely lived here."

"Why not?"

"His work took him all over the world and since he retired, he can't seem to settle in one place. Besides their yacht they own a villa in Spain, so they finally admitted they didn't need this house."

"Who keeps the grounds looking this nice?" Eden gestured toward the expanse of manicured lawn and the neat flower beds.

"There's a full-time gardener," Nick explained. "He doesn't live on the property, but he maintains the place and whenever he needs an extra hand, he hires temporary help."

"It seems such a waste. All this beauty and no one living in the house to enjoy it."

"I'm here," Nick reminded her. "And besides, hasn't Belle's Folly sat empty for a number of years?"

Eden slanted a glance at him and saw the amusement lurking in the depths of his dark gaze. "Your company is remedying that."

When they reached the wide double-door entrance, Nick unlocked it quickly and stood aside. Eden stepped inside and let out a sigh of pleasure. The large central hall was spotlighted by artfully placed skylights, the twilight highlighting the white terrazzo floors and casting shadows on the stark white walls. There were no obvious doors. The entire house seemed to beckon as she caught fleeting glimpses of rooms blending into each other like waves in the sea.

The living area was huge, two stories high with triangular-shaped glass windows reaching the roof line. Their steps echoed through the empty rooms as Nick followed Eden through the house. "Like it?" he asked.

"You need to ask? It's like living in the outdoors with none of the inconveniences."

They wandered through the living area and into an equally impressive dining area with glass French doors that led onto a sheltered patio fronting a section of the luxuriant gardens. Inside the kitchen, Eden stopped abruptly, her mouth forming an 'o' as she surveyed the gleaming cobalt-blue cabinets that seemed to be suspended in space. The lighter blue-and-white hexagonal ceramic tiles on the floor blended with the same shade of blue in the vertical blinds on the windowed walls.

Nick watched her with an indulgent smile. "It's not at all like Belle's Folly," he pointed out.

"No, it's totally modern." Eden was lost in appreciative exploration.

"You prefer modern?" Nick followed her over to the window.

"You saw my house in Houston," Eden replied.

"What about your attachment to Belle's Folly?" Nick waited for her answer, his gaze never leaving her face.

"I love Belle's Folly," Eden said simply. "But not to live in myself."

"Could you live here?" Nick's voice was suddenly serious and Eden turned to face him, brought back to the present by his tense posture and intense tone.

"Well, I suppose," she said. "I mean, who couldn't? It's fabulous."

"I'd like to buy it for us." Nick slipped the statement in so fast it made her head spin. He plunged his hands into his pockets and regarded her directly.

"Whoa!" She touched his arm lightly and felt the

tense straining of the muscles under her fingers. "There you go again, trying to rush me."

"I'm going to pursue you relentlessly." Nick's gaze deepened until his eyes were black and intense. "You're mine," he added, "I'm not going to stop reminding you that we belong together until I know you're convinced."

Eden felt a deep stirring of impatience. Something about his words was unsettling. "I don't belong to anyone, Nick." She spoke clearly, her words echoing in the empty room.

She saw the fabric of his trousers bunch slightly and realized that he was tightening his fists. The silence was electric until he broke it by laughing shortly and saying, "You're right. That was a poor choice of words."

Eden walked away from him and moved out of the kitchen, feeling uncomfortable for the first time in Nick's presence. Why was he so anxious to have her marry him? They loved each other, but they had known each other for such a short time. Wasn't he satisfied savoring each moment, allowing their relationship to develop naturally?

"It's getting dark," she said calmly as Nick came up behind her. "How about that dinner you promised me?"

"Coming right up," Nick said immediately, and Eden was relieved to hear that the tension had left his voice.

When they emerged from the house, Nick went back to his car and drove it to a spot beside hers while she walked over to the cottage and waited on the porch. She could smell the approaching rain in the air, a pungent musky odor that tickled her nostrils and made breathing difficult as it mingled with the sweet fragrance of the abundant flowers.

A thunderstorm was building again as dusk fell, menacing clouds billowing low over the landscape. Strong breezes stirred the water on the lake, foaming it into gentle swells that lapped against the long wooden pier. Her hair was lifted away from her neck and the cooling breeze felt good against her heated skin.

With bold force a streak of lightning zigzagged across the sky, followed by a deep rumble of thunder that muffled Nick's approaching steps. "Better get inside," he said behind her and she jumped, startled by his nearness.

As he unlocked the door, huge raindrops were beginning to plop down on the soft earth. Nick was carrying a grocery bag and Eden followed him into the kitchen, helping to unpack the assorted groceries. "Steaks," she enthused, lifting out the package of rich-looking meat.

"I was hoping we could grill them outside, but the rain seems to have put a stop to that." Nick pulled out two potatoes and deftly washed them before placing them in the microwave.

"Never fear," Eden announced. "I have a recipe that will save the day for any cookout."

"What's that?"

"Do you have a cast-iron skillet?" Eden replied enigmatically. As he pulled one out of the cupboard beside the stove she added, "And some rock salt?"

"Rock salt?" He looked at her as if she had rocks in her head and Eden laughed. "Just watch." Nick rummaged around and finally came up with a bag of the requested salt.

Eden turned on the oven and liberally sprinkled the salt in a thick layer in the skillet before sliding it into the oven. While it heated, they set the table and Nick made a tossed salad.

"Now for the steaks." Eden reached for a hot pad and carefully slid out the skillet, placing the two steaks directly onto the salt. Nick made a face as she sprinkled another layer of salt on top of the meat.

"What are you doing to those poor steaks?" he demanded.

"Don't complain!" Eden snapped the oven door shut and glared at him. "These are delicious. Probably unhealthy, but delicious," she admitted.

He shook his head disbelievingly and turned back to the salad. After ten minutes Eden whipped open the oven and withdrew the skillet. "Plates ready?"

"This I've got to see." Nick produced the plates and watched as she slid the steaks out of the salt and placed them on the plates.

They quickly put the rest of dinner on the table and sat down. "See?" Eden insisted as Nick took a bite of the steak and a surprised smile broke across his face.

"This is fantastic!"

"I know," Eden said primly, and they both burst out laughing.

While they ate, the storm began in earnest, blowing out its strength in driving rain and slashing wind. The water in the lake whipped up in frothy waves and darkness descended quickly.

"How was your meeting with Fred this morning?" Nick asked when they had finished eating and were sitting, still at the table, watching the storm outside the wide window.

Eden frowned, remembering Fred's harsh assessment of her. "Not too great," she said frankly.

"Oh?" Nick's gaze was unfathomable in the dim light.

"He seems to feel that you made a mistake choosing Sonnier's to handle the decorating job." Eden saw no point in softening what Fred had said.

"Just ignore him." Nick seemed unconcerned by what his office manager thought.

Suddenly the idea that had been niggling at the back of her mind all day took shape. Why had Nick asked her to take the job? After all, didn't he usually leave decisions of that sort to Fred? Why had he made this an exception? Was Fred's accusation true? The possibility bothered her intensely.

"Nick, why did you ask Sonnier's to take the job?" She spoke suddenly, almost unaware of making the decision to do so.

Nick paused in the act of pouring out a cup of coffee from the pot that had been brewing for the past few minutes. "I told you, Eden."

"Oh, I know what you told me," Eden said. "But why didn't you let Fred choose the firm? Isn't that how you usually work things. Delegate those decisions to Fred?"

Suddenly the atmosphere between them was charged and Eden realized that her words had been accusing, even hateful. Yet she had to know the truth.

Nick got up from the table abruptly and turned his back, pacing back and forth several times without speaking. Eden stared down at her hands, folded together on the table. "Why does my question upset you so?" she asked in a low voice.

"Eden—" he ran a hand carelessly through his hair "—I convinced myself that I chose your company because I felt it was the best possible choice. Yet would I have picked it if I hadn't fallen in love with you?"

"I don't know," Eden said quietly. "Would you?"

"I can't answer that question." Nick stuck his hands in his pockets and paced again.

"Can't or won't," Eden inserted carefully.

"Does it matter?" Nick turned back to her and demanded.

"Perhaps." Eden pushed her hand tiredly through her hair and stood up from the table. "I don't know myself."

"Eden, I couldn't stand by and let you go back to Houston without making a way to keep on seeing you. At the time, it seemed like a wonderful opportunity. And there's no question of your not doing a good job. I've seen your company for myself now. I know how good you are."

"But that's the point, isn't it, Nick?" Eden faced him with determination. "You made the decision, not Fred. You broke your own rule because of me."

"It's worked out," Nick said stubbornly.

"I think we've been less than honest with ourselves," Eden spoke softly. "We said we could keep business and ourselves separate. But we're not doing a very good job."

"I've never loved anyone as much as I love you, Eden." Nick came over to her and stood close beside her. "I guess maybe I'm pushing things."

Eden suddenly hated the tension and anger between them. She leaned against Nick and gave him a brief hug, leaving her arms wrapped loosely around his waist as she drew back and looked at him. "We're both tired, Nick. Maybe that makes this seem more important than it really is." Kissing him lightly on the cheek, she drew away. "I think I'll go home now. I've a full day tomorrow and I need some rest."

Nick looked as if he wanted to protest, but he restrained himself, getting an umbrella from the front closet and going with her to her car. "Talk to you tomorrow?" he said in a low voice when she was seated inside.

"Tomorrow." She started the ignition, unwilling to linger in saying good-night. Something was still bothering her, but she couldn't define exactly what it was. She simply felt she had to get some time alone, time to think before she and Nick talked any more.

"Good night." He kissed her warmly and Eden returned the pressure of his lips before driving away quickly.

WHEN SHE WOKE the next morning, she realized what was bothering her. Stretching slightly, she went into the shower and emerged a few moments later to dress in another pair of slacks and a crisp shirt. Her freshly shampooed hair quickly whipped into shape beneath the ministrations of her blow dryer and curling iron and before long, she was ready to go over to the main house.

Over coffee she assessed her situation. She loved Nick and she was sure he loved her. But so far, it seemed that love meant she had to give up her life in Houston, marry Nick, change her life-style. Slowly, but surely, she was being manipulated into changing many things about herself. Some of those changes were for the better but some were definitely not.

What was bothering her, indeed what had been bothering her for several days now, was that in every conversation with Nick about marriage, they could never actually discuss the method by which they could work things out. Underneath his agreeable exterior, she sensed that he had not yet given up on the idea that things working out meant that she would give up her job, move to Louisiana, marry him and become the epitome of his dream wife. And that meant he didn't know her very well, for she would never be anyone's dream wife in that sense of the word. She was too independent.

Somehow, she had to make Nick see what was happening. Until she thought of a way to do that, she needed distance, because whenever she was with him, she was overwhelmed by their attraction for each other. No matter how wonderful they were together, nothing would change the fact that she wasn't going to do all the compromising.

With that resolve, she put aside her own concerns and went to phone the moving company. They promised that packers would be available on Thursday, and after making sure that enough people would be sent to do the job in one day, she went up to complete the process of removing her personal belongings from the upstairs bedroom.

Karen called at eleven to cancel their lunch date. "Fred insists that I stay in to retype a letter," she explained, her voice nervous. "He's driving me nuts. I'm making all sorts of mistakes."

"You've got to stop this," Eden said definitely.

"I know," Karen wailed. "But how? I don't have the nerve to play that tape recording yet."

"When you get desperate enough, you will," Eden said, feeling badly about speaking so harshly but knowing that in the long run Karen had to take action and take it soon.

"Thanks for listening," Karen said. "It means a lot to know I have someone who understands what's happening."

"If you'd talk to Nick you'd find the situation a lot easier."

"I know," Karen said. "And I will. Soon."

EDEN SPENT THE REST OF THE DAY working furiously, eager to get through this part of the project. She was finding it more difficult than she expected to go through both her aunt's and her own personal possessions. Somehow, they were her last tie with the past and she felt as if a phase of her life was ending.

Nick called after work, but Eden explained that she was bogged down with work and they didn't talk long. She knew he could sense the strain in her voice, but she wasn't ready to talk yet.

Around seven she got in her car and drove along the river road, giving up at last when she realized that times hadn't changed. There was still no place to get a hamburger along this section of the river. Before going back to the house she stopped and bought a frozen dinner at the country store, letting the clerk warm it in his microwave oven so that she wouldn't have to heat up the ancient stove in Belle's Folly's echoing kitchen.

At last she fell into bed, exhausted, yet satisfied that things were ready for Tom's arrival. She was determined to concentrate on doing the best possible job before giving in to her thoughts about Nick.

CHAPTER NINETEEN

EDEN PICKED TOM UP at the airport early on Wednesday morning and drove him back to Belle's Folly. He was wildly enthusiastic about the plantation, exclaiming about its beauty as they drove in the entrance and swept along the drive to the house.

"But this is fantastic, Eden." He turned to her as they got out of the car.

Eden led him up the steps and unlocked the front door. "We've got our work cut out for us today," she explained.

Tom got right to work, getting out his camera and notebook and carefully snapping general shots of each room before beginning the item-by-item inventory.

He had brought the layout for the brochure on the Morgan collection. "It's all in storage now," he said as he handed her the layout sheets. "Barry inventoried the collection for us. We won't have any trouble finding a home for these things."

Eden was more than pleased by the proposed brochure. The collection was even better than she had remembered. Her excitement grew as she realized the potential use of the many pieces.

"When are the packers coming?" he asked as they moved into the living room.

"Tomorrow."

Startled, Tom paused to fix her with a gimlet stare. "Why all the hurry?" he demanded. "Problems with the flaming romance?"

"Tom!" she reproved. "I'm anxious to get back to Houston. If I stay away much longer, I'm liable to find you and Jenifer have taken over the firm." As he laughed she added, "How is our partnership agreement faring, anyway?"

"The lawyer says we'll need one last meeting to iron out the details before we sign the contracts." He snapped a shot of the sofa group and then grinned at her. "Haven't changed your mind, have you?"

Eden went over and squeezed his arm affectionately. "Not a chance. The more I think about it, the more I wonder why we didn't become partners before. You're going to be good for business, Tom."

Tom looked pleased by her compliment. "Guess what?" he asked as he moved around the room, pausing now and then to lift a vase and peer at it carefully or bending down to check the carving on a chair or table leg.

"You and Neva are back together," Eden guessed quickly.

"Well, I wouldn't put it quite so cheerfully," Tom said cautiously. "But the atmosphere is definitely less chilly."

"I bet the girls are happy about that," Eden said, thinking of his two teenaged daughters.

"Are you kidding?" Tom sounded disgusted. "They're frantic that we'll get together and find out that they've been playing Neva and me against each other for all we're worth."

Eden started to say something and then stopped as she heard a knock at the front door. "Wonder who that can be," she mused as she headed for the hall. "I didn't hear any car drive up."

Through the mesh of the screen, she could see the outline of a woman and she hurried to the door. "Yes?" she asked, opening it so that she could greet the person.

"Eden!" The other woman smiled hesitantly at her and for a moment Eden couldn't place the faintly wrinkled face surrounded by a wealth of snow-white hair.

"Why, it's Mrs. Avery, isn't it?" she said at last, feeling a surge of familiar pleasure.

"I wasn't sure you would remember me," the woman confessed, looking relieved as she entered the hallway.

"Come in and sit down," Eden urged, leading the way into the living room. When the other woman was seated, she said, "This is my partner." Completing the introduction, she said, "Tom, this is Mrs. Avery." Smiling at the woman, she added, "She and her husband are retired history professors. They own Cypress Gardens, which is our sister plantation across the river."

"Actually, that's the reason I came to see you, Eden," Jan Avery explained after the introductions were over. "It's about Cypress Gardens."

Tom ceased his inventory note taking and settled down in a chair to listen. "Yes?" Eden inquired. "What can I help you with?"

"Well, I'd heard you were remodeling Belle's Folly, so I wanted to know if you would work on Cypress Gardens as well."

"Oh, Mrs. Avery—" Eden started to refuse, but was stopped by Tom.

"Is Cypress Gardens also a large home?" Tom asked, his interest obviously whetted.

"Why, yes." Mrs. Avery seemed anxious to have someone listen. "It's fifty-two rooms. I'm afraid my husband and I have done little to decorate the place in the years we've lived there. Nothing, that is, beyond making a few rooms comfortable. We were so worried we might destroy something that we more or less made an apartment in one section and left the rest as it was."

"Then what you're wanting is a restoration." Tom seemed to understand Mrs. Avery before she could explain a thing.

"Why, yes." She seemed relieved to find that Tom was interested.

"Actually, the only reason we're working on Belle's Folly is because I'm the owner," Eden explained. "Our firm doesn't ordinarily work outside of Houston."

"I was so hoping you'd do it," Jan Avery persisted. "You see, I've called out several decorating firms from New Orleans. All they want to do is change the place, modernize it. I felt that you would understand my feelings about keeping things as historically accurate as possible."

"We do understand," Tom inserted smoothly in spite of Eden's dark looks. "Is there any possibility of my having a look at the place today?"

"Of course." Mrs. Avery beamed at him. "I could drive you over now and you could stay for lunch."

"That's great!" Tom agreed and before Eden could protest they were all three in Jan's car heading toward Cypress Gardens.

Tom walked patiently through every one of the fifty-two rooms, with Mrs. Avery carefully explaining what she wanted done. At one stage she left to answer the phone and Eden hissed at Tom. "We can't possibly take on this job and you know it."

"Why not?" Tom replied reasonably. "This could be worth a lot of income to the firm. Why turn down a good job?"

"What are you trying to do, Tom? Get rid of me? I belong in Houston."

"There's no reason why you can't take on jobs outside of Houston when an opportunity like this arises. You're bound to get more offers when people see what you're doing with Belle's Folly. Decorators are a dime a dozen, but people with your background on one of these plantations are not so readily available."

Mrs. Avery returned before Eden could answer him, but she thought about his words as they finished their tour and ate lunch. Jan was thrilled with their interest and after driving them back to Belle's Folly, she waited while Tom explained that he would work out a proposed bid for the job and get in touch with her.

"It's after two," Eden pointed out as they went back into the house. "We'll never finish getting the inventory done today."

"I can finish my photographs and together with the old inventory you gave me weeks ago and the notes I've already made, we'll have an inventory of every major piece. The storage documents should catalogue everything else."

As he finished clicking shots of everything in the house, Eden brought up the subject of Mrs. Avery. "Why did you encourage her so, Tom?"

"Because I think it's a good job and it's at least worth consideration," Tom said adamantly.

"We have jobs waiting in Houston," Eden objected.

"And now that there are two of us, we also need more jobs," Tom returned. "We've been talking about branching out. This might be just the spot."

There was no changing his mind and as he continued to express his enthusiasm for the idea, Eden began to get excited about it herself. It bore thinking about, anyway.

She had to rush to get Tom to the airport on time, but they made it just under the wire. "When are you coming home this time?" he asked just before he got on the plane.

"Home?" Eden said vaguely. "I'm not quite sure where that is anymore."

"You've been awfully quiet about your Nick today," Tom probed gently. "Problems?"

"Not really," Eden hedged. "He's a great guy, Tom."

"He must be," Tom laughed. "He's had quite an impact on all of us."

With that he got on the plane and Eden just had time to promise that she would be driving back over the weekend.

THE PACKERS ARRIVED at eight sharp on Thursday morning and at nine Karen arrived. She came running up the steps two at a time and met Eden on the front gallery.

"What are you doing away from the office?" Eden asked in surprise.

"I quit, that's what!" Karen's red hair was flying and her eyes were enormous as she stormed into the living room, stepping over the flattened boxes and scads of packing paper piled in the hallway.

"What?" Eden followed her in and sat down opposite Karen who perched on a chair.

"Remember that letter I messed up on Tuesday?" Karen worked to control her voice and bring it down to a normal level.

"What happened?" Eden asked patiently.

"I retyped it with Fred standing over my shoulder. He claimed to have read the new version, and he signed it so that I could put it in the mail that afternoon." She paused and her voice began to shake again. "This morning, when I got to the office, he was waiting for me. The letter was to a man in New Orleans about some office supplies we were purchasing. I messed up the figures and this time it's costing us money."

"If he signed it, the mistake is his responsibility," Eden pointed out reasonably.

"Not according to him, it's not," Karen said vehemently. "He had the audacity, the bald-faced nerve, to tell me that if I didn't quit being so unfriendly, he'd see that I was fired."

"He can't do that," Eden said firmly.

"You're darn right he can't. I saved him the trouble. I quit."

"This whole situation is ridiculous." Eden stood up and forced Karen to look at her. "Why haven't you talked to Nick. He's the boss, isn't he? You know he wouldn't fire you over something like this."

"It's the principle of the thing." Karen's hand was shaking and Eden paused long enough to suggest they move to the kitchen to get coffee.

"Here," she said a few minutes later, thrusting a cup of steamy coffee into Karen's hands. "Drink this."

As Karen sipped the liquid cautiously, Eden said, "You can't afford the luxury of quitting in the middle of a temper fit. You have Becky to think of."

"I know that." Tears came into Karen's eyes and Eden had to grab the coffee cup to keep it from sloshing.

"You can't go through life being a victim," Eden said brutally, hoping to shock a little sense into Karen. "Your husband left you pregnant and alone. Now you're going to let Fred's idiotic behavior cost you a perfectly good job with a company you like?''

"Eden!" Karen looked wounded.

Eden forced herself not to soften. "You better hope that Larry still wants to marry you because you're going to need some way to take care of yourself."

"That's a horrible thing to say!" Now Karen's eyes were blazing at Eden.

"It may be horrible, but that's how it'll seem to Larry if you run to marry him now."

"Oh, what am I going to do?" Karen moaned. "I know I shouldn't have quit. I just got so damn mad."

"It's time you learned to assert yourself a little," Eden said firmly.

"I'll try," Karen said shakily. "But how?"

"You've still got the tape recording?" As Karen nodded she went on. "Good. Now, call Nick and tell him you need to see him as soon as possible."

"I can't," Karen moaned. "I can't play the tape for him. It's so degrading. I feel ashamed that I let Fred talk to me like that."

"You're being ridiculous." Eden was losing her patience.

"Will you tell Nick first?" Karen pleaded.

"Why?"

"If you would just tell him, then I could talk to him. But I can't go into his office cold turkey and play that tape recording. I don't have it in me." Karen looked with such desperation at Eden that she couldn't say no, even though she knew she ought to.

"I'll call Nick," she said. "But that's all. The rest is up to you."

"Thank you," Karen said fervently. "You don't know how much I appreciate this."

Eden went in to the phone and quickly dialed the number of Nick's office. "Is Nick in?" she asked Kay a moment later. "This is Eden, and it's rather important."

"Eden?" Nick's voice came over the phone clearly a moment later.

"Nick, I need to talk for a minute. Are you alone?" Now that Eden was on the phone she wished she hadn't agreed to do this so hastily.

"What's up?" Nick's voice deepened in concern.

"It's about Karen," Eden explained. "Did you know she's quit?"

"What! I've been closed up in my office all morning. What's going on?"

"It's kind of a long story," Eden began helplessly. "But what it boils down to is that for several months now Fred has been making all sorts of comments to Karen, you know, sexual innuendos, things like that. Lately he's been getting angry at her refusal to have anything to do with him and finding all kinds of faults with her work. The upshot is that he threatened to fire her this morning and she quit before he could do so."

The silence on the other end of the phone was so tense Eden felt she could actually feel it. "How do you know about all this?" Nick asked finally.

"Karen's been telling me about it for several weeks now."

"Oh." That was all Nick said, but it conveyed a wealth of meaning. Such as, why hadn't she told him about it? Why had he been left in the dark?

"I'll speak to Fred immediately," Nick said at length. "Keep Karen there with you and I'll get back to you."

Karen was waiting anxiously when she got off the phone. "Well, what did he say?"

"He's going to talk to Fred. He said he'd call back." Karen seemed so nervous that Eden put her to work helping to direct the packers to keep her mind off her troubles. That didn't keep Eden from thinking about what had happened, though. She sensed that Nick was bothered by the fact that she had known what was going on while he hadn't. Well, he would just have to understand that she hadn't been able to betray Karen's confidence.

"They're here!" Karen's nervous shriek penetrated her thoughts a while later, and she went over to the window barely in time to see Nick and Fred reaching the top of the steps. Going to the front door, she opened the screen and waited for them to approach.

"Is Karen still here?" Nick asked abruptly, his dark eyes hooded by half-closed lids.

"In the living room," Eden replied.

Fred eyed her furiously, his short body tensed for battle. Without speaking, he followed Nick through the door, but Eden could practically feel the anger radiating from him.

Once in the living room, Karen and Eden sat down on the sofa while Nick chose a chair opposite them. Fred remained standing. "What's this all about, Karen?" Nick asked quietly.

Karen merely looked back at him, her eyes wide as she nervously glanced at Fred and then back at Nick.

"I don't know what kind of lies you women have concocted," Fred spoke belligerently, "but I'm not going to stand here and let you malign my character."

"Character, hah!" Karen snorted.

"Stop it, both of you," Nick interrupted. "Now, Karen, Fred claims that he didn't fire you. He has shown me evidence that you've made several bad mistakes over the past few weeks."

Karen stared down at the floor and looked miserable. "I have made mistakes, Nick," she admitted. "But it's because he's been standing over me like a hawk."

"I'll tell you what's going on here," Fred rudely interjected. "Those two—" he pointed his finger at Eden and Karen "—those two have made up some wild story in order to get rid of me. Ever since she came here—" and this time he pointed at Eden "—she's been trying to undermine my position in the company."

"That's ridiculous," Eden said angrily.

A muffled gasp from Karen told Eden that she was enraged by Fred's words. "Why, I have proof!" she said, and jumped up, searching the room anxiously. Locating her purse on a side table, she fumbled it open and drew out a tiny silver tape recorder. "Here," she said triumphantly, her hands shaking. "Listen to this, Nick."

Flicking the switch, she sank back down on the couch and held the recorder out where they could all hear. Fred's husky voice filled the room as he made several sexually suggestive comments, more than once addressing Karen by name.

The room became so quiet that it was difficult to tell whether any of the four occupants were even breathing. Fred's face turned a ghastly shade of gray and Eden actually feared for a moment that he might become ill. Karen looked calmer by the moment, her hands ceasing their shaking. Eden felt a knot form in the pit of her stomach as she looked at Nick. His jaw was clenched, a tight white line forming around his mouth as he listened intently.

Finally, as if he could take no more, Nick reached out and grasped the recorder, flipping the off switch and pocketing the instrument in one swift movement.

"Fred," he commanded quietly, "Karen. Come back to the office with me. Now." He stood up and strode toward the doorway, his back rigid, and after a moment Fred and Karen hurried after him. Eden sat listening to their retreating footsteps, not quite believing what had happened.

Never had she seen Nick so angry. He'd looked sick, too, as if someone had kicked him in the stomach. Knowing how much he liked Fred, she knew that he must be horrified by what he'd heard.

Slowly she rose from the couch and left the room, moving upstairs and trying to get back into the swing of directing the packing.

Karen called finally. The phone rang at four-thirty and Eden grabbed for it, thinking it might be Nick. It was Karen, her voice subdued, but firm. "It's okay, Eden. I'm still working for Nick."

"What did he do?" Eden couldn't refrain from asking, hating to gossip yet feeling as if she had to know.

"Well, first of all he told me he would transfer me to another department. Then he really let Fred have it. I almost felt sorry for him." Her voice lowered and she said, "It was awful for Fred. He broke down and told Nick he was miserable and lonely and yet he didn't know how to approach a woman normally anymore. I guess he had such a difficult time dealing with his feelings about what happened to his wife, he kind of went a little crazy."

"Did Nick fire him?" Eden held her breath.

"No," Karen said, "and I'm glad he didn't. He told Fred that he needed to talk to a counselor or a therapist so he could start living again." Karen paused and her voice dropped. Eden detected a hint of embarrassment as she went on. "Then Fred started apologizing to me and I felt so sorry for him that I offered to keep working for him. I did tell him I'm going to keep my tape recorder handy, though!"

"Sounds like you had quite an afternoon," Eden commented when she finished. "Feel better?"

"Immensely better. Thank you so much, Eden. I could never have done it without you." Her voice was exuberant as she added, "You're a real friend."

After they finished talking, Eden felt relieved

that things had worked out for Karen. What about Nick? Was it going to be that easy to talk to him? She sensed that he had been deeply perturbed by what had happened.

Going upstairs to check on the progress of the packers, she found that they were closing down for the day. "We'll be back early tomorrow to finish," the foreman told her. After they left, she showered and slipped into a fresh pair of slacks and a crisp shirt.

She had to see Nick. And she wasn't going to wait here to see if he came by. She would go to his house. Fifteen minutes later she was pulling into the now-familiar driveway where Nick's car was already parked.

So he had gone directly home without stopping at her house. That didn't bode well.

Going through the woods, she emerged at the cottage and paused a moment, hesitant to knock at the door. Firmly she forced herself to move forward. "Nick?" she called as she rapped sharply on the door.

It opened immediately, almost as if he had been waiting for her. His face was tired and his body seemed exhausted. Raking a hand through his hair, he managed a brief smile that didn't quite reach his eyes. "Eden."

"May I come in?" she asked, feeling suddenly awkward.

"Of course." He moved aside and let her lead the way to the living room.

She sank down on the sofa, her eyebrows lifting

as Nick chose a chair across the room instead of sitting beside her. "I spoke to Karen. She said you straightened everything out."

Nick didn't answer at first. Finally he said, "It was a hell of a mess."

"It seems to be over now," Eden pointed out.

"I'm afraid I can't be so trite as to say, 'All's well that ends well,'" he said brusquely. He startled her by jumping up and smacking a fist against his palm. "To think this has been going on for months and everyone, even a stranger like you, knew it except me."

Eden winced. A stranger. She would hardly call herself that. In the past weeks she had become more intimately involved with other people's lives than she ever had before.

"Why are you still so upset?" she asked finally.

Nick settled back down restlessly in the chair. "Why didn't you tell me what you knew about this?"

"It wasn't my business to tell you," Eden informed him. "Karen asked me not to tell anyone."

"Eden, I'm the man who loves you. And it was going on in my company."

"So?" she said reasonably. "That still doesn't give me a right to betray someone else's confidence."

"You're right, I suppose," he admitted at last and Eden breathed a sigh of relief.

"Why don't we go out and have dinner?" she asked, hoping to elicit some response from Nick.

"Okay," he agreed, but Eden could sense his reluctance.

"Nick, why can't you tell me when something is bothering you?" she asked directly.

In a low voice he explained, "It's very hard for me to admit to being hurt about something. I always hid any feelings of disappointment that I had as a child. There was no room for that at the orphanage."

"What are you disappointed about now?" Eden asked patiently. "That I was less than truthful about Karen? I've explained my reasons for that."

"No, it's more than that," Nick said honestly, looking earnestly at her. "I'm worried about us."

"Us?" she said blankly. "I thought you were the one who was telling me how everything would work out if we just got married."

"Maybe I was wrong," he said, and Eden's heart stopped momentarily. "I haven't admitted to myself how much this commuting back and forth is going to bother me." Nick looked as if every word were costing him great effort as he continued, "It's too much like my life as a child. The instability of never having any permanent relationship, always bouncing back and forth between my mother and the home. I want a wife who's around, not someone who only drops in every other week or so to visit."

Eden felt relief and desperation at the same time. Relief that at last they were getting to the source of what had been bothering Nick all along and causing him to withdraw. Perhaps it was true that the truth always comes out under pressure. But she felt desperate because she could see nothing to do about the situation. Or at least nothing that seemed desirable. She waited quietly for Nick to speak again.

The silence mounted between them before Nick burst out, "I love you so much, Eden."

His declaration seemed to spark her decision. "Nick," she said before she changed her mind. "Do you want me to give up the company and come live here with you in Louisiana? Just forget the commuting and make it a permanent change?"

"No." His answer couldn't have been more succinct or more definite.

Eden's heart raced painfully as she said, "Is that 'No, I don't want you to give up the company' or 'No, I don't want you'?"

"I don't know." Nick's answer came like a jolt out of the blue and Eden stared at him as if she didn't even know him. What had happened to make him this cold? Was it something she had done? Or had he simply decided that he really didn't want her around permanently?

Suddenly Eden knew that she didn't want to find out. Rising swiftly to her feet, she said, "I have to go now, Nick. I'm going back to Houston this weekend. That will give us both time to think." Without waiting for him to say anything else, she left the cottage and left Nick.

CHAPTER TWENTY

THE HOUSTON TRAFFIC was not just bad on Monday morning, it was impossible. Eden took out her frustration by honking rudely at the driver of a yellow sedan only to pull alongside and discover that it was being maneuvered by a withered old woman who looked scared and helpless. Smiling apologetically, Eden slowed down and continued on to the office in a subdued frame of mind.

She arrived before anyone else, unlocking the front doors and switching on lights as she went back to her office. Moving into the darkened room, she paused and slipped out of her jacket before flicking on the high-intensity lamp on her desk. Tom's neat printing leaped up at her from the front of a file folder and she picked it up, glancing at the memo on top.

"I worked on the Avery proposal before going home on Friday," he had written. "We should take this job. It's just your cup of tea, darling, a chance for you to shine. If we do a first-rate job, we might pull off that branch office in New Orleans after all."

"Great," Eden grumbled. "He never gives up!" She went into the employee lounge and put on the first pot of coffee for the day, avoiding all the while having to go back into her office and look at that file. She didn't want to see Tom's analysis of the Avery account. What good would a branch office in New Orleans be now that she and Nick might be calling it quits?

Because you know it's not over, her inner voice insisted, and Eden bit her lip in frustration. Of course it wasn't over. You didn't stop loving someone simply because you felt rejected. Why had Nick been so vehemently against her offer to concede? She had offered him exactly what she thought he wanted, a home, a family, a wife who stayed home and devoted herself to making his life easy and comfortable. What more could any man want from a woman?

Hearing the sounds of someone arriving, Eden went in to find Jenifer sitting down behind her own desk. "Good morning," she said pleasantly.

"Hello, Eden." Jenifer smiled warmly. "Tom put the Avery file on your desk Friday. Did you see it?"

"I saw it," Eden replied shortly.

Jenifer seemed to hesitate briefly before saying, "Tom said we might be opening a branch office in New Orleans instead of another one here in Houston." The inflection at the end of her sentence made the statement into a question.

Eden noticed her use of the word *we*. In the past few weeks Jenifer had grown professionally, her loyalty to Sonnier's seeming to advance in proportion to the independence of movement and action afforded her. "It's doubtful," Eden said kindly, walking toward her own office door.

"If you don't mind my saying so," Jenifer breezed right on as though she had no real doubts about expressing her opinion, "I think it's a marvelous idea."

"Really?" Eden paused by the door.

"There's only room for one Sonnier's office in Houston," Jenifer concluded. "If you started branching out here in the city, people would think you were a chain operation." As she spoke, the enthusiasm in her voice caught fire and she switched back to the use of *we*. "We don't want to lose that special, exclusive reputation that makes us what we are. Yet we do need to branch out, increase our contact with suppliers and designers in other cities. New Orleans is ideal. It's growing, it has aesthetic appeal, and best of all, it has people who can afford to buy what Sonnier's has to offer."

Eden was taken aback. "You seem to have given this considerable thought!"

"Oh, I have," Jenifer agreed heartily. "You see, I was hoping maybe you would take me with you. If you go to New Orleans, that is."

"You want to leave Houston?" Eden stared at her in surprise.

"I like working with you," Jenifer spoke sincerely. "Watch out, one of these days I may be your biggest competitor. In the meantime, I want to stay with you, learn from you. In New Orleans I would be in on the ground floor. That's important."

"Heavens." Eden smiled at her with a surge of

pleasure. "Before I'll turn you loose on the world, Jenifer, I'll think about offering you a chance at a partnership. You sound like too much competition to lose!"

Jenifer blushed slightly and said, "Well, maybe I'm rushing things a bit. I do enjoy my work and—" Here she paused and hesitated again. "Well, thank you," she finished lamely.

"Thank you, Jenifer," Eden said warmly, sincerely. "If we open in New Orleans, you'll be on the top of the list."

Going into her office and closing the door she sank down into the chair behind her desk. Looking around at the room, she realized that no matter what happened with Nick, she had changed. Even in a few short weeks he had been a tremendous impact on her life. She only had to look at Jenifer. Without Nick's example, she might never have opened herself up to help from other people, might have continued to do things single-handedly, driving herself on a lone journey that brought little reward in the end.

Had life been like that for Aunt Helene? Eden had never looked at her aunt in that light before. She had seen only the older woman's iron discipline, her total rule and control of the plantation and the sugar mills. Would things have turned out differently if she hadn't been so completely self-reliant? In the end, she hadn't really even let Eden into her life, always keeping her niece at a distance, locked into a mold determined by her unyielding devotion to principles she never questioned.

For years Eden had been set on one course, to establish the best decorating firm in Houston. Well, Sonnier's was well on the way to that success, but now it was worth more because it was a shared goal. Tom, Jenifer, even Barry and Glenna, all took pride in the eventual success of the firm.

Wasn't that the test of any love relationship? If it made you grow, complemented your life, made you into a stronger person, it was a worthwhile love. She had gained much from her association with Nick, no matter what else happened.

Offering to change herself for Nick had been her biggest concession to anyone, Eden realized. When he rejected that offer she had almost thrown away all the other changes in herself that had been clearly beneficial. With renewed resolution she flipped open the Avery file and got down to work.

Two hours later Tom knocked on her door and peeked his head in. "Hard at work?"

Eden glanced up and grimaced. "When did you have time to do all this?"

"I made it my top priority," Tom acknowledged, coming into her office and casually appropriating one of the chairs opposite her.

"I can see that," Eden murmured, lifting several of the carefully written pages in her hands. "How did you get all this information?"

"You forget how many years I dealt in antiques exclusively," Tom replied, pleased with himself. "I'm confident we could establish ourselves in New Orleans in a short time. There are a lot of decorators there, of course, but there's only one Sonnier's and now that I'm part of it, I like to think we're the best.''

"Are we ready to branch out that far?'' Eden asked the question carefully, hoping he would give it some thought.

"Yes,'' he said decisively. "We need to branch out. You did your job well, Eden. You've collected a team of highly qualified people, but now you need to put them to work. As your partner, I feel we can take on more projects, expand the business without losing our reputation for quality.''

"Why New Orleans?'' she asked bluntly. "Why not Dallas, Austin, El Paso?''

"Dallas isn't the place for Sonnier's work,'' Tom said, moving his hands expressively. "It's too modern, too fast, for your refined style.''

"It's not just my style now,'' Eden pointed out.

"Of course,'' Tom replied. "But my specialty is antiques, yours has always been combining the best of the past with present-day function. Jenifer is turning into quite a whizz at working with eastern, Oriental designs and mixing them with traditional-style decoration. To beat our competitors we need to concentrate on what we do best, and what we do best will be received better in New Orleans than in any other Texas city.''

"Just so you're not pushing me there thinking that's where I want to be.'' Eden fiddled with her pencil as she spoke, not looking at Tom.

"I feel sure your Nick is resourceful enough to find you wherever you end up,'' Tom said dryly. "No, I'm making New Orleans my choice because of business. It'll be up to you to mix in the personal details.''

"I'll think about it," Eden agreed finally. "That's all I can promise for now."

THE WEEK WENT BY both slowly and quickly. The days were quick, filled with a hundred varied activities that left no time for brooding. But the nights were a different story. By Friday night at six, Eden was wrung out from tossing and turning through a week of sleepless nights.

During the week she had considered and rejected several plans on how to approach Nick again. Should she try to talk to him about giving up her work completely again? Should she call him and pretend nothing was wrong? Should she do nothing and wait for him to seek her out? Her reserved nature dreaded the idea of making herself vulnerable again. No plan seemed right and as she turned into her street, she sighed tiredly.

Parking in front of her town house, she gathered up her purse and a stack of file folders and got out of the car, pausing just long enough to lock the door. Glancing up, she started at the sight of a man lounging on her front step. In the dusk, she couldn't see his face at all, but as he turned toward the walkway, she caught her breath.

Those wide shoulders, that long lean body, that black hair! It had to be Nick! Her heart beating rapidly, her stomach caught somewhere between her throat and her ribs, she started toward him. Maybe she was mistaken.

"Eden!"

Eden stopped, uncertain.

"Eden!"

Slowly she walked toward him, not knowing what to expect or say. He rose to his feet and waited, his hands jammed in the pockets of dark trousers, his pale blue shirt open at the collar. When she was barely an arm's length away, she halted. "Hello, Nick."

He looked tired, but to her eyes he looked absolutely wonderful. His jaw was dark with a day's growth of beard, his hair slightly untidy in the afternoon breeze. But he was the same Nick she had left in Louisiana. His expressive eyes, his mouth that she felt she knew as well as her own.

"Hello, Eden," he said again, taking his hands out of his pockets and stepping aside so that she could reach the door. She unlocked it mechanically, not waiting for him as he followed her into the living area.

"Would you like to sit down?" she asked stiffly, indicating the rattan sofa.

"I came to apologize, Eden."

She froze in the act of sitting down, then slowly sank the rest of the way down. What did he mean?

When she simply looked at him, he said roughly, "I still feel the same way, but I realize now that I didn't give your offer the consideration it was due."

"You don't owe me anything, Nick," she said with remarkable composure judging from the way she was feeling inside. "There's no need to apologize because you feel that way."

"I'm not sure you understand how I feel." Nick walked toward her slowly, burying his hands back in his pockets.

The silence was deafening and Eden wasn't sure whether the pounding she heard was her own heart or Nick's steps as he came toward her. "I'm willing to listen," Eden said finally, her voice breathless as she looked up and met his gaze.

He continued looking at her for a long, long time and Eden shivered despite the warmth of the room. "I fell in love with *you*, Eden," he said softly, emphatically. "But somewhere along the way, the real you got mixed up with some ideas I'd built up in my head about the way things were going to be when I got married."

Coming over to the edge of the sofa, he lowered himself down beside her, not touching her but making her aware of his presence in every pore of her body. "I had this image of a homelife that I'd carried with me ever since I could remember. Before long I began realizing that what we had between us was new and unique, not just a substitute for something I never had as a child. But I still couldn't give up those dreams, even though I felt selfish when I realized how unfair they would be to you."

Eden kept quiet, sensing that he had more to say. After a brief pause, he confirmed that by saying, "I haven't changed in my love for you, Eden. I love you more than I've ever loved anyone." His voice dropped lower and grew husky with feeling. "In fact, you taught me what love is all about. For all my conviction that I had myself together, I guess

I'd never really learned how to love someone in a way that meant anything.''

He reached out and rested his palm against her cheek and her hand came up involuntarily to cover his. She breathed in the scent of him, inhaling deeply, moving her face to let her lips brush across his palm as she closed her eyes. Words weren't necessary as he cupped his hand behind her neck and drew her to him, kissing her with such emotion that she melted against him, forgetting herself completely in the moment.

"Eden, Eden," he murmured as his mouth left hers finally and moved to linger on the smooth hollow of skin beneath her ear. "Tell me I'm forgiven.''

"Forgiven!'' Eden moved back and forced him to look at her with a gentle, nudging touch on his jaw. "I thought you were the one who was angry!''

"Never angry.'' Nick trapped her gaze with his own darkened eyes and pleaded with her silently to understand. "Just confused, bewildered.''

"That's how I felt,'' Eden admitted huskily. "I offered you what I thought was more than you wanted and then you didn't want it at all.''

"If I forced you to give up your life to come live with me, I'd destroy the very essence of you.'' Nick's voice was firm and sure, convincing her that he definitely believed what he was saying. Resting his hands on her shoulders so that their heat burned through her blouse and started a fiery path down her body, he said slowly and distinctly, "Marry me, Eden. Love me. That's all I ask. I'll be grateful for every moment I can share with you, but I'll never begrudge you the right to do whatever you want with your life. I've given up those old dreams. I'm ready to dream new ones together with you.''

"Oh, Nick." Eden wrapped her arms around his waist and leaned against him. "I could never ask for more than that. I love you so much." Her voice muffled against his chest as she slid her fingers along the buttons of his shirt, releasing them one by one so that her face could rest against his skin.

"Kiss me, Nick," she spoke in a tone that invited his compliance, and he met her mouth with his, eagerly seeking out and caressing the innermost recesses with utmost caring and a love that would not be denied.

"Maybe I could open an office here in Houston," he suggested quietly when they reluctantly broke off their kiss.

"Maybe you won't need to do that." Eden told him of the tentative plans for the office in New Orleans. "Tom is really eager about the idea; he seems to think it will work out great. I guess I still find it hard to trust his opinion totally, to share the reins of the company with someone else."

"It sounds ideal." Nick's voice held an undercurrent of checked enthusiasm, and Eden realized that he was reluctant to have her think he was too hopeful in case it didn't work out.

"It is sounding better and better," Eden murmured as she allowed her fingers to play restlessly down over one leg.

His eyes darkened and he pulled her against him

with a groan. "How soon will you marry me, Eden?" he whispered into her sweet-scented hair.

"As soon as we can manage it and that should be fast knowing what great organizers we both are," Eden replied gaily before their lips met again in a deep, unending kiss.

With a sigh of happiness Eden surrendered completely. Nick embraced her eagerly as they looked to the future into a life filled with enchantment, deep abiding love and the promise of joy.

EPILOGUE

EDEN LAID DOWN the last of a series of neatly lined blueprints and glanced at the clock on the opposite wall. Her smoothly polished desk was cleared of all except these last plans, and the calendar before her reminded her that today was Friday. It was also her anniversary.

Standing up, she stretched her cramped muscles and slipped into her jacket before going out into the hall. A moment later she was entering an office at the other end of the wide passageway. "Ready to go home, Jenifer?" she asked.

"In just a moment," came the breathless reply as Jenifer straightened up from a large square of cardboard, marked off in grids, that covered a goodly portion of the back part of the room.

"It looks like it might rain," Eden commented as she crossed to the floor-to-ceiling window on the side wall and peered out. Gray clouds marred the sky overhead but still didn't dim the glory of the luxurious gardens below and the sweeping oaks that reached higher than the window where she was standing on the second floor.

"This old building has stood through many a storm." Jenifer smiled and glanced around the room proudly. "Have you seen the article about us yet in Southern Digest?" she asked.

"Did you get a copy?" Eden replied eagerly, turning and holding out her hand when she saw the magazine Jenifer was offering.

A breathtaking photograph of Belle's Folly adorned the cover of the prestigious magazine, the double row of oaks lining either side of the wide lawns that led up to the stately entrance. "An Inside Look at Sonnier's," the caption below the photo read, and Eden thumbed quickly to the article with mingled feelings of pride and anticipation.

"Here, let me read it," Jenifer offered, taking the pages out of Eden's hands. "The South's brightest new star on the designing scene is headquartered in one of its oldest and grandest plantation homes—" she read out in a clear voice. Breaking off with a giggle, she said, "Isn't that great!"

Eden nodded her agreement, her eyes misty with pleasure and satisfaction. "Hey," she said suddenly, "I've got to hurry home. Don't forget, it's my anniversary. And don't forget it was Nick's idea to use Belle's Folly as our office in Louisiana. His new offices aren't nearly so grand."

"Oh, you two," Jenifer said disparagingly, a twinkle in her eyes nonetheless. "You'd think that after five years of marriage and two children, you'd be tired of each other."

"Not a chance." Eden's voice was slightly breathless and Jenifer shook her head.

"What about you and Barry?" Eden retorted as

she noted Jenifer's look. "Seems I've noticed a few stars in your eyes lately myself!"

Now it was Jenifer's turn to blush. "Barry's impossible," she claimed, but her flushed cheeks gave her away.

"At least you got him into some decent clothes for a change," Eden commented. "We're all grateful for your influence."

Jenifer held out her watch and pointed to its face. "We'd better be going. Too bad your car chose this morning to break down, but I'll be happy to drive you home."

"Thanks," Eden said.

The downstairs offices were already darkened and it took them only moments to finish closing the building. Jenifer seemed to take forever to fiddle with her car door and start the car. Eden tapped her foot impatiently and finally said, "For heaven's sake, Jenifer. What's got into you tonight?"

"Just tired, I guess." Jenifer stifled a yawn, but Eden glanced at her sharply, wondering if it had been real.

Finally they pulled to a halt in front of the rolling green lawns and modern graceful home where Nick and Eden had decided to live. Dixie had long since been followed by a line of never-ending progeny, but Eden could never enter the shady shell driveway without remembering the funny little racoon.

"Umm, no lights," Eden commented. "Wonder where everyone is."

"I'll come in with you," Jenifer inserted swiftly.

They went quickly up the walk and Eden reached

to open the front door. It was locked. "That's odd." Eden fumbled for her key and thought she heard Jenifer giggle. "Jenifer?" she said sharply, but when she turned the other woman was coughing lightly.

The key in the lock, she swung open the door and switched on the light. For a moment the contrasting brightness was shocking and then from all corners of the entryway, she heard, "Surprise, surprise!"

Nick came forward from the depths of the living area, a wide smile on his face as he joined his wife at the door. The wide-eyed little girl in his arms threw herself at Eden and said, "Mommy, it's your party!"

Eden looked over the top of the dark curls straight into Nick's eyes as he said, "Happy anniversary, darling."

A tug at her skirt made her bend down until she was at eye level with the toddler who stood slightly behind Nick. "I want my ice cream!" Nick, Jr. announced and Eden laughed, hugging him to her.

"When did you plan this?" she asked when she could disentangle herself from the two children.

"It took no time at all," Nick assured her with a quick hug of his own. "Just a little help from our friends."

With that Eden managed a look around at the others waiting in the hall. Karen and Larry surged forward with a leggy freckle-faced Becky in tow. Fred smiled from another corner, a genuine smile as he put his arm around the new lady in his life, Glenna. Last of all, Tom and Neva emerged from the shadows. There was a new maturity on Neva's face and a relaxed look on Tom's that indicated the many changes they had undergone.

Within minutes the party was in full swing. After a delicious supper, Eden disappeared upstairs to tuck Nick, Jr. and little Belle into bed. Nick caught her in the hallway and drew her into his arms, his lips meeting hers with a warmth that even five years of marriage had never failed to diminish.

"Let's sneak out the back door and go down to the cottage," he whispered seductively against her ear.

"Umm..." Eden murmured drowsily and contentedly. "You have the most delightful ideas. But won't everyone wonder where we are?"

"They won't wonder," Nick replied smoothly, a hint of laughter in his voice. "They'll know. We can't hide it, Eden. I'm afraid everyone knows how mad we are about each other."

"Do you mind?" Eden whispered demurely.

"Mind?" Nick's voice rumbled huskily in her ear. "I'd like to spend the rest of my life proving how right they are."

"Mr. Devereaux, you have the most delightful ideas," Eden repeated as she melted against him and surrendered to the ever-enchanting spell of love.

HARLEQUIN *SuperRomance*

Meg Hudson

BELOVED STRANGER

Author of THE RISING ROAD

December's other absorbing
HARLEQUIN *SuperRomance* novel

BELOVED STRANGER by Meg Hudson

As an anthropologist, Sara Westcott had come to
San Francisco to research the Russian community,
not to fall in love. Then she met Alexei Varentsov.

Alexei was an enigma in so many ways. He spoke
little of his past and never of the future. Sara's mind
held a thousand reservations—what if he were a
spy, a fugitive—but her heart was immediately lost
to this strong, gentle man.

She would live for the moment and not think of the
inevitable—the day she would wake up and find
Alexei gone . . .

A contemporary love story for the woman of today

These two absorbing titles
will be published in January
by

HARLEQUIN
SuperRomance

MOONLIGHT ON SNOW by Virginia Nielsen

Diane Armstrong would never forget the terror of having to land a small aircraft after her husband suffered a fatal heart attack at the controls. Nor would she forget her wanton reactions to the kindness of the man who helped save her life.

A well-bred girl, she was deeply distressed by her behaviour with Jim Forbes. But she determined to rebuild her shattered life without the help or comfort of the San Francisco executive with the alluring Southern drawl.

This self-sufficiency was dictated by her pride. But Jim Forbes demanded more of her soul than she had ever put to the test before.

WHEN ANGELS DANCE
by Vicki Lewis Thompson

Angie Nichols, public-relations consultant, needed Ben Scheaffer to make her promotional campaign a success. She was prepared to do almost anything.

Ben Scheaffer, computer genius, devoted himself to his floppy disks in a secluded Colorado cabin. As a retired Olympic skier, he knew the cost of fame and fortune—he wasn't prepared to stand in the spotlight again.

Their problems snowballed when they found themselves falling in love.